Sarah Abudawr

The Insiders

The Insiders

Judi Bevan

PIATKUS

First published in Great Britain in 1993 by
Judy Piatkus (Publishers) Ltd of
5 Windmill Street, London W1

**The moral right of the author
has been asserted**

*A catalogue record for this book is available
from the British Library*

ISBN 0–7499–0159–4

Set in 11/12 Linotron Times by
Phoenix Photosetting, Chatham, Kent
Printed and bound in Great Britain by
Bookcraft, Midsomer Norton

For John and Chiara

Acknowledgements

I would like to thank everyone who helped me with this book. Large numbers of merchant bankers, stockbrokers and captains of industry gave generously of their time on the basis they would remain anonymous.

On the legal side, Paul Bacon, Stephen Kamlish and Jonathan Goldberg QC guided me through the complexities. John Jay, Hilary Rubinstein, Gilly Greenwood and Susy Streeter gave me valuable criticism in the redrafting stages. Colin Murray proved an incisive yet sympathetic editor. I am also grateful to Mike Shaw for giving me the confidence to get started and Clarissa Rushdie for her continued encouragement. Most of all I would like to thank Judy Piatkus for being my publisher.

Chapter 1

Jack Armstrong flashed his most charming smile at the mirror which ran the length of the gym. He saw a tall, lean, lightly muscled figure. In his face, triangular green eyes glittered above prominent cheekbones and a clean jawline. It was a face in which women saw both sensitivity and strength – a winning combination he had found. A smooth, dark cap of hair was brushed forward into a fringe. He could pass for thirty-five, even on a bad day.

The reflection smiled back at him. There was a hint of jubilation which he noticed with a little shock – a chill almost – somewhere between his ribs. Then he tilted his chin towards the mirror in a gesture of defiance and considered his good fortune.

So Randolph was dead!

He pressed the plus sign on the treadmill to increase the speed. I am a winner, I am a winner, he repeated silently in rhythm with his pounding feet. Thud, thud, thud, thud.

The feeling of shock vanished to be replaced by cold, hard elation. He touched his forehead – it wasn't even damp yet. He turned his mind to running.

I am a winner, I am a winner. The words ran through his head as his feet paced the moving rubber belt. Thud, thud, thud, thud. Jack Armstrong had learned at Harvard Business School to cultivate a positive mental attitude to match a fit, hard body. He liked to think of his heart, pumping clot-free blood through wide, flexible arteries, making him the perfect executive machine. Now, after all the waiting, that machine was to be put to the test. He raised the speed of the treadmill once more.

1

A tiny inner voice whispered he had no business exulting in anyone's death. He dismissed it, but a picture of his seventeen-year-old son Mark, long clean limbs mangled in painted steel, whisked through his mind. He glanced up at the mirror to catch a fleeting expression of fear.

He had no business. No bloody business, his father would have said in rasping Lancashire, wheezing between the phrases. And to exult in the death of Randolph, of all people. His father would have been right, he thought. Randolph had been kind, fatherly, had paid him a good salary, well above the going rate. But not for one moment, one fraction of a second, had he ever treated Jack as an equal. The man in the mirror tilted his chin again at the memory of the last five years of oppression. Thud, thud, thud, thud. The dial told him he had been running 18 minutes, 42 seconds.

I am a winner, I am a winner, I am a winner. He smiled again, revealing large, even teeth. Jubilation won out.

Then came spite. That would teach him! Randolph had never invited him to his precious grouse shoots, or his fishing trips, or his expeditions to Glyndebourne. Jack glowed with vindication as the sweat formed on his skin. The reflection's eyes narrowed. Paternalistic not fatherly was the correct description of Randolph. He had let Jack know in a hundred small ways that what he achieved in business was one thing; what happened in their social lives, another.

Once a year Randolph invited Jack and his wife Rosemary to Sunday lunch at his family seat – a draughty converted abbey forty miles north of Chester. The first two years Jack had come away, his stomach churning with irritation and confusion.

He would go over the day. Randolph had been welcoming, his wife Hermione gracious, the food exquisite. Business had not been mentioned but Randolph had sounded Jack out for his views on the political situation, and the economic climate. In the afternoon, Hermione would show Rosemary the latest developments in the garden. Nothing could have been more pleasant.

The third year, Randolph's estate manager and his wife were also guests at the lunch and Jack had finally understood. Jack might be chief executive of Huntingdon Confectionery, the largest quoted confectionery group in the country, but to Randolph the chairman, son of the founder and owner of a fifth of the shares, Jack Armstrong was quite simply, one of the staff.

Highly paid, highly thought of, but staff.

There were no fishing expeditions or shooting parties for Jack and as the years had gone by he had felt his exclusion like a physical pain. Randolph reserved these treats either for those of sufficient social standing or those who could afford to pay. Charlie Briggs-Smith, a languid Etonian stockbroker born with all the privileges Jack lacked, regularly put together groups of eager young industrialists happy to part with £1,200 a day.

Thud, thud, thud, thud – he was panting hard now. It was Charlie who had rung with the news two hours before. Jack remembered how he had known instantly, from the first hello, had felt his heart leap in his chest in anticipation of the tragedy.

Randolph had been on tremendous form, reported Charlie, bagging twelve brace, double the nearest competitor, and irritating the hell out of his guests. After the standard shoot lunch of soup, steak and kidney pudding, sloe gin and port, one of the guests, who was also a major shareholder in Huntingdon, had engaged Randolph in a furious argument over his lack of expansion. On hearing this, Jack made a mental note to cultivate the shareholder.

To cool things down, Charlie had rallied the party to get ready for the afternoon's shooting. As they prepared themselves, Randolph had suddenly crumpled to the floor, purple-faced and moaning.

'While pulling his boots on?'

'I'm afraid so. Actually, it's more common than people being shot,' Charlie had said, seriously.

Jack wanted to laugh at the absurdity, the pathetic image. Randolph Huntingdon, the owner of 8,000 acres of the finest grouse moor, had collapsed in the boot room.

Charlie had sprinted up the stairs into the main house to call an ambulance, he told Jack, anxious to prove he had done his bit. One of the guests had come forward, had loosened Randolph's clothes and stopped his tongue from suffocating him. His wife Hermione brought blankets and stroked his forehead, unwilling to believe.

The rest of them stood around in a useless and embarrassed cluster and watched him die. It was Tuesday, September 3, 1985.

'But he was always so fit,' Jack had said with a flicker of self-interested unease. He also wanted to keep Charlie on the phone. 'He must have been one of the most active sixty-six-year-olds in the country.'

'Hermione says there was a congenital weakness in the family. Knocked off his grandfather and two uncles,' said Charlie.

Jack kept the conversation going, enquiring after Hermione and the other guests. Finally out popped the question. 'I suppose she didn't mention what she intended to do with the shares?'

There was a moment of stunned silence at the other end of the phone.

'No she didn't, Jack,' said Charlie eventually, his voice unsteady. 'He's only been dead three hours.' Charlie Briggs-Smith had never seen anyone die before.

Jack had made soothing noises and said goodbye. Charlie was quite sensitive for a stockbroker, he thought.

But he needed Hermione to make a decision on those shares just as soon as decorum allowed.

He pressed the plus sign again. I am a winner, I am a winner. He could manage another ten minutes before his massage. A pleasurable ache crept over him in anticipation of May Ling's delicate hands on his body.

He had often thought about leaving Huntingdon. But every time he had considered it, the thought of his personal investment in the firm stopped him. The company had been staggering along when he arrived, burdened by huge overheads. Jack had slashed the workforce, closed unnecessary plant, contracted out the distribution, had a new logo designed, launched an advertising campaign by Ogilvy and Mather, and installed computerised systems. Randolph had allowed all this, although it had hurt him.

Thanks to Jack the company operated like a well trained athlete – each part moving smoothly with the others for

4

maximum performance. But whenever he tried to take it further, to expand, to bid for another company, Randolph had always blocked him.

Not any more! Adrenalin surged through Jack's veins. In the next few years he would transform Huntingdon into an international company; world class, they called it in America. 'Huntingdon, a world class company,' he repeated to himself.

He would achieve what Randolph and his petty-minded family had never dared. He would work ceaselessly, he would inspire and lead, he would sell the company and its products around the globe. For a second he saw himself, solemn but glowing with pride, kneeling before the Queen as she wielded the sword.

The man in the mirror braced his shoulders, lifted his head and smiled again – as much as his straining lungs and heart would allow.

What a stroke of luck.

'And now, if you would follow me into the churchyard . . .' The Rector of St Bartholomew's led the mourners towards the Huntingdon family plot. It was textbook gentry stuff, thought Jack, picking up the faint scent of honeysuckle and late roses. A two-year-old boy who had just been walloped by his three-year-old sister began to howl as the minister set about burying Randolph's ashes. Everyone else was dry-eyed.

Jack remembered his own father's funeral, a bleak, ferociously cold affair where everyone seemed drenched in tears. His mother had clung to him desperately, wailing in that Irish way of hers, and he had wished guiltily that she would go away and leave him for a moment with the coffin. But she was oblivious of everything but her own grief. He had just turned twelve. He remembered the weight of her against him, the faint whiff of raw spirit on her breath, and the cold – the intense, vicious cold.

He shuddered at the memory of it, glancing up to lock eyes unexpectedly with a smooth-faced man wearing horn-rimmed spectacles who held Hermione's arm. Jack tried a sympathetic smile but the other man looked quickly back to the grave as if he had not seen it. To Jack he was the most important person there: Randolph's eldest child and only son, Paul Huntingdon, a leading defence barrister in Mansfield. He did not look in the least like Randolph, Jack thought. Maybe Hermione, her face closed like shuttered windows, had a dark secret.

A letter from Randolph's solicitors had arrived on Jack's desk the day before. When he read it, he realised this was the punishment of which the inner voice had warned. God was laughing at him and Mark would be spared. Randolph had left his entire 21.3% shareholding in Huntingdon Confectionery not to Hermione as everyone had assumed but to his son Paul.

The service ended and Jack watched the mourners slowly begin to move off towards the waiting cars. Paul Huntingdon and his wife walked either side of Hermione, the group slightly ahead of the rest.

'I'd have given my life for Paul to come into the business,' Randolph had said suddenly to Jack one evening, leaning across the table after a dinner in London where he had drunk too much port.

But Paul had never shown anything but lofty interest in the company, preferring the law. It was so like Randolph to have one last shot from the grave. The affection Jack had felt for Randolph in the early years suddenly resurfaced and Rosemary noticed him smiling.

The question was, would Randolph's tactic pay off? Jack's smile faded as he tried to imagine himself and the smooth-faced lawyer at board meetings. How, he wondered, would Paul react to his grand plan for Huntingdon?

He introduced himself at the reception afterwards in the library of the abbey – Randolph's favourite room. 'I shall miss your father. He was very supportive towards me,' Jack declared earnestly.

'I didn't think you had been getting on very well recently,' responded Paul in clipped tones. Hermione must have been talking.

'Well, we did have our differences.' Jack opted for disarming honesty. 'The truth was I wanted to expand the company and he was against taking over other firms. He knew we would use shares in a bid and that would dilute his holding.

He saw it as the thin end of the wedge. But I still had a lot of respect for him.'

Paul sipped his mineral water thoughtfully and said nothing. He was driving straight back to Mansfield to prepare the defence of a local drugs dealer.

'Now we've mentioned it – ' Jack could not restrain himself ' – have you decided what you want to do with the shares?'

'Certainly,' said Paul. 'I shall sell at the earliest opportunity.'

Jack struggled to contain the excitement in his voice. Was Paul offering him his freedom? ' Well, I'm sure that's sensible in your position,' he said. ' If you want any advice on a good broker to place the shares in the market, I'm sure Charlie Briggs-Smith could help you. He's over there somewhere. He was a good friend of your father.'

'Thanks, but, I've taken on Panmure Gordon as a broker already,' replied Paul calmly, his glasses glinting in the sunlight streaming through the mullioned windows.

'I'm not going to place them, I'm going to sell them as a single block to the highest bidder.' A smile played at the corners of his mouth. 'I've been told I'll get a much better price that way.'

The room seemed to shift on its axis. 'But you could end up selling them to a predator!' Jack said fiercely, trying to keep his voice from rising above the muted hum in the room. 'Don't you care if your family firm gets gobbled up by an asset stripper?'

Paul Huntingdon smirked. 'But I thought that was precisely what you were always trying to persuade my father to become, Mr Armstrong?'

Before Jack had time to respond, Paul said quietly: 'All I want is to be shot of Huntingdon Confectionery at a good price. I don't care if there is a bid for the company. I just want my money. It's nothing personal.'

'But what about the people who've worked for your father all these years?' asked Jack, incredulous.

'I'm told you've sacked most of them anyway,' replied Paul and Jack felt the full force of his antagonism. 'From what I hear, Mr Armstrong, you can look after yourself. Goodbye.' He turned and disappeared into the crowd.

7

The next morning, two hundred and twenty miles away in London, a black Bentley drove slowly along Birdcage Walk. This particular rich man's indulgence was not any old black Bentley. Leopold Stern, the founder and chairman of the mighty Stern Group, had lavished on his car the same attention to detail for which he was so well known in business.

This Bentley was a two-door model, specially custom made by Hooper, coachbuilders to the elite and the oldest Rolls-Royce dealer in the world. On the outside of the car everything was black – the paintwork of course, the bumpers, windscreen wipers, radiator grille. Against this unremitting black, the white number plate blazed like a beacon. Its message was simple – S1.

Inside, cossetted in sand-coloured leather, Paulette Stern was wishing her husband would stop talking on the telephone and look at St James's Park. In the intense, white sunshine of early autumn the trees had a photographic clarity. To look at the first golden leaves lying on the grass, each blade distinct, was almost to hear them crunch beneath your feet. The lake sparkled like tin foil.

'Yeah,' said Stern into the mouthpiece. 'OK, Peter, I'll look at it. But now I'm going to see the Queen.' He glanced at his wife, the wry sarcastic smile which had first appeared in teenage photographs twisting his mouth to one side and lighting up his hard black eyes.

He chuckled into the 'phone. 'In about half an hour,' he paused. 'Yeah, thanks, Peter.'

'Leo, look at ze park, you must remember eet for the rest of your life,' Paulette said as he put down the phone. His smile softened as he turned his head, taking in the willows caressing the water's edge. He reached out and took her hand, tiny and white, in his. 'Anyway she ees at 'ome,' said Paulette, gazing up at the Union Jack fluttering at the top of the flagpole.

'I'll be glad when this caper's over,' said Stern as the car swung through the gates of Buckingham Palace, pausing briefly for security.

Once inside, he was separated from Paulette by an equerry and led up the grand staircase lined with Gainsboroughs into a high-ceilinged room at the end of which stood a red plush kneeling stool with a rail.

8

As Stern had intended, the others had already arrived. They were thin, grey specimens of mankind, wearing the expression of schoolboys at prize-giving. Mostly they knew one another and stood around in groups, half chatting, half waiting, aching for something to happen.

The investiture was set for 11 a.m. but the letter had asked them to arrive half an hour early for a practice run. Stern stood apart, a bull of a man, tall and broad shouldered. His dark eyes and raven hair announced an unmistakably different breed from the rest – foreign and exotic.

There was just one celebrity, an actor who raised vast amounts of money for terminally ill children. The rest were industrialists, bankers, heads of institutions, civil servants. They had climbed the ladder slowly and painstakingly, getting in with the right people, keeping their noses clean. They were gentiles.

Stern was Jewish. He had always been his own boss, had risked everything, had worked sixteen hours a day, seven days a week; he was chairman, chief executive and finance director rolled into one. He alone was the entrepreneur.

He puzzled over his own lack of awe. The faint flutter of nerves in the car had vanished and he even found himself thinking of his last telephone conversation. Peter Markus was really on the ball. Randolph Huntingdon had been dead just a few days and already Markus was looking for buyers for the business.

Suddenly a couple of retired guards officers marched into the room in full uniform, boots dazzling, their backs like ramrods. Stern felt the tempo change. 'Good morning, gentlemen,' one addressed them, and began explaining the procedure with easy charm and efficiency.

'The investiture will take place in the ballroom. You will be approaching Her Majesty from her right,' he said. 'Continue until you are level with her, turn to face her, bow the head, take three paces towards the dais, put your left leg outside the stool and kneel on your right knee.' He smiled. 'And anyone who forgets what I say, just follow the chap in front and pray *he* has remembered.' There was a ripple of laughter and Stern relaxed.

He had made it; he had arrived. From Whitechapel to Buckingham Palace was a distance of only a few miles, but it

9

was a gigantic, audacious leap through the social strata. He was home and free. No-one could touch him now.

'The Queen may say a few words to you, but when she shakes hands that is your signal to go,' said the soldier.

Afterwards, Stern found he could barely talk. 'Well, what did she say to you? Tell me something,' Paulette begged. Even though she had been in the third row back, soft background music had muffled any words exchanged between the Queen and the recipients.

'She was very nice,' he said, getting into the waiting car and picking up a copy of the *Financial Times* lying on the seat. Strangely, he had found sitting in the hall afterwards watching everyone else come through, seeing their families choke back emotion, far more moving than his own investiture. One woman had been so overwhelmed he had felt tears welling behind his eyes – he who last cried when he was eight years old.

He turned to the obituary column. 'Randolph Huntingdon, who died earlier this week, aged 66, will be mourned by the food industry and field sportsmen all over the country.'

He hoped he would make it past that age, he thought, shuddering at the idea of his own death. His fiftieth birthday loomed in April.

'Claridge's, did you say sir?' asked the driver. Stern had a way of changing his mind at the last moment.

'Yup,' he said and turned to Paulette, still not quite in control of his emotions. 'We're going to celebrate,' he said. The phone began ringing but Stern held out a hand looking at Paulette. 'Take messages, will you?'

She kissed him. 'Darleeng, I'm so proud of you,' she said, her curiosity rekindling. Her Parisian disdain for the Royal Family had melted away the morning her husband's knighthood was announced. It must have been sensational, she thought. She had never known him stop calls before.

'No more calls for ten minutes,' Peter Markus told his secretary. 'And a cup of coffee.' He spun round a full circle in his wooden swivel chair, surveying his colleagues at their desks in the open plan office. They worked in their shirtsleeves, the cream of the public school system, in their early thirties, glued to the telephone or pressing the buttons of a calculator. Never in their lives had they worked so hard, got up so early, earned so much money.

Peter had risen at 6.30, breakfasted with an American banker at the Connaught, met a new client in his office at 9, made a dozen calls and taken almost as many. He needed time to think.

If they were really offering the Huntingdon stake for auction as Charlie had told him, he needed to find a buyer fast. Stern, or Sir Leo as he now was – the thought gave him some amusement – would only buy it to sell on to someone else. It was better than nothing, but he would prefer an industry buyer from the food sector where there was some proper logic. That way, he would pave the way for deals in the future.

In the City of London's merchant banking circles Peter Markus was the name on everyone's lips. His ideas were original, his manner persuasive and his brain high voltage. Not only did he come up with ingenious plans which entranced his clients (because they involved enriching them in money, or power, or both), he managed to pull them off with dazzling efficiency.

He examined his client list, and another list of possible buyers compiled by one of his assistants. 'The problem is most of these companies are already up to something,' he said to no one in particular.

'Whose fault is that?' said his secretary, wrily putting the coffee on his desk.

'Really,' he said in mock exasperation. 'Even I haven't got the entire top 100 companies on the go.'

Two of his colleagues exchanged glances.

He snatched up the phone on his desk the moment it rang and his secretary walked off shaking her head. 'Richard!' exclaimed Peter as if to a long lost friend 'I haven't heard from you for centuries. How *are* you?' He reached for a pen and began doodling.

'You think someone's trying to take you over?' he said delightedly, his azure eyes dancing.

'Well, no, I hadn't actually.' He punched out a number on the keypad and a list of shares appeared on the Stock

Exchange screen at his side. 'Oh! So they are, up 7p – but the market is pretty strong.'

A mischievous grin revealed two rows of perfect, pearly white teeth and the tone of his voice changed to unctuous.

'Well, Richard, you know the best form of defence is attack. I think I just might have an idea which could help.' He signalled frantically for his diary. 'Now, what are you doing at 4.30? Splendid, see you then.' He put the phone down and leapt to his feet, throwing on his jacket – double-breasted from Anderson & Sheppard – just to mark him apart. 'Where's this meeting with Ralph? At Warburg's?'

His secretary nodded. 'Yes, and you're lunching with Lord Hanson at the Connaught.'

'Look – ' he lowered his voice ' – you'd better tell Jamie to go to the work-in-progress meeting this afternoon. Can you ring the powers that be and apologise for me?'

'They're getting quite edgy, you know. You haven't appeared all week.'

He snorted. 'Well, they won't be edgy if I pull this one off, I can tell you. Come on, you.' He turned to his other assistant who jumped up from his desk. 'You want to meet Ralphie, don't you?'

Peter turned and swept out of the room with the younger man at his heels, scampering after him down two flights of stairs like an excited puppy dog.

On one level, the next three weeks sped by for Jack. There was so much to do after Randolph's death. So many people to reassure – banks, customers, suppliers, staff. He made a point of visiting the factories, of being seen to be in charge. The whole place was jumpy with anxiety. But deep inside him, where his ambition snuggled, like a cat half asleep, time crawled.

That last weekend in September, Jack appeared surprisingly cool, pretending everything was normal. He had been promised the result of the auction for Paul's share stake by lunchtime on Monday.

On the Saturday he worked zealously in the garden, raking up all the leaves into huge plastic bags. 'It's pointless doing it now, there'll be twice as many this time next week,' said Rosemary.

He winked at her. 'Where would you like to go for dinner tonight?'

He thrashed his son Mark at tennis. At seventeen Mark had speed, but at thirty-eight Jack had experience and strength and for once he held back nothing. Mark had not taken it well, slinking off sulkily to a friend's for the night. Jack had laughed at Rosemary's reproachful face. 'Life is unfair,' he had said, and she knew he was not talking about tennis.

On Sunday, he rose at dawn to play golf, arriving back for lunch hoping for some unofficial word of where the share stake had landed. None came. He hardly said a word over lunch. In the afternoon he went through his accounts, paying every bill he could find. That night he did not sleep well.

He was just kissing Rosemary goodbye at three minutes to eight on Monday morning when the phone rang. He picked up the hall extension. 'Yes,' he said, showing his irritation.

'Oh, good morning. Am I speaking to Jack Armstrong?' The voice was plummy English upper-middle-class and doing its best to be friendly.

'You are.'

'You don't know me but my name is Richard Butler. I'm the chairman of Butler's Biscuits and felt it only right that you should be the first to know that we are the purchaser of a 21.3% stake in your company.'

Jack's knuckles showed white round the telephone.

'I very much appreciate your letting me know so promptly,' he replied in almost as friendly tones. 'Can you give me some idea of your intentions?'

There was a slight hesitation the other end, and then the voice continued: 'We intend to buy more shares this morning to bring our holding to 25%, and we would like to come and talk to you about making a friendly takeover.'

A feeling of unreality closed in around Jack. 'Friendly and takeover seem to be contradictory words to me,' he said quietly. 'Anyway, I'm in Chester today.'

'Our helicopter is standing by at Battersea,' said the voice regally. 'We could be with you by 11.30.'

Jack paused. 'I would like to consult my board and our advisers before we have any meetings. Why don't we make it

13

tomorrow?' Rosemary stood a few feet away, marvelling at his self-possession.

'I don't think we can wait that long,' said the voice. The threat was too clear to be ignored.

'What about three o'clock this afternoon?' Jack made it sound like a gracious assent, rather than surrender.

'See you then.' There was a click as the receiver was put down and Jack realised he was still holding his briefcase in his right hand.

'Upper-class wally!' he shouted, slamming down the phone. It was covered in sweat. 'Fucking bastards!'

Rosemary quite liked it when he lost his temper. It was when her homely common sense came into its own. 'Is there anything I can do?' she asked soothingly.

He surfaced from his anger like a fish coming up for air.

'Yes, there is,' he said, putting an arm round her plump shoulders. 'Pack my case for me, and make sure I've got some decent shirts. I'm sure to be on the move soon.'

His mind clicked along like a production line.

'I'd better make a few calls from here before I leave,' he said, disappearing into the front room. He rang his finance director, his sales director, Charlie Briggs-Smith and the company's merchant banker, Brian Swinton, at home. By 9.15, Charlie, two of his corporate team and the banker were all booked on to the 10.30 flight to Manchester. The rest of the board were told to meet in the boardroom at 11. By mid-morning, Jack knew his life had moved into a new gear.

His inward fear and fury had given way to calm. It was as if he could see his thoughts moving through crystal, measured and precise like the parts of a clock.

'We should really be holding this meeting in our offices,' sniffed Brian Swinton. Jack ignored him. He knew Brian had a good brain but his personality always grated. There was something of the schoolboy about him, as though he could produce a whoopee cushion at any moment. A typical Randolph choice, thought Jack. The old goat had been too suspicious of the City to take on anyone of real calibre.

In any case, Huntingdon's head office in an elegant Queen

Anne house on the edge of Chester was infinitely more pleasant than the bank's branch.

Jack opened the meeting. 'Butler's has already announced to the Stock Exchange that its stake in Huntingdon is now up to 25%, and the price of Huntingdon shares has risen to 270p.' He paused. 'As you all know, the bulk of those shares has come from Paul Huntingdon, Randolph's son and heir. Your comments, gentlemen.' He sat back, playing with a pencil between long, slim fingers.

'The fact is Butler's has a very strong starting point,' said the banker. That's as obvious as stating it's autumn, thought Jack, watching the leaves blowing off the trees outside.

'But not assured victory,' said Charlie, sitting diagonally opposite him across an expanse of polished mahogany boardroom table. 'For that they need our recommendation, and it's up to us to screw as much out of them as possible.'

'How high could we go?' asked the finance director.

'I would think 350p would be a good place to start,' said Charlie, an arm draped lazily over the back of the chair. 'Then we could come down a bit.'

Jack considered Charlie. Greenbag's, his firm, was not even Huntingdon's official broker, yet he had more of a grip on the situation than anyone. Sometime in the distant past Randolph had appointed a Manchester stockbroker whose sole activity seemed to be taking groups of earnest young men and women round the plant twice a year. After each visit the shares would blip up 5p, or sometimes even 10p, which meant that they – being the managers of pension funds and insurance company money – had been impressed with what they saw.

Charlie was a different type altogether. A few years older than Jack, he gave the impression that buying and selling shares was something he did for fun – as a pleasant alternative to shooting, or going to the races, or chasing women. Jack suspected he had been Randolph's personal stockbroker, although neither he nor Charlie had ever said so. But Charlie would always bother to fly up to Chester for the annual meeting and join the thirty or so elite guests for lunch afterwards.

Some of the Huntingdon directors, Jack noted, looked quite excited at the thought of selling the company for 350p a

15

share. Thanks to him, they all had share options. There was fifteen years between him and the next youngest, but he had more options than any of them.

He let them argue the toss for half an hour. Then he took a deep breath.

'Well, gentlemen, it seems to me that you've surrendered before the battle has even started.' He looked round the table. His long body lounged against his chair but his face was taut, his eyes shining clear green with the light of battle. 'I intend to fight – and fight with every ounce of energy I have. Huntingdon is in great shape, I can see exactly why they want it.' He laughed a dry, disdainful laugh. 'But I'm not letting a bunch of southern wallies steal this company.' Charlie smiled good-naturedly at the slur, far too sure of his superiority to feel ruffled; but the little banker shifted with irritation on his seat.

'With all due respect,' Brian Swinton said, 'we must think of the shareholders.'

'The shareholders will do a great deal better with the present management over the next two years than selling out now to some crummy biscuit group,' said Jack. The pencil clattered on to the table with deliberate drama. 'We will *all* do much better.'

Nobody laughed at the pun. The emphasis on the 'all' was what caught their attention. They sat frozen in their seats, strangely in awe of Jack Armstrong, the rough diamond from Wigan – Randolph's whizz kid.

Charlie too sat still, observing the scene with the stirrings of admiration. For the first time in his career, Jack smelt real power.

The wind blew a flurry of leaves against the window and the moment passed. Jack lifted an elegant arm towards the Huntingdon directors for their response. They nodded dumbly. They knew that none of them could have achieved Huntingdon's renaissance. Before Jack's arrival, the company had ranked among the living dead, churning out the same products in the same packaging as it had for twenty years on ancient machinery. He had dragged the company into the twentieth century.

It would be foolish to oppose him now. Besides, only the

young finance director and the sales director, both recruited by Jack, truly understood how the company was run.

'Are we not forgetting that three members of the Huntingdon family own another 11 per cent between them?' The finance director broke the silence.

'Exactly,' said Jack. 'Do we really imagine Randolph would want us all selling out the moment he's cold in his grave?' He allowed another long pause and picked up the pencil, holding it between both hands, studying it intently. When he looked up his eyes were flat.

'I intend to fight, gentlemen, and fight to win.' His voice was just audible. 'I suggest that anyone who does not want to fight should leave the room now.'

The three older directors looked at their hands. The younger men struggled silently to contain their excitement, but Jack could sense it.

Everyone jumped as the phone rang. Jack had asked not to be disturbed unless it was urgent. Charlie picked it up, there was a pause, and then he replaced the receiver.

'Well?' demanded Jack.

Charlie grinned. 'Bridget in't kitchen says she doan't care 'ow important meetin is,' he said in a splendid imitation of a Cheshire accent. 'We've all got to go and eat us dinners.'

Chapter 2

Peter Markus sprang lightly from the chopper, as immaculate as a male model in *Uomo* magazine – and almost as good-looking. A skinny youth followed him and then the slightly stooped, rounded frame of Sir Richard Butler, great-grandson to Butler's founders, Philip Butler and his wife Edith. It was Edith who had dreamed up the recipe for the original Butler's biscuit and called it – with exquisite lack of imagination – the Oatie.

Sir Richard had mixed feelings about the visit. It seemed somewhat extreme to be hurtling north in a specially hired helicopter. But he had to admit he loved the excitement.

Sir Richard believed himself to be a force for good in the land – rather like his biscuits. A traditional product of a middle-class industrial family, he had been knighted for services to industry three years before. The investiture had coincided nicely with his fifty-fifth birthday party.

Until now, self-interest had told him investors should stick with the managers of companies (like him) who used their passion for the long-term view to explain their lack of short-term performance. In the great City debate of the 1980s – the long-term good versus short-term performance – he had taken what he saw as the ideological high ground, decrying takeovers as uncouth and unproductive.

He chose to forget that his father, Victor, had built Butler's into a gigantic food conglomerate selling more than 3,000 different products through a relentless string of opportunistic takeovers in the 1960s, earning him the title The Biscuit Baron. But then, like so many people, Sir

Richard was adept at keeping his thoughts in separate compartments.

He excelled at CBI meetings, lambasting the evils of City short-termism and sincerely advising fund managers to invest for the long stretch. He was, however, quick to berate the managers of the Butler's pension fund if their performance fell behind.

Imagine how his distaste for takeovers had sharpened when rumours began to reach him that predatory companies were eyeing his very own Butler's. Unlike the cautious Huntingdons, the Butler family had gone for growth. Share issues had reduced their proportion of the company and Sir Richard himself now owned less than half a percent.

He suspected any takeover would leave him out on his ear, without salary, car, secretary, business lunches, and most important, status; in fact, everything that made life worthwhile.

Then the press got hold of it. 'Predators are thought to be running their slide rules over Butler's', said the market report one day in the *Daily Telegraph*. *The Times* suggested a corporate raider was building a stake. A search of the share register showed nothing, but it was hopelessly out of date.

As he read the *Financial Times* one morning, seeing Peter Markus mentioned three times, he was reminded of a conversation with Peter the previous Christmas. They were at The Savoy for the Great Universal Stores annual cocktail party.

'What can companies do about predators?' he had asked Peter, as if talking about abnormally bad weather.

'Put the boot on the other foot, my dear man,' Peter had declared as if talking to a five-year-old. 'Start rationalising your portfolio – buy something, sell something.'

'What about all the people working for these companies that are bought and sold?' asked Sir Richard. 'It's not a game of monopoly you know.'

Wondering how such outdated views had survived six years of Thatcher rule, Peter had answered in the most caring tones he could muster. 'Of course it's disruptive, but if companies have the right parent, they will fare better in the long run – and isn't that what we are all concerned about?'

Perhaps, thought Sir Richard, young Markus was the man

he needed. And when he had called, Peter spotted a delicious opportunity to kill two birds with one stone.

It was a thundery early-October day and it seemed impossible to get any air into the Huntingdon boardroom. Jack took an instant dislike to Peter – all public school charm and slick patter, he thought. He noted Peter's finely chiselled features and thick wavy hair with a stab of male envy. At Huntingdon, Jack had grown used to being both the youngest and best-looking man round the table.

Sir Richard he judged as the ineffectual CBI type – too many lunches and not enough exercise.

They sat down. Tea was brought while Peter and Sir Richard muttered to each other and shuffled paper.

Finally, Sir Richard settled untidily in his chair and leaned towards Jack, his hands clasped on the table. 'The fact is,' he began in a fatherly way, 'we think you have a jolly good little company here.'

'So do we,' said Jack, eyes as grey as the sky outside.

Sir Richard smiled understandingly. 'If you will allow us we'd like to show you why we feel the two companies might prosper more together.'

He took Jack's silence for consent and motioned to Peter.

Aided by the skinny youth, Peter started on a flip chart presentation showing Butler's various divisions and how Huntingdon would fit in. As he worked, Jack felt a tongue of fear licking at the inside wall of his stomach. He was fascinated by how well the two groups would fit together, like a pre-ordained jigsaw. They had done their homework all right.

'There would clearly be a great deal of scope for cost cutting. We would aim to use the combined creative skills of both companies to develop new products,' Peter finished, archly emphasising the word 'both'. There was a ten-second silence.

Sir Richard looked at Jack, eyebrows raised. 'What do you think of our little show?'

'We're not interested in a bid from Butler's,' he said. His chin was like a point someone had neatly squared off, thought Sir Richard.

'But we haven't talked numbers yet,' Peter said, flashing his teeth in a disarming smile. 'May I?' He reached for the teapot.

Jack watched him while he poured until his cup was full and he was forced to look up. Jack's face was bland, implacable. 'Huntingdon has a prosperous independent future,' he said.

Brian Swinton began to wriggle around in his seat.

'We were thinking in the region of 270p a share, but of course we are open to negotiation,' said Peter.

Jack stared out of the window at the purple clouds gathering over the trees, his fingers slowly rolling a pencil against the blotter.

'Looks like you'll get very wet going back to your helicopter if you don't leave soon,' he said in his broadest Lancashire accent.

Back in the chopper, just five minutes later, Peter comforted his client through his mouthpiece. 'Don't worry, it was almost certain to be like that.'

Sir Richard's benign courtesy had turned to testiness, not helped by the wind bouncing the chopper around.

'Can I ask why we went to all this trouble then?'

Peter sighed. 'Because it puts us in a better light and if it had worked, we'd have got it cheaper.'

'Can't see me getting along with Armstrong for long,' said Sir Richard. 'He certainly plays up the northern hillbilly act.'

Peter had ambivalent views about Jack. 'He's chippy, but he's bright. He's well under forty and just as he thinks he's got the company to himself, here we are trying to take away his toy. He's bound to be a bit prickly.'

He forced himself to remember that what was a routine visit for him, numbing in its predictability, was a first-time novelty for his client.

As the helicopter swooped down the curve of the Thames into Battersea, Peter said: 'We'd better order some food for later, we've got a long night ahead of us.' The sun was setting, red on the water. 'What shall we have,' he asked. 'Pizza or MacDonald's?'

21

Alone in his office, Jack punched out a New York telephone number. 'Jean-Pierre,' he said sounding relieved. 'Well, I've told the buggers to sod off. What happens now?'

Charlie Briggs-Smith rang a small stockbroker in Jersey where he had an account in a nominee name. If he bought shares through it, his identity need never show up on the company's share register. 'Hi, Bob. Buy me another 50,000 Huntingdon before the opening tomorrow, will you?'

'You're not doing bad on the first lot,' said Bob, who had followed Charlie's lead two weeks before and bought a few himself. 'Think there's going to be a bid?'

'Almost certainly,' said Charlie, who was phoning from Manchester airport. 'Must dash, I've got a plane to catch.'

At 9 the following morning, Jack received his second phone call from Sir Richard Butler. 'I thought you ought to know we will be making a formal takeover bid for Huntingdon at 9.15,' he said, in treacly tones.

'Thank you for calling,' Jack said and put the phone down instantly.' Bereft of a Stock Exchange screen in his Chester office he had to rely on Charlie to tell him the bid – an offer of Butler's shares – was worth 280p a share at the then market price. There was a cash alternative, as was normal practice, slightly lower, at 270p. All told, it put a value of £80 million on the company. On the day of Randolph's funeral, two weeks before, it had been worth just £52.6 million.

Within three hours of the Butler's bid announcement, Huntingdon put out a statement. It read: 'The board of Huntingdon regards the offer from Butler's Biscuits as opportunistic, derisory, and failing totally to reflect the growth potential of the company. The board urges shareholders to take no action.'

Denis Jones studied the screen to the side of Sarah Meyer's desk. 'This bid's a bit of a surprise, isn't it? I thought Butler's was supposed to be one of your sleeping giants.'

Sarah looked up at him, irritation in her black eyes. 'The surprise was that Butler's was the bidder,' she said with an air of superiority. 'The Huntingdon share price has been telling us something was happening for a few days.'

'Tut, tut,' said Denis. 'All those naughty insider dealers, you mean.' His accent betrayed him as Essex man.

She sat back from her desk, dark bouncy curls framing a pale heart-shaped face, and resigned herself to a chat. She liked Denis. He was a good, old-fashioned spivvy stockbroker with a heart of gold, always ready to help out anyone in trouble. Dealing for the bunch of rogues he called clients, there was nearly always someone.

But he was also bright, she had realised, with a memory like a steel trap.

'Well, the market knew old man Huntingdon's share stake was on offer,' she said. 'It was almost certain it would go to a bidder, but I just didn't think it would be Butler's. If I'd known they'd taken on Hogarth Stein as their merchant bank, I might have considered it.'

'Yep. That young Peter Markus has really put Hogarth Stein's name back on the map. I suppose they'd die rather than admit it, though.'

'Mmm.' Sarah pointedly picked up her calculator and began working from some documents in front of her.

'Waste of time, research, if you ask me,' said Denis, settling his roly-poly figure on the edge of her desk. 'You'd be better off working for me, at the sharp end, acting on flair and intuition.'

Sarah looked coolly back up at him. 'Take up insider dealing, you mean?' she said, pondering the shortness of his hair. It looked painted on above his pink, puffy face.

'Well,' mused Denis, who had drunk his quota that lunchtime, 'there's nothing quite like a tickle from the chairman – or someone close to him.'

She affected deep shock. 'You're disgraceful,' she declared.

He grinned. 'Listen,' he said turning serious, 'you, the respectable stockbrokers' analyst, visit a company, have lunch with the directors, wheedle out of them how they are doing and send your report to your favourite clients first.

'Me, Denis Jones, the much maligned half commission man, gets the whisper on the figures from the guy that travels on the same train as the finance director and puts his best clients in.' He leaned on the desk, his round face thrust towards her, staring her in the eye. 'What's the difference?'

She smelt the whisky on his breath as she returned his gaze and suddenly her face lit up, eyes gleaming wickedly.

'It's just that your way is illegal and mine isn't, Denis,' she said, laughing.

She was tasty, he thought as he began electronically flicking through the pages on the Stock Exchange screen, using the key pad on Sarah's desk, but a bit too clever to fancy.

Denis had started work on the Stock Exchange Floor at sixteen as a 'blue button' – the lowest of the low in the hierarchy. He knew everyone of any note, and, alongside his official clients, dealt for a small circle of 'friends' who pooled their information. Members of this group would mutter an order in his ear over a drink, along with the supposed reason for buying. He would tip the others off, buying and selling within the fortnightly account so no money changed hands until the end. This was insider trading as practised among members of the Stock Exchange since its inception, although it had become illegal in 1980. The contract notes went to a front man in Jersey who took a commission. When the profits came in, the money would be cabled direct into an offshore bank account, usually in Switzerland. For some of his less sophisticated mates on the market floor, however, Denis would obligingly send a runner to pop over to Jersey and bring the money back in a suitcase. 'I'm never bored,' he would boast to his cronies, 'as long I can do the odd deal that's a little bit bent.'

His customers were mostly small-time rogues and stock jobbers. But the cream on the cake came from a handful of big hitters – international 'players' – heads of business empires, with tens of millions in the market at any one time. They would deal through several brokers, so that nobody ever knew their whole position.

Denis's biggest client by far was the newly knighted Sir Leo Stern.

In that autumn of 1985 the City of London still operated as a cosy club, as it had for two centuries, where the members closed ranks against the outside world at the first whiff of trouble. The motto 'my word is my bond' was rarely violated because the place would fall apart otherwise. Club officials dealt with rule breakers by censure or barring them from doing business for as long as six months.

Not much went wrong that couldn't be settled with a stockmarket official over a glass of champagne in Green's at the back of the Royal Exchange, or Jonathan's bar in the tall Stock Exchange tower. Such were the civilised, incestuous ways of 'self-regulation'.

Sarah had come to understand all this gradually in her four years on the research desk with Tulley & Co. She also knew that there was a tornado heading straight for this pleasant world. Big Bang – the ending of the small cartel of old established brokers and jobbers and the admission of big international bankers into the market – was due in a year's time in October 1986.

'Can Butler's afford to go higher?' asked Denis.

'Oh, sure. Butler's shares were inflated by bid hopes and Huntingdon was underrated for so long the shares haven't caught up yet.' She was rapping out the facts to impress him. 'They could easily pay another 20p. Butler's would still only be paying fifteen times earnings for Huntingdon, but should get it.'

'But I thought you rather rated that man at Huntingdon?' Denis enjoyed trying to catch her out.

'I do. He's pushed its profits up 25 per cent compound over the last three years, and without that family shareholding he could have done even better. But Butler's moved in pretty fast to pick up those shares and it's now in a very strong position.' Sarah was one of the few City analysts who had got to know Jack Armstrong. She liked following small companies where there was talented management.

'You've done your homework then, Miss,' said Denis with just a hint of teasing in his voice.

'Well, I am supposed to be the number two research analyst for the food sector in this firm, you know. I'm having lunch with Armstrong tomorrow, so I'll know even more then.' She grinned at him impishly.

'You're wasted in research,' said Denis.' Make yourself some real money. Come and work for me!'

To his surprise she looked up at him thoughtfully. 'You never know,' she said, 'I might take you up on that one day.'

Then she grinned. 'Especially if you let me talk to Sir Leo.'

'That reminds me – ' Denis turned suddenly businesslike ' – I've got a phone call to make. See you.'

Back in his own cubby hole he rang his favourite client. 'Leo – Denis. Our analysts here reckon Butler's will pay up, so you might as well hang on to your shares.' There was a pause.

'Well, what do you want with a confectionery company? Oh I see. Yeah, well.' Denis's tone was doubtful. 'If you must, I suppose – give him a ring, can't do any harm.'

He sighed as he put the phone down. Leo couldn't keep his fingers out of anything. It wasn't enough for him just to make a turn – he had to be playing power games. Oh, well, let him try and outsmart Hogarth Stein if it made him happy. It didn't make Denis happy though; he liked people to stick to what they were good at.

At two minutes to one the next day, Sarah Meyers scampered down the steps of Le Champenois restaurant, just off Bishopsgate. Her face fell short of classical beauty, although her dark oval eyes were large and her mouth generous. Her body was a source of annoyance to her with unfashionably rounded breasts and hips accentuated by a narrow waist. Sarah's true attraction sprang from an inner vitality, as if her heart sang perpetually of the goodness of life.

'Good morning, Miss Meyer, 'ow nice to see you,' the young head waiter greeted her with genuine warmth. The elegant, mirrored grey and white restaurant was already two-thirds full of young brokers and dealers, financial journalists and public relations people all out on company expenses.

She was the first to arrive as always. She liked a chance to see who was where and with whom. She ordered a glass of champagne and pretended to study the menu.

Jack had spent the week supervising the defence document from a temporary office in his merchant bank in London.

He spent a lot of time talking to the City food analysts, trying to win them over to his side. Sarah, who had singled out Huntingdon as a recovery stock three years before, was alone in inviting him to lunch – although he had no intention of letting her pay. She was one of the best in the field and she had

26

promised him her latest, and as yet unpublished, research note on Butler's Biscuits.

He liked Sarah. She was bright and straightforward, but somehow not his type. Not that it stopped him flirting with her. Something deep inside him needed to flirt with every female who crossed his path.

'Sorry I'm late. Someone rang just as I was leaving the office.'

'Don't worry.' She rose to allow him to kiss her cheek.

'How about a glass of champagne?'

Jack felt slightly thrown. 'I'm a gin and tonic man myself,' he said. 'Lunch is on me, by the way.'

She shrugged. 'If you feel your masculine ego can't cope with a woman paying – fine.'

'I like the outfit,' he said.

'Thank you. It's my new Jasper Conran,' she replied, allowing him to change the subject.

'I hear you City analysts get paid a fortune.'

'Not where I am. I could more than double my earnings if I went to an American bank. Our dealer in oils has just been offered over £100,000 – and he's younger than me.'

Jack's drink arrived and they raised their glasses. 'Long may it last,' said Sarah. 'It won't, of course. Everyone says when volumes drop off there'll be blood all over the street.'

Jack picked up the menu.

'They go in for exotic fish here,' said Sarah.

'So I see.'

They both ordered langoustine salad to start and Sarah chose the roast tuna for a main course. Jack had grilled chicken.

'If Butler's pay much more, I'm afraid you are going to lose,' Sarah said once they had ordered.

He laughed to cover his irritation. 'I thought you were on my side?'

She looked coolly back at him. She was intrigued by the way his face seemed to be made up of triangles. A broad brow and cheekbones gave way to a sharply slanting jaw which ended in a well-defined chin. His eyes and cheeks formed triangles of their own while his wide mouth made another with his chin. She wondered why he wore his hair in that absurd fringe.

27

'It's not my job to be on anybody's side,' she said.

He felt himself flush. 'But I had the impression you thought my team and I were doing a good job at Huntingdon.'

'Oh you are.'

'Then?' He spread out his hands in an uncomprehending question.

Sarah looked at him patiently. 'But if they pay enough, shareholders will accept.'

He grinned suddenly. 'You call a spade a spade, don't you, lass?' he said, playing up his accent.

She smiled back. 'Butler's is a great name, born of the spirit of Victorian capitalism. There are worse predators around.'

'Really? I wanted to ask you about the history.'

'Well, I take it you know the Oatie was due to an error of housekeeping by Mrs Edith Butler?'

'No, who was she?'

'She was the wife of the founder,' replied Sarah, amazed at his ignorance. 'One day she ran out of flour while she was making her favourite biscuits and hit on the idea of using part oatmeal. And hey presto – one of the best known biscuits of our time.'

'Yes, it's a strong brand all right.'

'At the time it became known as the perfect companion for tea – which had only just come into vogue. It became a massive seller in the early part of this century and all those ex-pats in various parts of the Empire took it with them, especially the currant variety.'

'It's surprising it survived all this time.'

'It nearly didn't. They expanded into cakes but stayed pretty small and provincial until the Second World War when both grandsons of the founders were killed. The shares passed to their widows who let an aged Scottish accountant run the company. It was fading fast when a southern cousin called Victor appeared and proposed a merger.'

'Why was he interested?'

'He had built up quite a healthy cake business in Guildford and saw Butler's and the Oatie as the perfect fit. He was Sir Richard's father.'

'Oh, I see.' Sudden comprehension lit up Jack's face.

'Yes. And he was the one who floated it and built it up in the fifties and sixties.'

'They don't really market those brands properly,' mused Jack.

'Exactly right.' Sarah's face lit up. 'Now just think what you could do for them.'

Their eyes locked. Jack's expression hardly changed, but she could tell he had already thought about it. She breezed on.

'Look, the Butler's share price is holding up very well. It's a fundamentally sound company as you will realise when you read my circular. The market obviously thinks it's a good deal. Why don't you negotiate yourself a seat on the board?'

Jack rang New York. He was beginning to fret. 'Jean-Pierre, are you sure I can rely on them to ring me?'

'Relax, old buddy. Plenty of time.'

Jean-Pierre Krandsdorf, New York's most controversial corporate lawyer, placed his feet carefully on the stool at the side of his desk and sipped mint tea. Carefully tended auburn curls framed tanned, intelligent features illuminated by blue eyes of Caribbean intensity.

Jack felt far from relaxed. 'It could be that what you see as blinding logic, hasn't even occurred to them.'

Jean-Pierre's perfectly manicured fingers toyed with a piece of walnut cake. 'Look, we've been over it. Butler's has virtually zero profit growth for the last three years. It's a company long on history and short on ideas. Unless they are complete morons they will approach you. Believe me, they need you.'

'Mmm. But do they realise it?'

'Listen. How long have you known me?'

Jack thought back to his first meeting with Jean-Pierre when he was working for an American conglomerate called Renasco. Jack would have been gobbled up and spat out if it had not been for the French–Canadian. He had saved him from making a fool of himself several times since.

But if, as he so confidently predicted, the Butler's directors were about to offer Jack a seat on the board, he felt they were taking an awfully long time about it.

Still, he had never known Jean-Pierre give bad advice and

29

he was the nearest thing Jack had to a best friend – even if he did prefer boys.

Peter Markus rang Jack just before nine the following morning, all lightness and brightness.

Could Jack possible come and have lunch the next day, just the two of them at Hogarth Stein's offices in the City?

Jack pretended to hum and hah about prior commitments and plane timetables but eventually agreed.

'Splendid,' said Peter. 'We're nearly two-thirds of the way down Cheapside, on the right coming from St Paul's.'

It was a lot grander than his own merchant bank's offices, Jack thought to himself as he walked into the rarefied atmosphere.

Opposite each other in the austere reception area hung two huge oil paintings of the founders, Joseph Stein and Edward Hogarth, in ornate gilt frames shining against the dark wood panelling of the walls.

Jack walked past them up to a long L-shaped desk, behind which perched two young receptionists in neat navy suits and crisp white blouses.

He treated the first one to a confidential smile. 'I'm having lunch with Mr Markus,' he said. 'Mr Armstrong?' she asked brightly without looking down at her appointments book. He nodded. 'Would you like to come with me?'

She took him briskly down a long corridor to a small lift. 'If you would like to go to the fifth floor, someone will meet you there.' She smiled a bright, clinical smile and was gone.

Back at her desk she rolled her eyes at her colleague. 'Gorgeous green eyes,' she said.

As he stepped out of the lift Jack was greeted by a grey-haired butler in a morning suit. He enquired if Jack would like to wash his hands, then whisked him with surprising speed along another long corridor to a small dining room. 'Mr Markus won't keep you long, sir, and someone will be along to give you a drink.'

There was more panelling and paintings. The walls sported one full-length portrait by Joseph Wright of Derby and two others he couldn't identify but were clearly the school of Constable. He assumed, rightly, they were originals.

30

A highly polished table was set for two, and on the sideboard stood a small selection of drinks including a large pitcher of tomato juice. There was also a bowl of fruit. Jack ate one of the grapes, feeling like a furtive schoolboy, before a motherly waitress appeared to dispense a tomato juice. After five minutes Peter arrived looking inordinately pleased with life.

He stretched out his hand. 'Jack, I'm so glad you could come,' he said with the emphasis on the 'so', as if they had known each other all their lives. 'I've *such* a lot of interesting ideas to talk to you about.'

Jack knew he was being deliberately charmed but despite his first impression of Peter, he found his wariness evaporating as the lunch progressed. He allowed himself to enjoy the sensation of feeling important.

Peter started off giving him a rundown on the bank.

'Like most London merchant banks, we're really German,' Peter explained. 'In the sixteenth century Joseph Stein's family were part of the Jewish Frankfurt banking scene – you know, the Rothschilds and the Goldsmidts. But the young Joseph did a runner and came to London in the early eighteen hundreds, setting up in Cheapside. And here we are!' he ended with a flourish.

'But where did the Hogarth come from?'

'Oh, he arrived at the end of Victoria's reign. Edward Hogarth was landed gentry from Yorkshire in search of excitement. Joseph needed the capital and took him on as an equal partner.'

Peter prattled on and by the time the butler had served the noisettes d'agneau Jack was bristling with impatience. Suddenly, Peter leant back in his chair. 'You're wondering why I asked you here.' He took a deep intake of breath. 'Has it occurred to you that Butler's might need your management talents?'

Jack almost laughed out loud to hear Sarah and Jean-Pierre's sentiments echoed so precisely.

'Not really,' he lied. 'How do you mean?'

'Well, you've done a good job at Huntingdon, and we know,' said Peter lowering his voice and looking conspiratorial, 'you would have done a lot more if poor old Sir Randolph had let you.'

Jack looked wise and stayed silent.

Peter continued: 'Butler's – we are speaking privately – has only got two efficient directors, the chairman and the finance director, and even they are merely adequate. The problem is they're long on history and short on ideas.'

Jack looked suitably impressed. 'And you think I might be able to help out on the ideas front?'

'Exactly.' Peter popped a potato in his mouth and chewed it thoughtfully.

He found Jack's accent intriguing. It was cultivated northern with hints of American, often when you least expected. It had integrity combined with sophistication, a gritty determination that had also seen life – just the sort of accent the big institutional investors in the City would trust.

'How would the newly created post of commercial director appeal to you?'

'On the main board?' This was even better than Jack had expected.

'Of course.'

'What kind of salary?'

'Twice what you get now, a car, a driver, all your house-moving costs paid, a non contributory pension and some generous share options,' he rattled off.

Jack took a large gulp of the velvety claret which had been poured into crystal goblets and smiled for the first time since they had sat down. Peter Markus might look like a male model, but Jack could probably get to like him after all.

The moment he got back to his makeshift office he rang Jean-Pierre. By the end of lunch Peter had agreed that he would talk to Butler's about increasing its offer by a modest amount in return for Huntingdon's recommendation, and discuss the detail of Jack's contract.

'Great stuff, old buddy, what did I tell you?' said Jean-Pierre. 'They'd be proud of you at Harvard. Gotta go, I'm in a meeting. I'll ring you when I get out.'

Jack put the phone down and smiled but he felt suddenly oppressed by a sense of anti-climax and gloomily poured himself a large whisky. What he needed was a woman.

Unexpectedly Rosemary came to mind. That was it. He

had hardly seen her or Mark since Randolph died. His face darkened as he thought of his daughter Susan, so many miles away. On a sudden inspiration he called through on the intercom to his temporary secretary, Amanda. She was flat-chested, but a paragon of efficiency. 'See what the next flight is you can get me on to Manchester this evening, would you?'

'Yes, Mr Armstrong.'

He hesitated a moment. 'And then I wondered if you could pop out and get me a bottle of perfume for my wife? Some-body was telling me about one called Mitsui or something like that.'

'Mitsuko, Mr Armstrong, by Guerlaine?'

'Clever girl.' He leaned back in his chair, a look of satisfac-tion on his face. Peter had told him that Mark Birley, who owned Annabel's nightclub, always made his girlfriends wear it. He would surprise her.

When his private line rang he picked it up eagerly, hoping it was Jean-Pierre.

But the voice at the other end was gravel, straight out of the East End of London. 'My name is Sir Leo Stern. We haven't met, but I am a significant shareholder in Huntingdon.'

Jack was intrigued. How the hell had Stern got this number and just how significant a shareholder was he?

'Yes, well, of course I've heard of you,' he said pleasantly.

'I'd like to talk in confidence to you about making a higher offer for Huntingdon – I think the current one is, how shall I put it, a bit mean.' Jack could hear the sarcasm.

He saw his new job, doubled salary, brand new car and possible knighthood disappearing into Stern's grasp.

'I'm not interested,' he said tersely.

'Don't be silly, my boy, it's in the interests of your share-holders.' The voice was quietly insistent, almost fatherly. 'I'm talking about a friendly deal here; it would be worth your while to talk to me.'

Never had the word 'friendly' sounded so menacing. Jack stood up – a moment such as this could not pass with him lolling in his chair. His long limbs tingled as if wired to an electric current. In that split second he knew that what he said next would change the course of his life.

'I'm sorry, I can't discuss the matter. Goodbye.' He put the phone down and instantly took it off the hook. Then he took two other extensions off the hook. In the outer office the secretary's extension began to ring. He shut the door and strode to the window, half expecting Stern to be outside. He felt like a trapped animal.

He needed advice. To talk to Brian Swinton was unthinkable. He would be bound to demand it be discussed at a board meeting. And the board, especially the non-executives with their 11 per cent, would be certain to want to consider a higher offer from the mighty Stern Group.

But from what Jack knew of Stern, there would be no job for him there. He would be out on his ear with six months' money if he was lucky. He thought of ringing Charlie, but he too would surely insist Stern go public with his higher offer.

Jack's mind raced. There was only one person he could turn to – even if he was on the other side.

He felt his shirt wet under his arms and realised he was sweating heavily. He mopped his face, his heart pounding.

He rang the Hogarth Stein number. 'Peter has just left I'm afraid,' said his secretary.

'I need to contact him urgently.'

'Well, you might try him in the car.' She gave Jack the number.

He dialled it feverishly. It was engaged. Finally he got through. 'Leo Stern wants to make me a higher offer.'

Peter, whose Aston Martin was a third of the way round Hyde Park Corner in the central lane, instantly recognised the northern accent. He flicked his left hand indicator and cut in front of a lorry which hooted frantically.

'Steady,' he said. 'These car phones are frightfully insecure, I'll be with you in ten minutes.' The wheels of the Aston Martin scraped the traffic island as he just squeezed through the exit down towards Victoria.

He smiled happily. 'Hey ho, another night written off.' How many sets of fees could he send out on this one, he wondered as he started punching out the number of the hostess of the dinner party where he was due in an hour. Just as well she was an old friend and not anyone important.

Jack waited in Joseph Waggstaff's offices, staring into space.

He checked his pulse rate. It was a steady 66 – a lot lower than Peter Markus's he would bet money on it. As for Leo Stern, he had twelve years on him. What did he have to fear from an overweight fifty year old?

He had come a long way since he had been turned down as a trainee by most of British industry. In his final term at the LSE he had trekked round a succession of big companies and been appalled by the dullness of the men who interviewed him and their obsession with class. Wherever he went he found public schoolboys on the board; grammar school boys down the line.

Then Rosemary, in those days a sleek blonde fellow student who rolled a joint with the best of them, had pointed out an advertisement in *The Times*. 'American food giant seeks trainees for British Division.' The company was Renasco, which made food products from popcorn to curry powder selling in sixty-five countries round the world.

He got the job, took Rosemary out to celebrate and she conceived their daughter Susan the same night. They had married three months later.

He drained the last of the whisky from the glass. It was just two months since Randolph had died, but he felt he was a different man on an unfamiliar planet.

The slim, gift-wrapped bottle of Mitsuko glimmered on his desk, complete with a silver bow. Rosemary's surprise would have to be postponed.

Chapter 3

'What the fuck is going on?' Stern bellowed down the mouth-piece at Peter. 'This is your bloody doing, I can smell it.'

'SIR LEO GETS A SWEET TOOTH' ran the headline on the front page of the *Daily Post* City section. 'Sir Leo Stern, head of the Stern retailing empire, is believed to be poised to make a higher offer for Huntingdon Confectionery . . .'

'I can assure you it was as much a surprise to me as to you, Leo,' lied Peter, doing his best to sound hurt. 'I had no idea you were interested in confectionery.'

'Well, I've had some snotty-nosed jerk from the Takeover Panel on to me three times so far this morning.'

An official from the City Takeover Panel had rung Stern's office first thing demanding he either deny the story (which would mean he would be unable to bid for three months) or admit it, in which case he would be forced to go ahead.

'Oh, don't worry about the Panel, Leo. It's full of tedious little clerks,' sniffed Peter.

He was proved right. In 1985 the Takeover Panel had more bark than bite – and Stern toughed it out, making no official statement either way.

But his temper was still simmering when Denis rang him just before ten to point out that Butler's had raised its bid to 300p a share. Stern instantly flicked to the page in question on the Stock Exchange screen in his office while telling Denis of his rebuff by Jack. 'If that story in the *Post* didn't come from Armstrong, I'm the Queen of Sheba.'

'Sounds like a stitch up to me, sir,' agreed Denis.

'Well, they'll be very sorry. Nobody stitches up Leo Stern.'

Sarah was delighted at the new offer. After her lunch with Jack the previous week, she had written a glowing circular on Huntingdon's prospects and predicted a higher bid from Butler's.

More important to Sarah that morning was the news that Denis's assistant, Tony, had given in his notice and would be leaving at the end of the month. The dealing partner, who worked on the Stock Exchange floor, reported via the open line to the office that Denis was 'like a bear with a sore head'. And when Denis appeared in the office, en route for his pre-lunch drink, he had not recovered.

'I hear Tony's off to make his fortune in Vancouver,' Sarah said brightly.

'Those bloody rogues out in Vancouver make London look like a tea party,' growled Denis. 'What these blokes will do for women.' But Tony, whose new young wife missed her family in Canada, could not be swayed.

Denis paused by her desk to play with the screen. 'I see Underwoods' new issue's been well over-subscribed.' He flicked to the Butler's announcement. 'I tell you, Leo is hopping up and down about that article in the *Post* this morning.'

'So it's true then?' Her dark eyes widened in interest.

'Oh, it's true all right. I told him not to get involved, but he can't resist it. Now he's been made to look an idiot. God help Mr Armstrong, mind you. Leo's convinced he leaked it.'

Excitement rippled up Sarah's spine. 'What can he do to my friend Mr Armstrong if he doesn't want to make a higher bid?'

'Oh, he won't go higher than £3. They obviously went for a knock-out once they realised Leo was in the frame. It's just that he hates to lose face – East End honour and all that. He'll get his own back.'

Denis called up the market overview on the screen. 'This market's really shifting,' he said, rubbing his hands with pleasure. He turned back to Sarah. 'I don't think these Australians are going to get Allied Lyons, mind you.' He looked down at her. 'I meant what I said yesterday, you know. Tony's job is yours if you want it.' Sarah didn't answer. 'Think it over and we'll have a chat tomorrow.'

Denis walked jauntily along Throgmorton Street and disappeared through a doorway under a large clock hanging at right angles to the street.

He went down a steep flight of stairs and made a sharp left turn into a wall of sound at one end of a long crowded bar. He was spotted instantly by one of his cronies. 'I'm told London & Edinburgh Trust are on the move,' he muttered in Denis's ear. 'Apparently the new finance director who's come from Rothschild's has been seeing the institutions and he's going down a treat.' Tony, his departing assistant, was standing by the bar looking sheepish. He handed Denis his first pint.

'I can only just about bear to drink this,' joked Denis. 'God, it's noisy in here. Even if I hadn't looked at the screen on the way out, I'd know the market was good. You can always tell.'

The bar was part of an establishment known as the Long Room – an eighth of a mile of subterranean restaurant. A huge double-sided open grill blazed at the halfway mark, the flames shooting high, hissing over steaks and chops. At each end of the restaurant was a bar, like two bookends – the 'long bar' where Denis and his cronies always drank and the much smaller 'short bar' where you went if you had some 'private business'. If any of your mates saw you there, they knew to leave you alone.

The restaurant acted as an unofficial canteen for the market traders who dined from a menu so short most of them knew it by heart. There was steak – small, medium and large, cooked medium, well done and rare; then chops and one fish dish. Roasts could be ferried in from the adjoining Oak Room by the ancient waitresses who served at the small tables, giving their favourites shameless preference. For a decent tip, they would happily part with a whole pad of blank receipts.

To Denis, it was home, workplace and club all rolled into one. He loved it.

A dealer from Wedd Durlacher came hustling, breathless, through the crowd towards him. 'Guinness Peat has just bid for Britannia Arrow and the shares are absolutely flying.'

Denis rocked happily on his heels. He'd bought a stack of those only yesterday. 'It's my shout,' he said. 'What's everyone having?'

Sarah sat at her desk, writing two lists – the pros and cons of working for Denis. She sat back and looked at them thoughtfully. Heading the 'cons' was loss of status – analysts were regarded as respectable; half commission men, or women, were not. There was the disapproval from fellow analysts to face, and possibly from her parents. So what?

Denis worked in the jungle – sometimes for the kings of the jungle, more often for the scavengers. She could sense the power out there, and the chance to make real money. Even before she had started writing the list, the tightness in her diaphragm told her the lure of the jungle was stronger.

Sarah had started at Tulley with no experience in stockbroking but a good academic record. Her schooling at St Paul's had been followed by a degree in Politics, Philosophy and Economics from Oxford. After graduating she had spent a year travelling, mainly in the United States and Israel. She had bluffed her way into a dogsbody job at Salomon Brothers in New York during that summer – and been smitten. But finding a job in the City had not been easy. Phillips & Drew had offered her a place as a trainee research analyst, but the size of the firm and the patronising attitude of the people who interviewed her had put her off.

After several similar experiences, she had allowed her father to introduce her to the senior partner of Tulley, who had been his personal stockbroker for twenty years.

Dickie Hardy-Blythe had been patronising too, but in a bearable old-fashioned way. She had liked the atmosphere in the office – it seemed like fun. And it was small enough for her to make an impact. People disappeared in those big firms. Tulley & Co was medium-sized with a dozen partners and although it researched only a few sectors of industry, it had a good reputation in those it covered.

Sarah had become assistant to 'the General' – an amiable grammar school boy made good. In surveys, he always came out among the top three food analysts in the City. Sarah felt a pang of guilt. He had been a good teacher and they worked well together.

Sighing, Sarah went in search of Dickie, and found him in his office on the floor above, pouring himself a whisky and soda as was his habit at 5.30 in the afternoon when he didn't take the early train.

'How's your father, dear? Furniture business going well, I'm told.' Dickie liked his pleasantries.

She nodded. 'Denis has asked me to work for him.'

'Mm, so I'd heard. Drink?' Dickie was never quite the old buffer he seemed.

'Oh, just Perrier.'

'So you want a bit more excitement, dear, do you?'

'I thought it was called a challenge.'

'Denis is a bit of an old rogue, you know,' he cautioned, pouring her Perrier water.

'Yes, but he's an honest sort of a rogue and he does have some interesting clients. I'd like to have a go at the sharp end. It's all very well writing a report on a company, it's not like risking the client's money, is it?'

'Of course, making money may not be so easy after Big Bang,' Dickie said. Not exactly pretty, he thought, but appealing; spirited yet vulnerable.

Oh God, he's going to block me, thought Sarah.

There was a silence as they both sipped their drinks. 'Listen, if it doesn't work out, I'm sure the General will have you back.'

A rush of excitement flooded through her. 'Oh, Dickie, thank you! I'll ring Denis at home later.'

Peter let the strains of the Queen of the Night's aria from the Magic Flute roll over him and tried to relax. The lorry in front of him belched out a cloud of diesel as it moved forward ten yards and Peter looked yet again in his wing mirror for the tiniest of gaps through which he could squeeze into the out-side lane.

The phone rang. 'Where are you?' It was his wife, Angela. 'In a slow crawl, just coming up to junction 7,' Peter replied miserably. 'There are road works. It should thin out soon.'

'I thought you were going to leave early.' A trace of irrita-tion entered Angela's well-bred voice.

'Darling, I was, but people kept ringing me up.' He looked at his watch. 'I'll make it by eight.'

'Oh God, Peter, if it was anyone important you would be

here.' Angela's patience snapped. She had invited two neigh-
bouring couples for supper.

'Don't whinge, darling,' he said and put the phone down.

As she picked out three bottles of claret from the rack,
Angela sensed the following two days were going to be hell.
Ever since Sir Leo Stern had been knighted, Peter had been
imploring him to bring Paulette for a weekend in the country.
Why they had finally chosen to come in November, she hadn't
quite understood. Thank God the chrysanthemums and dah-
lias were still looking presentable.

Stern had even chosen the week before the visit to try
and muck up one of Peter's deals. Angela, who prided herself on being able to handle most things, felt singularly
daunted.

It was pouring with rain when they awoke the next day.
Heavy, steady, splish-splash, puddle wonderful rain. 'It's
been sunny all week, and look!' raged Peter determined to
take it personally. Then he discovered that langoustines had
been ordered for supper and hit the roof. 'But you said fish or
kosher meat,' protested Angela, defending a thoroughly
bewildered cook.

'Yes, but not shellfish, darling. I'm sure I've told you a
hundred times.'

'Oh, yes, of course – ' Angela could never understand why
it was so important ' – only fish with fins and scales. Don't
worry, we'll have smoked salmon instead.'

Peter marched moodily round the house checking that
everything was just so, particularly in the Sterns' bedroom.
Angela had given them the yellow room with the four-poster.
The dish of burnt orange chrysanthemums on the dressing
table looked perfect, but he muttered under his breath when
he had to go looking for some mineral water.

Sir Leo and Lady Stern were not ordinary guests. Despite
himself Peter found something intimidating about a man
worth £300 million, even if it was only on paper. He loved to
take off Stern's accent and jibe at his nouveau riche ways, but
whatever he might say, he found the smell of that much
money as heady as the claret he bought by the case from Berry
Brothers in St James.

'This is really beautiful,' Paulette Stern murmured as the Bentley turned into the long driveway to the house, wheels scrunching on the gravel.

The rain had stopped and the sun shone down on the classic five-bay frontage of Charlton House, the red brick of the walls and cream of the pilasters standing out in sharp relief against the purple-grey of the retreating clouds.

The drive wound through wooded parkland so the house kept appearing and disappearing from sight through a lattice work of burnished trees.

Paulette nudged her silent husband. 'Don't you think it's beautiful?' she said.

'Yep,' he said, more to himself than her. 'This boy's certainly got delusions of grandeur.'

'Oh, Leo, you are such a killjoy.'

Stern hated being away from his beloved shops on Saturdays and did not bother to disguise it. Paulette sighed, her oval face solemn, knowing there was nothing to be done.

By the time they arrived at the front door, Peter was there to greet them, ecstatic that the sun had come out just in the nick of time. He helped Stern take out the bags. 'Let's leave them in the hall, someone will take them up later. Come and have a drink.'

A vast log fire crackled in the grate, but they stood at the French windows looking out on to the patio and endless lawn as Peter pointed out the main attractions.

To the left were tennis courts and beyond that Paulette could see old brickwork. 'It's a walled garden,' said Angela in answer to her query, 'and we've also put a pool in there.'

'Oh, is it heated?' Paulette instantly regretted she hadn't bought a costume.

Angela shook her blonde head. 'I'm afraid not.' Paulette was just as instantly glad she had left it behind.

But while Paulette was charming, the conversation over lunch struggled along.

Stern was moodily silent most of the time, demolishing his food at extraordinary speed and hardly listening to Peter explain to Paulette the history of the house. 'It was literally falling down when we bought it, I'll show you some of the photographs later.'

Thank heavens we've invited some lively people tonight, thought Angela.

But she found her eyes wandering towards Stern throughout the meal. There was a mesmeric quality about him. He sat, his broad-shouldered bulk overwhelming the reproduction Chippendale dining chairs, looking supremely bored. Yet he completely dominated the room. He's sexy, she thought. It was not a matter of his dramatic dark looks, or his imposing physique. It was the sense of restless energy under the stillness; like the seething liquid core of a volcano.

'What's it worth, Pete?' Stern cut into the conversation as Mrs Warren brought in the coffee. Peter pretended to think about it.

'Oh, about a million I should think.'

'And how much did you pay?'

'Three hundred thousand in 1977.'

'And you've spent?'

'Probably another hundred thousand.'

Stern leaned back in his chair and the flicker of a smile played on his lips. 'Well, you've got to have somewhere to live.' There was silence and then he said softly: 'I've got a bone to pick with you. How come you moved so fast on Butler's?'

Peter frowned at the tablecloth, then wagged his finger towards Stern. 'Naughty, naughty. I have no intention of discussing it in front of the ladies. Come and look at the garden.'

'Peter's father was French, you know,' Angela said to Paulette as they found themselves left alone.

'Oh, really?' Paulette raised a delicate eyebrow.

'Yes, he came from a French Jewish banking family – sort of poor man's Rothschild.' She laughed. 'But his father was an inventor. He left just enough for us to put down a deposit on this house. Fortunately some people who lost all their money were forced sellers, so we got it for a very good price.' Angela knew she was gabbling.

'Fortunately for you,' said Paulette pointedly.

Angela felt ill at ease with this immaculate French woman, with her perfectly cut dark bob and her dainty hands. It brought back her modelling days in Paris where, apart from

43

on the catwalk, her height had made her feel uncomfortably large. Wearing heels, she was only a fraction shorter than Peter. Paulette looked as though a puff of wind would blow her away. Angela noticed her shiver and put another log on the fire.

'Such a big house. Don't you have children?'

'No, we don't actually,' replied Angela, feeling quite apologetic. 'There seems to be a problem with my ovaries – although no one is quite sure what.'

Paulette's expression changed. 'I'm so sorry, my dear, I'm being tactless.' She moved forward and touched Angela's arm. 'They can do many things these days. Don't worry. You 'ave time.'

Angela changed the subject. 'Would you like to see round the house,' she asked, 'or would you just like to flop?'

Paulette did not share the English country obsession with grand houses. 'Flop, I think.'

Angela breathed a sigh of relief, then realised she was on the brink of bursting into tears. The French had a way of going straight to the point. 'Tell me,' she asked groping for a new subject, 'how did you meet Leo?'

Paulette's smile lit up the room at the thought. Stern had bulldozed his way into her life when she was twenty-three. She had only a faint memory of her own parents who had been murdered by the Nazis. She had been brought up by her uncle, a French lawyer, and his wife.

On leaving school she had set her heart on a career as a concert pianist, but after two painful years had realised she would not make the top grade. Turning to fashion, she had been working in the public relations department of Balmain when she had been introduced to Stern at a party on a visit to London.

The attraction to the powerfully built, loutish Englishman had been instant. But she dismissed him in her mind as '*vulgaire*' – uncivilised and uneducated.

He had followed her back to Paris and laid siege in the way that men like Leo Stern do when they want something. There were no cartloads of flowers or trinkets from Cartier – just Stern, with his intense eyes and razor sharp wit. His voice growled at her from the telephone; and he was waiting for her every time she set foot in the street.

Most of this she told Angela. 'He was impossible to resist,' she said, spreading her small hands with the slightest of shrugs. Then, with an apologetic smile: 'And he was so handsome.'

'What did your aunt and uncle think?'

'What could they do? They were so serious; he was so exciting, so funny.' Angela struggled to recognise the man of half an hour before.

'We had lunch one day – then a walk in the Tuilleries – finally dinner. We were engaged within a fortnight.'

Paulette started to laugh at the memory, the laughter bubbling up through the words as she talked. 'He had some tiny shops in a terrible area of London. He did not know a violin from a double bass.' She was crying with laughter. 'They would love to have stopped us.'

'Did they try?' Angela found she was laughing too.

'Oh, yes.' Paulette dabbed at her eyes. 'But in the end they gave in. You see, at least he was Jewish.'

On the far side of the lawn Peter stopped and turned back to the house.

'You can see it was originally a seventeenth-century building with a Palladian façade, supposedly influenced by Inigo Jones,' he told Stern who despite himself was enjoying the country air. But it had been absolutely ruined by all kinds of hideous additions under the Victorians. So I got Victor Hodges of Pantheon Designs to restore it.'

Stern nodded. 'Oh, yes, he's a good architect. Done some work for me in the South of France.'

Peter felt suitably gratified. 'So he got rid of the Victorian stuff and virtually remodelled the whole thing. He got stacks of awards, and all I got was a huge bill.'

Stern smiled. 'And who looked after it while all this was going on?' They began to walk on again.

'Oh, Angie. She's wonderful. Good solid shire stock. Doesn't seem to mind at all as long as she has her horses and can ride to hounds once a week.'

Stern could not see Paulette living amid builders' noise and dust for months on end. He had never understood the Gentile

45

passion for buying houses which were uninhabitable. They entered the walled garden where roses were now pruned back to spiky stumps. 'Now,' said Stern, purposefully, 'who leaked that story to the press?'

Peter knew he could evade him no longer. He looked contrite. 'Well, Leo, Butler's is my client on this occasion. I can't let you just come and ruin their party. The point was, Armstrong asked for my help.'

Stern's face was blank.

'You been reading about Jacob Clark?'

'What, the chap at Jaysee Textiles who called in the receivers last week?' asked Peter, puzzled at the turn in the conversation.

'That's him,' said Stern, turning to stare at the house. 'He's had a heart attack, too, they tell me.'

'Yes, that's right. Isn't there a possibility of fraud?'

'Yep, called in the police, I gather. An awful lot of his factories seemed to burn down.'

'Really?' said Peter, mystified.

They walked out of the garden on to the main lawn in front of the house in silence.

'He stitched me up once,' said Stern, his tone matter-of-fact. 'Quite badly.'

'Really?' Peter began to feel uneasy.

'It was three years ago. I went home and got one of the kids' plasticine sets and made a model of him. Then I stuck a pin right through his wallet.'

'It obviously worked.' Peter frowned as the sun disappeared behind a large raincloud. 'I think you've had the garden tour. Let's go back in the house,' he said, keen to change the subject.

But Stern had not quite finished. 'You can tell Mr Armstrong from me that I look forward to doing business with him in the future. Goddit?'

Peter had most definitely got it. Yet his primary emotion was relief that Stern's anger was directed at Jack rather than him. 'From what I hear, Leo, Jack has already felt your hand in his affairs.'

Stern's mouth curled a fraction at the corners. 'Why don't we see what the ladies are up to.'

No one had ever quite worked out where the money came from. True he had progressed from the Roman Road street market in the East End to a string of boutiques, but he could not have raised more than half a million on them at the most. Some said a distant relative had left it to him, others that he made it in the commodity markets. The most popular theory -because he loved to gamble, and because even in the City people are romantics – was that he won it playing Chemin de Fer at the Casino in Monte Carlo.

However he came by it, the crucial fact was he had a pile of cash in the bank when everyone else in Britain was up to their eyebrows in debt. He bought 75 per cent of a quoted department store company and changed its name to Stern Group. In the early l980s he grew at breakneck speed through a series of takeovers, diluting his own shareholding down to 47 per cent. Beyond that he refused to go, cherishing his ability to control the company. By 1985 he had turned the original six department stores into flagships of his empire and set up a chain of middle-fashion high street stores. He had also gone into food, forming Sandpiper Supermarkets, concentrating on delicatessen. Altogether there were over a thousand shops of different kinds and Stern Group was worth just under £600 million on the stockmarket.

That same wet November Saturday morning, Jack Armstrong had woken with a warm, satisfying sensation that all was right with the world. The day before he had persuaded the executive directors of Huntingdon to recommend the 300p offer from Butler's.

It had been a tour de force of salesmanship, he thought, especially after his 'fight, fight fight' stance at the start. Now, he told them, he could see the compelling commercial logic of the deal. He knew he had been blinkered by his own self-interest. He had feared to lose his job, and, indeed, all their jobs. But after long discussion, he had been persuaded by Sir Richard that the greater good of Huntingdon, its shareholders, its customers and its employees would be best served by accepting the offer.

He had also managed to convince his fellow directors, without actually committing himself, that there would be jobs for everyone. In fact, he said, life under the protective wing of Butler's would be just like staying independent, only better. 'With the extra financial muscle from Butler's and the synergies between the two companies, there is tremendous scope for Huntingdon as part of the bigger group.'

He had enjoyed himself and it had worked perfectly. After all, he had been known as 'silver tongue Armstrong' at Renasco. All that remained was to clear it with the non-executive directors on Monday.

When the sun came out he tried to persuade Mark to play tennis with him. 'It's pointless, Dad. You always go at it as if it was the men's finals,' his son had said moodily.

'There's no point in playing unless you play to win.' Jack wondered how he had come to raise such a wimp. The phone rang in the middle of their argument. It was Walter Huntingdon, one of the non executive directors and a member of the family who between them owned 11 per cent.

'Look, Jack,' he said hesitantly, 'we've been told some very disturbing things about you doing a special deal with the Butler's board. We really must meet.'

Jack felt as if someone had kicked him between the ribs. 'What total rubbish! I never heard such rubbish. Anyway, we're meeting on Monday.'

'I know, Jack, but my two cousins and myself are most concerned. I really must insist.'

It was too dangerous to refuse and he agreed to meet them for tea.

Jack instantly rang Peter, interrupting his preparations for Stern's arrival. Peter said it sounded like a tip-off, but refused to speculate from whom. Although he did not mention it to Jack, he strongly suspected his house guest.

On the last Tuesday in November, Butler's surprised the market by increasing its bid for Huntingdon another 20p to 320p with a cash alternative of 300p. The official statement read: 'The offer is being recommended by the full board of Huntingdon. Butler's has received irrevocable undertakings to accept the offer on behalf of a family shareholding representing 11% of the shares.'

The last sentence read: 'Mr J. Armstrong has been appointed to the board of Butler's as commercial director.'

Butler's had won – at a hefty price.

It had been touch and go. On the Sunday afternoon, Jack had been forced by the family shareholders to admit he had been offered a directorship at Butler's. They threatened to expose him if he did not extract a higher price. He had spent most of the Sunday evening on the phone to Peter.

He had been right that Stern, already on the vengeance trail, had tipped them off. He wondered how on earth Stern had found out, but the only way to molify the family was to force a higher price out of Butler's.

Using every ounce of guile on the Monday, Peter had managed to persuade Sir Richard Butler that Huntingdon was worth an extra 20p a share, valuing the company at £91.5 million.

Five days later Peter got the glad tidings that acceptances had gone over 50 per cent and the bid was unconditional. Sir Leo Stern took the share offer on behalf of his 2 per cent.

At the start of December, as Jack was negotiating a BMW 7 series as his company car and other vital details, Sarah began working for Denis. It was the nearest thing to a nightmare she had ever experienced.

Most of her time was spent in the 'box', a small underground office on the edge of the stockmarket floor. She hated the lack of daylight and the cramped conditions, and Denis insisted she be in for eight o'clock each morning instead of nine as previously.

Then she had to deal with the other market traders who teased her constantly, imitated her accent and nicknamed her Lady Sarah. But it was the relentless speed of everything that really wore her down, the continually flashing telephone lights, dealing directly with the clients and telling them what to do with huge sums of money. It scared the hell out of her.

On the Wednesday evening she went home to her flat in Islington, her head thumping, and burst into tears. She had made a terrible mistake, and worse, a fool of herself to everyone in the firm. The General must have been laughing his socks off.

Denis smiled at her woebegone face the next morning. He

had known it would be like this. 'C'mon, girl, cheer yourself up. I thought I'd take you out later.'

'That's very kind, Denis, I thought we weren't both supposed to be out together.' She hung up her jacket wearily.

'Ooh, special occasion! Young Ken can handle it for a couple of hours,' he said, waving his arm towards the office junior.

'Where are we going?' Her mood brightened a fraction.

'Leo's annual meeting at the Savoy. We're both invited to the lunch afterwards as well. In fact,' he winked, 'we'll just sneak in at the end of the meeting cos, as we both know, it will be full of old ladies asking why they can't get red jumpers in Cardiff.'

She laughed for the first time in days.

'And if you want to do yourself a favour, tell Leo to tuck away a few Antelope Leisure. My clever clients say they're right to have.'

'Why don't you tell him yourself?'

'Because I want him to trust you when I'm not here. We're a team now, girl.'

The meeting had just broken up when they arrived. Everyone was milling around with drinks in their hands waiting for lunch to be served in the next room.

Sarah looked around for Stern, hoping to recognise him from his photographs, but could not see him anywhere. They wandered through to the dining area and had just found their lunch table when suddenly he materialised at their side. He shook Denis's hand affectionately.

'And this is my new assistant, Sarah Meyer,' said Denis. Stern's eyes met hers, flicked slowly down the length of her body as if they were stroking her, then back up to her face. She stood transfixed.

He shook her hand, then turned back to Denis as if she had ceased to exist, taking him slightly on one side to whisper confidentialities.

She felt small, alone and abandoned. A waiter came by with a tray and took her empty glass, and she consciously shook herself. He had a lot of important people there, and a speech to make at the end of lunch. He had only just met her. Anyway he was Denis's biggest client, not hers. She would have to build up her own clients. Stern moved away to take his place and they sat down at large round tables, covered in starched pink linen.

'I see he's got the senior partner of Cazenove on one side and the Deputy Governor of the Bank of England on the other,' brayed the silver-haired man on her right. 'Not bad for a Jewish lad from Whitechapel, eh?'

Sarah treated him to a look of pure dislike and turned to the nervous-looking fund manager on her left. She beamed warmly at him. 'Haven't we met before, somewhere?'

At two-thirty people began to leave and she lined up with Denis to say goodbye to Stern. Unexpectedly he put a large hand on her shoulder. 'And what recommendations has Denis's new assistant got for me, I wonder?' he said fixing her in his dark gaze.

Her mind went as blank as the desert. Denis coughed.

'I'm told Antelope Leisure is undervalued at the moment,' she heard herself say.

Without blinking Stern said: 'Fine, buy me two hundred thousand when you get back to the office.'

She gulped. 'But don't you want to know the price?'

'If you tell me they're good value, I'm sure they are,' he said as he turned away. 'But God help you if you're wrong.'

As she and Denis walked out of the Savoy into the biting wind on the Embankment, she knew she was grinning from ear to ear.

'Anything happened while we've been gone?' asked Denis as they walked back into the box.

Ken was just hanging up the phone. 'Montana Properties whacked in an agreed offer for Antelope Leisure five minutes ago.' He motioned to the screen. 'They're up 50p.'

'My God!' Sarah looked at Denis amazed. 'Did you know about this?'

He turned on her crossly. 'Christ girl don't you think we'd have filled our boots with 'em if we'd known for sure?'

Sarah shuddered. 'And then we'd have all ended up in prison.'

Dennis patted her shoulder. 'Don't be silly. We'd have done it through nominee names in Jersey. You've got a lot to learn. I don't know what you're complaining about. Leo's really going to think you're the business.'

51

Chapter 4

Sir Richard Butler invited Jack for lunch with the other directors at the company's head office.

Jack could almost smell the money as he entered Butler's elegant Regency headquarters on the west side of St James's Square. He breathed deeply as he waited in the marble entrance hall, pillars at each corner. A tall Christmas tree bedecked with golden baubles stood in one corner while the lights from the chandelier bounced off the polished chequered floor.

In the executive dining room overlooking the square, a vast mahogany dining table was set for ten with antique silver. Dark portraits of the Butler family contrasted with ice blue walls, echoed in the blue and cream sculpted carpet, as thick and soft as marshmallow. Original cream mouldings surrounded the chandelier and softened the corners of the ceiling.

'My dear fellow.' Sir Richard moved forward to greet Jack shaking him warmly by the hand.

Sir Richard introduced him to the circle of middle-aged men holding drinks. A glance told him there was at least ten years between him and the next youngest, the finance director, Edward Williams. He had met most of them briefly before his appointment, but the three non-executive directors were new faces. 'We believe in the benefits of cross fertilisation of ideas that directors with other companies can bring us,' Sir Richard explained.

'Oh, I quite agree,' Jack nodded. 'At Huntingdon, the non-executives made an invaluable contribution,' he said, enjoying the secret irony.

He concentrated his attention on Edward Williams and a big bluff man called Bill Soames, the sales director.

'Glad to have you aboard.' Bill Soames proffered a well-padded hand. Strands of fading blond hair were combed across a shiny head. Peter had described him as ambitious, a smooth talker but undisciplined. Jack noted the round, palely lashed eyes in the fleshy face and sensed an enemy.

None of them, thought Jack as they sat down to smoked trout, looked over-bright or over-energetic. He noticed some of them were wearing ties bearing a Latin motto and smirked inwardly with contempt. How many of them would know the end of one MBA from another? They were flabby under their well-cut suits; their droopy jowls and rosy cheeks told him everything. None of them worked out three times a week, he would stake money on it. He thought fondly of his new gym in Piccadilly, so conveniently nearby. He had signed up only the week before.

There was a wariness in the air, perhaps normal in the circumstances, but the bonhomie seemed forced. Then it clicked into place. Where was the managing director?

He had been abroad on business when Sir Richard and he were tying up the deal. Jack had thought then how strange it was to go ahead with a mainstream appointment without the personal vote of the managing director. And now he was missing again.

'Unfortunately, Donald Appleton can't make it today,' said Sir Richard as if reading Jack's thoughts, and in a way that would have made further questioning seem rude.

'This wine is pretty good,' he said.

'Oh, yes, we have our own cellar here, pride of the Butlers,' boomed Bill Soames from across the gleaming expanse of table.

'And as you know, we have our own vineyard at Château Lamiffe,' added the chairman.

'Does it make any money?' asked Jack as a waiter brought tournedos served on a crouton smothered in rich pâté.

'Alas, no,' said Sir Richard, 'but it doesn't lose much and we reckon it adds cachet to the group.' Jack wanted to say he believed in cash not cachet, but resisted temptation.

After the Stilton, Sir Richard made a short speech of welcome and asked Jack if he had any questions.

'Well, I'd like to thank you for your warm welcome, gentlemen,' he said playing up his northern accent. 'Obviously I do have some questions, particularly about the non-biscuit divisions.' The face of a man at the far end of the table lit up at this. Jack later identified him as the director of herbs and spices. 'But I guess this is not the time or place. I'd like to come and talk to you all separately over the next few weeks if that's all right,' he glanced calmly from face to face.

Sir Richard looked fleetingly startled at the note of authority in Jack's voice, but nodded.

'One thing that has been puzzling me, not having the benefit of a classical education,' said Jack, waving away the 1960 Remy Martin, 'is what this Latin motto on your ties means.

'That is the Butler's motto – *Praestantia quocumque pretio*,' cried the marketing director. 'It means excellence at all costs.'

'Too much of that company's costs are going down the throats of the directors,' Jack said to Peter over a drink later that evening. 'I could take £100,000 a year out of the dining room alone.' Peter laughed. He was showing a flattering interest in Jack's progress.

'But the really odd thing,' said Jack, 'is that Donald Appleton wasn't there.'

'Well, he wouldn't be,' said Peter in a tone that made Jack look up. Peter paused and pressed the tips of his fingers together forming a triangle with his hands over which he regarded Jack, eyes glittering.

'Donald is not very well,' he said softly. The sound of a police siren penetrated the double glazing of the office and Jack felt the hair at the back of his neck rise. 'What the hell do you mean,' he asked equally softly, 'not very well?'

Peter's eyes had darkened to navy. 'He had a bad stroke four months ago, which is one of the reasons I was brought in. It coincided with the start of the bid rumours. They hoped he would recover, but it's pretty slow going.'

'But why hasn't there been an announcement?'

'Because, my dear man,' said Peter, using his I am talking to a five year old voice, 'they are terrified of a bid as it is, and revealing that they don't actually have a managing director would be tantamount to inviting rape.'

'Why hasn't it leaked?'

'Fear,' said Peter. 'They all know they'd be out on their ear if a James Hanson or Owen Green came along and took them over.'

'So the top job is wide open?' said Jack who was leaning toward Peter in a mirror image. Realising it he leaned back abruptly and stretched his arm along the back of the sofa.

'Indeed it is,' said Peter, 'and personally I think you are the man for it.' Jack looked at him with new respect as the pieces fell into place in his mind. It was so clear; so perfect.

'Why the hell have you waited until now to tell me?' he asked, already knowing the answer.

Peter looked amused. 'I wanted to be sure you were as good as I thought you were. You should be pleased.'

'I *am* pleased. I would have liked to have been privy to your plans for my future a little earlier, that's all.' It was a struggle to keep the terseness out of his voice.

'Listen, Jack,' Peter said soothingly, 'I'm sure you've got ideas of your own about how to merge Huntingdon into the group, but I've got a couple of little deals in other areas, which if you pulled off could well endear you to the chairman.'

'But surely some of the other directors must feel they are in line for the job?'

Peter nodded. 'There we may have a problem, particularly I suspect with Mr Soames. But let's meet early next week and I'll outline my strategy.'

Jack glanced at his watch. 'Yes, I've got to get the 7 p.m. flight to Manchester. I still haven't convinced Rosemary to move down.'

'Do you want her to?' Peter raised an eyebrow. He had noticed the way Jack's eyes followed attractive women and the way they returned his gaze.

Jack shrugged. 'Actually, we've been getting on rather well lately.' Ever since he had turned up with the Mitsuko, Rosemary's libido had gone onto overdrive. There were still areas where she drew the line, but Jack had always found others who would do what she would not. His mind drifted

55

briefly to May Ling and her infinite range of massage techniques. Now he was in London so much he missed her accommodating ways.

'My daughter Susan is working in Australia and Mark will be at university in a year,' he continued to Peter. 'I think I can persuade Rosemary to come south.'

Jack was well aware of his lack of knowledge in the ways of the City at this stage, but he did know a thing or two about management. It was here that he felt on firm ground.

As he had promised at the boardroom lunch, he made appointments with each director. He would saunter into their offices a few minutes early for his appointment and charm their secretaries. Once in their inner sanctum he would take off his jacket displaying his large Rolex, and sit casually on the other side of their desks, foot on opposite knee, playing with a pencil.

First he disarmed them by a mention of former glory, sometimes from years back. Then he would tell a story against himself. They struggled hard not to like him. When they met at each others' houses or on the golf course they cautiously agreed he was impressive.

'Arrogant though,' said Bill Soames.

'Oh, yes,' they chorused. 'He's arrogant'.

A few weeks later Jack had a clear picture of what needed to be done, and to whom. He also pinpointed his most daunting potential adversaries. Naturally they were the men who had most to lose. Peter he viewed as a divine instrument, sent to further his career; he resolved to pick his brains clean.

MEMO   February 4, 1986.
FROM: Jack Armstrong   TO: Sir Richard Butler
                                  cc Donald Appleton

Following our last conversation, I thought I would put some of my conclusions in writing.

1. The company is leaking money in many areas. The cost controls in purchasing, advertising and expenses are

loose and disorganised, with each division using a different system.

2. The subsidiary companies appear to be run like private fiefdoms with little control from head office. There are no mechanisms for monitoring these companies effectively and no means of rewarding or penalising managers according to performance.

3. Irrespective of their performance, no one of any seniority, appears to have been fired from Butler's over the past five years.

4. The head office is a freehold building housing more than 200 people. I would suggest you consider a sale and leaseback of the property, to free up some capital.

I would also propose halving the number of people, moving everyone on to the top two floors, and letting out the bottom two. I gather rents in this part of London are at a premium.

5. The way the financial information is collected is haphazard. At Huntingdon we are able to determine our stock position up to 24 hours. Full figures are filed to head office every month, and in some cases every week. That way there are no unpleasant surprises.

6. The Trade Unions, particularly USDAW, are far too powerful.

7. In sum, I believe there is a strong case for changing the way the company is structured along the model of Hanson Trust and BTR.

Stringent financial budgets and targets should be set for each subsidiary; managers given authority and responsibility and incentivised accordingly.

Sir Richard shuddered at the word 'incentivised'. He supposed rightly that Jack had learned it at Renasco. His gut told him Jack was spot on in everything he said, but he quailed at the prospect of putting any of it into operation. It would cause uproar. Jack had yet to meet Sean MacCready, the head official of USDAW.

A brief knock heralded the entry of his secretary with the noon edition of the *Evening Standard*. He stopped abruptly at the City page where the headline on the market report read: 'Bid talk lifts Butler's'. Not again! He thought he had stopped the speculation when he bought Huntingdon. 'Shares in Butler's Biscuits, the £550 million bakery group, jumped 12p in early trading on talk that Gary Weston's Associated British Foods is running its slide rule over the company. Analysts say the commercial logic of the two groups merging is compelling.'

He flung down the paper. 'What utter rubbish,' he said out loud. The phone rang. 'It's Mr Markus, sir,' said his secretary.

'Richard, I thought you ought to see what's in the *Standard*.'

'I've just read it. Do you know what's going on?'

'I was hoping you would tell me.'

'Well, as far as I know Gary Weston's on holiday and he's never breathed a word to me about getting together. As for the commercial logic – bread and biscuits are totally different businesses.'

'Probably just mischief then,' said Peter, sounding slightly disappointed. 'There's a lot of it about. Still, as I've said to you before, a little bit of action on your part wouldn't go amiss.'

'Well, dear boy, we bid for Huntingdon, didn't we?' He could feel Peter warming him up for another big fee.

Peter backed off. 'Of course. I meant more in the way of actually running the group. The institutions see it as a bit old-fashioned. You could do with a shake-up, a few management changes.' He paused deliberately. 'How is Donald, by the way?'

'Well, his doctors say he's recovering,' said Sir Richard with forced cheerfulness. 'He seemed a lot brighter when I saw him last week. He's even coming to the next board meeting.'

Jack won't like that, thought Peter as he rang off.

Sir Richard picked up his dictation machine.

MEMO   February 7, 1986
FROM: Sir Richard Butler   TO: Jack Armstrong
                                       cc Donald Appleton

I have given your last memo some thought and concur with much of what you say. However, in order to convince the board that the company is in need of such drastic action, I feel a more systematic investigation of the company is appropriate. I would therefore suggest you put such an investigation under way, for presentation at the March board meeting.

Jack read it grim-faced. Sir Richard was playing for time, going for a typical British compromise. Well, it could even suit him. A smile flickered across his face. The further he delved into the company, the more ammunition he found.

He had been given an office in St James's Square. And because his home was still in Chester, he had taken over the company flat at the top of the building, much to the annoyance of Bill Soames who had previously used it for entertaining his mistress.

As March drew near, the trees in the square came into bud. Working in a big company again was like breathing pure oxygen. He could afford to be patient – but he could see with dazzling clarity the scope Butler's had to become the world class business of his dreams. It just needed him at the helm.

His task now was to transmit his vision to Sir Richard. Jack knew the bid rumours had shaken his complacency, and whatever they said about Donald Appleton's health recovering, it was clear he would never be able to lead Butler's. Sooner or later Sir Richard would have to see that.

Jack soon discovered that Donald had always done the real work, while Sir Richard played the front man. He felt lost without him – alone in a world which had turned menacing and unfamiliar. Of the other directors he trusted only Edward Williams, the finance director, but the two men had little in common.

Sir Richard needed someone to show him the way ahead; someone to chat things through with over a whisky and soda;

59

someone to bolster his confidence, and to lean on. And in Sir Richard's moments of need, Jack Armstrong made sure he was that person.

A week before Butler's March board meeting Jack dropped into Sir Richard's office for a six o'clock drink, something he had made a regular event. Sir Richard was busily preparing a speech for the British Biscuit Bakers Federation dinner where he had been asked to propose the toast.

'I thought you'd like to see an advance copy of my report,' said Jack, sitting on the corner of the desk and placing a thick document before his chairman. 'I'll be sending it to the others.'

Sir Richard picked it up, as if weighing it. 'You've certainly been thorough.'

'I may as well warn you,' Jack said, 'this could be one of the liveliest board meetings you've seen for quite a while.'

Jack's report was forty pages of critical analysis, recommending savage rationalisation, new investment, redevelopment of surplus land and a cutback in the labour force by 30 per cent. It also proposed re-aligning the group into three major divisions, instead of the current seven. That meant four directors would lose their positions of power.

Intentionally, Jack arrived seconds before the meeting was due to start. The hostility in the room leapt at him as he entered. He walked with deliberate slowness to his place and sat down unsmilingly. 'Morning, gentlemen.' It was clear that they had all read it.

This was war and it was about time they knew it. The bright spring sunlight streamed in through the regency windows, bouncing off the polished walnut veneer of the table. 'Glorious day,' he said pushing his chair back a foot or so outside the neat circle. It focused attention on him as effectively as a spotlight.

No one spoke.

Sir Richard moved swiftly through the routine agenda. 'And now we come to 'any other business', the main item of which is the, er, report which Jack Armstrong, our commercial director, has, er, so kindly prepared.' There was no hostility there, thought Jack, just apprehension.

'Perhaps, Jack, we could just have a brief introduction from you, before I ask for comments.'

'Thank you, Sir Richard.' Jack drew a deep breath. 'Gentlemen, this company is in a mess. It is unwieldy, top heavy, overmanned at all levels and losing market share in key areas. Controls are weak – in some cases useless – and communication links virtually non-existent. I'd be grateful for your reaction.' His delivery had been cool and measured. But as he sat back he heard his heart pounding. The silence crackled around him as the sun made rainbows in the crystal water jugs.

'I'd like to know what gives you the authority to produce this document?' The speaker, as he had expected, was Bill Soames. His sales department had been strongly criticised for sloppy management.

Sir Richard's face was inscrutable. Again Jack drew a deep breath. 'In the absence of a functioning managing director, I took it upon myself to study the company.' He gave them all a steely glare. 'It seemed to me that somebody had to.'

Sir Richard coughed. 'Unfortunately Donald is unable to be with us today. He's not been feeling too well again.'

Bill Soames exploded. 'Well, for a start I can tell you, you wouldn't get two-thirds of this past our trade unions. Sean MacCready would have the entire company shut down within two days.'

Jack didn't comment. He had heard about Mr MacCready. 'Anyone else?'

'I object strongly to the idea of closing the Warwickshire plant and selling it off for redevelopment. The idea of merging it with the Staffordshire operation is ridiculous. The two culture's won't mix,' declared the cakes and pastries director.

'Yes, and we're not property developers, we're a food company. Stick to our last is what I say,' chimed in somebody else.

And so it went on. As Jack listened he realised even he had under-estimated the strength of the opposition. Not a single person had spoken out in favour of any of the measures he had suggested, although some had kept quiet, among them the finance director Edward Williams.

The non-executives held their peace, striving for dignity

61

but looking awkward and embarrassed instead. Bloody soft southern morons, Jack thought angrily to himself. Faced with this kind of opposition Sir Richard was bound to stick with the status quo.

'Well, gentlemen, I think we've had what I would call a fair and frank discussion,' cut in Sir Richard after half an hour. 'Do I take it then you are all perfectly satisfied with the way the company is run?'

Jack looked at him in surprise. There was a new edge to his voice and his eyes, deep-set under craggy brows, had lost their genial twinkle. Something of the original Butler drive had survived four generations of wealth and comfort after all.

Into the pool of silence, Edward Williams, glasses glinting in the sunlight, threw a pebble. 'If I might suggest, er,' he began diffidently, 'it seems to me that Jack's paper, into which I know he has put immense time and trouble, has hit, shall we say, a number of raw nerves.'

Bill Soames gave him a look which could have stripped the paintwork from several doors, but he appeared not to notice. 'Obviously, as it has come from someone who has only recently joined the company, there is a tendency to over-react, perhaps to be over-defensive.'

A number of heads bowed as their owners appeared to find something rivetting to read on the blotters in front of them. Bill Soames, Jack noticed, was doodling frantically. Edward Williams ploughed on, 'In order to cool emotions, I propose that we appoint a team of outside consultants to come in and give their independent view.'

The room darkened suddenly as the sun disappeared behind a rain cloud. 'An excellent idea, if I may say so,' said Sir Richard quietly. He looked slowly round the room, eyeing each director in turn. Jack was amazed at his sense of theatre – it must be all those speeches.

Sir Richard spoke again. 'Does anyone have any objections to that?' He was daring them to admit their complacency and self-interest.

'I just hope it won't be one of these American firms,' Bill Soames said petulantly.

'I think the executive committee is best suited to deciding

which particular firm gets the job, thank you, Bill,' snapped Sir Richard.

'Now, if there is nothing further,' the genial twinkle had returned, 'I don't know about you chaps, but I could do with a gin and tonic.'

During his review of Butler's Jack had dug out the rest of the history. Victor Butler had been fortunate in his timing when he bought out the widows. Britain was in the throes of the 'You've never had it so good' MacMillan era, and within five years, turnover had quadrupled. In 1959, he had floated the company on the stockmarket, valued at just £100,000.

By the mid-1960s he had become a legend as one of the most opportunistic, entrepreneurial figures of the time.

He bought pickle companies, spice companies, cereal companies, dried fruit companies, vineyards in France, beverage companies, meat processing companies, soft drink companies, not to mention other biscuit and cake companies which were grafted onto the existing businesses. By the late 1960s, Butler's was one of the largest and most successful food groups in Britain. In the process, Victor Butler's shareholding had dropped to just 2 per cent.

But Victor became more autocratic the older and richer he grew. He refused to encourage young talented men for fear they would threaten his position and by the late seventies, the company was in decline. To settle the succession issue, he put his son Richard on to the board and eventually made him managing director – though he had no great regard for him.

Richard, a qualified lawyer, was more cunning than his father supposed, and he recruited some capable, if not brilliant, directors.

Thus Butler's jogged along, missing out on the rationalisation of the food industry in the early 1980s. A combination of Victor's own arrogance and the general mood of the time also allowed the trade unions within the company to grow in strength, until they held it in a vice-like grip.

In the autumn of 1982, Victor was thrown from his horse while riding to hounds and broke his neck.

Richard promptly assumed the chairmanship, promoting a hardworking accountant called Donald Appleton to be managing director. The City, ever optimistic about new management, gave them the benefit of the doubt. They appeared to be a reasonable team and the City's increasing faith in food companies seemed largely justified.

Butler's profits rose by slightly more than inflation each year. Profit margins began to improve. Richard allowed his latent flair for self-publicity free rein, becoming a food sector 'pundit'. He could be found at CBI meetings and Institute of Director's luncheons saying precisely what everyone wanted to hear.

New investment was needed if the long-term interests of the food industry, and indeed the consumer, were to be served. Food companies were getting to grips with the workforce, costs were being honed and marketing improved. They were all jolly good fellows.

For these and other platitudes he was awarded a knighthood and became a regular guest at the little drinks parties at number 10 Downing Street. And he ensured that a steady stream of contributions to Conservative Party funds kept flowing.

Peter Markus began to produce acquisition ideas for Jack to consider. Butler's needed a massive clean-out, it was also good, he told Jack, for the market to see early signs of expansion.

In Peter's eyes, the deals provided the bread and butter fees of Hogarth Stein. They were also intended to indicate to Peter's superiors and colleagues that he was not only interested in the big headline-hitting takeovers.

The first acquisition Peter suggested was of a small private company making a variety of cheese and savoury biscuits at the luxury end of the market.

Sir Richard had been wary. Despite the successful assimilation of Huntingdon, he was distrustful of acquisitions. The phrase 'organic growth' – which had nothing to do with natural fertilisers – still tripped too easily off his tongue for Peter's liking.

Jack presented the deals as the first step in upgrading the group. 'I'm sure, Richard, you are aware that the whole country is moving up market, not just in food, but in clothes, furniture, you name it,' he explained carefully. 'I think buying a number of small companies making high margin, high profile products will help reposition our image in the marketplace.'

'But Butler's has always had a reputation for high quality,' Sir Richard said defensively.

'Of course,' Jack smiled, 'quality in the sense of using pure products and being totally reliable, but there's no glamour there. I'm talking about grafting on some glamour, Richard, some exceedingly profitable glamour,' he stressed, deliberately using his chairman's name, 'into a company – which already has a fine reputation.'

A second purchase, of a specialist nut processor, was made on the basis of the same logic. Peter's colleagues at Hogarth Stein were not fooled by these small deals. They knew he was grooming Jack for stardom. Like a trainer putting a young horse through its paces, Peter encouraged him, stroked him, gave him a lump of sugar or a slight kick now and again. He prided himself on his ability to spot individuals who would turn into big fee earners for the bank. Under Jack's casual, jokey manner and down-to-earth northern approach, he saw a ruthless ambition. It burned like a flame – and Peter knew just how to feed it.

Sarah awoke from a troubled sleep into the calm of her bedroom. She had been dreaming of the market, trying to sell shares in Stern Group. But the more jobbers she tried, the more they marked the price down against her and cut the size. 'Can only take a thousand, Lady Sarah,' they said grinning, wielding huge red crayons the size of baseball bats.

Then she became aware she was naked, although no one else seemed to notice. Panic rose in her as she tried to leave the floor but it was too crowded; everywhere she moved someone was blocking her and she didn't like to make too much fuss in case they noticed her nudity. Suddenly one of the jobbers became Stern and, without speaking, he had put a hand between her legs, thrown her over his shoulder and carried her from the floor. As he did so, she had felt totally safe – certain everything would be all right.

As Denis had predicted, the Antelope Leisure incident had imprinted her on Stern's consciousness.

'Know of any companies being bid for in half an hour?' he had asked mockingly when she turned up for the announcement of his annual profits in October.

She flushed. 'Your results are very good,' she said, trying to deflect him. 'All the analysts seem to think you are very clever.'

His face darkened and his lip curled a fraction. He tapped the side of his nose with a long finger. 'I have always found, my dear, that in this life you've got to be lucky to be clever.'

Chapter 5

As he entered Sir Richard's office, Jack sensed the tension in the air. Sir Richard looked as if he had not slept for days. 'Come and make yourself comfortable.' He motioned Jack to a soft green armchair.

'Is something wrong?' asked Jack. The secretary had said it was urgent.

'Well, two things really.' Sir Richard sank heavily into the couch. 'The first is that Donald has suffered another stroke, and it doesn't look as though he will recover this time.'

Jack strove to conceal his elation. 'The second is that Bill Soames is pressuring me to put him forward as the new managing director.'

It was as if someone slapped Jack hard across the face – even though he had been half expecting the news. He tried not to appear unreasonably hostile. 'And what are his credentials?' he asked, struggling to keep his tone level.

'Well,' Sir Richard sighed, managing a weary smile, 'he is a damned good salesman – and sales director. He has been with the company for fifteen years and knows how it works. He is also very popular with the other directors, and I understand he has unofficial support from a number of them.'

Jack picked up a pen from the coffee table in front of him and began to play with it. He could feel the sweat forming under his arms.

'Not Edward Williams, surely?'

'Er, no. Edward, being a cautious accountant, has never been able to forgive the level of Bill's expenses.'

'And how do you feel?'

Sir Richard rearranged himself in his chair. 'Well, of course, as chairman, it's my job to assess what the board wants.'

Christ, thought Jack, he's going to sell out for a quiet life.

'However,' Sir Richard studied his fingernails, 'I have been impressed by what you have done here. You already have a better understanding than anyone else here of how the company should develop, and you have shown great dedication to the job. You have bought two excellent businesses into the group, without over-paying.' He paused and looked directly at Jack. 'So if it comes to straight vote between you, which I sincerely hope it doesn't, I would support you.'

Jack stood up and walked to the window. It was a fine early spring day. The trees in the centre of the square were veiled in pale green and surrounded with daffodils. 'So that means there's you, Edward and me against the rest. Not brilliant odds, is it?' He spoke without turning round.

The steel Jack had glimpsed in Sir Richard at that first board meeting had vanished. 'Look, I've told him I'm not prepared to take any action until we see the report from the consultants which gives us until the end of June. My only fear is that Bill will leak the story of Donald's illness to the press, in which case we would be forced into a decision.'

Jack said: 'I shouldn't think he'll do that yet. He'll keep his ammunition back – I would.' He grinned and Sir Richard noticed for the first time the intensity in his eyes. 'Thanks for telling me – and thanks for your support. I need to go and think things over.'

Back in his own office, Jack called Peter and picked up the phone to summon his driver. On second thoughts a taxi might be safer. Half an hour later he was sitting in one of Hogarth Stein's anonymous meeting rooms. Peter lounged opposite, legs draped elegantly over an easy chair.

'So what you seem to be saying is that this clown gets to be managing director – unless we come up with a miracle.'

Even though his career hung in the balance, Jack felt a flicker of envy at the way Peter homed in to the heart of the subject.

'D'you know how these consultants are getting on?' Peter asked brightly, swinging his fashionably shod feet back on to the dark blue carpet.

'No.' Jack looked puzzled.

'I know someone there, actually.' Peter's face lit up with a wicked smile. 'I think I'll give him a ring. Now I must get on.' And he almost shooed Jack out of the office.

Two long days of torture passed as Jack brooded on how to wipe Bill Soames off the face of the earth. Several times he thought he had the answer, but then he would see the flaw.

He took to sipping vodka and tonic in the evenings to help his brooding and found to his surprise he sometimes got through half a bottle. It helped him to sleep, but at four thirty on the dot he would wake, gripped by a feeling of foreboding that kept him wide eyed until six. On the third day Peter rang him in the flat at 7 a.m. 'Got some good news for you,' he trilled down the phone. 'Can you make breakfast at the Howard Hotel at eight.'

'I'll be there.'

Peter was wolfing down croissants and studying the *Financial Times* at a window table when Jack arrived. He didn't get up, but flung down the paper in mock despair. 'God, some of these financial journalists deserve shooting. Couldn't organise their way out of a paper bag and they take the chairmen of world beating companies to task for being stingy with their dividends.' He had been reading about a favourite client in the Lex column.

'Well?'

Peter handed him the menu. 'Better order first, then we'll talk.' Jack got the impression he was being teased. But the pink dining room with its crystal chandeliers and painted ceiling, lifted his spirits.

'Tea and brown toast,' he said to the white-coated waiter, and turned back to Peter. 'Well?' he said again, wishing his head would clear.

Peter leaned back in his chair. 'Our friend Billy boy has been a bit naughty.' He sipped his orange juice, eyes twinkling, looking for all the world like a naughty schoolboy who had just discovered his most hated prefect in bed with the headmaster's wife.

Jack waited.

'Not all these lovely orders he's so good at getting are won

69

on pure merit, it seems. There are some extraordinarily happy supermarket buyers around.'

Jack's face lit up. 'You mean bribery?'

'Well not with cash. But young Billy runs an upmarket travel agency on the side with his brother. Favoured buyers get free trips to the Bahamas and other choice spots.'

'When you say 'favoured' you mean those who give him the biggest orders?'

Peter nodded.

Jack's face clouded. 'Yes, but this kind of thing goes on all the time. In my experience it's impossible to prove.'

Peter's eyes glittered like the Aegean at noon. 'My friend at the consultant has got a letter from a Mr Clean at Tesco's claiming he was offered two weeks in St Lucia if he doubled the size of his regular order.'

The pressure around Jack's head suddenly loosened. He leaned across the table towards Peter in a gesture of pure conspiracy. 'Right,' he said softly. 'When do we nail the bastard?'

Peter was only slightly taken aback. He recognised the look of naked ambition on Jack's face, and inwardly applauded.

'Well,' he said, with an expression of affected innocence, 'I think it is only our duty to tell Sir Richard.' He raised an eyebrow. 'Don't you?'

On Friday morning Bill Soames received a call from the chairman's secretary asking if he could possibly pop in and see him around 11 a.m. Bill Soames was only too delighted. He was forty-two, had a beautiful (if jealous) wife, two children, a 1972 Rolls-Royce, a great job, a sexual arrangement with his secretary which suited them both, and a lucrative little business on the side. What more could any man want? he thought – except to be managing director of one of the country's biggest food companies.

He hummed to himself in the washroom and smoothed his sparse hair over his pink head. The sales force was doing well – and if he and his brother could give a little help where it was needed, well, what was the harm?

'Such practices are highly unethical,' said Sir Richard in his most censorious voice. 'I suggest that you resign to pursue other business interests.'

'And if I don't?'

When Bill Soames had walked into the chairman's office he had met not the cosy little welcome he had envisaged, but a hostile threesome comprising Sir Richard, Jack Armstrong and Peter Markus.

So, that goody goody at Tesco's had shopped him. He should have paid attention to his intuition. But he could not believe that such a trifling issue could wipe out his record with the company.

'Are you sure you want this publicised? If I refuse to resign, you'll have to fire me, and that could be unpleasant. Can this company afford to have a scandal on its hands with the managing director lying on his deathbed?'

'I think the company can afford it more than you can,' said Sir Richard. 'You will never work again, certainly not in a comparable job, if this gets out.'

Bill Soames felt a sick churning in his stomach. 'My service contract is for two years,' he said, his defiance fading.

Sir Richard wasted no time. 'It will be honoured in full and you can have my word that our conversation this afternoon will not go beyond this room.' Jack and Peter nodded in agreement. 'I suggest you clear up your things and leave immediately.'

'Today?'

The three men watched the reality hit Bill Soames. Standing against the doorway in his blue suit he seemed to shrink like a balloon seeping air, a look of disbelief in his round pale eyes.

'I think that would be sensible,' said Sir Richard.

When he had gone, the three men looked at each other shamefaced. It had been like witnessing a killing. They had all been glad it was someone else standing there, suddenly deprived of his livelihood.

'I think we could do with a drink,' said Sir Richard.

'Not for me, thanks, I must dash.' Peter was as ever late for his next meeting.

'I'll get our press guy to put out a statement on Monday. Does it have to go to the Stock Exchange?'

'I should say so, and it would be best to do it today,' advised Peter. 'Get it in around 3.30 so they will just put it on the screen before close of play. On a Friday afternoon all the newspapers are frantic. With any luck, no one will notice it.'

'Is there anything that young man hasn't got an angle on?' wondered Sir Richard aloud when he had gone, offering Jack his private box of Monte Cristo cigars.

'Not much,' said Jack, smiling wrily. He chose a cigar and sat down to light it.

Sir Richard sipped his single malt.

Someone really ought to tell Jack to take the label off his cigar before smoking it he thought.

The following week, just before the start of Royal Ascot, Butler's issued another low-key announcement to the Stock Exchange. 'The managing director of Butler's Biscuits, Donald Appleton, is retiring due to ill health. The board is grateful for his valuable contribution. Jack Armstrong, the commercial director, has been appointed to the new post of chief executive.'

A few days later, Rosemary walked wearily from the heat of the summer afternoon into the shady calm of Claridge's, clutching a sheaf of estate agent's particulars. She was half an hour early for her six o'clock meeting with Jack, but could not walk another step.

A waiter led her into the large room on the left of the main lounge area and she sank down into one of the soft chintz-covered sofas. She ordered some tea and sat waiting, feeling highly conspicuous. Rosemary had never been to Claridge's before, but it frequently cropped up in Jack's conversation along with other London hotels as a place where the rich and powerful met. So she was surprised to find herself in a room decorated in what she considered terrible taste. Over-blown roses crept up sickly green walls, while large lamps and a deep peach carpet gave the room more the air of a dowager's boudoir than of a top class hotel. Still it had a certain comforting feel, she decided, as the waiter arrived with her tea.

'It seems gentlemen, that there is a party going on here in London to which perhaps, we should be invited.' The words were spoken softly in clipped Teutonic tones, but she heard them quite distinctly.

They came from the group at the next table and the more she examined the constituent parts, the more they intrigued her. The speaker looked around thirty-five – thin and pale. His fair hair was combed straight back without a parting and seemed to merge with his ivory skin, clear and flawless from brow to chin, showing no hint of blood running below the surface. He sipped his tea delicately with a finely bowed mouth. Behind thick rimless spectacles, eyes of palest blue glimmered, fringed by fair lashes.

Rosemary shuddered. He was the sort of man who would pull the wings off flies while ordering the extermination of whole races.

The man next to him was his opposite – short, podgy and tanned – while the third member of the party looked Spanish or Italian.

Just then Peter Markus arrived and headed straight for the group. 'Hello, Max, how nice to see you.' He shook hands with the short podgy man who said, 'Peter, this is Klaus von Gleichen, and Dimitri Grigia.'

'Delighted to meet you, gentlemen.' He sat down and addressed Klaus. 'I gather you feel you're missing out on the action in London.'

Rosemary had only met Peter once and he did not register her sitting there on her own. By the time Jack arrived at ten past six, the group had already gone and when she described them, Jack had no idea who they might be.

'One thing's for certain,' she said, handing him the sheaf of estate agent's bumpf, 'we can't afford more than a pokey three-bedroomed house in any of the areas you like.'

It was Jack and Rosemary's turn to spend a weekend at Charlton House. 'He's a serious rising star,' Peter had told Angela when they were fixing dates. 'He's going to make me famous.'

Rosemary was horrified at the prospect of the weekend. She had been brought up by down-to-earth socialist parents to believe she could hold her own in any company. And so she did – normally.

But Jack had unsettled her strangely in describing Angela. Not only was she blonde and willowy, she was also a former Paris model. Rosemary knew that over the years of motherhood and schoolteaching she had become mousey and dumpy, but until now she had not consciously thought about it.

She decided to buy some new clothes in London. Not knowing the London shops she headed for Harrods and wandered through countless rooms – the Designer Room, the Suit Room, the Younger Set, searching through endless racks of clothes. Anything she liked was the wrong size, wrong shape wrong length. She spent more than two hours miserably struggling in and out of them. The mirrors were strategically placed to give an all round view and at one point she caught sight of a dimpled wobbly bottom, only to realise it was her own. Eventually she paid £60 for a blouse she did not care for very much.

The smell of coffee lured her towards the queue at the Dress Circle restaurant. I need the energy, she thought, as she helped herself to a glistening Danish pastry and a coffee. The only spare place was at a small table next to a formidably smart woman. She looks as snotty as they come, thought Rosemary. Still, there was nowhere else.

But as she bent carefully to put the tray down on the low table, her shoulder bag slid treacherously down her arm, jerking the tray and sending the coffee cup leaping in the air. Half the contents spilt over the tray.

She felt her face turn crimson, sure the entire restaurant was watching. She knew she was ridiculously close to tears. 'Here, use these.' The young woman held out a bunch of paper napkins.

'Oh, thank you.' As she looked round surreptitiously, she saw to her relief that no one was paying any attention.

Finally she sorted herself out and sat down with a sigh smiling gratefully at her neighbour, who surprised her by smiling back. 'It's happened to me,' she said sympathetically. 'Those shoulder bags are killers.'

Spurred by guilt at her character misjudgment, Rosemary poured out her problems about the weekend. 'I can't seem to find anything I like here, it's so confusing.'

'Well, I'm supposed to be buying garden furniture,' said the other woman gloomily, 'but they won't deliver for two months. My husband is already furious with me.'

Rosemary nodded sympathetically. 'But why don't you try Harvey Nichols next door for your clothes?' suggested the woman. 'It's smaller and easier to find your way around. It's quite pricey, though.'

'Oh, money's not the problem,' said Rosemary, 'just so long as I look the part. My husband keeps telling me how glamorous the host's wife is.'

'Well, just you trot along to Harvey Nicks, I'm sure you'll find something,' said the young woman comfortingly.

What lovely blonde hair, thought Rosemary enviously as they parted. Help came from the strangest quarters.

Within an hour she was kitted out in clothes which miraculously made her look pleasantly rounded rather than dumpy. Jack would be proud of her.

Charlton was in its full summer splendour. An extra gardener had come in to help prepare for the annual opening to the public, which Peter had forgotten about when he had invited Jack and Rosemary. The Women's Institute was due to descend at 2.30 in the afternoon bearing their tea urn.

But the weather was gorgeous and as Jack's brand new silver BMW turned through the gates, both he and Rosemary let out sighs of appreciation and envy which Peter would have found most gratifying.

'Horse chestnut trees always look so British,' said Rosemary as the car's wheels scrunched along the drive.

By the time they arrived at the house Jack felt strangely on edge. Until the moment he had turned into Peter's drive he had been sure he had everything he desired in life.

'Hello, you two, come round this way.' Peter greeted them from the garden, waving for them to go round the side of the house. They followed the path blazing with phlox and marigolds which led them to a vast expanse of perfectly clipped lawn. Peter led them on to the patio. 'Angie's just getting some fizz.' He broke off and called into the house: 'Darling! Hurry up, we're all dying of thirst around here.'

There was a clatter of heels as Angela appeared with a tray

75

of glasses and a bottle, concentrating hard. 'Sorry!' she said, without looking up, 'Mrs Warren is having a crisis about what to do with the mange tout.'

Turning to Rosemary, Peter noticed her round face had turned bright pink and she was staring at Angela in a strange way. Angela put the tray down with a sigh of relief and straightened up. Then she saw Rosemary.

'Well, my advice clearly paid off,' she said after a pause. They both burst out laughing, managing to explain their story in between bursts of giggles.

'How about you, did you find anyone to deliver the garden furniture?' asked Rosemary.

Peter winced and Angela gestured in despair to the one small table and four chairs.

'But we are having lunch outside as it's just us,' Peter cut in firmly. 'That is if anyone's bothered to prepare it,' he added in long suffering tones. At that moment Mrs Warren, who thought of Peter as a tyrannical two year old, appeared with plates full of lobster and salad.

After lunch Angela showed Rosemary round the house while Jack got the obligatory garden tour.

Daunted by the grandeur of most of the house Rosemary decided she liked the sitting room best, decorated in shades of yellow, from palest primrose to old gold. 'I love all these country scenes,' she said of the framed oil paintings.

'Oh, I've spent weeks in Sotheby's and Christie's over the years. Mind you, I'm always on the lookout. You can often find something lovely buried away at the back of a village shop.'

'We're going to have to buy a house near London,' said Rosemary miserably, thinking of the work ahead. If this was life in the south, she would rather stay in Chester.

'Well, you must come shopping with me. Have you never been to an auction?'

Rosemary shook her head, feeling angry and out of her depth. 'It's such fun,' Angela rattled on. 'And also I know one or two nice antique shops here and there.'

She saw the look of confusion on Rosemary's face.

'I suppose if you have lived in the North all your life, the thought of moving down here must be quite unnerving,' she said. Rosemary could be quite attractive if she slimmed down and had her hair cut properly.

'Yes, it is. It won't be so bad for Jack, but I have all my friends there.'

'Well, now you have us,' said Angela firmly. 'How long have you been married?'

'Nearly twenty years.'

'And you have children?'

'Yes, two. A girl and a boy.' Rosemary hoped Angela would not enquire too closely about the age of the children. She had been three months pregnant with her daughter Susan at the wedding. Her mind flashed back to her mother's terror that people would notice her thickening waist under the bouquet.

'Unfortunately Susan has settled in Australia. She and her father never really got on.'

Angela felt in need of a diversion. 'Don't you love the view from this window?' Looking out they could see Jack and Peter walking slowly along the paths of the rose garden to the side of the tennis courts. Hills rose gently behind them in the distance.

'It would be great to paint,' said Rosemary. 'I used to be quite good.'

'You should take it up again. One really shouldn't let talent waste away. I'm totally hopeless at anything artistic.'

'Well, you wouldn't know it from the house,' Rosemary retorted.

Angela was staring curiously out of the window again. 'I bet they're talking about their next deal,' she said.

Not a single dead head marred the white blooms as the bees flew happily from flower to flower. 'I'm not doing any more deals for at least six months,' Jack said. 'That company needs major surgery. You can't sack whole factories of people and buy new companies at the same time. It makes for bad feeling.'

'Mm, well, I see your point, but these markets don't last for ever.'

Jack was enjoying Peter's persistence. 'By the way,' he said with deliberate casualness, 'I've asked Greenbag's to be Butler's official broker.'

'You're not going to fire Michael?' said Peter horrified.

'No, no, he's happy to stay in on a joint brokerage basis.'

'Mmm,' said Peter, and felt his control slipping. 'Well, remember, Michael's connections are impeccable. Green-bag's are pretty good but I'd watch that Charlie Briggs-Smith if I were you.'

'Why?'

'Oh, Charlie's an affable, good-hearted soul. Just a little sharp that's all.'

'Like your friend Sir Leo,' Jack bit back.

'Leo's OK – just can't resist playing the game.'

'Well, he nearly ruined mine,' said Jack.

'Do you play tennis?' asked Peter, deliberately changing the subject. 'We could have a game later on.'

As they went downstairs to join the men for tea Rosemary caught sight of Jack still with Peter in the garden. He was strolling around waving his long arms in expansive gestures, the line of his jaw at right angles to his neck. A shiver of unease went through her. He was becoming obsessed with his image. All this City stuff brought out the worst in him.

Peter had noticed the change too. He remembered Jack's panic the night Stern had wanted to make a higher offer. At that moment he would have done anything Peter had told him. But since he had become chief executive of Butler's, his attitude had altered. Three months ago Jack would never have appointed Greenbag's as joint broker without asking Peter first. It might behove him to remember just who his friends were.

Jack sensed he was being put through his paces. 'He still treats me like a northern hillbilly,' he told Rosemary as they dressed for dinner.

''Appen he's right, lad.' She twirled in front of the mirror in her new dress and high heels, and sighed. It was an improvement but there was a long way to go. Jack felt a moment of lust. There was a new sexual awareness in her – or rather a harking back to an old one. He took hold of her, a hand on each shoulder and kissed her hard on the lips. 'Being the wife of a successful man obviously suits you,' he said gruffly.

Then he turned back to the mirror and carefully arranged his fringe.

Peter had invited an impressive selection of people to dinner. Rosemary sighed with relief to see all the wives wearing similar dresses to the one she had bought in Harvey Nichols. But Angela, dressed simply in black, with diamond studs in her ears, outclassed them all.

At dinner they ate carrot and coriander soup, noisette d'agneau, mange tout and salad, followed by warm pear tart and cream.

Rosemary found herself next to a local farmer. After ignoring her for the first ten minutes, he turned to her. 'Do you ride much?' Before she had time to answer he carried on, 'We've had appalling trouble with these animal liberation hooligans around here,' Rosemary remembered Angela saying he was master of the local hunt. 'Tried to sabotage us, you know.' He speared a piece of rare lamb with his fork. 'But I showed 'em. I got together a rival army of farmers and locals and laid in wait for 'em. Really gave 'em a good hiding. Broke a few ribs. Upset the police a bit but it worked, worked like a charm.'

Stunned by this vision of life in the shires, Rosemary could think of no response.

'I blame a lot of it on those lefty school teachers. Her companion now addressed the whole table. 'They're a lot of long-haired layabouts, talking all that tosh about equality. It's about time Mrs Thatcher sacked a few of them.'

'Well, she could always try paying them a bit more and then she might get better quality.' Rosemary suddenly found her voice. Everyone stopped talking.

'Hah! They throw around the tax-payer's money enough as it is with all this fancy technology they keep demanding in the schools,' said the landowner. Rosemary ignored Jack's warning glance.

'I happen to be a schoolteacher.'

Several people sipped their wine in the silence which followed.

'Well, we do want our young to be able to compete internationally?' said the man on her right who was a publisher.

'And how, my dear fellow, will they be able to compete

internationally if they can't read and write and have heads stuffed with left wing nonsense?' the master brayed.

'If your beloved Mrs Thatcher would invest some money in education, which is supposed to be an area she knows something about, standards would rise.' Rosemary heard the shrillness in her own voice; she could feel her temper rising.

Jack tried to look unconcerned, but did not want everyone to think he was married to a rabid socialist; she was not as left-wing as she had been at the LSE – she had even voted SDP last time – but rabid by the standards round the table.

Peter wished Jack had his wife slightly more under control. Dudley might be a boring old fart, but he was influential in local politics and retained some surprisingly high-powered contacts in the City.

'Rosemary's right,' said the publisher, putting his hand firmly on her arm, 'the better educated people are, the more of my books they'll buy and the richer I'll be.' Everyone except Rosemary laughed, thankful they were out of a corner.

'Let's move into the drawing room for coffee,' Angela suggested, seizing the opportunity to break up the party just in case they re-grouped.

'It's a wonderful fireplace, isn't it?' A fellow guest who had been introduced to Jack as a corporate lawyer joined him in front of the large open fire, lit on all but the hottest summer evenings. 'Are you enjoying Butler's?'

'It's a challenge. I guess I've a tough year or two ahead of me.' It was Jack's stock reply.

'Well, if you need any legal advice, do give me a ring. One of our special areas is redundancy and trade unions.' His new friend smiled knowingly. 'So we might be able to help as time goes by.'

Jack felt the warm glow of flattery as he realised the man had done his homework.

Later on when Peter was dishing out the 'stickies', another guest sought Jack out.

'Are you going to change the corporate image at Butler's?'

'I hadn't given it a lot of thought yet,' he lied.

'Well, I'm sure you will, and when you do, remember we are the leaders in corporate design.'

By the end of the evening Jack's ego was on the wing. 'You know I might have misjudged Peter,' he told Rosemary as she lay silently seething in the red brocade four-poster. 'I think he really rates me. I think he really wants to help.'

In the last week of June, Rosemary found the perfect house for them in Esher and the independent consultant's report on Butler's arrived. It was even more critical than Jack's bombshell. Nine months after he had joined the company, he finally got down to work.

It took three stormy board meetings, but Jack got his way. Biscuits was to merge with cakes and pastries, pickles with jams and preserves, and spices with beverages.

Three divisional managing directors and more than thirty senior managers took generous redundancy packages in the restructuring.

Jack knew speed was vital if people were not to become demoralised. He also believed in getting rid of the management first. Then at least the workforce knew you had started at the top.

The frozen food side was put up for sale. Unless they were set on becoming market leaders, it made little sense to keep spending money on upgrading the plant.

As at Huntingdon, he contracted out all transport and distribution and centralised the financial controls.

Designs for a state-of-the-art computer system were commissioned. Jack was determined he should be able to gather up to date information within seconds on any part of the group. As he had said at the last board meeting: 'There will be no hiding place for inefficiency.'

A new sales director was found through a highly recommended head-hunter called Jane Brompton who had managed to land one of Beecham's hungry young stars.

He replaced weak managers and eliminated his own former post of commercial director. After all, the job had only been created as a glorified bribe.

But he left Edward Williams as finance director. Edward, Jack found, made up in competence what he lacked in imagination. He was a meticulous detail man – an ideal executor of Jack's ideas.

81

Sir Richard continued his CBI and Food Federation circuits, blocking his ears to the screams of pain from his own company. 'It is for the best, it is for the best,' he would murmur to himself over a lonely whisky and soda in his office. These days Jack did not drop by for his evening snifter so often.

But Sir Richard's talent for public relations and contacts in industry and government made him an ideal chairman and, in the eyes of the investment community, a perfect complement to the youthful aggression of Jack Armstrong.

By the autumn of 1986 it was clear to the outside world that the group was under entirely new management. As the City braced itself for Big Bang and the evenings drew in, Butler's share price began to move steadily upwards.

Chapter 6

The ants had left the anthill. The structure which had teemed with life and industry stood deserted, the inhabitants scattered to new homes, some cast out for ever. Big Bang had arrived in the Stock Exchange.

Where there had been swarms of men doing deals, gossiping and hustling, there was emptiness. The tiny cell-like traders' boxes around the market floor had been cleared of years of clutter: Pirelli calendars, dart boards with half the numbers missing, dog-eared playing cards and mountains of old copies of the *Financial Times*.

Now the cells were locked, silent for the first time in decades of gossip and rumour; of booms and busts; of share ramps and scandals; of fortunes made and lost; of dreams and nightmares.

On the trading floor itself, the only octagonal pitch still in full operation was that of Smith New Court, the stock jobber reborn in the new guise of market maker, but still a staunch believer in the traditional way of trading in stocks and shares. One other pitch trading in share options was also in business. The date was 27 October 1986.

Denis looked around sadly. For more than a year now he had known this moment would come. But while the turmoil of each day had continued with the jokes, the whispers, the tips so hot they burned your fingers, and the handshakes sealing each bargain, it had been hard to imagine this emptiness. Now the place felt like a ghost town.

He walked over to the Smith pitch. 'How's it going, Wally?' he said to the slight man standing despondently by the white board. Denis saw defeat behind his eyes.

'It won't work, Den. We'll have to do like the rest and go upstairs.'

'Come and have a drink in a minute?'

'Sure.'

Denis walked slowly across the empty floor, his normal jauntiness gone.

'Bloody Big Bang.'

In the Long Room there was the same eerie stillness and most of the 'regulars' were missing. Behind the bar, Rose looked miserable.

Denis rang one of his closest mates from one of the 'phones just outside the bar. 'Sorry, Den, but I can't leave this blooming screen.'

'How's it going?'

'Total chaos. It's a telephone market at the moment, till everyone gets the hang of the screens, but business is OK.'

To Denis he sounded depressingly cheerful.

'I'll have a large malt, please, Rose,' he said to the barmaid.

'Arntcha going to 'ave a pint first?' Her face was all motherly concern.

'I'll have them together,' said Denis by way of a compromise.

'How about a drink for a poor starving journalist then?'

At his elbow, tanned and smiling, stood a diffident-looking young man, a lock of black hair flopping over his forehead.

'Hello Patrick,' Denis said. 'Christ! You been away or what?'

'Yeah'. I went to Greece for a late break. I've been back a week, though.'

'Still can't find anyone to iron your shirts I see,' said Denis whose own clothes always looked just pressed. 'I suppose you're down here reporting on the first day of Big Bang?' Rose had pulled Patrick a pint automatically.

He nodded. 'Your very good health.' He sipped his beer, 'Everywhere's the same. I popped into Corney and Barrow in Old Broad Street, and Green's – not a soul in sight.' His voice carried a clear Irish lilt.

'Well, they can stuff their Big Bang right up their arses – and you can quote me on that,' said Denis, tossing back half his whisky. Thank God he was going to see his lady friend that afternoon. It would take his mind off everything.

'Listen, before you incriminate yourself totally, I should tell you you are talking to the new City Editor of the *Sunday Herald*.'

'Good grief! Patrick Peabody a City Editor. Where's my drink? I feel quite faint.' Denis gulped at his whisky. 'You've gone legit then, have you? Just work one day a week, I suppose. So you won't need any more tips for the market report?'

Patrick, who had known Denis for five years, smiled indulgently. 'There's plenty of space for tips,' he said. Then he frowned. 'Also a lot for features on Big Bang.'

Denis shook his head. 'I'm not sure I can talk to City Editors. Sounds a bit grand to me.' He gazed into his beer, his face broody. 'Tell me one thing?'

Patrick nodded.

'Do City Editors buy drinks?'

Patrick grinned and caught Rose's eye. 'I think you'd better give Mr Jones a large malt. And have one yourself.'

Once that was out of the way they got back to business.

'What's going to happen to Tulley, Denis?'

'This for quoting?'

'Just for background. I won't mention the name of the firm.'

Denis relaxed. You could never be too careful with journalists, even those you knew well.

'Well, like all these medium-sized firms, it's going to be difficult for us to keep the business. It'll be all right while turnover holds up, but these new big firms have already been after our bright guys at amazing salaries.'

'What about commission rates?' Up until Big Bang, all London stockbrokers had enjoyed a fixed minimum commission, but overnight it had become a free-for all.

'The institutions will crucify us,' said Denis. 'What have we got to offer them that's special? The big American banks who've bought stockbrokers, like Citicorp with Scrimgeours, have spent fortunes on new technology making sure their execution is as fast as anyone's. And they've got top-class research. Young Sarah Meyer in our office was offered a job doubling her salary as a food analyst.'

'Why didn't she take it?'

''Cos she's in love with me.' Denis grinned. 'She's put all that boring research behind her. Ah, here's Wally. What do you want, Misery?'

Wally looked ready to drown himself. 'Just a light ale, please, Den.'

'I suppose they're still buying stocks and shares, are they, with this new fangled high technology?' Denis asked.

'Looks like it. A lot of action in the food sector as it 'appens. Butler's is going very well.'

'Oh, yeah.' Denis perked up. 'Sarah's very taken with this new chief executive they've got. Used to follow him at Huntingdon. It's one of the few stocks I'll still let her research. He's very secretive with most of the press, so I gather.' He glanced at Patrick and took another large gulp of whisky. 'All I know is my clever clients have been tucking them away.'

Patrick scribbled something in his notebook which had appeared from nowhere. 'Clever client' meant someone who knew something he shouldn't.

Denis scowled at him. 'No quotes.'

Patrick shook his head.

'So what will happen to these personal relationships the City is so famous for?' He had 1,200 words to write on Big Bang.

'They're bound to become less important,' said Denis. 'Everyone's moving from firm to firm, department to department, and most of them are stuck in front of screens. We won't see each other over there,' he motioned towards the Stock Exchange, 'or over here, it looks like.'

'But you'll talk to each other on the phone?'

Denis looked at him as though he was simple. 'Yeah, but what can you say on the phone. All the jobbers – sorry,' he corrected himself, 'market makers, have got tapes in. Have had for months.'

The bar was still half empty and he despondently took a sip out of his pint. Wally was nodding. 'It's the end of an era, you can tell your readers,' he said. 'We'll all be sitting in front of screens next week.'

What constituted promiscuity? Sarah wondered as she

watched Simon Weatherstone pull on his underpants. One lover a year? Two, five, ten?

'They're a lovely colour,' she said, 'I love that strong pink.'

'Yes, I know.' He smiled shyly. 'That's why I wore them.'

She felt unexpectedly touched. Simon was the first person she had made love to since she had thrown Rob out. Rob had been her first love at Oxford, a wild free spirit who would never have worn Y fronts, let alone in her favourite colour.

Rob had been caught in a time warp. The rest of their friends had long since stopped dropping acid and taking speed and had become 'normal people' with jobs and mortgages. The occasional joint at the occasional rock concert, fine, but Rob could never put it behind him. He wanted life in the fast lane, out of control, out of his head.

She would arrive home, tired after work, and he would be ready to go, dragging her out to clubs until she begged to leave at two in the morning. Often she would go home alone, leaving him to take revenge on her by disappearing for days at a time. Once he had brought another girl back to the flat. Their rows had grown increasingly violent and a year ago it had become a straight choice between her job and him. He had gone – noisily. But she still missed him with a raw, searing ache in her soul.

She had been tempted by Simon's devotion and persistence. She had told herself there was nothing wrong with being adored and that Simon was an intelligent, kindly young man. Already, half an hour after he had reluctantly lifted himself off her, she knew it was a mistake. How seductive flattery can be when you are lonely, she thought to herself as he combed his hair in her mirror.

He had made love to her carefully, tenderly, caressing her body as though it were glass, ready to shatter at too demanding a touch. He had buried his face between her legs and licked her patiently, caringly, until she came. Then he had entered her softly, moving inside her gently until he finally gave way to his own orgasm with a burst of frantic sobs.

It had been very nice, Sarah thought, as he sat on the edge of the bed and regarded her with dark spaniel eyes. 'Are you sure you want me to go?' he asked.

'Honestly. I'm not sure I'd be able to sleep if you stayed and I have to get up at six now I work for Denis.'

'I hate not seeing you in the office,' he said. 'It used to make my day to watch you walk in every morning. You just breeze in and out now.'

Just as well, she thought as she smiled up at him. 'Thank you for a lovely evening,' she said. 'Can you make sure the front door has closed properly as you go out?'

He gave her one last, lingering kiss and as he left the room she gave a sigh of relief. Remorse followed. What right had she to play with a young man's feelings just to dull the pain of missing Rob? And now she would have to find a way of telling the poor boy. 'Look, I'm sorry,' she would say, 'I thought I was ready for another relationship but I'm just not. You know I'm very fond of you and I hope we'll always be friends.' And he would accept it and continue to make her coffee every time she appeared in the office. God! She hated herself sometimes.

As the London parks turned golden, Jack completed on the third perfect house in Esher Rosemary had found for them. The previous two had fallen through. At the end of October they moved the family home to the South for the first time ever and Rosemary thought she would never wake up happy again. She missed her vegetable garden most. She missed the ability to pluck a lettuce from the earth and serve it up as salad half an hour later. She missed her friends, the warmth of the people, Mary Salter next door. But she missed her garden most.

Angela Markus came to her rescue. She liked Rosemary's straightforward northern approach. Paris had taught Angela about taste and style, but she knew them for what they were. On the surface the two women had little in common, but they were soon calling each other daily, hooting with laughter at the antics of their husbands. Angela helped Rosemary furnish the Esher house and re-model herself into a sophisticated corporate wife. In return, Rosemary provided the mothering Angela had lacked – and an intimacy she had left behind with her schooldays.

In November, Jack took on the trade unions.

Under the restructuring plan, the old-fashioned cake manufacturing plant near Newcastle was to be closed. To replace the production, there would be a brand new cake plant built in Birmingham next to the biscuit factory. It would make delivery of raw materials and distribution easier and cut costs dramatically. It would also involve making 400 people in Newcastle redundant.

It was one of the moves Bill Soames had claimed was impossible, because of the strength of the local union.

Jack's experience with unions was limited to Huntingdon, where they had been quite reasonable. Warned by the other directors of the type of intransigence he would meet from Sean MacCready, the senior official and a persistent trouble maker, he decided to fly up to Newcastle one crisp Wednesday morning and beard the lion in his den.

The 'lion' was tall and skinny with a look of glittering truculence in his blue Irish eyes.

Jack met MacCready in the airless plant manager's office which overlooked the factory floor. Butler's industrial relations manager and the managing director of the cakes and pastries division were there too, officially to support Jack. He was not so sure. Rumours of the plant closure had been circulating all week and Jack's sudden visit had confirmed it in the minds of the workers.

MacCready entered the meeting still wearing his overalls, bringing with him two 'comrades' as he called them. He ignored Jack's outstretched hand from behind the desk.

'Well?' was all he said.

'I would prefer it if you would sit down, gentlemen.' Jack gestured to three chairs.

'I would prefer it if we didn't,' said MacCready. His lips curled at the word 'gentlemen'.

Jack and his colleagues were faced either with standing up, which would have made them feel ridiculous, or talking up to the three union officials. Jack chose the latter.

'Perhaps it might be simpler if I read you this announcement which is due to go to the Stock Exchange and the press tonight?' Three pairs of eyes stared coldly.

Jack cleared his throat and read: 'The management of Butler's Biscuits has decided to merge its cake and pastry making facility in Newcastle upon Tyne with its biscuit factory near Birmingham. The management believes this will provide substantial cost savings and increases in efficiency and productivity. It regrets the loss of jobs but relocation costs will be paid to those wishing to work in the new plant. Redundancy payments are currently being negotiated with the unions.'

He looked up. MacCready's face was blank. He turned to leave. 'Where are you going?' Jack snapped.

'To tell my members they've lost their jobs.'

'That's not true, and you know it,' said Jack. 'There are and will be jobs in other parts of the country. When the new plant is built your members will be given first choice of jobs. This closure won't take effect for at least a year and we can negotiate a settlement to help the workforce at this plant adjust to the changes with the minimum disruption to their lives.'

MacCready tipped his head backwards so that his chin and adam's apple stuck out. He looked down at Jack through contemptuous eyes and wondered how he could ever have considered working in management.

He could have said a lot. He could have said that there was no settlement on earth that would help men and women adjust to the trauma of losing their livelihood. He could have said the prospect of men uprooting their families from Newcastle and moving to Birmingham was utterly impractical. He could have said that arriving by helicopter to fire people lacked sensitivity and tact. He could have said he had been looking forward to management overplaying its hand ever since they had overlooked his talent.

But he knew better. Instead he said: 'Mr Armstrong, I am not empowered to negotiate anything until I have talked to my members.' His accent was heavy scouse. 'When I am empowered, we shall doubtless make contact.'

With that he turned swiftly and vanished.

For a moment the room fell silent. 'Does that bastard expect me to wait around all day, or what?' asked Jack. He had expected a closely argued confrontation, worthy of his time.

The managing director, whose own job was on the hit list, looked at him wearily. 'I wouldn't bother. He'll call a union meeting that will last the rest of the day anyway.' He lit a cigarette.

The noise of the works siren suddenly filled the stuffy office. 'That's it.'

'What?'

'The meeting.'

Below on the factory floor Jack watched the machines slowly come to a stop as each person abandoned work. Within two minutes it was empty.

He made as dignified an exit as possible in the circumstances.

Inside the canteen, the traditional place for union meetings, Sean MacCready heard the engine and rotor blades of the chopper taking off for London.

'There they go,' he told the meeting. 'The fat cats of management. But they've gone too far this time. The balance of the scales of justice screams out for redress. This proposed exploitation of labour has became intolerable. It is time to stand up for our rights.'

There was loud cheering, but thrashing out a resolution took until well after five that afternoon. It read: 'This union deplores the decision of the management to close the Newcastle plant at the loss of 431 jobs. This union rejects the management's invitation to negotiate terms and will withdraw its labour until the management reconsiders its decision.'

The next day, no one at the Newcastle plant turned up for work, bar a few harassed managers who drove through the picket line stone-faced.

By the end of the week two-thirds of Butler's baking capacity was at a standstill and regional officials from USDAW were unsuccessfully attempting to persuade MacCready to go to ACAS for arbitration.

'I don't understand what he hopes to achieve by this.' Jack was genuinely puzzled. 'He must realise we won't go back on our decision.'

The industrial relations manager sat nervously in Jack's office in St James' Square. He had never in his ten years at Butler's seen anyone stand up to MacCready for more than an afternoon.

91

'He's used to getting his own way, sir. There have been thoughts of moving the plant in the past, but he's always stopped it dead in his tracks.'

'Really! Well, nobody bothered to tell me.' Jack turned to the lawyer he had met at Charlton House. 'I suppose they are legally within their rights?'

'Oh, yes. They had a vote at the first meeting and all the action has been quite voluntary. If I understand your colleague, MacCready is the type of professional union official whom people believe is invincible.'

'I suppose it's the power which is so attractive,' said Jack.

The lawyer looked up. 'My experience is these people are inspired by simple Marxist ideals. Their real raison d'être is to destroy the system.'

'So he's not buyable?'

'I very much doubt it.'

'Why can't I just sack him?'

The industrial relations manager gasped in horror. 'You'd have the whole of the union out, right across the country.'

The lawyer shook his head. 'Not these days. But it's illegal to sack anybody just because you don't like the look of them, or because they are causing you a bit of trouble.'

Jack swivelled his chair to look out of the window. A biro turned between his fingers. 'It seems to me this man must have done something wrong in the fifteen years he's been with Butler's,' he said, almost to himself. He swung the chair back towards the industrial relations manager. 'Find it.'

The industrial relations manager looked terrified.

'But how?'

'And find it fucking fast!' Jack's tone turned menacing. 'I don't care how much it costs. Hire outsiders, check the records, find his enemies. I want him nailed.'

Sometimes, he thought later as he poured himself a large vodka, terror was the only thing that worked.

Peter had been pestering Jack to have lunch with him, and two days later they met in Wiltons in Jermyn Street.

'So you see,' concluded Peter, 'it's a perfect fit.' He gulped down another oyster and leaned back on the banquette. They were seated in one of the private booths.

Jack regarded Peter across the starched linen with suppressed admiration.

He loved the idea. It had style, logic, and above all it had audacity. It was the kind of deal he had always dreamed of – in the same league as Guinness's bid for Distillers, of Burton's takeover of Debenhams. If he could pull it off, it would put him on the map and bring his vision of creating a world class company a few steps away. The target Peter suggested had often crossed his mind in his search for acquisitions and he had done some work on it already. But it had seemed too ambitious. Now here was Peter presenting it to him as if it were the most reasonable thing in the world.

'What about timing?' he asked tersely, determined to conceal his excitement.

'Well, as I've said before, these markets won't go on for ever. But we need to do our homework very carefully. And it is vital to get your share price up before we go for it. I'd say, late summer or early autumn next year.'

'Won't someone else beat us to it?'

Peter demolished his last oyster and dabbed his mouth. 'It's a risk. I can't really see any other British company being that aggressive – apart from Hillsdown Holdings – and it's too big for them at the moment.'

'It's pretty big for us.'

Peter made a triangle with his fingers and his eyes darkened to navy.

'Listen, Jack, it's do-able.'

Suddenly they both laughed out loud.

MEMO

November 16, 1986.

From: Jack Armstrong   To: Edward Williams

Please get together the details of our manufacturing operation in Italy? Could you make this a priority?

93

Jack stopped pedalling, watching the numbers on the dial of the bike disappear. He was gasping for air. He had just been given a new, tougher work-out. Still, he would live, he decided, and started on his bench presses.

His investigators had discovered two relevant facts about Mr MacCready. The first was he had been narrowly beaten to a middle management position in the cakes division seven years before. Shortly afterwards, he had stepped up his activity in the union. Secondly, his wife came from Siena. MacCready was a fluent Italian speaker and spent every family holiday in Italy.

The information lacked the kind of ammunition Jack had hoped for. That weekend he brooded silently. Even Mark had remarked on it. Eventually Rosemary cracked.

'For heaven's sake, Jack, whatever is the matter. Or have you taken a vow of silence?'

He told her the problem.

'Why not offer him a high-powered job in Italy?'

'But the industrial relations manager says he's a committed Marxist. Not buyable.'

'Oh rubbish,' said Rosemary. They were reading the newspapers on the sofa. 'He'd never have gone for that cakes job in the first place if he were that committed. How old is he?'

'About forty.'

'Well, he must be sick of being a Marxist by now. You remember my Marxist phase at the LSE? It became excruciatingly boring. All those meetings.'

Jack grinned. 'You were the sexiest Marxist I've ever come across.' He slid an arm round her waist. 'You're losing weight,' he said in surprise.

'Mmm, a stone and a half so far.'

Something in her tone aroused him. Now they were in London, he missed the regular attention of May Ling. Somehow he had been too busy to find a replacement.

'Come back upstairs,' he pleaded.

'What's wrong with here?' She looked at him, her eyes dancing, and started to unbutton his shirt. 'No one else is in this weekend.'

Some time later, as she rode him on the living-room floor, her body arched away from him, breasts moving just out of reach, he had fleetingly wondered why he bothered to play around.

When he returned from the gym a slim dossier was lying on his desk, with a note attached. 'This is all we have in Italy. Edward.' It was a canning operation, mainly tomatoes and tomato puree, but also plums and peaches. Called Pommodorro Rosso, it was based in Puglia in the south of Italy and had a turnover of £5 million although it never seemed to make a profit. Study of the file notes revealed the plant was also subject to frequent strikes and shutdowns.

'Bloody perfect,' murmured Jack to himself.

All he had to do now was to sell the idea to MacCready. He would assume the mantle of humility and return to the plant. He would request a one to one meeting, to talk man to man. After all, they were both working class lads – it should be like tickling a trout.

Jack requisitioned the manager's office for the afternoon, ordering tea and biscuits for four o'clock and pale ale and sandwiches for six. He had brought with him a number of minor adjustments to the plan to close the plant.

MacCready was less openly truculent this time. The strike had lasted for more than a week and some of his members were beginning to complain, and to press for negotiations.

But he saw quickly that Jack was not offering anything new. There was a slight slowing down of the closure, some additional help with moving costs, a tweak on the redundancy payments but nothing which he could take back to his members and say: 'We've won.'

He became sullen and immoveable. There was no way Jack could put the Italian pitch to him in that mood, but he hung on, hoping some kind of opportunity would emerge. At six, when the beer arrived, they were still at a stalemate. Then, for an instant, Jack saw a look of weariness come over Sean's face.

He tilted his chair back on two legs and forced a sincere-looking smile. 'It's a tiring business, negotiating.' MacCready almost smiled back. It was now or never.

'Of course we've both got our jobs to do. I have to say I

95

think you do yours very well.' Jack slowly poured the beer. 'It's a pity this trouble has come up, because there's a problem in Southern Italy near Puglia that I wanted you to sort out for us.' He pushed MacCready's glass towards him. What was he thinking?

'It would have taken you away from here, of course, which I don't suppose you'd have liked, but you would have been ideal for it. Still, never mind.'

MacCready had frozen in his chair. There was a moment's silence. Jack felt the hostility blowing around his ears. He was not going to play.

'Well, we'd better get back to the matter in hand.'

Sean suddenly came to life.

'What problem?'

Calmly and slowly, Jack explained about the Italian factory, how it was leaking money, how it needed someone with both financial nouse and skill at dealing with unions.

'I gather you were once considered for a job managing one of Butler's subsidiaries?'

MacCready's nostrils flared.

'Are you trying to bloody buy me off?'

Jack looked at him levelly. 'Yes, of course I am.'

MacCready's pale, bony face relaxed and he took a mouthful of beer, swilling it round his mouth slowly.

'Well, it won't work,' he said, almost to himself.

When the two men emerged from the manager's room at seven, MacCready had rejected every single proposal Jack had put to him.

The plant stayed closed and MacCready stepped up the pressure through his friends in the press. The stalemate was all over the local newspapers the following day and soon picked up by the nationals. The most worrying coverage for Jack was in the *Financial Times* which carried nearly a third of a page on it. Another story scheduled for that page had bitten the dust at the last minute.

The article sent the shares plunging more than 10 per cent in two days, despite the fact that Butler's public relations department was telling everyone the strike could not spread.

Peter rang Jack. 'We can't launch a major takeover bid with your share price plunging,' he chirruped.

Sir Richard asked him to pop in for a drink.

Sarah and half a dozen food analysts rang him to ask what exactly was going on.

Jack decided to play for time and stepped aside from direct negotiations. The industrial relations manager called for a meeting with the union, which was increasingly keen to negotiate. It was agreed to take the matter to ACAS. In return, the men would go back to work, but with a ban on overtime.

The City did its sums and calculated the cost of the strike would be far less than the overall savings Jack was making in his restructuring. In any case, in a year of great change, they knew it would all be lost in below the line special provisions. The share price not only recovered, but began to move up to new ground.

Chapter 7

The dispute rumbled on like a controlled forest fire. Each time they neared a solution, MacCready would find another point to haggle over, another spark to inflame his members. Jack told the board the problem was contained. But he knew, as they did, that while Sean MacCready stayed in office, Butler's would never be safe from disruption.

In December, when the work to rule had shrunk to three plants, Jack launched a personal tour of the company to boost morale and see how the restructuring was going. 'I don't interfere, but I think they need to know who the boss is,' he told Sir Richard.

His visits struck terror into the managements of the subsidiaries. They were planned with military precision. He would give two days' notice, then arrive by helicopter early in the morning, half an hour either side of the appointed time. A tour of the factory with the works manager would follow. Jack would charm everyone from the cleaners to the shop steward, flashing his warmest smile and always singling out one lowly staff member to ask about her mentally handicapped child or sick mother. The girls on the line all fell in love with him and the managers would begin to relax. He had a gift for remembering names and would call out to the workers as he left 'See you next time, Sid. Keep up the good work. 'Bye, George.'

At lunch he would turn coolly distant, then aggressive, firing questions at them. 'How many workers have you sacked? What is the stock turn? Why are the gents' toilets a disgrace? Why isn't production higher? What are you paying for pallets these days?'

When answers were fudged he would ask for the correct information to be produced before he left. Over pudding he would become jovial again, even telling one or two risqué jokes. He always enjoyed the ensuing cackle of nervous laughter.

As he left he would say: 'Remember, the future of Butler's rests with you guys.'

By the time he swooped back into the sky in the early afternoon, they would be glowing with enthusiasm. He was using a helicopter so often he asked Edward to look into the logistics of buying one.

Jack could not understand the City. 'You tell them something bad and the shares go up,' he said to Charlie Briggs-Smith and Peter later that week. 'Ever since we announced those terrible half-year results, they've been racing upward.'

It was ten days before Christmas and they sat at a small table laden with nuts in the Savoy's American Bar. The atmosphere was thick with festivity.

Charlie was taking Jack out to dinner as a 'thank-you' for making Greenbags joint broker, and had invited Peter along too. Their motive in courting Jack, was after all, identical.

'I saw Mummy kissing Santa Claus,' sang the pianist in the corner rather too loudly.

'What the City likes is certainty,' Peter shouted above the music. 'It now knows the extent of the bad news, so people can look forward. They see a new strong man at the top of a hitherto moribund company – *et voilà.*'

Charlie laughed and added: 'Which is why the time is rapidly approaching for you formally to introduce yourself to the City.' He waved energetically at a waiter in an attempt to order a second drink.

'Oh, yes?' Jack's tone was cautious.

'Well,' said Charlie, abandoning his quest as two white jackets whizzed by, 'you've proved you're a strong leader in the mould of our great heroine, the beloved Margaret, by axeing hundreds of jobs and dragging Butler's into the 1980s. You made a tough, brief, statement with the results; now you have to tell them how you are going to take the company on to glory.'

'Exactly,' added Peter, popping a salted almond into his mouth. 'And, most important, make lots of lolly for them.'

And us, they both thought.

Jack looked unimpressed. 'We've still got the strike on our hands. I'd like to get rid of MacCready for good before I start prancing round the City.'

Charlie finally entrapped a waiter. 'A large gin and tonic, and two more glasses of champagne – and the bill, please,' he called after him as he disappeared at the speed of an Olympic athlete. Jack still held out against the City habit of drinking champagne at all times.

'Sure, but you have contained it.' He saw Jack's face darken. 'Or the City thinks you have,' he added.

'Fear and greed,' said Charlie. 'They are the only two emotions in the City that really count.' Jack laughed – a dry, choking sound. He produced a leatherbound notepad from his inside pocket. FEAR and GREED, he wrote, the only two emotions that count.

'What a cynical bunch you are.'

'Oh, hell, I think we've been spotted by the press,' said Peter, looking delighted. 'Do you know Patrick Peabody? He's the new City editor of the *Sunday Herald*?'

Before Jack had time to answer, an affable Irish voice said: 'Now what big takeover are you plotting here?' Peter stood up and shook the speaker by the hand. 'Patrick, how very nice to see you. You know Charlie.'

'But do you know Jack Armstrong?' Patrick looked blank. 'Of Butler's Biscuits?' Patrick's face lit up. 'Oh, yes, of course, you've been doing sterling work, I hear. I had lunch with Hector Laing last week. He was really singing your praises.'

'I'm dreaming of a White Christmas, just like the ones I used to know,' sang the pianist.

Jack leaned forward and shook the outstretched hand. Randolph had hated the Press and forbidden press conferences at Huntingdon, so journalists were still largely a foreign breed to him. He took in Patrick's dark good looks and rumpled blue suit with interest.

He knew from Peter that the *Herald* was the most influential of the Sunday papers when it came to swaying City opinion. Charlie clearly knew it too.

100

'Come and join us for a drink.'

'I'd love to,' said Patrick, flipping a long lock of hair off his face, 'but I'm already late for dinner.' He glanced anxiously at his watch, then looked speculatively at Jack and smiled.

'Oh, well, it is Christmas. Just a quick one. I'll get them.'

You'll be lucky, thought Jack, but a waiter appeared the moment Patrick raised his hand.

'He has a way with waiters.' Charlie winked.

For an hour Patrick regaled them with anecdotes. Then, picking a moment when Charlie and Peter were distracted by another of their mutual clients two tables away, he leaned towards Jack. 'So what's happening with this strike of yours? I'm told it's still something of a problem.'

Jack's defences rose. 'It's contained. The effect on our profits will be minimal,' he snapped.

Patrick smiled his lazy smile. 'Don't worry, I'm not trying to make a big issue out of it. When it's finished though, it would be great to be the first paper with the story.'

By the time he left, making them all late for dinner, he had persuaded Jack to have lunch with him.

The Savoy Grill's frock-coated manager, Angelo Maresca, greeted Charlie like a returning hero. 'Meester Breegs-Smith, what happens? I theenk you dissapear in Beeg Bang.' His cherubic Italian face alight with good humour, he guided them to a table on the far side of the room. He lovingly tucked them in, while another waiter carefully spread their starched white napkins on their laps. Giving them one last, fond smile, Angelo was gone, leaving them to the discreet care of his staff.

Jack wondered how much money Charlie must have given him over the years. The best tables, like theirs, were set back against the panelled walls and the diners were mainly immaculate middle aged men, deep in earnest conversation.

Charlie sat back, content. 'I do like it here. Do you realise all the panelling comes from one single yew tree?'

Jack noticed the occasional steel haired dowager, out with her husband. In the centre of the room was a large table, set for a Christmas party. He and Peter, he realised with a jolt of pleasure, were the youngest people in the room.

'Who's that with Professor Roland Smith over there?' he asked as the waiter arrived with the menus.

'Dunno,' answered Charlie, 'I'm starving. He's astonishing, that man. He's chairman of so many companies I've lost count. I think I'll have the smoked salmon and roast duck.'

Charlie and Peter got back down to business. 'What we've got to organise is a roadshow,' said Charlie.

Jack frowned. 'What he means is a rehearsed presentation that you make to half a dozen separate institutions on the same day,' said Peter.

'I know, I'm not a complete idiot.' Peter could be incredibly patronising. 'I did a roadshow during the bid for Huntingdon. I still don't understand why you can't get all the institutions under one roof and do it, instead of seeing them individually.'

Charlie shook his head. 'They don't like it, that's why.'

'It's not done,' agreed Peter.

'And what do I say on this roadshow?' Jack had yet to warm to the idea.

'Well, that's what we wanted to talk through with you.' Across the table Charlie winked at Peter.

When the cigars came round at the end of the meal, Charlie and Peter both chose one. 'I don't suppose I can tempt you?' Charlie said to Jack. 'You're so terribly fit.'

'Well, Sir Richard and I occasionally indulge. And they go well with armagnac,' he said, staring pointedly at his empty glass. 'I'll have a Monte Cristo.'

Charlie ordered more drinks while the waiter lit Jack's cigar. Another Armagnac wouldn't hurt him. He agreed with Charlie, he thought, as he surveyed the Grill Room through a cloud of perfumed smoke. He liked it here.

He also liked Charlie. He had endeared himself to Jack by introducing him to the hitherto closed world of field sports. 'You know Hermione still has shooting parties on Randolph's old estate,' he had said one day after a meeting in Jack's office. 'You should come along sometime.'

The invitation gave Jack intense pleasure. But it also gave him some discomfort. His experience was limited to some clay pigeon shooting he had done on joining Huntingdon, in the unfulfilled hope of an invitation from Randolph.

'I'd love to,' he said. 'Need to get in a bit of practice, though.'

Charlie had sensed his unease. 'Tell you what, there's a tremendously good chap at Holland & Holland in Northolt. It's one of the best places. Have a few sessions with him first.'

The first date had been set for January.

Jack stayed in the company flat overnight after dining with Peter and Charlie as he was due to fly to Hong Kong at lunchtime the next day. When he dropped into the office before leaving, Amanda, whom he had poached from Brian Swinton, put a pile of mail before him.

'I think there's one there you'll quite like,' she said drily.

On the top lay a thick, white card inviting him for drinks with the Prime Minister at Downing Street. When Amanda brought his coffee in five minutes later, he was on the phone to Rosemary. 'And guess who's invited me to a party?'

But he sighed as he got into the car to go to the airport. The trip had been forced on him by the head of the spice division. A Hong Kong Chinese, he had taken violent exception to Jack's idea of centralising the buying – and losing thirty local staff. He saw it as an erosion of his empire.

Jack did not want to fire him, as he was an extremely able man, constantly being approached by other companies. Jack had learned from his two years in the Far East for Renasco that the Hong Kong Chinese love flattery almost as much as they love money. And he judged he had a chance of winning the man round if he took the trouble to see him personally.

The only consolation was that Jean-Pierre, whose passion for the Orient continued unabated, had said he would be passing through on his way to Peking. He had not had a chance really to talk things through with his old friend since he became chief executive.

By the time Jack was settled into his first-class seat with a glass of champagne in his hand, he felt more cheerful. He was looking forward to dinner. Cathay Pacific's caviar portions were mountainous.

Seventeen hours later he checked into the Mandarin Hotel in

Central. From the window in his room, Hong Kong harbour lay before him, alive with small craft of all shapes, ancient and modern. The Star Ferry ploughed its way across the water to Kowloon Side where a new hotel had risen since his last visit. It was good to be back.

A bell boy arrived with a letter of welcome and a telex from Jean-Pierre saying he would check in the next day; two waiters came bearing Jasmine tea; the laundry manager and the hall porter range wanting to know if they could be of service.

Having dispatched the laundry boy happily clasping some Hong Kong dollars, Jack cut himself a slice of papaya from the basket of fruit on his table, and headed for the shower.

He noticed Jane Brompton the moment she walked into the Captain's Bar where he was reminiscing over a Singapore Sling with an old colleague from Renasco named Frank. He saw a halo of auburn curls framing a striking face with high cheekbones and a strong jaw. It was a face of womanly determination. To Jack's surprise Frank waved at her. She joined them, smiling.

'This is Jane Brompton,' said Frank. 'She's a headhunter.'

'Of course.' Jack slid from his bar stool to shake hands. 'We've never met, but your company has found me both a sales and a marketing director in the past five months. I've been very impressed.'

'And you are . . .?' She looked bemused.

'Jack Armstrong, Butler's Biscuits.'

'Oh, yes.' Her large cat like eyes widened. 'You've been really shaking things up there.' Jack leaned on the bar, trying to look nonchalant. 'But you really should change the name of that company, you know. Butler's Biscuits sounds so old-fashioned.'

For a moment he felt affronted by this woman telling him what to do with his company name. Then he caught the smell of her perfume, lemony yet warm.

'Well, you may be right,' he said. 'Maybe we should meet up in London and talk about it?'

She looked amused. 'I'd love to.'

As she sat down he noticed her legs, firm and slightly

freckled, with dainty ankles. He pulled up a stool for her. 'So how do you know this old rogue?' Jack motioned to Frank.

'I head hunted him from Renasco,and we've been friends ever since.' Both she and Frank giggled over a shared memory.

'Jane occasionally lets me buy her dinner when she's passing through Hong Kong.' Frank looked smug.

At eight o'clock Jack's managing director, Sam Woo, and his English assistant arrived. They looked startled on seeing Jane.

'Have you been after my guys?' Jack asked her directly. He could sense their embarrassment.

'Yes, I have,' she answered just as directly, her wide red mouth smiling. 'But they won't come.' Everyone laughed and they split up to go to dinner.

As he had suspected the main gist of Sam Woo's argument was that too many people would lose face. In other words he felt his domain was being contracted – and there was no compensation.

Jack did not offer any solutions that evening. He wanted to let the man sweat a little. Although he was threatening to resign, he had been with the company for nearly twenty years and Jack sensed he would prefer to stay.

The following night Jack had arranged to meet Jean-Pierre in the Captains Bar and go on to eat in The Pierrot.

Jack's relationship with Jean-Pierre puzzled everyone. Jack had always excelled at all the masculine sports; his vanity centred on his ability to attract women; his considerable charm could swiftly give way to tough northern aggression. Why did such a man fraternise with an overt homosexual like Jean-Pierre Krandsdorf?

When he arrived, Jean-Pierre was already sitting at a table, dressed impeccably in a pale tropical suit which threw up his smooth tan. But to Jack's irritation he was with another man – a short podgy creature with tight greying curls and coarse orange skin, leathery from years of Florida sunshine.

Jean-Pierre stood to introduce them. 'Jack, I'd like you meet Max Schlosstein, one of the smartest arbs on Wall Street.' They shook hands, Jack towering above him. The man's face crinkled in what Jack took to be a smile. He spoke with the nasal whine of the Bronx.

105

'You remember when we first met, old buddy?' said Jean-Pierre.

Jack nodded. He had been attempting his first takeover – of a small moribund company. But it had been far more difficult than he had anticipated. The arbitrageurs had grabbed 60 per cent of the shares.

'Max here was one of the guys who agreed to deliver,' said Jean-Pierre. 'I seem to remember you had over 10 per cent of the stock,' he said to Schlosstein.

Jack warmed marginally towards the little man.

'I obviously owe you a drink,' he said, and ordered Singapore Slings all round. 'What are you doing in Hong Kong?'

'Oh, I got some old friends here,' Max answered guardedly. 'I'm leaving tomorrow if this typhoon that's coming in lets me.'

'Oh, they fly in anything around here,' said Jean-Pierre.

'You got quite a lot of action in London these days,' said Max. 'That Guinness bid for Distiller's was pretty dramatic stuff. You know Boesky was in there?'

'So they say,' said Jack, suddenly wary. 'Is Boesky out on bail now?'

Max nodded, grinning. 'We all have to be a bit more careful these days.'

Jack wondered just how well Max Schlosstein and Boesky knew each other.

'I thought London was all pretty small beer to you Wall Streeters.'

'A profit is a profit,' said Max, 'it doesn't need a passport.' He chuckled throatily. 'You have some big players too. Like Leo Stern. He and I go back a long way.'

Jack decided it was time to turn on the charm.

Later, over dinner, Jean-Pierre said: 'Max may not be the most wonderful human being in the world, but you never know, he could be useful.'

Jack nodded. 'You look great by the way,' added Jean-Pierre. 'How's the sex life?'

Jack smiled wrily. There were times when Jean-Pierre's curiosity verged on the voyeristic. He felt he should mind, but somehow he didn't. Part of him even found it quite exciting.

'I left May Ling in Chester, and since then life has been too hectic. Funnily enough, Rosemary seems to have redis-covered sex. Maybe I'm getting too old for playing around.'

Jean-Pierre looked at him with one eyebrow raised. 'Not you, sweetheart. You and I have the same type of drive.'

He savoured the expression of uncertainty on Jack's face. Then he let him off the hook, and laughed. 'It's just the gender that varies.'

Jack laughed as well, relieved. He'd never been entirely sure whether Jean-Pierre found him attractive or not. He always declared it was out of the question if anyone asked, but it was more the case that he had made a conscious decision right at the beginning of their relationship. If Jean-Pierre preferred men, that was fine, just so long as it didn't involve Jack.

And, after all, Jean-Pierre had been known to go with women too. There was one memory they both shared of a drunken New York evening when they had ended up with the same woman in Jean-Pierre's flat. She had been black, lithe and adventurous.

Jean-Pierre had presented her to Jack in the way a father gives a shiny new sports car to a teenage son. Initially she and Jack had made love in the bedroom. She had writhed and shuddered under him like no other woman he had known. Later they went back to the living room where she had sucked Jean-Pierre off while Jack had taken her from behind.

It was a memory he had tried to eradicate. But occasionally the image would come unbidden into his mind – most vividly the look of ecstasy on Jean-Pierre's face as he came, seen over the pulsating velvet back of the woman as Jack thrust into her. There had been one moment, one very fleeting moment, when Jean-Pierre's eyes, wide with imminent orgasm, had gazed straight into Jack's. Neither he nor Jean-Pierre had ever referred to the evening again.

They ordered. Or rather, Jean-Pierre ordered. It took him a good five minutes, chatting with the young Chinese waiter as if they were old friends.

'Do you know him?'

Jean-Pierre grinned, his eyes gleaming wickedly. 'Oh, I've seen him here before a few times.'

107

Jack asked his advice about Sam Woo.

'Pay the guy.'

'But he's already earning as much as I am. The rest of the board won't like it.'

'Look, this is Hong Kong. You and I both know that. The directors in London may not like it, but they understand it's a different world. It's a drop in the ocean in the scheme of things and the guy can say he's the highest paid director in Butler's.'

He picked out a mushroom from the sauce and delicately popped it into his mouth.

'Yes. You're probably right.' Jack stared vacantly across the room.

'What the hell is it then? You look like you're bustin' to tell me something.'

Jack leaned back in his chair, enjoying the moment, a slow smile spreading across his angular features. 'I can't tell you what it is, but I've got plans to pull off a really big one next year.'

Jean-Pierre stared at him.

'Sure you can tell me.'

Jack glanced around to make sure no one was listening. 'It could more than double the size of Butler's.' He was almost whispering. 'Turn us into a truly global food business. We'd have a distribution network in four continents, a quarter of the cake and biscuit market in the US, and 12 per cent of the European soft drinks business.'

Jean-Pierre's classical features expressed both interest and scepticism.

'These stock markets are looking mighty frothy, dear heart.'

'And it would make us number one in almost everything in the UK.'

'You still haven't told me the name.' The waiter started to take plates away, but Jean-Pierre had ceased to pay him any attention.

'The only problem is this fucking strike,' said Jack. 'There's a shop steward whose neck I'd like to wring. I even got a telex about it this morning.'

'You'll find a way,' said Jean-Pierre. 'Now what about the name?' he persisted.

Jack wrote it down on a napkin.

Jean-Pierre looked at it for a while and slowly tore up the napkin, his face a blank. Then he raised his Caribbean blue eyes to Jacks. 'Rather suits your style, old buddy,' he said softly.

Jack saw Sam Woo early the next morning. He proposed a new title plus a twenty-five percent bonus payment for overseeing the rationalisation. Sam Woo said goodbye with much smiling and bowing.

As Jack checked out of the Mandarin they told him the typhoon was still heading for the island. When he arrived in the first-class lounge he made straight for the bar and ordered himself a large bloody Mary.

'Heavy night?' enquired a voice behind him. He turned gingerly.

Jane Brompton was wearing a grass green cotton shift and scarlet lipstick. She looked as fresh as if she had just been picked.

The Cathay captain sounded as chatty and cheerful as if the typhoon was a mere breeze. Then along came the first round of hot towels and away they went, roaring up the narrow runway into the harbour at full throttle. The plane hurled itself into the air and instantly began bucketing about. Its huge frame creaked and groaned, the lights flickering on and off. Inside the cabin no one moved or spoke. Jack glanced across to where Jane was sitting and saw her face, white and stricken with fear. Suddenly protective, he caught her eye and smiled reassuringly as the plane plunged a couple of hundred feet. She managed a half smile back, like someone drowning, but grateful for the contact.

The turbulence was soon over, and when he looked at her again she had regained her composure and was laughing at something her neighbour had said. But he could feel the vibrations across the plane. He would make that lunch date soon. After all, he didn't want her waltzing off with all his good managers. She was someone it was better to have on your side.

He got back to London to find Sean MacCready threatening

109

an all out strike again. 'But he's extracted the best possible terms for his members.' Jack had gone straight to see Sir Richard. 'Apart from not closing the plant, they've got every damn' thing they wanted.'

'He still seems to have some strange idea he can stop us from closing the Newcastle plant.' Jack heard the question mark in Sir Richard's voice.

'No way,' he said. 'That plant has to be closed for sound economic reasons. You know that. It's for the good of this company and its shareholders.'

Sir Richard nodded, but there was little conviction in his face. Jack put an arm round his shoulders. 'Come on, Richard. We don't give into blackmail.'

Nevertheless, he went to bed in a deep depression. It was five days before Christmas. It did not look good to be at odds with the workforce at that time of year.

He was reading his mail gloomily the next morning when the phone rang. A deep scouse voice said: 'Is that Mr Armstrong?'

'Yes,' he snapped. He did not want to talk to MacCready.

'My name is Vickers, George Vickers, and I'm shop steward in one of the Newcastle bakeries. I wondered if we could talk, unofficial like, about the strike.'

'Go ahead,' Jack said quietly.

As he listened his spirits lifted. The man told him that MacCready had been so tough, he was losing sympathy with the main body of workers. They felt management had been as fair as it could; they'd seen several managers sacked too and wanted a settlement before Christmas.

'What can I do about all this?'

'Well if you were to ask him to put it to the vote – a proper ballot like – we'd support you.'

Jack could not imagine why he hadn't thought of it before.

'It's just that he's fooled you all into thinking he had unanimous support. So it's never been suggested,' said George Vickers as if reading his mind.

'Well, thank you kindly, Mr Vickers, I'll certainly think about what you've said.'

In the front room of a terraced house on the outskirts of

110

Newcastle, Sean MacCready's wife Lucia was also helping Jack's cause. Her father had contracted pneumonia, and his death, expected in the next few days, would leave her mother alone.

'Let's go back to Italy,' she pleaded. 'You could get a job with your Italian. You could even work on the farm for a while. I'm so sick of it here. Unions, unions, unions. Rain, rain, rain.'

Sean looked at her tear-stained face and thought of the countryside around her father's farm in Puglia in the south, where the earth was red with iron, just five miles from the Pommodoro Rosso factory. He wondered how on earth Jack Armstrong could have come up with an offer so perfect. He thought too of the last union meeting. They had given up, he could tell. There had been mutterings about holding a ballot.

He put his arms around his wife and sighed. *'Va bene. Andiamo,'* he said simply.

Jack bought Rosemary a two-pound box of Prestat truffles. Amanda had told him they were the best chocolates money could buy. He laid the box reverently on her lap and kissed her on the mouth.

'You were right, the bastard's given in. He wants to go and can tomatoes in Puglia.'

He had thought briefly of refusing MacCready, of humiliating him by calling for a ballot as George Vickers had suggested. But common sense told him the opportunity of getting MacCready out of Britain, and into management, should not be missed. He could never go back to the union again.

'You know I've always liked and respected you,' he had told MacCready on the phone. He had almost heard the man soften at the other end of the line.

By Christmas Eve redundancy terms for the Newcastle plant were settled, and for the second time in his career Sean MacCready began to think about buying a suit.

Sir Leo Stern perversely threw the company Christmas party in the second week of January. When Amanda handed Jack the heavily embossed invitation, he sat quite still for some time, looking at it.

111

Did he want to be friends – this man who never took no for an answer? Or did he simply want to get the measure of an enemy?

Well, he thought, as he scrawled a 'yes' in the right hand corner as a signal for Amanda to accept, he would jolly well go and find out.

The invitation was for 6 p.m. and, not wanting to appear too eager, Jack aimed for 6.30. His pleasure at the thought of the party and the inevitable confrontation with Stern had given way to tension. Yes, he would admit to tension; pleasurable tension that is. There was nothing Stern could do in the middle of Claridge's after all. But why had he been invited? He had asked Peter who waived it aside in his airy way. 'Leo loves playing games.'

As Jack had hoped, by the time he arrived, Claridge's ballroom was already seething. Stern stood at the entrance with two of his directors receiving guests, his face like granite. Jack attempted a cordial but tough, 'Hello, Leo, nice of you to invite me.' But he had shaken hands and had been somehow moved past into the ballroom before he realised it. Stern had not even bothered to speak.

A sea of dark-suited men and a loud babble of conversation enveloped him. 'Hello, Jack.' Geoffrey Maitland Smith, the assiduously polite chairman of Sears, greeted him. Butler's supplied a number of products to Selfridge's food hall and some of the other department stores. They were soon joined by a corporate lawyer and a banker. After the round of parties and dinners in the run up to Christmas, Jack knew a surprising number of people. What was more gratifying – they were eager to talk to him.

He soon understood that an invitation to this party was no measure of good feeling. As well as friends, colleagues and suppliers, anyone Stern could possibly conceive of as a rival was present. To the right, Ralph Halpern the chairman of Burton chatted to Sir Terence Conran and the Dixons' boss, Stanley Kalms.

To the left, Jack could see an enclave of property men. As a retailer, Stern needed to know about shop sites and had a reputation for being well informed.

Gerald Ronson, the chairman of Heron International, broad-shouldered and puffing on a huge cigar, held forth to

Peter Hunt the head of Britain's biggest property group, Land Securities. John Ritblat of British Land stood with them, his smile flashing on and off like a neon sign, eyes darting around the room.

The City glitterati was out in full force. Senior stockbrokers and merchant bankers seemed to be everywhere.

Peter materialised out of the crowd, snatching a canapé from one of the waiters who was attempting to penetrate the crush.

'Nobody can talk about anything but Guinness,' he said crossly. The Guinness scandal had broken a year before but was still an obsession in the City.

'It's already made life much tougher for everybody,' Peter grumbled.

'I thought Roger Seelig was your arch enemy. I'd have thought you would be delighted to see him in trouble.' Peter was never happy, it seemed to Jack.

'Rivalry is one thing, but we're all in the same business. Morgan Grenfell should never have just fired him like that.

'Ooh, look, there's Michael Richardson talking to Geoff Mulcahy,' he said, easily diverted. 'I suppose they're congratulating each other on beating off Dixon's.'

'Oh, here's Leo,' he said, and melted into the crowd. Deserter, thought Jack, taking a large gulp from his glass.

'Glad you could make it.' Stern stood directly in front of him, face implacable.

'It's a magnificent party. I'm honoured to be invited.' Jack was a couple of inches taller than Stern, but he felt smaller, and generations younger.

'Oh, I wouldn't be too honoured if I were you.' Stern's upper lip curled, the tone was mildly mocking. 'I just like to get everyone under one roof once a year, that's all.'

His dark eyes bored into Jack. 'You should have talked to me, my boy. We could have dealt.' Jack struggled to hold his gaze, his mind a blank. He could hear his heart pounding.

'Well,' he said eventually, 'I believe I did the best deal for Huntingdon sharehol—'

'Leo, Colin here tells me you haven't actually met each other,' Peter's voice cut in.

Rescuer, thought Jack, wondering if Stern knew about his side deal with Butler's. Stern's expression did not waver as he shook hands perfunctorily with the stocky, cheerful-looking man at Peter's side.

Suddenly someone was plucking at Stern's arm. 'Leo, Leo, she's here, you must come.' The tone was beseeching.

'Excuse me, gentlemen.' Jack saw Stern's eyes shine for a moment like a child about to blow out the candles on a birthday cake. Then he strode into the crowd.

Peter raised an eyebrow and moments later there was a stir at the door. Jack could just make out the unmistakable blonde-coiffed head. Then he saw the face, the pearls at the throat, the square shoulders of a royal blue silk jacket.

A murmur of surprised appreciation went round the room. 'They never announce beforehand that she's coming because of security,' Peter said in Jack's ear. 'Well, clever old Leo,' said one of the property côterie. 'You've got to hand it to him, it takes pull to get the Prime Minister along.'

Roadshows normally fall to the stockbroker, and a few days later Charlie started rehearsing Jack. He wanted to impress Jack on the minds of the men and women who invested money for the large institutions – the big insurance companies, the pension funds of large companies and the unit trust groups.

With Butler's year end coming up fast in March, Charlie urged Jack to get it out of the way before the 'close' season – the six weeks' information blackout before the financial results.

Thus in early February 1987, Jack, Edward Williams and Charlie set forth armed with a slides and charts to show their wares. 'Don't expect too much response,' Peter had warned. 'Fund managers are not the liveliest bunch, as I'm sure you've already realised.'

For Jack, it was the nearest he would ever get to showbusiness and he treated it that way. His lanky good looks and eloquent delivery caught his audience's attention, while his northern accent made them believe he was honest.

But what really impressed them was that he had taken action – and shown himself adept at dealing with both management and the unions. Most of all, he wore his ambition on his sleeve – an ambition they judged, in this bull market of bull markets, would make money for them all.

Chapter 8

'Up do-o-wn up, up do-o-wn up, up do-o-wn up, up do-o-wn up.' Sarah finished the final turn and skidded to a halt. Where was Simon? She had lost him again. She looked back up the mountain, dotted with skiers. 'This way, Sarah!' He swooped past her, skinny black legs sticking out beneath a billowing cerise jacket. Skiing brought out a new side of Simon. Gone was the diffident boy from the office.

She started off again in her methodical way as the instructor had taught her. Weight on lower ski, she told herself, lean into the valley . . . Aaagh! A skier in a sunshine yellow outfit swept from behind her and crossed almost immediately in front. She shuddered at the sound of skis scraping ice.

'Shall we take the bubble up and then ski to that place we found on Monday for lunch?' suggested Simon when she got to the bottom.

'Great,' said Sarah, gasping for air.

They had taken a whole chalet with a group from the office, mainly dealers and their girlfriends. It was to be on a strictly friendly basis, Sarah had insisted, so she was sharing a room with another girl. As ever, Simon had gone along with what she wanted.

Sarah stuck her skis and poles next to his in the snow outside the wooden restaurant, willing herself to remember their position. 'Ooh, look, there are still some seats outside,' she cried.

This was the moment she loved. She loosened the clips on her boots, shook her hair free from her hat, sank down on a chair and tilted her face to the sun. Two of the others from their chalet joined them. 'I'm going to have cheese omelette, frites and chocolate cake,' she declared.

'Good idea,' said Simon. He ordered the same, with some white wine. The sun poured down on the mountain peaks from an unbroken blue sky. 'Oh, bliss.'

Desks and screens were in another universe, shrivelled into a dark corner of the mind. Altitude and exercise honed her senses. 'It's like being on top of the world,' she told everyone in earshot.

Sir Leo Stern was also gazing at the mountains – from a different angle, from a different restaurant. He and Paulette had taken a suite at the Suvretta House in St Moritz as they did every year in the last two weeks of February. It was guaranteed to be full of people they knew, and their sons Jacob and Daniel adored it.

Stern liked skiing less than his family. Ten years of practice and lots of private tuition had turned him into a tolerably good skier but like Sarah, what he really enjoyed was sitting in the sun and eating lunch. If there was someone with whom to talk business, even better.

Opposite Stern, his pale irises shielded by mirrored glasses, sat Klaus von Gleichen. Next to him Max Schlosstein guzzled goulash zuppe.

'So Leo,' Klaus's accent was clipped RADA English edged with the merest trace of German, 'what do you want us to do with our three per cent in Butlers?'

'Sell it.'

Stern stared moodily at the mountain, his dark eyes glowing with malevolence. Originally he had wanted to use the stake in Butler's to frighten Armstrong. Last year, he would have laid money one of the big European food groups would pounce on the biscuit group. There had been well-informed talk that Nestle, the giant Swiss group, was sniffing around. And the rumours on Wall Street had said Nabisco was also 'running the numbers'. The big American companies, he reflected, talked a lot but rarely moved. They had a lot of things against them, not least a lousy accounting treatment of goodwill.

'The price is up by a third,' said Stern. 'Do yourselves a

116

favour. Take a profit.' The waitress put a huge coupe of ice cream in front of him, topped by a giant swirl of whipped cream and finished with chocolate sauce. He stuck his spoon in absent-mindedly.

'You do not want us to sell to anyone in particular?' asked Klaus, his voice neutral.

'Nah. I'm afraid Mr Armstrong, aided by my good friend Peter Markus, has been a bit cleverer than I anticipated. They've turned that company from prey to predator in a remarkably short time.'

'Well, Leo,' Klaus applied some white sun block to his mouth, 'you are always telling us that nobody ever went broke taking a profit.' He glanced at Schlosstein. 'But it's not much fun.'

Schlosstein shrugged. 'A profit's a profit.'

'Well, if you want fun,' Stern said, pausing from his sundae, 'you might try putting some of your profits into a company called Empire Foods.'

'Why?'

'It's nothing definite. I just have a hunch that when Mr Armstrong decides he wants to play takeovers, he might well turn his attention to that company.' The corners of his mouth twitched.

A svelte skiier in palest turquoise stopped dead in front of them in a shower of snow. 'Darleeng,' cried Paulette, 'you 'avn't eaten lunch already, 'ave you?' She sounded aggrieved as she kicked off her skis and clomped up to the table, her tanned face glowing with health. She kissed Stern on the cheek. 'Oh, darleeng!' she said as if scolding a child, 'you've been very, very naughty,' seeing the now empty bowl.

'Never mind,' he said, patting her behind, 'I'm sure you'll put me on one of your horrible diets when we get back to London.'

'I think it would be nice to get out of the milling throng and ski to that village everyone keeps telling us about this afternoon,' said Simon, draining the last drop of wine from the glass. The others all murmured assent.

'It's not off piste, is it?' Sarah asked, feeling the butterflies start in her stomach.

117

'Well, you can go off piste if you really want to,' teased Simon studying the map, 'but in fact the simplest route is mainly blue runs with just a couple of reds.' Sarah smiled with relief.

'Yes,' said one of the others, 'Ron and Jigger went yesterday and said that apart from one steep red path it's a doddle.'

The butterflies started up in Sarah's stomach again. But she said nothing. She was sick of being the wimp of the party. Two chairlifts and an easy skim down a blue run and her confidence had returned. It was, after all, a marvellous day.

The others in front had turned off on to a path through the trees. This must be the red bit, Sarah thought uneasily as she felt herself gathering speed down the slope which became bumpier and bumpier. The surface seemed like polished glass and the path was too narrow to turn in. Against her will she leaned back on her skis, knowing it would increase her speed but unable to defy her instinct. Ahead of her, she saw one of the girls shoot up in the air with a whoop over a big bump and disappear as the path veered off to the left.

A wall of virgin snow lined the right of the path, its unbroken sparkling surface at waist level. As she hurtled towards that big bump, a vision of her chin hitting the deck, blood and teeth everywhere, flashed before her and she knew there was only one way to stop. Deliberately, she flung herself to the right.

She lay listening to the silence, buried up to her armpits in powder snow. The sun shone warm on her face. The problem now was how to extract herself. One ski had come off and she could just see the tip a couple of feet in front of her. Slowly, carefully she extricated it and placed it at right angles to the slope. Then she began struggling to get herself out, but the harder she tried the deeper she seemed to get. There was nothing solid to use as a lever.

After several minutes, she sank miserably back into the snow with a groan, steaming hot with the effort. It was typical of the others just to go on and leave her. Even Simon had abandoned her! Tears of self-pity begin to prick at the back of her eyes.

'Now what have we got here?' said a deep male voice.

Relief flooded over her, swiftly followed by astonishment as she looked up to her left and there, resplendent in an ice blue anorak, salopettes and a contrasting bobble hat, stood Sir Leo Stern.

Some knight in shining armour, she thought.

'I know the snow's nice, but do you really want to go rolling in it?' he asked. Neither of them expressed any surprise at meeting in such an unlikely spot.

'I was going so fast, it was the only way to stop,' Sarah gasped.

'Here grab hold of this.' He positioned himself firmly and held out his ski pole. Within a minute she was out.

'This makes a bit of a change from wheeling and dealing for Denis Jones, doesn't it?' A glimmer of a smile played at the corners of his mouth.

She struggled to think of a witty reply and felt her face burning; there was something about him that made her feel five years old. She stood there awkwardly on one ski, brushing ineffectually at her ski suit.

'I'll wait until you've got your skis back on.' His voice was suddenly gruff, or did she imagine it? She stumbled around, her dark curls caked in snow, hat skewed. He held out a steadying arm as she finally clicked the other ski on. She was like an overwrought puppy which needed taking off somewhere quiet and calm. She couldn't be much older than Daniel, his eldest son. He had always wanted a daughter.

She regained some composure. 'You've been very kind.' Her huge eyes smiled up at him. He was on the point of inviting her to come and have dinner with them at the Suvretta House, but something held him back.

'My pleasure. Now you go on ahead. You'll find it widens out once you get round that bend.'

To her annoyance she found he was right.

'What happened to you?' Simon sounded anxious. He had sent the others on ahead.

'I'm sorry. I lost my nerve and fell into the deep snow.' She did not confess she had done it deliberately. 'But luckily someone rescued me.'

'Oh. That was nice.' She could hear the unspoken question

in his voice, the hint of jealousy. As they edged forward in the queue to pick up the chair lift, she knew she was smiling. It served him right for leaving her behind.

'Yes, it was actually,' she said. And as the chair swept them up into the air, she could feel her pulses racing.

At the beginning of 1987, the pundits had predicted a buoyant year ahead for the London stockmarket. The Chancellor, Nigel Lawson, attacked 'short-termism' in the City but forecast a good year for the economy.

The government's big privatisations, British Telecom and British Gas, had gone better than anyone had dared dream and subscribers who had held on to the shares could boast to their friends of a healthy profit. Mrs Thatcher's vision of a share-owning democracy seemed to be becoming reality.

There were a few warning voices. The economy was growing too fast, declared the analysts at the big broking houses. The stock market was historically high and the reverse yield gap (the difference between the yield on shares and gilt-edged stock) was yawning alarmingly wide.

Alan Budd at the London Business school predicted respectable growth in output of 1987 and inflation below 5 per cent. But for the longer term, he was more cautious, writing prophetically in the *Financial Times*: 'A more important question is whether the policy will set Britain on the right path for a sustained recovery with low inflation, or whether the government will succumb to the temptation to push the economy along more rapidly now at the cost of high inflation (and the painful process of correction) later on.'

At the beginning of 1987 as the bulls gathered for their last stampede, these words of caution fell on deaf ears. The market knew only that in an election year, Margaret Thatcher's government was unlikely to upset the applecart, and responded accordingly.

Each day the FT-SE index of 100 leading quoted companies leaped upwards as if it had springs in its heels; new companies, often with little in the way of solid assets, flooded on to the market to a euphoric reception. In May, the specialist retailer Sock Shop, a tiny company with only a handful of outlets, mainly in tube stations, was oversubscribed fifty times.

By March the FT-SE, known as the 'Footsie', had rocketted a staggering 30 per cent and seemed unstoppable.

Even sapling companies shot skywards, using their shares to snap up their smaller, weaker or sleepier brethren. In those extraordinary months in 1987 when the wildest dreams became reality, the world divided sharply into predator and prey. The corporate Tarzans at the head of fast-growing companies looked abroad for new jungles to conquer.

Inspired by Hanson and White, 'doing well over there as well as over here', many turned their eyes across the Atlantic to the United States, the biggest market of them all.

When Martin Sorrell, the young accountant who had deserted Saatchi & Saatchi to buy into a tiny supermarket trolley company three years before, successfully took over J. Walter Thomson, Madison Avenue's most famous advertising name, the City cheered.

Food companies are more stable by nature and were not at the heart of the action. But there were exceptions, such as the ravenously acquisitive Hillsdown Holdings, headed by Harry Solomon. Hillsdown had made a name for itself as one of the most aggressive groups. It also specialised in highly profitable chilled recipe dishes.

Butler's, too, proved an exception.

Jack had put over his tale well. As Sarah concluded in a research note for the General: 'Jack Armstrong has achieved much in the year since he took over as Chief Executive of Butler's Biscuits last March. The number of divisions is down from seven to four core businesses, the workforce is two-thirds what it was a year ago, and the board of directors has shrunk from fourteen to eight. The frozen food side has been sold for £44 million. In short, an in depth restructuring has been effected at all levels.

'The management's intention is now to grow in the areas where it has market strength. So far we have seen four smaller strategic acquisitions in high value added areas. The year ahead promises to be one of considerable progress for this company.'

Around this time, Jack had a new Topic screen installed in his airy office overlooking St James's Square. It gave him a

121

special kick to see what his share price was doing, minute by minute, hour by hour. He also liked to keep track on the competition. There was one company whose shares he watched with special relish as they drifted aimlessly along that springtime. It was called Empire Foods.

As the tulips bloomed in the square below, Peter, Edward and Jack discussed takeover strategy. 'What about the Monopolies Commission?' asked Jack.

'We should squeak through.' Peter sounded genuinely confident. 'There's no way we have more than the maximum market share in any product area. I can get my completed document to you within the week.'

'When can we do this bloody deal?' demanded Jack. He was indulging in ever more frequent fantasies of receiving a knighthood. 'Are we the only ones to notice that Empire Foods is begging to be attacked?'

Peter recognised the tone. Clients always began to panic as a deal drew near.

'Well, despite what I said about the state of the market, I still think we should wait until July. When we go, we need to have all our ducks in a row,' he said firmly. 'And you need to get yourself a proper PR man. That in-house toady you've got at the moment won't do at all for a bid on this scale.'

Jack nodded. Rodney James was competent enough with the trade press, but someone more heavyweight was called for to handle the financial press – someone who knew his business backwards. 'Who would you suggest?'

'Well, you're going to need a specialist. Someone who knows which City editor to go drinking with, and which journalists to avoid.'

'David Bang,' they both said at the same time. Peter looked startled.

'I met him at your party,' Jack reminded him. 'You weren't terribly nice about him.'

Peter pursed his lips. 'No, but he knows an awful lot of journalists and for some strange reason they seem to like him. He has a veritable piggy bank of favours owing to him. If anyone will deliver the goods, he will.'

'Fine. Ask him to give me a ring and I'll get him in. But why can't we do this deal sooner?'

Peter explained carefully. 'It's now March – Empire and Butler's year end. Both companies will produce their financial results in late June and if I've done my homework right,' he smiled his arch little smile, 'comparisons will be odious.'

'Is it worth approaching them to see if they would recommend our offer?' Jack stood at the window gazing out into the square.

Peter hesitated. 'It might be, nearer the time, when they're feeling vulnerable after their results. If they did agree, then it might be cheaper. And at least we know that Bertie Underworth is too stupid and too old fashioned to leak any approach to the press and push the shares up.'

'You know him?' Jack frowned at this casual reference to the chairman of Empire.

'Of course,' Peter said disdainfully. 'Before I started acting for you I'd been trying to find a new chief executive for him for ages. I even suggested a little reverse takeover with another company, but he's too much of a stick in the mud.'

'I didn't think you were supposed to advise other banks' clients.' Jack knew Baring Brothers had been Empire's merchant bank for years.

'Rubbish,' said Peter. 'You should know me better than that by now. Since Big Bang, all that traditional stuff has gone out the window. The American way is to come up with an idea and sell it to a client. The client uses you for that one transaction – they don't have to fire their official bank.'

Jack scowled. 'So just which company will you be advising in this bid?'

'Oh, come on, Jack,' grinned Peter. 'All that was before you came along. Anyway, you know I never do defences.'

Denis and Sarah sat on the low couch upholstered in a tweedy beige in Sir Leo Stern's office. It was designed for a man who barely noticed his surroundings.

Sarah had worked for Denis at his 'sharp end of the business' for more than a year and now fully understood why he called it that. But, wearing and infuriating though it could be, she loved the exhilaration that came with it.

In the run up to Big Bang, Tulley had been something of a wallflower. All around, partners of stockbrokers (who actually owned their businesses) were selling out for fairytale sums to the American, Swiss and British banks. But Tulley had been left suitorless.

Dickie had pretended not to mind. After all, he said, he had enough money, he enjoyed City life; he could just go on doing what he had always done.

Everyone knew this was whistling in the dark. Dickie understood better than anybody that the competition was about to get a whole lot hotter, commission rates were set to crumble and, as Denis had told Mickey, Tulley had nothing special to offer.

Then, at the eleventh hour, in the September, a Saudi Arabian bank put in an offer, making the wildest dreams of Dickie and the other five partners come true. The only pity for the partners was that they were financially tied in to the business by 'Golden handcuffs' for two years. So they couldn't put their feet up just yet.

Denis had worried at first that the new owners would object to doing business with Jews – which would have eliminated over half his clients. But although Saudi officially refused to trade directly with Israel, the Arabs appeared supremely relaxed about the nationality of the clients.

Stern did not relish the idea, but like the rest of Denis's Jewish clients felt he was dealing with Denis rather than the firm. He had followed Denis to Tulley from another stock-broker five years before. Sarah talked it through with her parents and in the end decided if it was all right for Sir Leo Stern, it was all right for her too.

'So I want you to start buying tomorrow,' Stern said to Denis in his worst bully boy voice. Sarah looked at him with intense dislike. He had ignored her for the whole of the meeting. He had been abrupt and stonefaced for the past twenty minutes, bawling Denis out about petty mistakes and demanding a huge cut in his commission rate. He had taken off his jacket and, for the first time, she noticed a roll of fat curving over the top of his trousers; his eyes were flat and emotionless in a face dark with stubble. She wondered how she had been so taken with him; he really was just a financial thug as everyone said.

'And what about the young lady here?' Sarah inwardly

124

jumped to attention. 'Can she manage if, God forbid, some-thing happens to you?

'Sarah's got a natural talent for the business. I'd trust her with my own portfolio,' said Denis.

Sarah felt Stern's dark eyes resting on her.

'And what do you think, my girl?' His tone was half sneering half hectoring.

'I shall certainly do my best, Sir Leo,' she said brightly.

'That wasn't the question,' he snapped. 'Will you or won't you be able to handle this share buying exercise in Empire Foods should your master here go sick?'

An icy calmness came over her. 'Don't worry, I'm sure I will be able to cope,' she said quietly.

Once outside she turned on Denis. 'Why do you put up with it? How dare he behave like that? All that money you've made him.'

He put an avuncular arm round her. 'Darlin', he's my biggest client and he's a one off. I respect his brain, and most of the time he's a pussycat. But every now and then he feels the need to push people around. Maybe something went wrong with his potty training. Who knows?'

Sarah laughed, her anger evaporating. 'It won't last,' continued Denis. 'He'll be nice as pie for months now, you see. You'll soon be fancying him again.'

For Jack, the days blurred into a mass of frenetic activity – meetings, phone calls and arguments which carried on far into the night. He became locked in seemingly endless confron-tation with nit picking lawyers who appeared to delight in blocking whatever he or Peter wanted to do. Emerging at nine or ten in the evening, he would end up drinking late into the night with anyone he could find.

He relied a lot on Jean-Pierre's advice. From the other side of the Atlantic, he sometimes saw things more clearly.

'There is only one important point about this deal,' he had said when Jack first put him completely in the picture. 'You have to win – and it really doesn't matter how.' He had paused to emphasise the point.

'With the smaller acquisitions, if you lost – *tant pis*. With this one, old buddy, your corporate balls are on the block.'

125

Jack had felt fear as Jean-Pierre spoke. But it was the fear of a mountain climber as he stands at the base camp and looks up to the snowy peaks. It made Jack's heart beat faster and his eyes shine brighter. It did not keep him awake at night.

He invited Jean-Pierre over for the board meeting where he planned to break the news of the bid to Butler's directors. He was going to need every atom of his silver-tongued talents to win them over and Jean-Pierre always boosted his confidence.

Peter was coldly furious. He had hoped to keep 'the poof with the tinted hair' as he privately called him, out of it. They had met only once and taken a cordial dislike to each other; both uncomfortably aware they had met an intellectual equal.

But Peter sensed the bond between Jack and Jean-Pierre was too strong to break, so reluctantly he agreed to his participation in project 'Star Wars' as the bid for Empire had been code named. If Jack wanted to load the company up with superfluous fees that was his business. And who knew? Jean-Pierre could come in handy with his high-flying friends in New York. Peter reckoned that Jean-Pierre and Leo Stern between them, should have Wall Street sewn up.

The visit suited Jean-Pierre perfectly. 'Bluett's have several vases they want to show me,' he had said. 'My oriental porcelaine collection is becoming truly awesome!'

David Bang had been one of the most beautiful young men of his generation. Tall and golden-haired, with rugby-players' shoulders and gently mocking eyes, he had been every hostess's delight throughout the 1970s. But fifteen years later, two restaurant meals a day, a drip feed of fine claret and armagnac, Sullivan Powell cigarettes, Monte Cristo cigars, 3 a.m. bedtimes and 7 a.m. power breakfasts, had done their worst.

In the spring of 1987, having celebrated his forty-first birthday on 23 March, he would have passed for forty-six. His friends now fondly referred to his once celestial face as 'lived in'. Twice a year he would have a purge, learn a new sport, join a gym, take himself off to a health farm and swear off booze. For a few weeks he would look tremendous, feel great and resolve never to slip back into his old ways. Then would come the crisis – a bust-up with a treasured client; one of his best account executives quitting for a rival firm; yet another mistress announcing enough was enough – and he would disintegrate into his old self.

But whatever the state of health or looks, he retained a magical allure for women; and for men come to that. But by 1987, with the AIDS scare, he rarely took men to bed. He thought it unfair on his wife.

In 1980, he stormed out of a large successful public relations and advertising agency and started up on his own, specialising in advising quoted companies. It had been tough going at first, but gradually as the City and industry responded to Thatcher policies, business took off. The new issue boom came at just the right time for him. The unlikeliest entities started coming to the stockmarket, turning their owners into paper multi-millionaires overnight.

While merchant banks such as Hogarth Stein made a killing, giving financial advice to these companies, David used fair and sometimes foul means to secure them the right coverage in the right newspapers at the right time.

But, like Peter, it was on the back of the takeover boom that he really made his reputation. Merger mania could have been invented especially for him. He thrived on crisis and tension, relishing the war-like atmosphere of big contested bids. He thought of them as medieval battles, each king sitting in his tent plotting strategy, sending out spies and inspiring his troops. The smell of fear in a boardroom, when it seemed they must lose – and then the jubilation when they won – was better than any drug. It was nature at its most savage, red in tooth and claw.

He had been half expecting a summons from Jack. He had noticed the way Peter Markus danced round him at the Christmas parties, like a worker bee feeding the Queen. There was clearly going to be action.

'I need your help,' Jack said simply when they met. 'I'm thinking of doing a deal which will take my company into the big league – the world class big league.' David noted the emphatic use of the word 'my'. He also noted the speed at which Jack had downed his drink. 'Any chance of another?' He raised his own glass and Jack's eyes lit up. At midnight they were still talking and a new bottle of Bell's had been started.

There was no usual beauty parade where half a dozen agencies make presentations of their wares. Minimal discussion took place with the rest of the board. Within the week David Bang Associates was appointed to handle all Butler's financial public relations for the next twelve months.

David decided they should start winding up the publicity machine in May. 'We need a couple of good profiles in the cuttings. *Management Today* or the *Investors Chronicle* will leap at the chance.' With any luck they could follow those up with a feature on Management page of the *Financial Times*.

Empire Foods' results were due to be announced on Tuesday, June 16 and all the market intelligence indicated they would be terrible. It was decided to release Butler's figures on the same day, in the hope of some interesting comparative press coverage. The weekend ahead of the results they would couple an interview with Jack with a leaked news story in one Sunday newspaper of the good profits expected from Butler's on the Monday. Flattering photographs of Jack and Sir Richard would be sent out with the press announcement. The daily papers would do the rest.

The stockbroker's analysts were to be given no hint that their profit forecasts for Butler's were several million pounds below the true figure. That way the profits announcement would send the shares soaring.

'Won't that turn the analysts against us?' asked Jack. 'Some of them have been pestering my secretary every week for an interview.' David nodded, puffing on his Sullivan Powell.

'Yes, they will be a bit annoyed at first,' he said. 'But from then on you are going to be so charming and so indiscreet about aspects of the business that they will be putty in your hands.' He warmed to his theme.

'In fact, we should take them on a jolly round some of your overseas activities just after the results.'

'Butler's nearest overseas operation is Hong Kong,' Jack retorted, suddenly cold. 'Apart from that, most of our subsidiaries are in the UK.' He had hoped David was doing his homework. 'That's one of the reasons we're bidding for Empire.'

'Oh, well, somewhere in a nice part of England, far enough away for them to stay in a decent hotel overnight,' said David, unperturbed. 'We can fly them up, helicopter them round a couple of plants in the afternoon, and give them a fantastic dinner in the evening where you can make a surprise appearance.'

Jack recovered his good humour. 'Bribe them, you mean?'

'You're getting the idea, Jack,' said David mockingly. ' You are getting the idea.'

Charlie's role at Greenbag's was to ensure that Butler's shares were supported both in the run up to the bid and during it. By June he told Jack and Peter they could expect some of the most powerful institutions, and some 'high net worth' individuals, to have bought substantial shareholdings in Butler's.

'So basically they will be given inside information about our results?' Jack had said, turning to Peter.

'Tut tut,' Peter had rejoined. When Charlie Briggs-Smith tells them they ought to have a couple of hundred thousand Butler's, they have a couple of hundred thousand Butler's – they don't want chapter and verse. They know the rules.'

'And what about these individuals?'

'Oh, just big players who enjoy punting in the market,' said Charlie vaguely.

'I don't know where they find the money,' muttered Jack. He was coming to realise that what he had always regarded as generous managerial salaries were petty cash in City terms.

Chapter 9

'We're just about up to five per cent, Leo,' Denis muttered into the mouthpiece, then covered it with his hand. 'Tell him I'll ring back,' he said to Sarah who was holding a note under his nose. The finance director of a company they were about to float was in a panic.

'So what's the next step? ' asked Stern blandly. Mentally Denis sighed. He was not feeling well and he didn't want to play games. 'Well, as you know, Leo, the rules are that you must disclose all shares once you get over five per cent. Your cover will be blown. How much higher do you want to go?'

'High enough to be able to control which way the bid goes,' said Stern.

'Well, five per cent might be enough,' said Denis hopefully.

'No way,' Stern snapped. 'I need nearer ten per cent to be sure.'

'So disclose and carry on buying,' suggested Denis. 'No way,' said Stern again. 'I want to see their faces when they find out.'

'Martin from BZW on the line,' mouthed Sarah.

'Sell a ton of Ikey at best,' ordered Denis. 'Sorry, Leo. What have you got against Armstrong anyway?'

Stern ignored the question. 'How about one of your other clients buying just under five per cent and then selling to me nearer the time?' he suggested.

'Fine, Leo, but that's called a concert party and it's illegal as we both know. If it's another one of my clients it will look very suspicious, and knowing my clients I wouldn't trust them to sell to you when it came to it anyway.' He was enjoying the irony. 'How about one of your overseas friends?'

'That's not suspicious?'

'Sure, but you are the great Sir Leo Stern and I am a spiv broker. One of your friends just happened to build a stake, got bored and decided to sell to you – it happens. Anyway, we don't know for sure this bid is coming. And we shouldn't be talking about it on the phone.' He held up two fingers indicating two minutes to Sarah who had one of the big unit trust groups on the line.

Stern said: 'Well, I've got one or two friends in the American arbitrage community who owe me favours – they could afford a few.' He had decided not to mention his Swiss associates. He was saving them for a fail safe back-up. 'You'd better come round here and talk about it then, say five o'clock.'

'I'd rather it were six, Leo.' Denis put the phone down and took the other from Sarah. 'Hi, Merv my old son, what can I do you for?'

But he did not hear the answer. In slow motion Sarah saw Denis claw at his tie, his face a grimace of pain as he slumped to the floor.

It was not until two hours later, after the ambulance had been and Sarah had made the difficult phone call to Denis's wife Irene, that she remembered the six o'clock appointment with Stern. She considered handing the business over to Dickie, but an inner voice warned against it.

Dickie had always been jealous of Denis's relationship with Stern and might contrive to screw things up. Three months ago she would have leapt at the chance to deal for Stern but ever since he had bawled Denis out, she had found it impossible to think of him without shuddering. She shuddered now as she remembered how Stern himself had asked if she would be able to cope if Denis went sick. She wondered if he were psychic and walked out of their cubby hole to the coffee machine. A shiver of excitement replaced the fear. I simply have to do the professional thing, she told herself. My personal feelings do not come into it.

Back at her desk she braced herself, picked up the 'phone and dialled Stern's private line.

Leo Stern liked to think of himself as a simple man. He

131

believed in buying something for one price and selling it for a higher one – thereby making profit. He cared not at all about what he was selling – the point was he made a profit. That was business. For fun he liked to gamble. When he stayed at his house in the south of France he was a regular at the casino in Monte Carlo, just twenty minutes along the Bas Corniche.

Nothing gave him greater pleasure than to leave the casino with a wallet full of winnings, pick up a *Financial Times* and treat himself to a Café Liégoise sitting in the sunshine outside the Café de Paris.

For Stern, the stockmarket was a microcosm of everything he loved most. He relished its wild swings, the uncertainty, the way a company could fall from favour in a matter of days. Most of all he enjoyed the big, fiercely fought takeover battles which sent the adrenalin coursing round his system.

But if he was honest it was the power of being a big player in the stockmarket gave him the greatest pleasure. When he bought a share stake, the knowledge that what he did with it could decide the fate of top managers and thousands of workers satisfied a deep hunger in him. If those top managers were also members of what he considered the British establishment, it was icing on the cake.

He also enjoyed the attention of the City, relishing his power over the public school boys whom he believed sneered at him over their Sunday lunch parties in the country. He knew them to be anti-Semites and took his revenge by making them dance to his tune.

He was British – a citizen of the land of his birth – but according to Jewish tradition also a stranger.

At home, with his family around him, entertaining his friends, he rejoiced in the fact. When he occasionally attended synagogue he rejoiced in the fact. He worked long hours to raise money for Israel and for Jews in trouble all over the world. Once a year he spent a week in his apartment in Herzlea, just outside Tel Aviv, where a number of his old friends now lived.

But when he lunched at one of those blue-blooded firms of City bankers he would feel keenly the chill of his difference – not simply the difference of race, but also of class.

His greatest satisfaction was the knowledge he possessed

something which levelled out those differences. That something was money.

At five to six Sarah pushed open one of the plate glass doors of Stern House, just behind the teeming rush hour crowds of Oxford Street. A small lift with grey walls carried her to the sixth floor where a receptionist sat behind a large desk with a few flowers on it. She pondered at the lack of ostentation in the head office of a man who, according to Denis, had a quarter of a billion pounds in the market at any one time.

Stern kept her waiting on one of the functional leatherette chairs until twenty past six. Various conversations ran through her head. They all ended with her saying: Well, if you can't be civil I'm not prepared to act for you,' and sweeping out, leaving him . . . Leaving him what? The phrase ricocheted around her brain. What possible effect could a twenty-seven-year-old half commission man's assistant have on Leo Stern?

'Hi, Sarah. How's Denis?' She jumped as he strolled into reception holding out a large hand, his shirt sleeves rolled up over muscular arms. His tie was pulled down, his collar open. He had come to greet her personally!

'Well, he's still in intensive care,' she heard herself say. 'His heart stopped twice but they managed to bring him back – Irene's there.'

She struggled to keep control as she heard her voice waver. She had not realised how fond of Denis she was until today. He was the one who had given her a chance; had kept his faith in her in a world of male chauvinism and brought her face to face with her own talent.

Stern heard the waver and ignored it. 'He'll be fine,' he said firmly, dismissing the prospect of any other outcome. 'He's far too much of a rogue to die young. Come inside.'

Stern's own office was light and airy with a large window to the left of a huge leather-topped desk bearing three telephones, a humidor, and nothing else.

To the right was the sofa where she and Denis had sat last time and a couple of easy chairs round a low oval table. As he eased his bulky torso into a chair, motioning her to sit opposite, she noticed his hands for the first time, large but with

133

long tapering fingers. The second finger of his right hand had a kink at the end, as if it had been broken at some time. She had a strange, fleeting vision of that finger on her clitoris. His voice broke into her thoughts.

'Now, young lady, we have some work to do. I don't want you to think I'm entirely callous but Denis wouldn't want things screwed up just because he's out of action.'

'You're sure you want me to handle it?'

She felt Stern's dark eyes boring into her, like hot coals. 'Oh, you think I should start from scratch with one of those wallies in your office, or perhaps a completely different broker? Tell a whole new team my plans?' His tone was harsh and sarcastic.

Part of her wished he would. She could walk out of there and never see him again. She could go back to research. The General would have her back. For a microsecond escape beckoned, but flattery beguiled her. Leo Stern is the biggest single player in the London market and he wants you, Sarah Meyer, to deal for him, it whispered.

The thrill of collusion stole over her. 'No, of course not.' Her voice sounded clear and confident.

'Right, that's straight.' His tone softened. 'I think you know what we're up to but I'm just going to tell you what you need to know and no more – it's better that way. You're officially an insider already. OK?'

She knew he was telling her he trusted her and that knowledge made her feel strangely calm. Yet somewhere deep inside, the fear still lurked.

'Greenbag's is broker to Butler's Biscuits and they've asked me to help out in a bid that they hope will be coming in due course.' He glanced out of the window abstractedly. 'As we know,' he almost muttered, 'nothing in this life is certain.'

He turned to her again. 'As a result, I have been given the opportunity to buy shares in both companies.' A wintry smile lit his face. 'So when Jack Armstrong finally has the balls to bid for Empire Foods, which we both have a shrewd idea is the target company, I'll have made so much money on my Empire holding, I won't mind buying a few more Butler's to keep up the price. That way, they might actually win.'

She nodded, her conscience suspended.

'I've agreed to help support the Butler's share price, and no doubt along with others have been buying shares to show what, er, great faith we have in the management.'

Stern smiled knowingly at her and she discovered she was smiling right back – the same, intimate smile of conspirators.

'Now all that buying has been done by Greenbag's.' He paused. 'What Mr Armstrong and Greenbag's don't know is how many shares I have bought in Empire.'

That you are nearly up to five per cent and want to go higher but don't want to disclose, she thought, petrified by what she had heard Denis say on the phone that morning. But she said nothing.

He rose abruptly and walked to the window. 'Now as it happens, I have a business associate in New York who for reasons of his own wants to buy some Empire shares. And before his heart attack, Denis agreed to buy them. In his absence, I'd like you to get on with it.'

A warning siren shrieked in her head, but she could think of no retreat. He had not spelt out that he and this associate would be acting in concert. He thought he was protecting her from that knowledge.

'Why not do it through an American broker?' She felt suddenly desperate to give the business away. He sat down again and looked at her intently.

'Because they don't understand the London market; they would come in like charging rhinos and push the price up.' His voice softened. 'You, on the other hand, will do it like Denis has taught you, quietly and sensitively, through several nominee names, preferably in Switzerland.'

Goose pimples prickled her skin and she jumped when the phone shrilled out. He moved to his desk to pick it up.

'Yep,' said Stern.

'Yep . . . Nah . . . OK.' He put the phone down and turned back to her. She could feel her heart hammering in her chest as their eyes locked. She had a sudden desire to rip off his shirt. He looked down at her for what seemed a very long time.

What is this American's name?' She found her voice.

'Schlosstein,' he said, leaning against the edge of his desk. 'Max Schlosstein.'

The siren in her head shrieked again. She had read about him in the *Wall Street Journal*. 'Isn't he a friend of Ivan Boesky?'

Stern's lips twitched. 'They did occasionally work together,' he replied. 'But I'm sure Schlosstein's straight.'

Sarah knew it was rubbish. Nobody could be sure any of those American arbitrageurs were 'straight', least of all a friend of Boesky's. But she was past redemption.

She led him away from Schlosstein. 'There was a strong rumour that Nabisco was looking at Empire early this week,' she ventured.

'Yeah, but that's wrong. Put about by Denis, I shouldn't wonder,' retorted Stern. He sat down again, looking at her keenly trying to work out how much she really knew about Denis's tactics. What would happen if he ran a finger up her glistening leg? The thought came from nowhere. He ignored it.

'He's a past master at pumping up a share on a false rumour and picking them up as they fall back once everyone realises it's a ramp. Not a bad technique for you to pick up.'

Her eyes glittered. 'I've been trying to learn.'

He rose to his feet again, this time in dismissal, and her whole body sighed in relief.

'But I don't have to tell you your business. It's Friday night and way past sunset. You and I should be in the bosom of our families.'

'I'm not very frumm, I'm afraid,' said Sarah.

'Me neither, but I do try occasionally. Where do you live?'

'I've bought a flat in Islington, to be near the City, but my parents' home, where I'm going now, is just down the road in Portman Square.'

'How convenient. Do you ever go to Upper Berkeley Street?' he asked, referring to the Reform Synagogue there.

'Sometimes,' she replied, 'I like the choir, but my parents are United Synagogue.'

'It's awfully Middle Eastern that United, isn't it?' he said, and they both laughed.

'You'd better give me your home number. Here's mine.' He scribbled on the back of one of his cards and Sarah did the same.

136

He walked her to reception. 'I'll get Schlosstein's details across to you first thing Monday – you can take it from there.' He held out his hand. 'Watch out for snowdrifts.'

His expression did not change, but he saw Sarah's creamy skin flush pink as he shook her hand. He stood watching her until the lift doors closed.

Sarah lost no time on Monday morning setting up two Swiss nominee companies with Tulley's bank in Zurich and another in Jersey just to be on the safe side. She cancelled her lunch appointment, knowing New Yorkers arrived in their offices at 8 a.m. their time or 1 p.m. London and she did not want to be out when Mr Big rang.

The call came from the personal assistant to Mr Max Schlosstein at 1.46 p.m. and she smiled with satisfaction that she had read them right. No smart Wall Streeter was going to catch her on the hop. Lines of credit were set up and an address given where contract notes should be sent. She was to call every day with a report, even if she had bought no shares.

It was the first day of the fortnightly account and as she had suspected the price was falling as everyone realised the Nabisco rumour was a spoof. By 3 p.m. the price of Empire had drifted down 6p to 281p. She told Ken to buy a couple of blocks of 50,000 shares through two different market makers, preferably ones they had not used to buy Empire shares recently. Not a bad start.

Sarah had found a new clarity of thought. It was if her brain had been in soft focus before and now Stern had tuned it in. This was her long awaited opportunity to prove herself. Not just to the partners of the firm who treated her as a kind of pet, not even to Dickie or her father who thought that she had gone raving mad switching from research. Not even to Denis who already believed in her, but to herself.

The warning sirens in her head were silent and she wondered why she had been in such a funk. All around, shares were being ramped, markets manipulated. Officially, she did not know Stern was operating a concert party. Nobody had told her. Her job, as Denis had so often told her, was to carry out instructions from her client. And that was what she would do. If I get this right, I'm made, she told herself.

After work she set off to visit Denis. The ambulance had taken him straight to the London Hospital in a tatty part of East London, and there he had stayed. He had been moved from intensive care to a private room, although it could hardly be described as luxurious. Only Irene had been allowed to visit him over the weekend but restrictions had been lifted that morning. Sarah knew he would want to know the news.

As she edged her red Golf GTI through the gates she saw a gleaming black Bentley gliding towards her. Even before she read the number plate, or could make out the face in the passenger seat, she knew it was Stern.

Her heart did a double somersault – very quickly – and then she felt absolutely normal. No. She felt slightly surprised. Very surprised! Their cars were side by side now, but Stern was busy on the 'phone and had not seen her. She did not know his driver so she just drove on robot-like and eventually found a parking space. She turned off the engine and sat as still as ice, listening to the thudding of her heart.

So he wasn't just a financial thug. He had been to see Denis in hospital, gone well out of his way. He cared. He was a real human being after all.

The Cherry trees in St James's Square were heavy with pink blossom when Jack called a full board meeting to explain the bid for Empire to his fellow directors.

Edward Williams knew the details already. The quiet accountant could hardly bear to reveal his own name, let alone a company secret, and Jack trusted him completely. Not that Edward approved of these big hostile bids as he believed they inevitably distracted management from actually running the business and brought out the worst in everyone. But although he quietly expressed this view, he sensed Jack was unstoppable. He had prepared a sheaf of arguments and figures to back up the bid, prepared to take on any opposition.

But the other directors had also been infected by what they read daily in the City pages and greeted the news enthusiastically. After the dreary months of cutbacks and sackings they relished the idea of doing something positive. Launching a

138

major bid fulfilled their need for excitement and daring. There was much talk of 'challenge' and 'new opportunity' and they readily gave their agreement for Greenbag's to start quietly building a stake in Empire. As a final coup de grâce Jack even managed to persuade them to vote through a change in the company name from Butler's Biscuits to Butlers Group, dropping the apostrophe in the process. Jane Brompton had been right he decided. To thank her for the suggestion, he took her to lunch at the Savoy Grill.

David Bang had been delighted about the name change, as it provided a brilliant 'peg' on which to hang all manner of flattering newspaper articles about the group's metamorphosis under Jack's leadership. At the end of the board meeting he asked Edward to address the directors on security.

Edward looked around the table half apologetically. 'The greatest danger,' he said, 'is that our intentions towards our target may leak. I must point out, gentlemen, that what we have been discussing this afternoon is price sensitive information. I take it you all know what that means?'

There were nods all round. 'Using that information for profit, not that I am suggesting anyone here would – ' a pale smile crossed his face ' – or passing it on to anyone who might use it for profit, is a criminal offence, punishable by a prison sentence of up to two years.'

There was a murmur of surprise. 'So it is imperative that you do not tell anyone – and I mean anyone.' He paused for effect. 'That includes your wife, your children, golfing partners, bank managers, mistresses – anyone. I hope I make myself clear?'

'Thank you, Edward,' said Jack. 'And the reason some of you may be surprised about the prison term is that no one has yet been sent to prison, although, as I am sure you are all aware, we are waiting to hear what happens to Geoffrey Collier.'

'You're becoming quite an expert on the ways of the City,' Sir Richard commented over the board lunch afterwards. These had become more frugal after Jack became chief executive although he had noticed the good wines appearing again.

139

Well, they were in stock after all, he thought. And it was only once a month.

But he resolutely refused to allow brandy and port at the end of the meal. Lately, he had schooled himself not to drink at all at lunchtime as once he started he invariably overdid it. He could not afford to spend his afternoons in a blur.

'I'm not quite up to speed on this Collier chap,' admitted the new sales director.

'Collier was at Morgan Grenfell and used knowledge gained from the corporate finance side to make a fast buck in the shares of a bid target,' replied Jack.

'Went over the Chinese Wall,' chimed in somebody else.

'Yes, you know the problem with a Chinese Wall?' said Edward. Jack stared at him in disbelief. Surely this immaculate, reserved, accountant was not about to tell a joke. 'It's got chinks in it,' said Edward with a shy smile. There was a ripple of amused laughter.

Sir Richard was right. Thanks to Peter and Charlie, Jack felt quite an old City hand. He had bought shares for himself in a couple of blue chips and even some in Stern group, which had given him a pleasant sense of irony. But if Stern was as tough as everyone seemed to think, his shares must be worth having – and they had been highly recommended by his broker.

Peter's team at Hogarth Stein slaved sixteen hours a day putting together a detailed document on Empire Foods, code named Darth. 'The first rule,' Peter told Jack, 'is to know more about the target company than they do.'

'Aren't these code names a bit over the top?' asked Jack.

'My dear fellow,' Peter had said, 'we can't have documents wizzing about with 'bid for Empire Foods on them'. The thing would leak in five seconds. So we create code names and refer to those at all times.'

'It really is like toy soldiers,' replied Jack wrily. 'I suppose that's another £10,000 on your fee.'

Peter ignored him. 'So it's Star Wars for the whole operation. We'll call Butlers Skywalker and Empire Darth.'

'How about sending some of our lads out to one or two of Empire's local pubs to pick up the gossip?' suggested Jack.

Peter raised an eyebrow. 'Mm, I was going to suggest that actually. It can't do any harm.'

Jack wondered uneasily how much it was all going to cost. But Peter refused to be drawn by his jibes and he supposed it would be difficult to tell until it was all over. He considered asking for an estimate of how much it would have cost so far but a little voice whispered it would be better not to know.

One morning a week later an ambitious young salesman called Tim Freeman presented himself for a job interview at Empire Foods. 'Your record looks excellent,' said the personnel manager, a thin man with a fleshless nose. 'But I'm slightly mystified by why you want to leave Butlers. ' We can only offer you another thousand a year at this stage.'

The glossy young man before him showed the merest hint of embarrassment, then smiled ingenuously. 'Without being disloyal, Mr Matthews, I haven't really seen eye to eye with the new management at Butlers and feel I might be happier at a more traditionally run company.'

Mr Matthews could hardly believe his ears. For months he had attempted to stem a tide of hungry young men departing for other companies, telling him they saw no future with a fuddy duddy company like Empire. And now here was someone coming the other way.

'Well, that's very nice to hear.' He said smiling paternally at the young man. 'We may even be able to make it £1500.'

A few hours later, Tim Freeman sat in Jack's office giving him a blow by blow account of the interview.

'Well done,' said Jack. 'But don't let picking up two salaries go to your head. I expect a full report in a month.'

'Don't worry, sir.' A shadow crossed the confident young face. 'You will protect me if anything goes wrong?'

'Why should anything go wrong?' Jack asked, a slight edge to his voice.

'Oh, I'm sure it won't, it's just that . . . well, I'd like to feel sure you would take responsibility for the idea.'

'Of course. I'm surprised you even feel the need to ask,' said Jack, sounding slightly hurt. 'But I'm relying on you to make sure it goes right. Let's be positive,' he said. 'There's a big promotion in this for you if it goes well.'

141

The idea had come from Jean-Pierre who said it was common practice in the United States. Somehow Jack had forgotten to mention it to Peter until it was a fait accompli.

When he did tell him, Peter hit the roof. 'If he gets caught, it will look appallingly bad for us,' he fumed, horror stricken at the thought of his senior partner, John Young, finding out.

'Hogarth Stein would never put their name to something like that. It's over the line Jack. I really should resign from the deal.'

Jack never knew how seriously to take Peter, but it seemed clear he himself had overstepped the mark.

'Jean-Pierre said it was acceptable practice,' he protested.

'Spying? Acceptable practice! Don't be ridiculous. You must understand, Jack, that what is *on* in the States, is not necessarily *on* here. If you want Hogarth Stein to be your adviser you can't go off on a frolic like this without telling me.'

'Well, he won't get caught,' said Jack airily. 'He's a bright lad, and I'll take full responsibility if he does.'

'What if he decided to blow the whistle?' Peter shuddered.

'Relax, Peter. He'd blow his own career out of the water if he did that. Have another drink.'

Peter gradually allowed himself to be mollified, mentally adding £100,000 to his bill.

Jean-Pierre had booked seats for every production at Glyndebourne that season. He invited Jack and Rosemary to the Marriage of Figaro, judging it to be about Jack's level. Rosemary was shocked by her delight at the prospect of this evening of privilege. She had spent the winter struggling with her emotions each time they went to the Royal Opera House, sitting guilty but spellbound while Jack slept.

But Glyndebourne was the ultimate rich man's perk, and to make matters even more grandiloquent they were to drive down in Sir Richard's Rolls-Royce. Having enlisted Angela's help in buying her outfit, Rosemary arrived at St James's Square in a floor-length silk print with a matching jacket. 'I know we're eating in the restaurant but Angela tells me it can be pretty draughty just having drinks.'

They had chosen a popular if wet evening, finding Charlie Briggs-Smith and John Young and their wives all huddling

142

under cover by the bar, glasses of champagne clutched in shivering hands. Only the hardiest were setting up their picnics for the interval in the bedraggled gardens.

'Where's Jean-Pierre?' asked Rosemary as the first bell sounded. 'He's got our tickets.'

Jack looked around and caught sight of him bidding goodbye to a dapper man with a magnificent head of wavy black hair, worn, like Jean-Pierre's red curls, a fraction too long.

'Who was that?' enquired Jack as they slid into their seats in the stalls.

'A player, old buddy, a player.' Jack could tell he did not mean the musical kind.

'What a neat little theatre,' exclaimed the American girl Jean-Pierre had brought along as his partner.

To Rosemary's annoyance Jean-Pierre and Jack could talk of nothing but business throughout dinner, speaking in semicode. She attempted to talk opera with Jean-Pierre's guest but as the two men began to argue, it became impossible not to listen. 'I just think it would be a good idea if you went to talk to our friends about doing a joint venture,' said Jean-Pierre firmly.

'Why on earth should we want to do a joint venture?' snapped Jack.

Jean-Pierre's turquoise eyes glittered. 'Of course you don't actually want to do a joint venture, old buddy. But just think of what you might learn talking about it.'

Jack shook his head. 'Not without discussing it with Peter. I had a bit of trouble over that other idea of yours.'

'It's paid off though, hasn't it?'

Jack grinned fondly at his friend. 'OK, I'll think about it.' Only the day before Tim Freeman had rung him with information on Empire's long-term sales projections on major product lines.

Rosemary yawned ostentatiously and kicked Jack under the table.

'Let's talk about this tomorrow. I can see we're boring the ladies.'

'At least we're warm,' said Rosemary, 'I'd hate to be out there eating smoked salmon on the grass in that vicious wind.'

'But it is so British,' drooled the American.

143

'Yeah,' cut in Jean-Pierre, 'freezing to death is very British.' They all laughed and Jack glanced round the room to see who he knew.

'Talking of our friends,' he said quietly, gazing across the room to a large table. Bertie Underworth, the chairman of Empire Foods, was holding forth, his double chin jiggling as he talked. Jean-Pierre followed Jack's gaze.

'Do you suppose he's the host?' he asked. 'That's £500 for Glydebourne tickets paid for by stockholders, plus the bill for dinner.'

The light of battle lit Jack's eyes. 'Stop staring JP, they'll notice.'

But for the rest of the meal he could not stop watching them for more than a few seconds. Something disturbed him about the gathering but he could not put his finger on it. One of the guests told a funny story and everybody broke into laughter including Bertie, his mouth wide open as he laughed, his chins wobbling obscenely.

Jack could feel the hair rising on the back of his neck as he watched. He felt like a game hunter stalking his prey, watching the quarry at play in its natural habitat, unaware of danger. In the mêlée of braying voices, clinking glasses and raucous laughter in that most privileged of restaurants, he sensed the jungle around him, heard a twig snap in the undergrowth. It only needed the wind to shift.

'Who's that next to Underworth?' Jean-Pierre asked. To the right of the Empire chairman sat a haughty-looking man with an aquiline nose and hooded eyes.

Of course, that was what was wrong!

'It's Stuart Anderson, the head of corporate finance at Marlow,' Jack said slowly, a shiver of excitement running through his whole body.

'I thought you told me their merchant bank was Barings?' said Jean-Pierre, puzzled.

'I did,' said Jack.

'But isn't Anderson the great defender over here?' Jack nodded and saw the light finally dawn in his friend's eyes.

Obviously, the wind had already begun to shift.

David Bang had fixed dinner with Patrick Peabody and Jack

for eight at Claridge's for the following Wednesday evening. 'Make a change from the Savoy for him,' said David.

At eight-thirty Jack and David were still waiting at their table on the terrace some steps up from the main body of the restaurant. Patrick had neither arrived nor telephoned and Jack had turned edgy ahead of what promised to be the first serious interview in the run up to the bid. He grew stonier faced by the minute as David tried to keep him amused with anecdotes about his better known clients.

By twenty to nine, even David was inwardly cursing Patrick for the cavalier way he treated people. 'You mustn't take it personally', he said. 'Patrick is one of those people who's always late.'

At ten to nine a waiter approached the table and David's heart sank. Surely Patrick wasn't going to stand him up? 'Meester Peabody 'as been eld up, but weel be weeth you soon.'

Finally Patrick arrived in a fluster and David waited for the cutting remarks from Jack. He was absolutely charming.

'Don't worry about it at all, we had lots of things to discuss,' he told Patrick. 'I expect you would like a drink?'

Throughout the meal Jack behaved like a virtuoso. He fleshed out the strategy behind the company name change, was gossipy about the food industry in general, had all the Butlers financial facts at his fingertips, giving Patrick a helpful steer on the forthcoming profits (David had prepared a crib sheet as a back up), and parted with his home telephone number without a murmur. He also gave the impression of a man firmly in charge without appearing to be an egomaniac.

Patrick scribbled away in his spidery longhand, while Jack wondered how he would ever read it back. 'Am I going to be able to quote Jack direct in this story?' Patrick asked David.

David shook his head. 'We-ll, we were planning to put the announcement out Monday afternoon – the Stock Exchange would give us a lot of trouble.'

Jack looked dismayed, feeling the last hour of what he considered verbal brilliance was about to be wasted, but Patrick came to the rescue. 'Why don't you pop it into the Stock Exchange on Friday night, and issue a press release on the Sunday for Monday's papers,' he said to David in a conspiratorial tone.

David frowned, pretending it went against the grain. 'That sounds fine to me,' said Jack cheering up. How about another Armagnac?'

Patrick sent a photographer round the next morning and on the Thursday evening David dropped into the *Herald's* offices near St Pauls. Patrick gave him a warm glass of white wine and he gave Patrick another copy of the crib sheet with the facts and figures. If he got them wrong, David would feel that at least he had done his best.

Around seven on Saturday evening he picked up several early editions of the *Sunday Herald* straight off the presses in Fleet Street and turned to the City section. Pity it was on a left-hand page, he thought, but as he read the article he relaxed. There was a good picture of Jack looking purposeful, the tone was friendly and there were no major errors. What more could you want?

He sent one straight down to Jack's Esher home. Everyone else could bloody well wait till the Sunday, he thought, especially that shit Peter Markus.

At nine o'clock David picked up his wife and drove round to an old friend's house for a very late and drunken dinner.

The phone rang at eight o'clock the next morning.

'Hello,' he said struggling to surface through the clatter of his hangover.

'What the hell do you call this rubbish in the paper?' Jack's voice was colder than permafrost.

'I thought it was very good,' David said weakly.

'I've counted four major mistakes, the article is buried away and the photograph should be burnt.'

David wanted to say: You should count yourself lucky and be grateful.

Instead he said, 'Let me get the paper and ring you back in two minutes.'

He retrieved the paper from the car, begged his wife to make some coffee, splashed his face with cold water, took four aspirin, settled back in bed and lit a cigarette.

'OK, Jack,' he said in honeyed tones when he rang back, 'let's go through it slowly.'

146

Chapter 10

The crowd roared as the winning horse streaked past the finishing post. Even the elegant guests in Sir Leo Stern's box, their tummies full of fresh salmon and strawberries, were yelling their heads off.

'And it's Paean, the winner,' said the commentator over the loudspeaker. Rosemary clapped her hands with glee. 'Wasn't it absolutely thrilling?' said the stick-like woman at her side. 'Do you ride?'

Angela tore up her ticket sadly. 'I nearly went each way on Sadeem.'

'Second place at seven to two wouldn't have been worth it,' said Peter, patting her shoulder condescendingly. 'Paean was six to one,' he purred. A breeze ruffled the ladies' dresses and they trickled back inside to the pale green rectangular dining room.

'Oh, not more champagne,' groaned Angela, sitting down at the long dining table that took up most of the space. 'I do love these flowers. Could I possibly have another cup of coffee?' she asked the waitress.

Charlie came in grinning broadly. 'Even easier than the market,' he said.

'You had it too?' preened Peter. 'How much did you put on.'

Charlie looked abashed. 'Oh, a couple.'

'Two hundred?'

'Er, well, no actually, two grand.' He looked around uneasily for his wife. Peter laughed unpleasantly. 'Post election euphoria, I suppose. You brokers are doing even better than I thought. Still, this market can't last.'

'Oh, I agree,' said Charlie. 'When a potty little franchise operation like Tie Rack is over subscribed eighty-four times, you've gotta be near the top.'

'Oh do stop talking shop,' exclaimed Angela, rolling her eyes at Rosemary. They were both wearing identically shaped hats – a flat wide brim with a tiny domed crown.

'Did Leo have it?' Angela looked round for him but he had disappeared.

'Gone off visiting again,' said Peter. 'Half the companies in the Footsie seem to be here today.'

Jack had been secretly thrilled by Stern's invitation. It was his first time at Royal Ascot and the previous year numerous people had irritated him with their tales of how awful it had become: how crowded; how tacky; how they let any riff-raff into the Royal Enclosure.

Now he would see for himself.

From the moment they walked through the tunnel into the grandstand that morning he had been enchanted. Never had he seen so many pretty girls dressed to the nines, all in one place, all smiling, quite a few of them at him. In fact, everyone was smiling, even the lift attendants.

Only two things rankled. The first that he still did not have a Bentley to park alongside the others; the second that they took his mobile phone away at the gate.

But the novelty of the day swept him up. He sauntered along, completely at ease, knowing his tall long-limbed frame suited the outfit. Rosemary looked wonderful in speedwell blue. Angela had finally persuaded her to show her knees.

What captivated him was the carnival atmosphere of the whole event. The air tingled with excitement as people studied their form cards, knowing even a humble fiver could turn into a small fortune on the right outsider. Inside the stand, the sound of laughter, clinking glasses and rustling money mingled together.

On the third floor Stern greeted them in his box, magnificent in his morning suit, offering them a glass of Roederer Cristal. A Cabinet minister, a director of the Bank of England and John Young had already arrived with their wives.

Not quite everyone, Jack noted with satisfaction, had a Royal Enclosure badge. Fortunately, Peter had arranged a

148

sponsor for him and Rosemary, who despite the waiting list had somehow come up with the goods.

After the first race Jack stayed outside, gazing down at the racecourse, mesmerised by the sea of hats as the crowd in the stand dispersed. He'd let the winners do their crowing out of earshot. He had only put on £50.00, but losing it made his stomach churn.

'You should never nurse your wounds in public.' Stern had materialised at his side.

Jack's face relaxed into a smile. 'Is it that obvious?'

For a moment Stern liked Jack Armstrong. He saw the ingenuous smile of a man who had never risked his money or reputation – and lost.

'You're still young. You'll learn to write it down to experience,' he said pleasantly. 'Come and have some coffee.'

Over the previous few months, a guarded truce had broken out between Stern and Jack. Stern had become an active buyer of Butlers' shares, helping to boost the price until it had broken through its all time high – Peter seemed to trust him, assuring Jack they could count on Stern when the going got tough.

'As long as we see him OK.' Peter had thrown the line away.

Jack had begun to understand the game. At Renasco, he had learned how to deal with Third World suppliers. In the West it would have been called bribery, but in the Far East it was the normal way of life. The City too had its own way of doing things. The smooth smiles, the jocular handshakes, the impeccable suits and endless champagne masked a ruthless end game – the pure and simple pursuit of profit. In that pursuit, some rules, he understood, were there to be broken, or at any rate bent.

Jack shied away from it, not on moral grounds, but as a potential threat to his career. But there was no one more ambitious than Peter, he had realised, or more jealous of his own career. Surely if he stuck with Peter, he would be OK?

It was not as if they were setting out to bribe Stern. After all, he was hardly short of a few bob. It was more a matter of pride.

He had realised that Stern needed to feel he was getting the edge over you in order to help. It might be a new line of soft cookies at a special price fixed for the next two years to be sold in his food halls, or perhaps a joint promotion between Butlers and Stern Group where Stern paid a fraction of the cost. Jack shrugged mentally as he thought about it. Whatever it took.

'Come on, Angela,' Rosemary broke the post-race torpor. 'Let's go and see who we can spot in the Royal Enclosure – we've got to go once – and I simply must pick up my winnings.' She smiled wickedly at Jack who pretended to ignore her.

'It's hell down there,' warned Paulette Stern, stunning in emerald silk Valentino.

'It must be wonderful to have an unlimited budget,' sighed Rosemary, who had discovered the allure of designer clothes – and that she could barely afford them.

'Jack doesn't do badly.'

'Oh, come on, you know the perks of the job give a false impression. We've got no capital and the mortgage is huge. We were better off in Chester.'

'You'll be joining the Conservatives soon,' Angela said, laughing as Rosemary shook her head violently. 'How's the house coming along?'

'That's what's gobbling the money. I need a second mortgage for the curtains. It's your fault, introducing me to all these posh shops. I'd never heard of Colefax and Fowler before I met you.'

'Oh, it always seems like that. You'll love it when it's done, and we'll find you some darling little knick-knacks to finish it off at the local antique shops in Wiltshire.'

Rosemary smiled at the way Angela called everything 'darling'. 'You still haven't taken me to Sotheby's.'

'We'll do that in the autumn,' promised Angela. 'What is it?' she asked as Rosemary clasped her arm. Angela followed her gaze further down the course to where the bookies had their pitches set out. They saw Stern towering over a dapper figure with glossy black hair, deep in conversation.

'I'm sure that was the man Jean-Pierre was talking to at Glyndebourne,' said Rosemary, unaccountably intrigued. 'He said he was a player, whatever that means.'

150

'Someone who plays the market,' said Angela. 'I have a feeling I've met him with Peter. Baron something or other. I think he's in property,' she trailed off. 'Come on, I want to look at the horses, I'm fed up with all these people.'

They were just coming out of the lift on the third floor on their way back when Jack rushed up to them, followed by Peter and Charlie. 'Thank God there you are!' Jack's face looked bloodless.

'We've got to go, something's come up.'

Peter cut in. 'Leo has very kindly lent us his helicopter. Can you two go back to London in the cars?' Both women sensed that wifely indignation would be wasted.

'Of course – good luck,' said Rosemary drily.

The men disappeared into the lift and the two women walked slowly back to the box, each unsure of how much the other knew and unwilling to betray their husband's confidences. 'Well, I suppose this is the deal that Jack's been so excited about for months,' Rosemary tried.

'Peter is always wound up about some deal. But from the look of them we should know very soon,' said Angela diplomatically.

They found Stern alone, standing in the left-hand corner of the box, his broad back turned to the room. He was muttering into a portable telephone in fluent French.

He finished his call and turned round, his eyes aglow with secret knowledge. He leaned his powerful frame against the wall and placed the mobile phone on the table, his brow gleaming with perspiration.

'How ever did you get that in?' asked the Cabinet minister coming in from the balcony. 'They confiscated mine at the turnstile. The Queen doesn't like them, would you believe?' He sounded quietly amused at Stern's ability to cut through red tape.

Stern ignored him, regarding the two women solemnly. 'I'm afraid ladies, your husbands have deserted you,' he said mockingly. 'But don't worry,' his eyes glittered, 'I shall look after you to the very best of my ability.'

The little room began to fill up with guests returning to watch the next race. Plates of sandwiches and cakes now stood on the table. Paulette appeared with a visitor from

151

another box, her face lighting up at the sight of the food. She spread her hands, open palmed, in a gesture which said there was nothing in life more desirable than to be a guest in that tiny privileged room, with her, at Royal Ascot.

'Do lets 'ave tea, everyone.' In her husky French accent, the invitation sounded wonderfully exotic.

A few minutes later, Stern's four-seater chopper lifted gently into the air, its stainless steel body gleaming in the sunshine. It turned to avoid flying over the course, then headed towards London.

As they gained height, the splendid view of Royal Ascot grew smaller by the second until they were flying over the rolling green fields of Surrey.

The three men barely noticed.

They talked in semi-code through the earphones because they were hooked into the pilot.

'How much is the Darth price up?'

'Fifty pence the last I heard. The market rumour seems to be an unspecified predator. But Darth have had 212s out on their share register. They think they've uncovered a hostile shareholding.'

'Is it us?' Jack's eyes locked with Charlie's opposite.

'Could be. But I think we've covered our tracks pretty well.

'What shareholding have we got now?' asked Jack.

'Just under five per cent.'

'Any clue who else?' Peter to Charlie.

'Stern's bought quite a bit. There's vague talk of an overseas player but nothing specific.'

'How soon can we do it, Peter?' Panic gripped Jack at the idea of another company snatching his prize.

'I can go tomorrow morning,' Peter answered, emphasising the 'I'. 'It's up to Charlie – think you can underwrite it?'

'Shouldn't be a problem, but I'll be happier when I've talked to a couple of the big boys this evening.'

'For heaven's sake be careful, we don't want the price any higher.'

'I'll wait till after hours – what do you think I am?' Charlie said in hurt tones. 'An American bank?'

Jack gazed out of the window as Peter and Charlie

152

chuckled. This was the moment he had been driving towards for the last eleven months. Before that even. Since he joined Butlers in October 1985. No. Further back than that. In a moment of vivid clarity he saw the last two years laid out like a map before him. It was Randolph's death, that late summer afternoon, which had led inexorably to this moment.

The chopper had already found the River Thames and was following it down to Battersea.

'Anyone think to organise a car?' asked Jack.

'Leo said he'd do it,' said Peter.

They looked at each other, the same thought in all their minds. Leo was being just a mite too helpful.

A black Mercedes with tinted windows awaited them at Battersea. 'Goodie! Two car phones,' chortled Peter. 'Trust Leo.' He gave one handpiece to Jack.

'I suggest we get Richard and Edward round to our place.' He began punching out a number. The Embankment was mercifully clear and they were in the City in twenty minutes.

They dropped Charlie off at Greenbag's and went straight to Hogarth Stein. The traffic was light here too. 'Everyone's at Ascot,' said Peter.

'Not quite.' Something about the tone of Jack's voice made Peter pay attention. 'Look.'

As the car waited at the traffic lights in Lombard Street, they saw the imposing figure of Stuart Anderson bidding farewell to Bertie Underworth and the Empire finance director. The two directors folded themselves into a blue Volvo and for a brief moment Stuart Anderson stood on the pavement, not ten yards from them, gazing after the car, an unmistakable look of disdain on his patrician features. For a moment, he reminded Jack of an elderly jungle-wise panther; one which could still move fast when necessary.

'Thank God this car's not S1!' Peter exclaimed, looking the other way. They could never be sure whether Stuart Anderson spotted them or not. But as he turned his elegant frame away from the traffic to re-enter the Marlow offices, Jack saw the shadow of a smile cross his face.

By six o'clock David Bang and Edward Williams had arrived at Hogarth Stein, closely followed by three lawyers. For

153

seven hours Peter, Jack, David and one of the lawyers argued over the wording of the four-page press release which would tell the world Butlers Group was making the biggest bid yet in the history of the food industry.

Meanwhile two of Peter's team beavered away at the more straightforward task of drawing up the sub-underwriting letters which had to go to the institutions first thing in the morning. The bid for Empire involved the issue of new Butlers shares. Hogarth Stein guaranteed to buy those shares and then laid off the risk through the sub-underwriting to the major City institutions using the services of a broker – in this case Greenbag's was running the operation. The system meant that should the worst happen and everyone plump for the cash alternative, the shares would still be taken up.

For the first time since they had begun planning the bid all those months before, the code names were abandoned.

By 1 a.m. most of them were beginning to feel the strain. Everyone sat in shirtsleeves and there was a grey weariness around people's eyes. The room looked like a war zone. The only two smokers, David Bang, who was wishing he had not drunk so much claret at lunchtime, and one of the lawyers, had managed to fill three ashtrays to overflowing. Piles of papers, plates of stale sandwiches and half eaten pizza covered the huge oval table.

Jack and Peter were running on adrenalin. They both looked fresh and calm. David marvelled at their concentration. Worse, they kept finding new improvements. What with the lawyers haggling over a contentious point in every line, it seemed they would never be finished.

Finally, at 2.30 a.m., the sheaf of computer print-out was handed to a typist to transfer on to headed paper for the press release.

'Why don't you go home?' Peter said to Jack. 'You can sign the underwriting agreement and leave it in escrow till the morning. We want you looking spruce at Greenbag's at around 7.30. If we're lucky, we might have some copies of the press release.'

Jack looked alarmed.

'No, no, don't worry, they will be here,' soothed Peter.

Jack had never felt less like sleeping in his life, but he knew there was no more he could contribute. He took one of the fleet of taxis Peter had waiting outside the bank, their meters ticking away. Jack would have liked to go and get drunk, but even most of the clubs were near closing now. Peter was right, he needed some sleep.

Back at St James's Square, he found a message on his answering machine from Rosemary wishing him good luck and telling him not to bother ringing. He selected a clean shirt and his new red tie and put them in the wardrobe next to his new summer-weight suit that had been delivered just the day before. He admired himself in the mirror and winked at the reflection. He pushed his fringe back from his face then let it fall back again. The image in the glass smiled. He was finally in the right place at the right time.

He yawned, suddenly tired, and eased himself between crisp sheets. He would have to miss his workout again, he thought, just before sleep swept him off. He was looking forward to ringing Bertie Underworth in the morning.

At exactly five to nine the next morning every single telephone extension on the executive floor of Empire Foods exploded into life. Miss Paget, secretary to the chairman Bertram Underworth, had just placed his cup of tea (made weak with one teabag for a whole pot) on his leather-topped desk when the cacophony started.

Bertie was already on his private line to Stuart Anderson, but broke off at this telephonic dawn chorus. 'Tell them nobody is available to comment, just take their numbers,' he ordered. 'But don't promise anything.' She nodded her dark permed head and scurried away to tell the other secretaries. His tone was firm, but she had seen the panic in his eyes.

For weeks the atmosphere had been one of preparing for war and Miss Paget realised hostilities had now broken out in earnest. It had been an abnormal morning. When she had arrived at her usual time of 8.30 she had found Bertie already in his office – he rarely arrived before ten.

'That upstart Armstrong got me out of the bath to tell me he was launching a bid,' he frothed. 'Said he wanted to come round and talk it over. Bloody nerve!' Miss Paget had never before heard her boss swear.

Bertie Underworth had worked for Empire Foods since the age of twenty when, after two years in the Army, he had joined as the second ever graduate trainee. By dint of good fortune, a certain amount of hard work and a talent for corporate politics, he had risen through the ranks to become chairman in 1980. He ran the company with a modicum of efficiency and had been instrumental in pulling it out of the tough times of the seventies. But with eighty per cent of the business overseas it was all too easy to let the managers do their own thing, just so long as they produced reasonable returns.

Empire had some of the best brand names in biscuits, tea, coffee, preserves and spices; it owned a vast meat business in South America and a baking company in Canada.

Empire also had valuable property assets around the world, not least the five-storey piece of real estate on Hyde Park corner. It had been the group headquarters since the late fifties when the legendary Jack Cotton had sold it to the chairman for what then seemed an outrageous price.

Bertie was wedded to Empire by sentiment for its history and affection for his own comfortable lifestyle. He intended to fight, which was why he had brought in Stuart Anderson, a merchant banker renowned for seeing off unwelcome predators. Less flamboyant than some of the Young Turks of Peter's generation, he was shrewd, experienced and totally amoral.

Jack slept deeply and dreamlessly. His driver picked him up at six and drove him through a clear, June dawn to Greenbag's offices, stopping so that Jack could buy the newspapers outside the Ritz on the way. Nothing of any relevance seemed to have happened since the election he thought as he thumbed anxiously through, starting with the *Financial Times*, going through the *Telegraph*, *Times*, *Independent* and ending up with the *Daily Mail* and the *Post*. The clearing banks seemed to be in an awful mess with their third world debt.

All the market reports commented on the leap in the Empire price the day before, speculating on bid rumours. But the *Post* was the only one near the real story. Headed SHARE STAKE LIFTS EMPIRE, it read: 'Well informed

156

buying of Empire Foods sent the price flying 53p to 322p yesterday as hopes of a bid grew stronger. Rumour has it at least one hostile shareholding of just under five per cent has been uncovered by the company. Possible bidders include Hanson Trust, Nabisco and Butlers Group which recently changed its name from Butler's Biscuits.'

Jack grunted in annoyance. You would think they could have mentioned his dynamic new management and all the changes over the past year, he thought. In fact the author of the piece had put in a flattering paragraph about Jack; but the City editor, who was an old acquaintance of Bertie Underworth, had cut it out.

Charlie had reserved a room for them on the second floor and put a dozen or so chairs out. The senior lawyer was there, poring over the draft of the press release; Charlie and another partner were listening to the 7.30 news.

'Wall Street dropped 30 points last night on fears of higher interest rates,' said the partner when it had finished. 'Should we perhaps sight our first shot a fraction lower than 360p?'

'If we want to look serious, I think we should have a serious-looking price,' declared Peter imperiously from the doorway. Charlie nodded agreement.

'But we're already offering 50p more than we'd planned,' protested Jack.

'I know,' Peter tried to sound sincere, 'but the game has moved on. We have to go at a reasonable premium to the price in the market. It's still only an exit price earnings ratio of twelve.'

The lawyer looked up from the press release, regarding them over his gold-rimmed glasses. 'I suppose we can prove their assets are grossly under-utilised?'

Peter sighed. 'Well, on my reckoning, if you revalue the property, they're making about four per cent return on their assets.'

'But how do we know our valuation is good?'

'Jones Lang Wootton doesn't normally get that kind of thing wrong,' said Peter acidly. 'If anything they will have been overcautious.'

The lawyer smiled thinly. It was his business to be unpopular. Clients were quick enough to shout 'negligence' if something wasn't spotted. It was a bit like pulling teeth. If you left the rotten ones in they sued, but they hated the pain of extraction.

'I think I've done my worst,' he said, handing Peter the draft release which was going out on Hogarth Stein headed paper. 'You'd better have a look.'

'Now, Jack, how many people do you want to talk to the press at Butlers? We have to put a list of telephone contacts,' asked Peter.

'Just me.'

Peter raised an eyebrow. 'What? Not Edward? He's pretty sound. Or Richard?'

Jack's jaw set. 'Just me,' he said firmly. 'And put my home number in Esher on it as well.'

'What about me?' David Bang had arrived wearing a Prince of Wales check suit with a royal blue silk handkerchief spilling out of his top pocket. He was still celebrating the Tory election victory.

Jack suddenly relaxed, smiled broadly and put his arm around David's shoulders in greeting. 'I think that sounds like a gradely idea, lad.'

'So that's you for Butlers, me for Hogarth, and David – work and home numbers, OK?' Peter said crisply, scribbling them in. He could do without Jack hamming up his Northern bit.

'Now, I suggest you talk to the salesmen before you ring Bertie. You'll be more in the swing of it then.'

'What do I tell them?' Jack was holding a folder bulging with notes.

Peter waved it aside. 'Look, don't bother with a long song and dance. Just say the two companies fit perfectly. Butlers is on the up; Empire is on the down. The records speak for themselves and we should all make pots of money.'

David grinned and lit a Camel cigarette – he'd run out of Sullivan Powell. 'That's what I like about you, Peter, succinct.'

'Well, someone's got to be with you PR chaps around.'

'Have we got Underworth's number?' asked Jack as some coffee was brought in.

'Yup. He's silly enough to put it in *Who's Who*.' Peter

handed him a piece of paper with the number on it.

'Well, I'd like to do it now and get it over with.'

Peter looked at his watch. 'You've got ten minutes before the sales boys arrive – if you really want to wake him up.'

Jack smiled grimly. 'Nothing would give me greater pleasure.'

He sat down at the table and started dialling.

'Could I speak to Mr Bertram Underworth, please?'

There was a silence.

'And you don't know his new number?'

Another silence.

'Yes. Sorry to have bothered you.'

Jack put the phone down, looking as if someone had punched his stomach. 'He moved three years ago – so much for *Who's Who.*'

For a moment Peter and David looked stumped.

'Hang on,' said David, producing a tatty black book, 'I think I know someone who plays golf with him.'

Five minutes later Jack tried again.

'Is that Bertram Underworth?'

There was a pause.

'Well, I'm sorry about that,' Jack continued pleasantly, 'but I felt it only right that I should inform you that my company, Butlers Group, will be launching a 360p a share bid for Empire Foods shortly after the market opens this morning. I'd very much like to come and talk to you about it later today.'

There was a pause.

'Well, I thought you should know before it became public knowledge. Goodbye.'

He put the phone down, his face one huge grin, and swung round triumphantly in his chair. 'I got the silly old fool out of the bath.'

Just then Charlie came in followed by a stream of sleepy-looking men in pinstripe suits and white shirts.

'These are some of our crack salesmen and they are going to make sure the institutions sub-underwrite your deal,' said Charlie. Through his excitement Jack felt a tremor of envy at the way Charlie always appeared so relaxed. He never seemed to take his hands out of his pockets.

Charlie called for the salesmens' attention, briefly told them about the bid and introduced Jack.

He took a deep breath. 'Good morning, gentlemen.'

Jack gave Peter a lift back to Hogarth's. 'They should know if the sub-underwriting is placed by early afternoon,' said Peter reassuringly.

'And if it's not?'

'It will be,' said Peter, getting out of the car, 'barring Mrs Thatcher getting shot. Let's just be thankful the election is out of the way.' He waved and tore up the steps of the Cheapside office, his expression moody. He had a million things to do before joining Jack at the press conference.

Jack arrived back at St James's Square at precisely the moment the bid flashed up on the Topic screen. As he strode along the corridor to his office, all the phones started to ring. He felt like a war lord leading his people into battle. He found Amanda juggling with three calls.

'Start putting them through,' he ordered. He swept through her office into his own, threw off his jacket and sat down at his custom-built mahogany desk. Only then did he notice he was shaking with excitement.

Chapter 11

'It's permanently engaged,' said Sarah to Denis.

'Will be, won't it?' retorted Denis. 'Every analyst and reporter in town will be on to them. God knows why.' He was reading the statement on the screen. 'What a load of waffle!'

'Analysts are supposed to find out something extra, that's their job,' Sarah pointed out.

'How's the market taken it? That's what counts.' He pressed 'JUMP' on the keypad to get the Empire share price. It was 380p, 20p higher than the offer. 'Yeah. Well, that's telling us they'll have to pay more. So it's just a sighting shot as usual.'

Denis's private line rang. Guess who? thought Sarah, hating herself for wishing Denis was still away so that she could talk to Stern. Denis had returned to work a fortnight before, two stone lighter and under instructions to take it easy. He went home early most afternoons, but nobody had yet managed to make him change his drinking habits.

'Well, I should stay with it, Leo,' Denis said into the mouthpiece, winking at Sarah. 'The market thinks they'll go higher. Mind you, this is one helluva frothy market.' Sarah listened to the conversation avidly, straining to hear any mention of herself.

She had dealt for Stern for nearly two months, talking to him daily although she had not seen him since their first meeting. But even when she was not working for him or Schlosstein, he filled her thoughts.

She told herself Stern was a fifty-year-old international tycoon who had no interest in her other than professionally.

161

Even supposing, just supposing, he did find her attractive, everyone knew he was devoted to Paulette. So if there was no hope, why did she waste hours of her time imagining?

She began flicking through the other announcements on the screen to divert herself.

'Really? That must have been fun. OK, 'bye.'

Denis put the phone down. 'Leo, of course, was entertaining Jack Armstrong of Butlers at his box at Ascot yesterday.' One of the lights on the key and lamp started to flash. 'Never invites me to Ascot,' he grumbled as he picked up the phone. 'Jones,' he bellowed into the mouthpiece. Or me, thought Sarah.

David booked the Fitzalan Suite at the Howard Hotel for the press conference. In the middle of Ascot week there wasn't a lot else going on and he hoped for a big turnout. Each journalist on his extended invitation list had been rung by one of his team; the nationals he rang himself, occasionally talking to two writers on the same paper. It was vital everyone who had a special interest in either Butlers or Empire was included.

He was just leaving the office for the fourth time when Patrick Peabody rang.

'Thanks for the story.' There was more than a note of sarcasm in his voice.

'I promise you, Patrick, this was not due to happen for weeks. It all started leaking yesterday and they decided to go before the price ran away.'

It was nice to be able to tell the truth once in a while, David thought, holding the phone under his chin while he lit up.

'Mmm.' Patrick sounded half convinced. 'Well, it would have made a sensational story on Sunday.'

'Honestly, Jack Armstrong and Peter Markus were both at Sir Leo Stern's box at Ascot yesterday. They rushed back when the price started to move.'

'Oh, that will make a nice intro to my feature,' cooed Patrick, sounding more cheerful.

'Oh God, please don't say it was Stern's box. They'll know it came from me.'

'Well, I do need an exclusive angle for this week.'

'How would you like to be the only journalist with a one-to-one interview with Jack Armstrong?' David's voice turned to honey.

'Fine,' said Patrick dubiously, 'just so long as he tells me something he hasn't told everyone else at the press conference today.'

'Don't worry, we'll find something juicy for you,' said David. 'Though heaven alone knows what,' he said aloud to himself as he headed towards the door for the fifth time.

Charlie rang Peter at noon. 'The underwriting should be done by two, they're lapping it up,' he said.

'Well done. Are you coming to the press conference?'

'Don't think so, I don't like the press en masse,' said Charlie. 'I think one of our other partners might look in.'

'Fine. Thanks again.'

Peter allowed himself a brief moment of self-congratulation as he looked at the Topic screen. The Butlers price had dropped back only 10p and Empire shares were 380p – and that broker had wanted to cut back the price! He sniffed. Should he ring Jack? No, he'd let him suffer. Instead he called John Young, Hogarth's senior partner.

'It would be terrific if you could make it to the press conference at the Howard, fly the flag for the shop as it were.'

John Young agreed, even though it meant cancelling his lunch with a senior industrialist. But a successful bid of this size would do the bank no end of good in these competitive markets. He would like the world to know that it had his blessing. And why should Peter get all the glory? He really was a bit too high-profile sometimes.

David had judged it right. Journalists were trooping diagonally across the chandeliered lobby of the Howard Hotel, like ants in search of sugar.

The *Financial Times* had sent both a company news reporter and one of the Lex column writers – always a good sign. Most important, there was someone from every national paper including two City editors.

Altogether there were about forty people, and he'd drafted

in a half a dozen of his own employees to swell the ranks. By midday, the room looked bursting at the seams.

He hoped Channel 4 News did not make it. He found the cameras and lights disrupted the proceedings in return for thirty seconds coverage on a programme nobody watched. He had arranged for the Financial World Tonight to interview Jack afterwards.

David's main worry was holding Jack back. Normally company chief executives were so overcome with nerves they had to be fed large drinks beforehand to enable them to perform. Jack, however needed to be kept away from alcohol, and even without it appeared dangerously confident.

The Guinness scandal, which had broken upon the City like a tidal wave, was just beginning to fade in people's memories. Especially Peter's, thought David. He had noticed his tendency to push the authorities to the limit, apparently just for the hell of it.

Each chair had a copy of the press release on it, plus a copy of the latest Butlers figures, plus some press cuttings comparing Empire unfavourably with Butlers. There were also pictures of Jack and Sir Richard Butler, luckily taken for the annual report, but several newspapers had sent their own photographers.

The Howard had put a raised dais at one end of the room with chairs and a long table draped in green baize bearing water jugs. Stiff white name cards for the directors of Butlers and Hogarth Stein faced the audience.

Although it was already two o'clock, David gave them ten minutes to read the press release and for Peter to arrive. Most of them were sitting, heads down, busily underlining. Others were already scribbling questions. Mike Walters of the *Daily Mail* had his pen poised and was gazing hard at Jack. David didn't like the look of it. Mike had a line in awkward questioning that could throw the most experienced director.

The phone near him rang. 'The boy wonder's arrived,' said a minion sotto voce. 'Fine, send em down straight away.'

The noise of gossiping journalists fell as the five entered the room and took their places on the stage, Sir Richard in the middle, Jack and Edward either side of him.

Jack wore a midnight blue single-breasted suit with a pale

blue shirt (he had read somewhere that blue signified power) and a navy tie with spots. David had persuaded him not to wear his red tie. Red, this same article had said, indicated a strong sexual drive. 'It's hardly appropriate for a takeover bid,' David had snapped. But he had failed to make Jack brush back his fringe. 'I like it, it's me,' he had declared.

Sir Richard looked perfect for the occasion in a ten-year-old Geives & Hawks pinstripe suit which he always brought out for big City appearances. Peter was his normal dashing self in chalk stripe double-breasted grey flannel.

David strode to the front of the room and banged a glass on the table. A lesser PR man would have thanked them all profusely for taking the trouble to come. David just said: 'I think you have all had time to read the press release and I'd like to hand straight over to Butler's chairman, Sir Richard Butler, to say a few brief words. Then we'll throw it open to questions.'

Sir Richard rose, exuding gentlemanly charm. 'First of all I'd like to welcome you all here this morning to hear about what we think is the most exciting event in the sixty-two-year-old history of Butlers. We believe we have a great deal to offer Empire, and that together we would form a food group of world beating standard.'

The audience stirred with anticipation.

'Most of the credit goes to our chief executive, Jack Armstrong, who has helped revitalise the company over the past year, so you can expect him to answer most of the questions.' Sir Richard paused. 'The floor is now open.'

'You seem to be expecting shareholders to accept some dilution of earnings?'

Neither Jack nor Richard realised it was a question for several seconds. Then Peter nudged Richard who looked at Jack.

The angles of his face cast sharp shadows. 'Yes, that's right, if you keep to the most conservative estimates of both companies' profits for the coming year.'

'Can't hear, can't hear,' cried several people at once.

There was a hiatus while David fiddled with the microphone.

Jack started again. 'But we do anticipate that in the event

there will be no dilution, although we cannot definitely predict that at this stage.'

The questions carried on at this kind of technical level. Jack was lucid and confident, friendly yet dignified. You would have thought he had done it a hundred times before, thought David. Why did Jack's aptitude make him so uneasy? Suddenly a question snapped him out of his reverie.

'Why did the share price rise so dramatically yesterday?' it was Mike Walters of the *Mail*.

'I wish I knew. As you know we were forced into announcing the bid early because of it,' said Jack.

'Perhaps Mr Markus can enlighten us.' Mike Walters' voice held its usual mocking tone.

'We really have no idea,' Peter said.

'Do you suspect insider dealing, Mr Armstrong?' Mickey Freeman of the *Daily Post* chimed in.

'It has to be a possibility,' said Jack before anyone could stop him. David cursed himself. How could he have forgotten to brief Jack on the answer to that question. It was obvious it had to come up.

A few more questions about market share in the various sectors followed and at ten to three, as people were beginning to drift back to their offices, David brought the meeting to a close.

As most of them began to file out, a couple of reporters came up to the dais.

'Any idea who might have been buying yesterday?' It was Mickey Freeman again.

'None at all,' answered Jack curtly, having just been ticked off by Peter.

'Have you complained to the Stock Exchange?' Freeman wasn't going to be deflected, but Peter had walked up behind him.

'The authorities will be looking into it, just as they look into all abnormal price movements,' he said tartly.

'Just you write about how good our deal is, lad, and don't worry about share price movements,' added Jack. David shuddered as he overheard.

'Mr Armstrong, I wondered if you could go through the different biscuit brands of the two companies and how they overlap?' asked a wide-eyed young woman from the *Grocer*. Jack gave her his most disarming smile. 'It will be a pleasure, my ear. Why don't we go and sit down?'

'Well, that should keep him out of harm's way,' sighed David to Peter. 'I've arranged some lunch upstairs if you want it.'

'I really can't stay.' Peter was looking distracted. 'I've got so much on. I'm hitching a lift with John.'

'But you will be back for the analysts at four?' David struggled to imagine what was more important than this deal.

'I'll have to be.' Peter winked and was gone.

One of David's runners rushed in brandishing a bundle of *Evening Standards*. David had briefed the City editor first thing.

BUTLER'S BITE AT EMPIRE read the headline on the first City page.

'The increasingly aggressive food combine, Butlers Group, this morning made a bold bid of 360p a share for Empire Foods, which has interests in four continents.' Thereafter it was pretty well much a crib of the press release. There was a huge picture of Jack, with the caption: NEW BROOM ARMSTRONG.

Jack, who by now expected a few inaccuracies, thought it pretty fair. He especially liked the bid being called bold.

Even David cheered up. 'Now I don't want you all squiffy for the analysts later on,' he said as he led them into the dining room upstairs, 'but I think we deserve a little celebration.' A waiter was pouring out glasses of Dom Perignon. They all murmured assent. 'To us,' David toasted.

As they lifted their glasses, Peter was sitting in the back of one of Hogarth Stein's Daimlers speeding westwards and talking on the car phone to Sir Leo Stern.

'Are you sure we have to meet now, Leo? I've got an overconfident chief executive and a £2.8 billion bid to handle.'

'Positive.'

'Well, I'll be late.' Peter sounded peevish.

'I'll wait.' Stern put down the phone, got out of his Bentley and walked through the side entrance of Claridge's.

The wining and dining of the previous months had paid off and the analysts' meeting went like a dream. The mood was good humoured and it was clear they liked the commercial logic of the deal even though most of them believed Butlers might have to pay a higher price to clinch it.

Jack rang Amanda who reeled off a string of messages. Salomon Brothers and Shearman Drussel, two leading American investment banks, were among the callers. Jack rang them and listened to two almost identical pitches about how they could help him win the bid.

Peter went through the roof when he told him. 'You can be absolutely sure they've been on to Empire in just the same way,' he warned. There were also a couple of callers claiming to have small stakes in Empire and asking for special terms in return for their acceptance.' Tell them it's against the takeover code to give any shareholder better terms than another,' Peter instructed.

At six-thirty Peter whisked Jack downstairs to an impromptu drinks party hosted by John Young and with all Peter's team present. The other Butlers directors had been rounded up by David Bang.

'The toast is "Star Wars",' said John Young. They grinned at each other like schoolboys who had become blood brothers. Jack felt weak with happiness. Peter kept his counsel; it would be pointless to ruin a perfect day.

It had been a far from perfect day for Bertie Underworth and his board. Never had such chaos reigned. Stuart Anderson had advised him to call a full board meeting as soon as possible, but rounding up the fifteen directors was quite another matter.

Most crucially, the finance director had left two days before for a touring holiday of the Pelopponese.

Eventually, enough of them had turned up to hold a semblance of a board meeting at 11.30. The telephones did not stop ringing all morning and even Miss Paget began to veer towards the hysterical. The calls divided into two categories. The first came from journalists, stockbroker's analysts and fund managers all after information.

The second group were advisers selling their wares –

merchant bankers, brokers, PR men and mysterious 'consultants'. Shearman Drussel and three other American investment banks had been on as Peter predicted.

The most extraordinary people seemed to have got hold of Bertie's private line number, but he dared not take it off the hook in case it was Stuart or one of his missing directors. In the end he disguised his voice and pretended he was just passing through the office.

The truth was he had no idea what to say.

Those who could not get through on the telephones resorted to the fax which began disgorging messages like a fruit machine hitting the jackpot.

Stuart Anderson was in his element. He liked nothing better than a panic-stricken board of directors. He congratulated himself on leaking the story of a mysterious share stake to his old fag at Winchester, who now worked for one of the few remaining agency only brokers.

It was Stuart who had made Bertie Underworth start searching the share register and send out section 212 applications. They were a new weapon against predators, legally compelling the true owners of secret nominee holdings to identify themselves.

He had not been entirely surprised to find Butlers or Sir Leo Stern there but he was surprised at the amount. Three per cent had probably cost a minimum of £70 million – big money even for Stern.

Stuart did not imagine for one moment that Stern had bothered building a holding of that size, using several nominee holdings, on a whim. As Stuart had hoped, putting the rumour round the market of a hostile stake had flushed out the bidder and pushed the share price well up in the process. Now Butler's had bid, it might be interesting to see what the Sunday newspapers would make of Stern's holding.

Up on the lushly decorated executive floor at Empire, Stuart walked slowly and deliberately through Miss Paget's domain and into Bertie's office.

He exuded the confidence of someone who knew his business – in sharp contrast to the four directors standing in a huddle to the right of Bertie's desk.

'For the last time, I'm telling you I cannot comment at this stage,' thundered Bertie into the phone. As he looked up and saw Stuart's imposing figure, relief flooded his podgy features. 'I'm afraid I have to go now, I have a board meeting.' He slammed the phone down and took it off the hook.

'Stuart, am I glad to see you!' He came round the desk and grasped his hand, while the other directors turned to stare mutely at them. Miss Paget popped into the office like an anxious moorhen. 'The boardroom is ready now, sir.'

'Excellent,' declared Stuart in his plummy baritone. Taking control, he gestured to Bertie to lead the way. 'Shall we go through?'

At the end of the impromptu party at Hogarth Stein, Peter told them all to go home and get a good night's rest. 'If you're anything like me, you haven't seen your wives for ages and are desperate for sleep.'

The last thing Jack felt like was a cosy night at home. This was one evening when he would celebrate. Everybody who needed to be talked to had been talked to. His interview with Patrick was fixed for lunch the following day and apart from the inevitable meetings with Peter and Charlie, his diary was clear.

He summoned his car and rang Rosemary from it. She sounded delighted to hear from him. The bid had been mentioned on the news and an excited neighbour who had been shopping in the West End had brought round the lunchtime *Standard*.

'You must be exhausted. I'll get something delicious out of the freezer.'

'The problem is I've still got a couple of meetings – things to sort out. I think it's best if I stay up here tonight.'

Jack heard her sigh with disappointment. 'Well, when will you be home?' Her tone was tart.

'Honestly, love – if I could make it any different I would.' No reply.

'There shouldn't be a problem tomorrow.' Still no answer. 'I promise.'

'OK,' said Rosemary wearily. 'I know it's important, but so is your family.'

'I'll see you very soon.'

He rang Jane Brompton's number.

When she opened the door of her flat, Jane looked as though someone had turned on a light inside her. For a moment she reminded him of someone but he could not work out who. It was like a half remembered dream.

He took her in his arms and kissed her full on the lips. There was no resistance, but little response. He pulled away from her and saw an expression of amused surprise.

'I'm exhausted and slightly drunk,' he said.

'You had better come and sit down in that case.'

She led him through into a comfortable room and motioned him towards a large black leather sofa.

He stayed standing and held out his hands and drew her towards him. She smelt of Shalimar.

'I've wanted to do that ever since I saw you in the Captain's Bar.'

She smiled at him, her cat-like eyes still wary.

'You're very attractive.'

'Am I?' He felt suddenly off balance.

'You're lucky to find me in. I should be on the way to New York, but the trip was delayed at the last moment.'

'It must be fate,' Jack. He could feel his erection growing.

Suddenly she smiled and moved forward so that their bodies were touching. She pressed her hips against him and kissed him full on the mouth. They stood straining against each other, tongues entwined. Her hand stroked the bulge and slowly she unzipped his trousers and began gently caressing him. He stood, eyes closed, as she slowly sank to her knees and enveloped him in soft, wet warmth. Just as he felt himself losing control she moved on to the sofa and spread her legs, hitching up her skirt.

He saw dark stocking tops held by black and red suspenders which cut into the cream of her thighs as she laid back. And between her legs only red, springy curls. She summoned him with her eyes and, kneeling in front of her, he bent his head to the red fur, inhaling the pungent perfume. His tongue found her clitoris which grew hard as he licked it, round and round, over and over again.

Then he knelt up and thrust into her with a violence he had not felt in years. Her nails dug into his back and above the

171

sensation he could hear her shrieking and shrieking. His body moved, pounding and pounding until the tone of her cries changed, deepening into long, gasping sobs of relief and he felt the sperm shoot into her in sweet explosions.

It was only afterwards he realised that neither of them had removed a single garment.

His driver picked him up at seven the following morning and Jack collected the newspapers at his local newsagent, settling back comfortably in the back of the car with a pleasant feeling of anticipation.

BUTLER'S BOSS SUSPECTS INSIDER DEALING screamed the headline in the *Post* over an article of which two-thirds was devoted to the possibility of insider dealing and a third to the bid.

He would fire David Bang! He turned hurriedly to the others papers, hoping for something more balanced, but they were all the same. INSIDER DEALING WORRY AS BUTLERS BIDS £2.8 BILLION FOR EMPIRE, thundered *The Times*. Even the *Financial Times* had used the insider dealing angle as the headline.

He glanced up at the rear view mirror and caught his driver watching him as he thrashed furiously through the newsprint. 'I'll never understand journalists,' he said loudly to justify himself. He wanted to swear loud and long but here was this man – a new driver who could well be a spy for Empire – and so he contained his anger to a few explosions of blasphemy.

Every article covered the bid details as well. But Jack had this time been so sure of a euphoric response that even the balanced coverage seemed sour and mealy mouthed.

The tone of the Lex column he felt was positively vitriolic. The concluding paragraph read: 'Mr Armstrong's leadership has yet to prove the test of time and with Butlers barely reorganised a bid of this size could be premature. In any event, Butlers will have to dig considerably deeper into its coffers to win over Empire shareholders.' Jack made a note to write to the Editor.

The *Telegraph* gave a grudging acknowledgement that the companies fitted well together and that Butlers was undergoing a transformation; but it was sniffy about the price.

His temper simmered all the way to St James's but he decided against using his car phone. He did not want to be cut off in mid-stream.

Why the hell hadn't David warned him about that kind of question, or Peter for that matter? Here were these experts who handled big bids all the time, or so they kept telling him, and yet they failed to keep him briefed about routine questions. At a minute past eight he sat down at his desk and lifted the telephone.

David was on his third cigarette of the day, expecting the call.

'You are being paid a small fortune to make sure this kind of thing doesn't happen,' ranted Jack. 'If I had been warned of this kind of question and told how to answer we'd have had some decent press coverage today.'

There was a pause. 'You're absolutely right,' David said quietly. 'I take full responsibility for not briefing you and I'm prepared to knock ten thousand off my fee for the mistake.'

For a moment Jack was completely lost for words, just as David had intended. Then he said: 'And how do you intend to put matters right?'

David took a long, relieved draw on his cigarette – at least he'd still got a client.

'Look, Jack,' he said calmly, 'This seems like a crisis, because it's the first morning after the bid. But this story will die surprisingly fast. In future, if anyone asks you about it, just say it's in the hands of the authorities and you can't comment. By the end of the week, everyone will have forgotten about it. We can put a lot right at lunchtime with Patrick, but we do need to give him an exclusive for Sunday if we want him wholeheartedly on our side.'

Jack forgot his anger and began mentally flicking through the possibilities.

'How about telling him about our new count-line brand?'

'New chocolate bars are fascinating to the *Grocer*, marginal to Patrick at this stage. It might come in useful later on.'

Jack was silent, racking his brains.

'What about your plans to sell Empire's UK biscuit brands if there is a Monopolies problem?' suggested David.

So far only the *Financial Times* had mentioned the

possibility of a reference to the Monopolies and Mergers Commission. Despite Peter's confidence, the two biscuit operations came perilously near to taking twenty-five per cent of the British biscuit market.

'Shouldn't we tell the Stock Exchange first?'

Jack was learning fast, David thought.

'Then it would cease to be a story.'

'There must be a way round it,' snapped Jack.

David drew on his cigarette. 'We could drop it round last thing on Friday. The Takeover Panel won't like it, but tough titty. I think you'd better not mention it to Peter, though.'

'I don't like going behind his back. Let's talk about it at lunch,' he said as his private line began to ring.

It was Peter, keen to keep the advantage, airy and bright. 'Not bad coverage, nice picture,' he said breezily. But Jack could hear the edge to his voice.

'You know bloody well it's a disaster, with them all latching on to this stupid insider dealing business. I pay you chaps a bloody fortune to stop this kind of thing happening.'

'Blame David, not me. If I hadn't stepped in, it could have been a whole lot worse,' said Peter loftily. 'Anyway, everybody will have forgotten about it by next week . . .'

Amanda put her head round the door enquiringly.

'Hold on, Peter. What is it Amanda?'

'The telephone engineers are here – are you happy with the list.' She put a piece of paper into his outstretched hand.

'What about Sir Richard?' Her eyes widened a fraction. He nodded. 'Well,' she hesitated, 'if you're really sure.'

Jack smiled wrily. 'I'm sure,' he said, and waved her away. 'I'm having handsets directly connected to this office put on the desks of every executive in this building,' Jack told Peter proudly.

Peter decided to stay out of office power games. 'Just remember we have sixty days to play with,' he said. 'It's a long time and the most important days are the last four. Now I need to come and see you. Are you free at 10.30?'

Jack felt thankful David had arranged lunch with Patrick at the Savoy Grill. Nowadays he felt completely at home there. It was partly Angelo's consistent welcome and partly the

174

clientèle itself; wealth and material success swirled round the tables like an invisible miasma, touching everyone. The moment Jack stepped into the Grill Room's atmosphere he felt more alive, more potent.

Unlikely combinations of people – Adam Faith and the politician publisher Jonathan Aitken, Jeffrey Archer and Peregrine Worsthorne of the *Sunday Telegraph* – sat deep in conversation over the day's special, be it bangers and mash or liver and bacon. It was the City's substitute for public school meals.

One of the few magnates who never ate there on principle was Sir Charles Forte. He had been trying to take over the Savoy Group for years.

Jack arrived with his head bursting with the news Peter had broken to him at their morning meeting. His rage of the early morning had given way to obsession. How was he to turn sentiment to his advantage?

They ordered glasses of champagne and David lit a Sullivan Powell, eyeing Jack speculatively. Something was up.

'Stern's got just under five per cent of Empire,' Jack said.

David blew a smoke ring. Yes, of course, he should have guessed.

'Well, that's all right isn't it? He's a friend of yours.'

'Not exactly,' Jack said. He took a sip of champagne and told David about the row at the time of Butlers bid for Huntingdon. How he had always suspected Stern would take his revenge; how he had never felt quite happy about the surface displays of friendship; how Peter and Charlie had told him not to worry.

'I always have worried, of course,' said Jack. 'Something in the pit of my stomach told me he would try and get his own back.'

'Well, five per cent is not necessarily crucial.' David's voice was soothing and then he brightened.

'Why don't we give the story to Patrick?'

'No way. We would have exactly what happened this morning. He'll write all about Leo and give two lines to me – I mean, Butlers.'

'Possibly,' said David evenly. 'But once you've given him such a big exclusive story, he will be on your side for the rest of the bid. The *Sunday Herald* can be very influential in the last two weeks – it would be worth it in terms of goodwill. Ah, here's Patrick now.'

Patrick appeared in the entrance, talking animatedly to Angelo. Even then he kept them waiting, stopping to talk to people at three different tables. He finally ambled up looking sheepish. 'Sorry about that.' They all shook hands.

'Well, now you have eventually arrived, Patrick, I'm going to leave you two to have lunch together,' announced David. Jack looked startled.

'It's all right, I won't bite,' Patrick said in his Irish lilt taking one of David's cigarettes from the packet on the table. He and David exchanged smiles that spoke of a pre-arranged deal.

'Come on, Jack,' urged David, 'you know Patrick well enough by now. You don't need me.'

He grinned. 'Ok, but if I say anything I shouldn't, I'll still blame you.'

'What else am I here for? Have a nice lunch,' David said and was gone.

'The only problem is – will it hold for Sunday?' Patrick was moving his turbot round the plate.

'I understand they are planning to announce it on Monday or Tuesday.' Jack leaned forward confidentially. 'But I thought you would like to be the first to know.'

Patrick smiled. 'I love it. But I'll have to ring Stern and get him to confirm it.'

'Well, it's absolutely true, I assure you,' Jack bridled.

Patrick put his hand on Jack's arm. 'I don't doubt you for a second,' he said. 'But people get awfully annoyed if you don't check.'

Jack leaned towards him. 'So do you think you'll be able to write something positive about the deal for Sunday?'

'Oh God, never ask a journalist that,' exclaimed Patrick. 'You and I get on well, but that kind of question is like a red rag to a bull.'

His face crumpled into a smile. 'But I don't think you'll be too upset.' He put the last piece of turbot in his mouth and leaned back contentedly. 'It's a great story.' Then his eyes snapped open. 'Oh, ho! See what I see.'

176

Being guided through the tables to the back of the room by an animated Angelo were Stuart Anderson and Sir Leo Stern.

'God! Anderson must have something on Stern to get him to come down here,' said Patrick. 'He never usually eats outside Mayfair.'

Jack felt his blood turn icy cold as Patrick prattled on.

'He's a wily old devil that Anderson – he must know about the stake. God, this story will never hold.'

Jack had ceased to give a damn about Patrick's story – but at that moment he would have given anything in the world to hear what Stern and Stuart were saying to each other.

Patrick ran the story as the splash on the first City page. He was pretty pleased with himself, even though the *Sunday Telegraph* and *Observer* had followed it up in their second editions.

For once, Jack was not disappointed with the coverage of the bid. A grateful Patrick had gone overboard. Not only did he run a huge feature, detailing the recent history of Butler's in glowing terms and forecasting a glorious future for the combined group should the bid succeed, he also devoted half his influential comment column to the subject, hailing Jack as one of the most brilliant new managers to emerge this decade and prophesying that he would be 'a Lord Hanson of the 1990s'.

Jack read the piece over and over again with a mixture of disbelief and euphoria. David had been right, he realised. He began to understand. Journalists could be bribed just like everyone else – but their weakness was for information, not money.

Sarah read the story in bed on Sunday morning with intense concentration. Then she lay back on her pillows and smiled to herself. If they only knew about Schlosstein's three per cent, she thought, that would really get them going.

David, meanwhile, added back the £10,000 he had so kindly offered to cut from his fee.

First thing on the Monday morning, Empire shares shot up. Then the market, knowing that Stern was not a serious

177

counter bidder himself, let the Empire stock drift back to only 7p above Butlers offer price of 360p.

Jack had feared worse and when the drafting meetings to put together the formal bid document began in earnest that week at Hogarth Stein, even the lawyers seemed in high spirits.

Chapter 12

Sir Leo Stern decamped to the South of France. Or at least Paulette and their two teenage boys did, taking up residence in a pale primrose Edwardian villa on the rocky hills above Beaulieu-sur-Mer. The house stood halfway up a steep winding road, lined by pines, prickly pear and wild poppies in the spring. It was just over a kilometre from Beaulieu, a town perfectly placed midway between Nice and Monte Carlo.

Inside the balustraded tribute to Edwardian frivolity, the marble-floored rooms were decorated in palest blues and greens and sparsely filled with Louis XV French furniture. In the small sitting room overlooking the terrace stood a white baby grand piano on which Paulette Stern kept always a bowl of perfect flame roses. She would often play in the afternoons, and occasionally to guests after dinner.

Paulette enjoyed the house more than her London home which after years of constant attention had acquired a museum-like quality. Les Palmes had an uncluttered air of tranquillity, the terrace overlooking the Beaulieu marina and the azure blue sea stretching to the horizon. To the right was the hilly peninsular of St-Jean-Cap-Ferrat and she could play 'spot the yacht' as they made their way from the harbour of St Jean over to Monaco. Throughout the day helicopters would flit along the coastline like lone wasps, apart from the Nice to Monaco service every half hour, where they travelled in pairs.

From the end of June each year Stern spent each weekend there, flying into Nice in his private plane and being helicoptered up to a flat piece of land just behind the house – a privilege which had cost him a sizeable contribution to the local mayoral funds. Each August, he settled in for the month.

He loved the house, not just for its architecture or its commanding view of the best-hulled harbours of the Cote d'Azur, but for its location. Within twenty minutes he could be playing roulette in the Casino in Monte Carlo, betting calmly on the birthdates of his two sons. Twenty minutes the other way and he could be checking in at Nice airport.

On the ground floor, at the back of the house, Paulette had a small study from which she conducted her own mainly charitable affairs. Her first love was promoting promising young musicians.

One of the second-floor rooms had been converted into an office for Stern, with a Louis XV desk, two telephone lines, a fax machine and a computer that hooked him into the company system in London by satellite.

His shops had such sophisticated point of sale and stock control equipment that he could call up the sales figures for that day within ten seconds.

Stern relished the aspect from this room, overlooking the paved garden and the swimming pool – naturally in the shape of a modified S. On two sides of the paved area grew a profusion of tropical trees and shrubs: oleander, pines, eucalyptus, scarlet hibiscus, and a mass of climbing roses. Along the outer edge of the garden stood three ionic columns in between which pink and red geraniums tumbled from mock grecian urns and jardinières. A simple wooden bar at the far end saved the bother of running to and from the house for drinks. At the entrance to the garden, two perfect palm trees reached for the sky surrounded by the fleshy blue spikes of agapanthus.

It was to this paradise on earth that Stern invited Jack and Rosemary, Peter and Angela, and, to her intense astonishment and rapturous delight, Sarah Meyer, with whomever she cared to bring. She cared to bring no one. She had finally consigned Rob to the past and Simon simply was not up to it.

So, gritting her teeth, she went alone.

'What does he want?' Jack asked Peter over tea at Wimbledon.

180

Peter was his guest for the men's finals. Butlers centre court seats were one perk Jack did not intend to relinquish.

'Well, we won't know unless we go.' Peter adored the South of France.

Jack frowned. 'I don't know whether it's on for me to accept his hospitality. It wouldn't look very good if the press got hold of it.'

'We can't really risk upsetting him,' said Peter. 'He might use our refusal as an excuse to hold out against the offer.'

'Or to sell his stake to a white knight,' said Jack grimly.

They flew out on the Friday night accompanied by Stern who laid on an extra helicopter to take them to the house. When they arrived Paulette ushered them into the garden where they were offered pink champagne in fluted glasses and tiny crisp tartlets filled with best beluga.

They were then shown their rooms, each with a *mazuza* on the door and the palest grey marble bathrooms en suite, and invited to appear for dinner an hour later at 8.30.

Sarah had spent over £1,000 in Whistle's and Brown's kitting herself out for the weekend – worth every penny, she thought as she unpacked. As Paulette noted with a French woman's eye, the simple dusty pink linen tunic Sarah wore that night emphasised both her youth and her sexuality.

Dinner was a 'simple affair', Stern announced, starting with fresh asparagus, followed by loup de mer and tiny green beans, and ending with goat's cheese and wild strawberries.

The conversation centred on the area. 'Garbo used to come and stay in a house just up the road in Cap d'Ail, and David Niven's house is just below us,' Paulette told them.

'Too many bloody property developers living here now,' said Stern tersely. 'There's only one place I like more, and that's Venice, but it's impractical.'

He sat at the head of the glittering table, dark and imposing. He loved the way an overt display of wealth could impress even the most sophisticated people. Jack, of course, was a pushover. Stern never understood these men who worked all their lives for other people's companies, always living at the edge of their means, constantly insecure and at the mercy of the board of directors if they put a foot wrong.

181

Jack's ambition was obvious enough, but he showed no interest in making serious money.

During the 1970s some of these corporate slaves had got away with blue murder, mind you, but not any more. Thatcher had brought the meritocracy back into fashion. What a wonderful woman she was, he thought. She had given the country a huge kick up the backside and made it OK to be rich again. She had shown the strengths of a free market – so that fat-cat non-performing directors were no longer safe.

Over the past four years Stern had been involved in half a dozen of the big takeovers. He was one of the few British investors with the financial firepower to match the American arbitrageurs – and knew that in that pool he was still small fry. Boesky was reputed to be worth over $1 billion at his height.

Boesky had been a fool though, he reflected. He had turned up with major shareholdings in every big American company on the end of a takeover approach for years – it was too blatant.

With hindsight it had been only a matter of time before his arrest in November, 1986. The SEC had been monitoring his dealings for months. Boesky had believed his own publicity, Stern thought, something he had resolved would never happen to him.

In any case, apart from the financial press, who reported his ever rising profits with increasing mystification, occasionally demanding greater disclosure in his accounts, the newspapers left him alone. That's what he liked about the Brits – nice and laid back.

Peter was altogether more sophisticated, Stern mused. He must have a dozen clients in the top 100 companies in Britain. It was evident from the way he lived that he wanted to be rich, but there was a level at which he didn't have the balls to take the necessary risk. Stern could sense Peter eyeing up the silver, the wine, the china. And despite his pretentions and rich friends, Stern could tell he was impressed.

Through his reverie he noticed Sarah talking animatedly to Jack. Her dark slanting eyes were flashing.

'I really do think all this stuff you businessmen come out with about short-termism is hogwash – the market decides,' she said firmly.

Stern felt unexpectedly tender towards her. She had guts and a good brain too. Something about her smile reminded him of Paulette, but Sarah was more robust – rounder and less refined. More like him. Apart from Paulette and himself, she was the only other Jewish person in the room. Yes, he thought again, she could be his daughter. If their first baby, which Paulette had miscarried in her third month, had been born, he knew it could have been just like Sarah. Paulette had been sure it was a girl.

Jack laughed at Sarah's vehemence. 'You'd never guess you were a stockbroker. But do you really want to see European food companies snapping up everything British?'

Peter broke off his cross-table speculation about the artist of one of the pictures on the wall. He could tell Jack had drunk just a couple of glasses too many.

'Jack hasn't been entirely indoctrinated yet,' he said, winking.

But Jack gazed at Sarah, suddenly belligerent. She was only an analyst after all. 'If you don't mind my asking, why exactly are you here?'

'Young Sarah here is one of the best little stakebuilders in London, that's why,' said Stern, his voice cutting through the conversation like a knife.

For a moment all that could be heard was the rustling of the palms in the breeze. Sarah shivered.

'But I thought your broker was Greenbag's?' said Jack.

'Greenbag's is one of my brokers, certainly,' Stern replied. 'But one needs horses for courses as anywhere else, and sometimes,' he added mockingly, 'one has a conflict of interest.'

In a flash of insight, Peter realised that Leo had used Tulley to build up the stake in Empire. That's why there had been no gossip from Charlie. He hadn't been able to understand it at the time. At the very least they normally dropped a few hints. How silly of him not to realise, he chastised himself mentally. Now it all made sense. Or almost. Sarah may be reasonably bright, but she could not possibly do all Stern's work for him single-handed.

'Who do you work for at Tulley, Sarah?' Peter asked.

She looked diagonally across the table at him. 'Denis Jones

is my boss,' she said, uncertain as to how much she should say.

'And he's a partner, presumably?' Peter persisted. Sarah hesitated, glancing at Stern.

'Let's just say he's one of the shrewdest market operators in London,' said Stern.

'And dare one ask why he's not at this splendid occasion?

'He had a massive heart attack two months ago,' said Sarah.

'And the doctor doesn't think frolicking in the South of France is advisable just yet,' Stern helped her out again. The sight of all our topless beauties might just polish him off.'

'Leo,' Paulette intervened from the other end of the table, 'why don't you tell them your latest news?'

Peter and Jack exchanged glances. Surely he wasn't going to launch a counter-bid himself after all? Peter's mind raced round the possibilities.

Stern looked faintly embarrassed. 'Well you know that I love music,' gushed Paulette. 'I'm very interested in the work of the London and City Ballet Company which is full of amazingly talented people.' She shrugged. 'But it is 'opelessly managed. Well,' she took a deep breath, 'Leo has agreed to be chairman of the board and give financial advice.'

Jack and Peter dared not look at each other. Leo Stern and ballet just didn't seem to mix. Peter had a vision of Stern in tights and leotard, and quickly tried to think of something else.

'Well, I think that's wonderful,' said Sarah crisply. 'The arts need people like Leo. If these ballet and opera companies were run properly they wouldn't need so much money from the Arts Council.'

'But won't it mean that they'll have to perform non-stop popular works like Swan Lake and Sleeping Beauty?' asked Rosemary, coming to life.

'Nah.' Stern recovered from his embarrassment. 'I think a lot of the reason these kind of companies lose money is just down to sloppy management. There are too many chiefs and not enough Indians. And a lot of them still don't have a clue about marketing. The English National Opera and the London Philharmonic Orchestra have shown what can be done with a professional approach.'

184

Angela raised an eyebrow at Rosemary. Stern had clearly done his homework.

'Anyway,' said Paulette, 'no one must breathe a word as it's not official for two weeks. It must still be formally approved.'

A wave of envy swept through Sarah. Paulette had everything: Stern for a husband, pots of money, two handsome sons – and she was beautiful. Her dark bobbed hair shone in the candlelight, framing her delicate face as she smiled happily at her guests.

'Do you think it's warm enough to sit on the terrace for coffee?'

Down to their right, the lights of St Jean-Cap-Ferrat sparkled like jewels casually scattered on to black velvet. And as they sat in the still night air, rich with the scent of pine. Sarah felt suddenly shrouded in loneliness.

She was putting on a convincing show but she hated being the only one without a partner. She had been in love in her teens with a medical student, but he had not been Jewish and, worse, got another girl pregnant and married her. Even now, when she thought about him, it was like touching a wound to see if it had healed. Then there had been Rob. These days she played safe with the company of family and old friends. In any case, she worked so hard that she was exhausted in the evenings and the weekends flew by.

But tonight, although only twenty-seven, she was sharply reminded she was still single in a world where to be a couple was a requirement. Successful people were married – it was part of the package. And for the first time, she consciously admitted that Leo Stern was the only man for whom she had felt real attraction since she left Oxford.

She liked Paulette, although she sensed a reserve on the older woman's part. There was a slight unease between them which she could not quite pinpoint; it was not there with either Rosemary or Angela. Perhaps it was her own guilt, or perhaps simply that Paulette's feminine antennae had sensed a rival.

Throughout the evening there was absolutely no hint of the 'real reason' behind the weekend. Neither Jack nor Peter were surprised – it was far too early.

185

Paulette stood by the window in their white-draped bedroom. 'It all seems to be going very well, darling.' She looked down at the lights twinkling below. Stern stole up behind her and put his large hands on her shoulders. Instantly she stiffened. 'It was perfectly organised as usual,' he said, his voice suddenly gruff. He bent to kiss her long, stem-like neck. But she stood frozen as he moved his hands round to her breasts.

'Darling!' She turned towards him, her face troubled and defensive. 'Darling, I can't. Not with all these people in the house. Try to understand.'

He sighed and moved abruptly away. These days there was always something. It was over a month since they had made love.

On the Saturday, Stern's white and blue motor launch roared them through the transparent sea. Sarah sat to the side, the spray hitting her face as the boat cut a foaming swathe through the water, a little Union Jack fluttering proudly on the bow. They zoomed past Nice, Antibes, Juan-les-Pins, Cannes and finally came to the Lerins islands of St Marguerite and St Honorat, named after a devout reclusive monk and his sister.

They walked round the monastery of St Honorat, where cream-robed monks moved silently among the tourists, and bought oil of lavender from the small shop. Later, they lunched at Chez Frederic's on baby moules and langouste, sitting at vine-shaded tables.

In the afternoon the boat whisked them back to Beaulieu where they lay around the pool or napped in their rooms. Stern disappeared, presumably to work. In the evening he had booked them into La Réserve, famous for its elegance and good food. Afterwards, he informed them, they were off to the Casino in Monte Carlo.

By this time Peter and Jack were beginning to wonder when Stern would make his move. There had still been absolutely no attempt to talk to either of the men alone.

'Don't tell me the whole weekend is just a bloody goodwill exercise?' said Jack to Peter that afternoon as they sat at the pool bar during the afternoon, trying to avoid the sun.

Peter shook his head. 'He's not that subtle. Just you wait.'

186

They arrived at the sugared almond pink hotel bang on eight o'clock and sat in the bar looking out on to the sculpted garden in the centre of the building. The whole atmosphere was of discreet elegance. 'Quite understated for Leo,' whispered Angela to Rosemary, and they giggled. From the lounge, the other side of the courtyard, two surprise guests watched them arrive.

'I'd like to introduce you to some friends of mine whom I've invited to join us.' Stern's voice cut across their desultory chatter a few minutes later. Jack recognised Max Schlosstien instantly but not the man next to him.

Pipe cleaner thin, with pale skin and colourless hair swept straight back, his face looked bloodless. The contrast between him and Schlosstein, with his crinkly hair, eyes like black olives and leathery Florida tan, could not have been more marked.

'This,' said Stern putting his arm around the tall pale man's shoulders who visibly winced, 'is Klaus Von Gleichen, a friend of mine from Switzerland.' The man bowed, expressionless, with the faintest suggestion of heels clicking. 'And this is the famous Wall Street arbitrageur Max Schlosstien.' The fat man raised a podgy hand, glittering with jewellery. 'Hi, gang.'

So this was the big hitter for whom she had been buying all those shares in Empire. And he sounded so tall on the telephone! Sarah was glad he gave no sign of recognition when they were introduced. Stern had obviously primed him to be discreet, but it didn't look as if it came naturally.

Peter recognised his accent as coming straight out of the lower East Side of Manhattan.

'I do love the alligator shoes!' whispered Peter to Jack once everyone had started to talk again.

Carefully chosen by Paulette, dinner that night was definitely not a simple affair.

They sat at a round table on the terrace looking out into a black sea, unbroken by light. 'We seem to have a magnificent view of absolutely fuck all,' declared Peter loudly. Everyone laughed and even Stern smiled tolerantly.

The table was a shade too small for nine people, but ideal for Stern's purpose.

He sat with Rosemary and Angela either side of him. Jack was next to Angela, and Peter to Rosemary. Opposite Stern was Paulette with Klaus on her right and Max to her left. Sarah sat between Peter and Klaus.

Peter cross-examined the two strangers who both appeared to be in the area quite by chance. Klaus had been invited to the wedding of his cousin in Cap D'Antibes, and Max was visiting some American friends who had rented a villa at St Jean for the summer.

For a while Jack and Peter relaxed. 'Didn't you get involved with Dixons' bid for Woolworth?' Peter asked Max, remembering his name being mentioned.

Schlosstien grinned. 'I nearly lost my ass, you mean. In retrospect I was real glad that the Woolworth stock was so hard to get hold of.' He shook his head. 'I mean, I thought Dixons had it made.'

'Most of us did,' Peter agreed. 'Looking back, though, I wonder if Dixons would have been able to handle it?'

Schlosstein shrugged. 'Who cares? All I know is I lost three million green ones.'

All eyes turned on him.

'And have you done much in the London market since?' Peter persisted. Something made Sarah glance at Stern. He had frozen in his seat like a cat about to pounce.

'This and that,' said Max. 'I picked up quite a few shares in a group called Empire earlier this year.'

A large fist thumped into Jack's solar plexus. Sarah held her breath. Please God, don't let him mention her.

'Oh, really, what a coincidence?' The German's voice was light and clipped. 'I too have been buying Empire shares.'

Peter was white. 'You do realise, gentlemen, that Mr Armstrong here is in the middle of bidding for Empire?'

'Wow, really?' exclaimed Max. 'You're with Butlers? Well, waddayouknow?'

Klaus von Gleichen's ice blue eyes glimmered palely behind his gold rimmed glasses. In the silence, Sarah followed his gaze to the flower arrangement on the table – pink and white roses in the shape of a modified S.

'Let's be clear about this,' Jack pushed his chair back a

couple of foot from the table, 'exactly how much of Empire do you own, Mr Schlosstein?'

'Please call me Max. Well, let's see now . . .' He glanced at Sarah, but something in her expression stopped him from asking her for an update. 'At the last count I think it was just under three per cent.'

'And you?' Jack jabbed a finger in the German's direction. Klaus answered instantly. 'About two per cent.'

'And how about you, Leo?' Everyone could hear the undercurrent in Jack's voice. Stern was lounging back in his chair, one arm hooked over the back, his black eyes expressionless. There was the merest suggestion of a smile around his mouth.

'I'm still at 4.9.'

'So there's ten per cent sitting round this table?'

'By remarkable coincidence, Jack, it does rather look that way,' Stern said pleasantly. Everyone stared out into the black sea.

Sarah was fascinated but puzzled. Stern had laid his cards on the table. What did he expect now. An offer? Over dinner in a public restaurant? It was inconceivable.

The cheese arrived. 'I do love the way they bring the knives and forks with each course. You don't have to worry about which ones to use,' Sarah blurted out. Everyone burst out laughing.

Peter knew exactly what Stern expected. He certainly did not want crude bargaining to begin then and there at La Réserve. But in due course, before the end of the bid which now had forty-six days to run, he would expect a favour – and a pretty big favour at that, thought Peter wrily. He just hoped they would be in a position to deliver.

Just before midnight, the pudding was rushed to the table. By the time she had put the last spoonful of hot passion fruit soufflé in her mouth, Sarah knew she had eaten the best meal of her life.

The next morning dawned calm and sunless. A thin layer of pale cloud merged the sky into the sea which lay flat and still, so different from the sparkling blue tumult of the day before.

Peter and Jack decided to go for a walk.

189

'Isn't this what you call a concert party?'

'Of course it's a fucking concert party,' said Peter irritably, 'but it's impossible to prove.'

'They are both friends of his. He introduced them as friends.'

'So? That doesn't mean he knows what shares they buy. One's in Zurich, the other in Manhattan.'

'He's a crooked bastard,' said Jack.

Peter laughed. 'Devious rather than crooked, I'd say. He sails close to the wind, but he's a great survivor. He's been around a long time.'

'What do you suppose he wants?'

They stopped to admire an icing sugar white Edwardian villa, set back from the road.

'I think I'd better have a private chat with him sometime next week,' said Peter thoughtfully.

Sarah went for an early swim in the pool to clear her head. It was a wonderful part of the world, she thought, flipping over on to her back and admiring the house. It brought back memories of childhood holidays. She was just drying off on one of the sun loungers when Stern's voice made her jump.

'How did you enjoy last night?'

'Oh, fantastic,' she replied, 'the food was absolutely magnificent and . . .'

'Nah, nah, you know what I mean – how did you enjoy the cabaret?' He pulled up a chair beside her, disconcertingly close.

She laughed. 'Well, I don't know what you are up to, exactly, but as Denis would say, you certainly put the frighteners on those two.'

Stern smiled, running his eyes over her tiny waist and plump thighs, still glistening with water. He just stopped himself from reaching out and smoothing the droplets away.

'Armstrong tucked me up once.' The smile vanished. 'No one ever tucks me up and gets away with it.'

Something occurred to Sarah. 'And who have you been using to buy von Gleichen's shares then?'

'Sshh, don't talk like that. You never know who's wired for

sound.' His voice was very soft. 'You've done very well, Sarah.'

Without warning he bent over and kissed her briefly on the mouth. 'See you later.' And he was gone.

She picked up a magazine but her hands were shaking so hard it was impossible to read.

Chapter 13

Hogarth Stein and the lawyers thrashed out the nitty gritty of the formal offer document over two weeks of fourteen-hour drafting meetings. Jack did not bother to read it until the final stages and Peter turned a bit tetchy when he decided to rewrite the first two pages. But then, he thought, winking at himself in the mirror, he was the client after all.

The dial on the treadmill showed four more minutes to go. Jack admired his tan, kept fresh on the sun bed, and attempted a smile. But he was panting so hard, all he could manage was a grimace for a fraction of a second. He had let all this wheeling and dealing divert him from his programme.

'You are about to go through the most gruelling few weeks of your life,' Charlie had warned him a few days before.

If it was going to be as bad as that, he'd better be fit. From now on it was going to be three times a week without fail. He would make his secretary book it into his diary and stick to it.

He had been drinking far too much at night. It was the stress, he told himself, but he must try and ease off. At last the dial showed twenty minutes and thankfully, he brought the treadmill to a stop and walked across the floor.

It was about time Peter gave him a formal quote for the cost of this bid, he thought, clinging to the pulse measuring machine like a drowning man. He really ought to put it to the board.

Rosemary took Angela to the Summer Exhibition at the Royal Academy. 'I'm amazed you've never been,' she said as they were standing in front of a large orange and yellow abstract. 'Well, I can quite see,' Angela said, looking around dubiously, 'that you could pick up some *interesting* pieces here.'

Rosemary sighed good-naturedly. 'I think I'm going to have to find myself something more – what would Peter say? challenging to do soon. Mark will be off to university this year. His A-level results will be through in August.'

'At least you've had your family.'

'Children aren't everything, you know,' said Rosemary. She knew Angela longed for a baby. 'Didn't you go to see a new man last week?'

Angela nodded and they moved on to a seascape. 'He says there's nothing wrong and I should just relax about it. It's what they all say.' She sighed impatiently.

They do say that if you consciously try too hard, it blocks things,' said Rosemary.

'I thought Jack wanted you to buy a house near us,' said Angela, changing the subject. 'You could do it up.'

Rosemary wrinkled her nose. 'I'm not a born interior decorator like you. But I'll have to find something – Jack is never home these days.'

Angela picked up the wistful tone in her voice. 'Typical. You lose two stone, turn into a glamour puss, and he's never home.' She smiled and put an arm round her friend. 'Still, I appreciate it.'

'It's all your doing anyway.'

'Maybe you should start your own business?'

'Doing what?' said Rosemary miserably,

'Oh, I don't know. Paulette Stern promotes young musicians.' Angela paused as they moved on to a new room. 'Or you could get a lover.'

'Now there's an idea,' said Rosemary. They stopped in front of a mauve and red daub entitled 'Self Portrait'. 'He'd have to be better looking than this fellow, though.'

For Jack, things suddenly seemed very flat. The defence document from Empire was not expected for nearly two weeks and until it was published, there was nothing more

Butlers could say. Any company thinking about making a counter bid would almost certainly wait to see it.

Jack rang Jean-Pierre in New York to fill him in on the details of the French weekend.

'By the way, what do you think of Shearman Drussel?'

Jean-Pierre chuckled. 'Been after you, have they? They're heavy hitters, lots of firepower, one of America's finest investment banks. It won't do you any harm at all to talk to them.'

'What about Peter?'

'Be up front. Tell him you've seen them. Keep the arrogant son-of-a-bitch on his toes.'

'Well, it's bloody boring here, after all the excitement.'

'Why don't you come over for a couple of days, old buddy, get to know a few of the local boys?' Jean-Pierre sounded in high spirits. Why not? thought Jack.

To his surprise, Peter was all for the idea. 'A bit of goodwill on the other side of the Atlantic never hurt anyone,' he said.

He would not have felt so charitable if he had seen Jack the following evening.

The oeufs aux caviar are real good,' urged Jack's host, Dan Hershfield.

'Fine,' he said. 'And I'll have a plain fillet steak.' There were no prices on his menu, but he decided that was not his problem.

'Any preference on wine, Jack?' He nodded, relieved. Everybody else but him had started on Badoit.

'I'm a claret man myself. Don't go mad on my account, though.'

The American engrossed himself in the thick wine list, reflecting the vast catacomb-like cellars running beneath Hays Mews, and serving both Mark's Club and Annabel's. Jack, in a quest to learn more about wine, had read somewhere the cellars held more than 12,000 bottles of claret and 2,000 bottles of champagne.

'Say, why don't we try the Petrus, '61?' said the American.

'Sounds good to me.'

He was flattered that they were prepared to spend what he guessed must be more than £200 on a bottle of wine, but

194

irritated at the blatant desire to impress him. Placed with his back to the wall, Jack had a clear view of the long, cosy room – perfect for watching the rich and powerful come and go. Cabinet ministers and heads of vast business empires all dined at Mark's Club.

Jack Armstrong from Wigan glowed inside. The room tingled with power and he was a part of it. Beneath the low hum of conversation he could sense matters of great significance under discussion.

'We at Shearman Drussel feel we could do a lot to help your bid along,' Dan was saying, 'without in any way treading on Hogarth Stein's toes. We have the utmost respect for Peter Markus.' Both his colleagues nodded along with Mary Ann Weinberger, a corporate lawyer from Texas.

'Our New York office could certainly help in interesting US investors in Butlers shares,' said Bobby.

'Or even selling Empire shares,' said Dan.

'Very interesting,' said Jack as the food arrived. 'Frankly, gentlemen – and lady – I think you're wasting your time and money on this occasion. We might do business in the future though. This won't be the last acquisition.'

Bobby smiled broadly, showing huge, even, American teeth. 'Exactly,' he said. 'You know it seems to me no one really understands the use of debt in this country. Look at what Drexel Burnham has been doing with junk bonds in the States. There's no reason why that shouldn't happen . . .' He broke off.

'Say, isn't that Sir Leo Stern?'

Stern was just entering the dining room, filling the doorway. Jack felt the force of his physical presence from the other end of the room. In the soft light, Stern looked demonic with his thick raven hair swept back, so long it almost touched his collar. His skin was glossy and tanned; his suit taut across massive shoulders.

His whole bearing spoke of a man for whom success was second nature. He and Paulette, who followed him – fragile and golden in white lace – went over and shook hands with one of the diners.

Stern moved away and his eyes locked with Jack's. He paused for a second, taking in the strangers at the table, then nodded and allowed the hovering waiter to guide him to his table.

'Do you know him?' asked Mary Ann, wide-eyed.

'Oh, only slightly,' said Jack. He felt as if someone had plugged him into the mains. 'We do a bit of business now and then.' But before they could question him further he turned back to Bobby.

'What was all this about using debt?'

Two mornings later he was heading for New York. He felt his mood lift the moment he entered the Concorde lounge at Heathrow. He instantly spotted Sir Hector Laing, Richard's great chum at United Biscuits (even though they were supposed to be deadly rivals), and Lord King, the British Airways chairman.

He waved at Sir Hector, helped himself to some coffee and buried himself in his *Financial Times* like everyone else.

'It's going to be awfully hot in New York, you know.' Jane Brompton was standing before him in a cool biscuit-coloured cotton suit.

His heart skipped a beat. 'What are you doing here?' he asked, beaming at her. 'Sit down.' He took his briefcase off the seat next to him

'The same as you, I expect, going to do business,' she replied, smiling back at him. 'I'm thinking of linking up with one of the New York firms of headhunters on a reciprocal basis.'

'Sounds good.' He paused awkwardly. 'Look, I know I should have phoned you, but you can imagine how hectic it's been.'

'Oh, don't worry,' she said airily. 'I've been incredibly busy myself. It's just amazing at the moment.' She sat down, crossing her immaculate legs.

'Actually, half the reason I'm going to New York is to get out of the office for a couple of days. The City market has been absolutely frantic – there just aren't enough good people to go round, or even mediocre people with experience come to that.'

'I've heard some of the salaries are pretty phenomenal.'

'Oh, quite barmy really.' Jane hit her head lightly with the side of her hand. 'I placed a twenty-two-year-old dealer, with three years experience, at £150,000 basic the other day. I don't see how they can justify it. But the competition is so fierce at the moment, with the American investment banks recruiting, no one seems to care.'

Jack noticed she gestured almost constantly with her hands. The long tapering fingers tipped with shiny vermilion nails stirred a memory.

'Anyway, what about you?' she asked. 'I can't open a newspaper for seeing your picture.'

Jack laughed and stretched his arm along the back of her chair, fingers just brushing her shoulder.

'Oh, come on, it's the hype that goes with the bid. I'm just a straightforward Lancastrian,' he said. 'But they tell me I have to do it.'

He could tell by her look that she was not fooled.

'How are your flying nerves?' he asked, remembering Hong Kong.

'Funnily enough, Concorde bothers me far less than those jumbos.' Her face lit up in a smile. 'And you've got to admit, it was a pretty hairy take-off.'

'Why, Jane, there you are. I thought you were going to miss the flight.'

An elegant young man with a shock of blond hair stood before them.

'No, I was just chatting to an old friend. Jim is one of my directors,' she said to Jack. 'He's travelling with me.'

Jack was just finishing his coffee after lunch and congratulating himself for not drinking on the flight when he saw the Greenbag's senior partner swaying down the aisle towards him, grinning broadly.

'I say, I've never had to come this far back in Concorde to talk to somebody I know,' he said. Too much champagne, thought Jack, but the remark irritated him. He had noted that everyone he knew was further forward than him – even Jane.

'I didn't see you in the lounge,' Jack said, resolving to do something about it on the return flight.

'I only just made it,' the man confessed. 'I'm going to see a

197

possible buyer for the firm.' He lurched forward, tapping the side of his nose. 'Very hush hush.'

'It won't be if you drink much more champagne,' he said crisply. He did not like the sound of it. Greenbag's had always been so proud of its independence. He read the notes Peter and David had prepared on what to say to the American institutions and arbitrageurs, then he gazed out of the window at the curve of the earth and thought of Jane Brompton's thighs.

At Kennedy she eluded him. The steam-bath heat of New York in July enveloped him, making him instantly sweaty. One of Jean-Pierre's limousines was waiting to whisk him off to his hotel. He looked around one last time and regretfully slid into the air-conditioned coolness of the car. He had not even asked where she was staying.

Peter had insisted Jack stay at the Pierre on Fifth Avenue instead of the Plaza which he loved. It was so near to Central Park he could go jogging before breakfasting at the huge oval coffee shop on the ground floor where he always saw some-body famous.

But Peter was adamant. 'My dear man, you are the chief executive of a group leading the biggest takeover in the food industry in Britain. It has to be the Pierre.' He had paused. 'Or the Carlyle, I suppose, but the Pierre's more your style – and it's just as close to Central Park as the Plaza.'

If this was his style, he thought looking around the cool marble lobby, he could live with it.

It was still mid-morning in New York and straight away he called Jean-Pierre who had arranged an 11.30 meeting and lunch at 12.30. Jack had forgotten how early everything hap-pened on the East Coast.

When he got back to the hotel after lunch, he found a message to ring Miss Brompton at the Plaza. He rang her immediately. 'How did you know I was here?'

'Where else would you be?' She laughed and invited him for a drink either before or after dinner. Naturally he opted for after. He would get some sleep now, he decided, collap-sing on to the vast bed.

He had arranged to pick Jane up at 10.30. As he was waiting in the bustling chandeliered lobby he spotted Max Schlosstein, also clearly waiting for someone. He was gazing at some overpriced swimwear in one of the shop windows at the main entrance.

Jack introduced himself. 'Jack Armstrong, Butlers Group.' The leathery features looked vague. 'We met in Hong Kong – and in the South of France with Sir Leo Stern.'

'Sure.' Schlosstein's face contorted into a smile and he stuck out a tiny hand. Jack noticed that the face of his Cartier watch attached to the solid gold bracelet was surrounded by a tiny row of inset diamonds.

'Of course I remember. It's just the different environment,' He paused. 'As a matter of fact, there'll be some news for you tomorrow.'

Jack felt a flutter of fear as he looked down at the man. 'Really?'

'Yeah. Klaus has sold his stake in Empire to Leo.' Jack stood, frozen to the spot. 'But couldn't they – I mean, isn't it possible they would get more if they stuck with it?'

Jack was desperate to avoid spelling out that Butlers would go higher in the bidding, but anxious to put the message across.

'Oh, that's the view I take,' said Schlosstein, showing a fine set of gold fillings. 'But it's horses for courses. Leo's given them a good whack above the market.' He winked broadly. 'He must really rate you.' For once Jack was stuck for words.

'Look, here's my date,' Schlosstein excused himself. 'You'll see tomorrow, it'll all be announced.'

A willowy blonde towered over Schlosstein, bending to let him kiss her. He took her arm and waddled out into the balmy night.

Jane appeared in a white strapless dress with a bolero jacket, preceded by a cloud of Diorella. 'Is something wrong?'

'I need to make a phone call. I'm sorry – can you wait here?'

'Of course.' She looked crestfallen.

He dialled Peter's home number. It was 3.30 in the morning in London. 'Yes,' said an abrupt voice.

'Peter – Jack. Sorry to – wake you.'

199

'You're not the first,' Peter said tartly. 'I suppose you've heard?'

'Von Gleichen has sold to Stern.'

'Yes. Leo rang me ten minutes ago from New York. It will be on the screen at 8.30.'

Jack wondered uneasily where Stern was staying. 'But can he do that?' he asked.

'Buy shares? Yes, of course.'

'No, at so much above the market price, I thought all shareholders had to be treated equally?'

'My dear boy, by us they do. But by each other it doesn't matter. Stern can pay double if he wants to.'

Jack put the phone down. He was learning. It took two brandy alexanders before he smiled again and Jane was beginning to wonder if she had lost her touch.

As if coming out of a dream Jack gradually became aware of her – the curve of her breasts held firm by her dress, her tiny ankles as she crossed her legs, the way she held his gaze with her clear green eyes a little longer than she needed to. He began to ache with desire.

They went to the bar at the Sherry Netherlands, just across the corner of Central Park from the Plaza. They talked and talked until it was past midnight and he judged too late to go dancing. They wouldn't get to bed before three, and not to sleep before four – and he had a 7 a.m. breakfast meeting.

After the sexual intensity of their last encounter he felt paralysed by shyness.

'I'd better be getting back,' he said reluctantly. 'I'll walk you over the road.' He could not tell whether she looked disappointed.

Outside the temperature was still in the mid-seventies. On the corner of the park, one lone pony and trap was left where in the day there were half a dozen.

A tense silence fell between them.

'Why don't we go for a stroll in Central Park?' Jane's voice was studiedly casual.

'I thought it was supposed to be dangerous,' said Jack. What was she playing at?

'Not this end,' she retorted scornfully. 'Anyway, where's your sense of adventure?'

200

She took his arm and as they walked he could feel her breast moving against him. The green smell of the park surrounded them and they stopped to look at the water. He could see another couple some way in front of them. 'You can't see how dirty it is at night,' said Jane. Almost in a trance he ran his hand over her bare back and began stroking her neck.

Slowly she turned towards him, her lips slack, eyes half closed. He ran his tongue inside her upper lip and they melted into each other. For a while they stood, pulling and pushing at each other's bodies.

'Can't we go back to the Plaza?'

'Too boring,' she said.

Wordlessly she took his hand and began leading him away from the path to where the larger shrubs were.

'What are we doing?'

She took off his jacket and laid it on the ground.

She moulded her body to his, fingers dancing over him. He gasped with pleasure.

'But . . .'

Her extraordinary eyes shone in the darkness.

'Pretend you're a rapist.' She guided his hand to the zip at the side of her dress – under it she was wearing absolutely nothing.

She took him hot and throbbing between cool hands, then engulfed him in her mouth. She stopped and turned her face up to him. 'Rape me.'

He pushed her down, pinning her shoulders to the ground, kissing her mouth. He felt her struggling under him, then suddenly she lay still and he licked his way down her quivering body, her neck, her breasts, her silky white stomach.

She writhed at his touch, gasping and murmuring his name, arching up to him. Then suddenly she turned over to kneel facing away from him.

'Now! Now, please,' she groaned. His self-control gave and he thrust between the round soft buttocks into the warm wetness, grasping at breasts slippery with sweat.

She pulled one hand down into her fur and he felt her shudder and groan, and then came the agonising sweet explosions of his own orgasm. They collapsed, panting on the ground.

201

Gradually the noises of New York at night impinged. A police siren wailed somewhere further up Fifth Avenue. There was the erratic sound of many horns of different key honking irritably against the dim roar of the traffic.

Then there was the sound of footsteps on the path below. 'So I said to her, why have we had kids if all you wanna do is woik?' drifted up to them in a strong Bronx accent.

They froze. The footsteps walked past and the voice faded. Jane started to giggle.

'Come on,' said Jack suddenly gripped with fear. Visions of sensational newspaper headlines flashed through his mind.

They emerged cautiously from the undergrowth, brushing each other down. They walked along companionably enough, trying to disguise the awkwardness they both felt, admiring the old-fashioned high rise buildings which dominated that end of the park.

The bright lights of the Plaza lobby seemed from another world. He saw her to the massive double lifts.

'Goodnight. I'll call you in London.'

She kissed his cheek and walked into the lift. The image of her face – half smiling and half rueful as the doors closed – stayed with him as he walked back to the Pierre, and followed him into his dreams.

The next morning passed in a whirlwind of activity. Jack was returning to London on the 1 p.m. Concorde and at the airport he just found time to buy Rosemary some diamond ear studs, the kind she had always wanted.

There was hardly anyone he recognised on the flight back, but he was gratified to be given a seat in row B, even though, in all the rush, he had forgotten to fix it.

Exhausted, he tried to sleep, but every time he closed his eyes he saw still frames of the night before. He could still feel her soft body writhing under him, smell her perfume, hear her urgent whispers. He had to see her again. He had to see her again soon.

Chapter 14

The Star Wars working committee sat round one end of the board room table, studying Empire's defence document.

'I have to give Stuart credit,' declared Peter. 'He hasn't done a bad job considering the ghastly state of that company. But you could drive a coach and horses through most of the points.' David nodded in agreement.

'First,' said Peter crisply, 'they fire their main guns at us for lack of experience overseas, and even cite one or two of Butler's past disasters.

'Well, that's true, of course,' said Edward cautiously.

'Yes, but they've hardly done a brilliant job themselves,' said Peter scathingly, 'and our so-called disasters were pretty tiny – and five years ago.'

'Exactly,' broke in Jack. 'The whole point is that if we succeed, we'll use the Empire middle management. They've plenty of experience but are desperately frustrated. We'll have to recruit one or two young hungry guys, though.'

'Great,' said David. 'We can say we intend to realise the potential of their senior and middle management in our response.'

'Exactly.'

Peter continued, 'Then they've gone for us on Monopolies grounds. Well, frankly, if the two companies do have over 40 per cent of the chocolate cookie market in this country, I'm sure we can sell part of it – there's no shortage of willing buyers.'

Everyone nodded. Peter already had two lined up.

'Then, of course, they've attacked our profit record,

which,' Peter glanced uneasily at Sir Richard, 'is mainly down to people who are no longer on the board.'

'I notice they've kept remarkably quiet about their own profit record,' said Jack, keen to deflect criticism of Sir Richard.

'Yes,' David chuckled, 'they've got a wonderful graph of sales shooting up then a very sotto voce black and white one of profits which have gone nowhere for four years.'

'I thought you said they would make a profit forecast for the current year, Peter?' said Jack.

'Yes, but they'll save it for later in the battle. They'll be running round like crazy trying to find everything bar the kitchen sink to throw in.'

'And then there's the regional argument,' pointed out the sales director. 'Wicked Butlers pushes up unemployment in the North.'

Jack grinned. 'Our generous contribution to the Conservative Party should help us there. I stepped it up to £50,000.'

'Shrewd move,' said David. 'However ridiculous these political arguments are, we have to fight them.'

Peter made a face. 'I suppose you're right, but it's so tedious.'

Sir Richard came to the rescue. 'We have, of course, got a Conservative MP on our board. He's the only non-executive Jack didn't boot off.'

'Brilliant,' said David. ' Why don't you, me and our MP form a working committee to address the political aspects of the bid?'

'Excellent idea,' said Peter, much relieved.

Jack cut in. 'Just a moment!' They all looked up at the sharpness in his tone. 'I hope I'll be able to put in my views as well. I do come from that part of the world, you know.'

'Yes, of course,' David agreed smoothly. 'But you can't do everything, Jack. Any moment now, you'll be making institutional presentations all day long.'

Jack's chin lifted and his face set. 'I'm aware of that, David,' he said in a tone which silenced everyone. 'But I need to know every detail of what's going on. Is that clear?'

Peter and David exchanged glances, recognising the symptoms. It was chief executive tremens.

In the first half of 1987 the British stockmarket soared by more than 40 per cent. And when the Tories won the election so decisively on 11 June, it continued heavenwards for five weeks until, on 16 July, the FT-SE index hit 2443.4.

Few realised it at the time but the market had peaked and would not touch that level again for more than two years – and then only fleetingly.

Big contested takeover bids fell out of favour overnight. Perhaps, people said over their City lunches, just perhaps, there might be something in the argument about predatory takeovers being bad for business, after all.

The Butlers share price began to drift down with the stockmarket – reducing the value of its bid for Empire. Every time Jack looked at the screen, he saw a red figure next to Butlers name, indicating a fall in the price. It made him feel sick.

But mysteriously the Empire share price was going the other way. Every day it put on a couple of pence and was now 20p above the value of the Butler's offer.

'It's Von Gleichen's sale to Leo that set this off,' raged Jack to Peter. 'You keep telling me Leo's on our side. Can't you control him?'

'I'm sure when we need him, he'll be there,' said Peter with a confidence he was far from feeling. Leo was being unusually tricky, even for him.

Charlie went into action. He approached two of the big institutions who had been tipped off about the bid and had a profitable slice of the action in Empire.

If they would pick up a few million Butlers shares now, Charlie promised, Greenbag's would buy them back at the same price if necessary. He fervently hoped it would not be necessary. As they began buying the Butlers price started to edge up again against a falling market.

'It just shows what a tremendous following Jack Armstrong has in the City,' said Peter to every journalist he spoke to. But neither he nor Charlie could discover who was doing the buying in Empire shares.

Charlie, Jack and Edward set off on their roadshow. Charlie acted as the warm-up man, introducing Jack and Edward and cracking a couple of jokes.

Jack talked the audience of fund managers through a sophisticated slide show giving a brief history of Butlers and the changes since he himself became chief executive. He took them through each business, highlighting the good performers, whisking over the bad ones.

Then came a vastly distorted chart of rising profits over three years, including another 30 per cent increase projected for the current year.

'Clearly, gentlemen, you realise that increase is what the analysts believe we will make,' Jack would say, po-faced. 'I don't want to get into trouble with the Takeover Panel for giving a profits forecast at this stage.'

He would then launch into a complete annihilation of Empire. Peter's team had gathered together every single unflattering comparison with Butlers it could.

At this point Edward would do his turn, pointing out the financial 'synergies' between the two companies. After Jack's northern aggression, Edward's dry self-effacing manner provided Southern credibility, although by this stage – particularly in the afternoons – some fund managers would be 'resting their eyelids', as Charlie put it.

The morning of the first presentation, Jack awoke with a sore throat. The following day it was worse and by the third day he had developed a streaming summer cold.

He pushed on, dosing himself with Coldrex and whisky. But, quite often, when Charlie or Edward were talking, he would get an uncontrollable fit of sneezing. Charlie began to suspect it was deliberate.

After all his fitness training, the cold made Jack feel the fates had turned against him, and the blank politeness of the fund managers depressed him even more. He sensed their condescension and hated them for it.

On the Wednesday night, when his symptoms were at their most ferocious, he decided to sleep late the following morning. He was still asleep when Peter rang at seven in the morning.

'Poor old Stuart,' chortled Peter. 'He must be absolutely fuming – Shearman Drussel of all people! That man Walt Bratvurst is supposed to have the biggest boot of all the American banks in London.'

'What the hell are you talking about, Peter?' Jack snapped. 'I've got a filthy cold and I've just woken up. Say that all again slowly.'

'Sorry, I thought you always got up at six,' said Peter unabashed. 'Empire – you know, the company you're bidding for – has appointed the American investment bank Shearman Drussel as joint advisor along with Marlow.'

'But isn't that a bad thing? Why are you so pleased?'

'Because, my dear man,' said Peter in his speaking-to-idiots voice, 'what the American banks know about British takeover bids you could write on my thumb nail. They even have this ridiculous idea that bid targets should play down their worth to deter the other side from going any higher.'

'Oh, really?' said Jack. 'Will it stop Empire shares going up?'

'Well, it might. Look, I only got hold of the news myself last night and I thought you ought to know as soon as poss.'

'Yes, of course. I'll ring you later.' Jack put the phone down, his eyes streaming, and reached for the tissues.

'Really!' exclaimed Peter to his empty flat. 'Sometimes you get no thanks at all for being on the ball.'

Stuart Anderson was absolutely fuming. 'But where is it that I'm supposed to have failed? The defence document was extremely well received.'

'Yes, of course it was, Stuart,' grovelled Bertie Underworth at the other end of the phone line. 'We feel you've done a splendid job. It's just – well – the non-executives felt another approach, as it were, might add to our fire power.' Bertie could feel little beads of perspiration running down his forehead. He hoped to God Stuart wasn't going to resign.

'It really wasn't my decision. I'm only the chairman and chief executive.'

The idea of resignation had indeed entered Stuart's head, but left it almost as quickly. Walking out in a fury would do no good, either to his personal reputation or that of the bank.

'We haven't formalised our fee arrangement yet, have we, Bertie?' he said instead. 'Er, no,' Bertie was relieved.

'Well,' Stuart's tone turned a shade warmer, 'as I understand our American brethren arrange things in advance, I think we should do the same.'

'Fine,' said Bertie weakly.

'We'd normally charge a straight £4 million for a defence like this, but as this is the first time we've acted for you and we hope to keep you as a client, we'll try and keep it down to £3 million. Does that sound about right?'

Bertie was blinking in disbelief. 'Well, I'll have to clear it with the board.'

'Of course. I'll let you have something in writing very soon.'

Stuart put the phone down feeling a lot better and dialled his mistress to tell her how clever he had been. He could, at least, make them pay for their stupidity.

By the summer of 1987, Stern Group was capitalised at £1.5 billion, making Stern's 46 per cent worth £690 million. On top of that his share portfolio had nearly doubled in value over the previous two years to around £400 million. Aside from these tranches of wealth there were the few million invested in pictures hanging in his house in St John's Wood and Beaulieu. In short, he was well past being a billionaire – and in sterling.

Jack Armstrong had committed the cardinal sin in Stern's book – he had snubbed him. The fact that Jack was no more a member of the establishment than he was made matters worse. Jack should have joined forces with him instead of rushing into the arms of Sir Richard Butler. He should at least have had a conversation.

Stern had set about teaching him a lesson, and so far it was going rather well. Jack and his advisers were clearly rattled by his stake in Empire, which since his purchase of von Gleichen's holding was now officially up to 7 per cent. Stern had made so much profit out of buying Empire shares, despite paying over the odds for von Gleichen's stake, that he knew in his heart he could call it quits with Jack. But it amused him to keep the game going a bit longer.

At the beginning Stern had expected a counter bidder to come along, but as yet there was no sign. He was also watching the unsteadiness of the Butlers' share price with some pleasure. He did not underestimate Greenbag's – they were his official broker after all – but sooner or later he knew he could count on a call from Charlie.

The third week in July the market got fit of the jitters. The Butlers' price plummeted, at first taking the Empire price with it. But then, once again, mysterious buying from Switzerland and America pushed the price up.

Stern's international intelligence network would normally have discovered who the buyers were within twenty-four hours. But whoever it was – or they were – had been too skilful even for him.

Charlie and Denis both failed to come up with the answer but agreed the size of the buying indicated a serious competitor. Peter began priming Jack to tell him that Butlers would now have to raise its offer, probably with a cash sweetener on top of the share swop.

Breakfasting on his terrace at Beaulieu the following Tuesday morning, Stern was ladling dollops of wild strawberry jam on to a croissant when the phone rang. It was day thirty of the bid.

'I think I've an idea who our buyer in Empire is, Leo,' muttered Denis Jones in his ear.

'Should a man with a delicate heart be up at six in the morning?' asked Leo, delighted to hear from him. There was an hour's time difference between England and France.

'Leave it out. You want to know or not?'

'Fire,' said Stern.

'It's an American outfit called Renasco.'

All Denis could hear was the sound of Stern taking another bite of croissant, so he carried on.

'I'm told they're going to make a bid when the market opens.'

'Which market?'

'Er – good point. Ours, I think. If they waited for Wall Street it would be two o clock and the price could run away – the rumour is all round the place.'

'Price?' The munching noises continued.

'The word is 400p in cash. That's 40p above Butlers' offer on last night's closing price.'

Stern chuckled. 'I like it.' His tone changed. 'You going to be about this afternoon?'

'Sure.'

'I think I'd better come back for this. I'll drop in this afternoon.'

'Hold on,' said Denis. 'It hasn't happened yet.'

Stern grinned as he looked over the terrace to the glittering Mediterranean below. 'Denis, old son, you are not my favourite broker for nothing. See you later.'

He put the phone down and gazed down at the Marina. Paulette lay sleeping upstairs, beautiful and untouchable. Sarah's face, her black eyes laughing, flashed into his mind. He had nearly asked Denis if she would be there too, but had thought better of it.

Sarah and Denis both arrived at their desks at 7.30 these mornings. With the market now opening at 8.30, it had become necessary. Sarah marvelled at Denis's recovery – on the surface it was almost as though the heart attack had never happened. The warning had partially served its purpose. At least he had given up cigars.

She was so used to working with him now that sometimes it was like being part of the same person. They communicated in a kind of verbal shorthand.

At eight o'clock on the dot the announcement came up on the screen. Renasco was bidding 400p in cash for Empire just as Denis had predicted.

'Good old Martin,' he muttered, reading the details carefully. The funding had been put together by Salomon Brothers in America and Morgan Grenfell in the UK.

Denis rang Stern, but he had already left for the airport.

'Leo's rubbing his hands,' Denis said. 'Let's see if they're buying in the market as well. Ring a few of your faces, will you?'

Sarah was already punching out a number. 'Hi, Keith, what do you think of the Renasco bid? Are they? What have you done? Anything else I can do for you?'

Five minutes later she and Denis had pieced together the picture. Renasco's brokers were bidding institutions heavily for stock at the new offer price. On the whole the fund managers were selling part of their holding, but hanging on to the majority in the hope that the bidding would go higher yet.

Jack was trying Peter for the third time when he came through on the private line.

'I'm on my way round,' he said, shooting the Aston through amber lights at London Wall and slowing to a halt in front of a lorry the other side, 'but the traffic is terrible.'

'I'll call a working committee meeting for ten.'

'And I'll ring Charlie.'

'You know it's my old firm,' said Jack.

'That's fantastic. You must have lots of inside info. See you.'

Jack reached for his first cigar of the day.

At ten, the key directors of Butlers, Peter and Charlie, gathered in the board room in St James's Square, a file of papers in front of each one.They hung their jackets on the backs of their chairs and helped themselves to coffee. Only Peter and Edward noticed the new picture behind Jack's chair.

'As I see it, Renasco has the advantage of cash in a wobbly market and the disadvantage of being foreign,' Peter said.

'I was under the impression you thought all this stuff about stopping foreigners from taking over British companies was bullshit.' Jack looked puzzled.

'Of course it's bullshit,' Peter agreed. 'That doesn't mean we can't use it to our advantage. But what I really mean is they don't understand how the London market works.'

'But they've got a British advisor,' chimed in Edward.

'From my experience, American clients always have a habit of thinking they know best,' said Charlie.

Jack, whose face was grey with tension and lack of sleep, suddenly brightened.

'That's right,' he said, the memories flooding back to him. 'The directors are completely bone headed about taking any advice that is different to what they are used to. When I was there they had a management manual for every division, and any fresh suggestion was like spitting in Church.' He grinned and reached for a biscuit.

It was exactly two hours and seven minutes after the announcement.

'So,' he felt fully in control now, 'when do we raise our offer?'

211

'Er,' Edward coughed politely, 'shouldn't we first assess whether it's in the interests of our shareholders . . .'

'Of course it's in their interests,' Jack retorted. Then he caught himself. 'Peter's done the sums. We can go a lot higher yet.'

'The problem is that unless we raise our offer sharpish we can't buy shares in the market, and they can,' said Charlie. 'What's more they are,' he added.

Peter had been lounging back in his chair, but now he put both hands on the table, pressing his fingertips together as he did when he was going to say something important.

'It really isn't a question of if, or even when, but how much,' he said in his most serious voice. 'Obviously we will now have to include a cash alternative to the share offer, and we need to decide whether this is going to be the final offer or just another shot. I suggest we all clear our diaries and reconvene at Hogarth Stein as soon as possible.'

Jack nodded agreement. 'Yes, let's do that. But I'd like to say now I think we should make this the final offer.'

Charlie and Peter exchanged glances but said nothing. The meeting broke up.

'I didn't know you were a soccer supporter,' remarked Peter in an amused tone as he was putting on his jacket. The picture on the wall behind Jack was an oil painting of a football match, a canvas of bright greens and blues, full of movement.

'That's my team,' said Jack proudly. 'Jim Hogan of Wingways introduced me to them. He's one of my best customers.' He stared fondly at the picture. 'And they've asked me to be chairman next year.'

'Dare I ask if Butlers is sponsoring them?'

Jack lounged against the door frame and treated Peter to a disarming smile.

'Yes, we are. But don't 'worry, it will all be disclosed in the annual report. I was thinking of reproducing that picture actually.'

Peter shuddered mentally. He'd seen the signs too often before.

'Mr Armstrong,' Amanda had appeared in the doorway, 'Bertie Underworth is on the phone.'

Everyone in the room froze in mid chatter.

'Peter, you stay with me,' said Jack. 'I'll see the rest of you at twelve.' They began to file out.

The atmosphere became instantly charged. Jack and Peter pulled their chairs round the phone, their differences forgotten. 'Put him through on the squawk box,' ordered Jack, referring to the loudspeaker attachment on the phone which allowed the whole room to hear the conversation.

He motioned to Peter to sit down. 'I'll talk, you listen.'

Amanda put the call through. 'Good morning, Bertie. Grand day don't you think?' began Jack, his voice heavy with irony.

'Wonderful,' said Bertie weakly, glancing anxiously at Stuart Anderson, seated in charcoal grey elegance on the opposite side of his desk.

'I – I wondered if you would like to come round and see Stuart and me for a cup of coffee?'

Jack raised his eyebrows at Peter. He nodded.

'Only too pleased,' said Jack, grinning as he locked eyes with Peter. 'Shall we say 11.30?'

Sarah got back to the office from lunch with one of her favourite clients in bubbly mood to find Stern sitting at her desk.

'I hope you've sold a lot of shares for me,' she teased, her stomach turning liquid.

'I'm still in a buying mode,' he said unsmilingly. 'I'm told Underworth and Armstrong met for talks this morning,'

'Oh, really?' said Sarah. He was making her feel she was dragging her heels in the information flow.

'Any announcement?' She stood uncertainly by the desk.

He was looking at the screen. 'Nah. I reckon Underworth would prefer Butlers to the American, though. Probably trying to stitch up an agreed deal.'

Sarah recovered her poise. 'Mm, they'll have to go a lot higher though – and offer a cash alternative.'

'Which is good news for major shareholders like me,' Stern said 'How about having dinner with me tonight?' He was still looking at the screen, expressionless.

'I'll just check if I'm free,' she said automatically. She

grabbed the thick red *Economist* diary an inch from his elbow. She was supposed to be having dinner with an old college friend but he could wait. 'Yes, that seems fine.' Her voice seemed to be coming from a great distance.

'Great. I'll pick you up at eight.' He stood up to go, moving towards her like a field force. For an instant she thought he was going to kiss her.

'You'd better give me your address.'

'Sure, I've just had some cards printed.' She fished in her handbag and handed him one with a brittle smile.

'See you later,' he said, and was gone.

She could hear her heart knocking against her chest as she put the diary back in its rightful place. What the hell was she going to wear?

He probably just had some time to kill, she told herself as she laid out her favourite white lace underwear. His reputation was as a strong family man in the best Jewish tradition. And he had a beautiful wife, she thought as she lay in the bath. He probably saw this as a little treat for her efficiency over the past year. She must not read too much into it.

But as she threw the third outfit despairingly on to the bed, her mind kept returning to that moment when he had kissed her. It had been just a spontaneous, never to be repeated gesture, she told herself.

She pressed the dress she finally selected, cleaned her shoes, plucked her eyebrows, sprayed herself with Shalimar and spent a full half hour putting on makeup that normally took ten minutes.

At five to eight she was ready. She slipped a compact disc of Mozart's clarinet concerto into the player, sank into her favourite armchair and tried to relax.

The telephone at her side rang. She looked at it as if it were on fire and waited for three rings before picking it up. 'I'm in the car,' Stern growled, 'how exactly do I find this place?'

Peter and Jack decided to treat themselves to dinner at Mark's Club.

'You boys will be all right while we're gone, won't you?' said Peter to his team. 'We'll see you before midnight.'

In Charles Street, the doorman outside nodded good evening as Peter rang the bell.

Inside it was half empty. 'It's summer and it's early,' said Peter, settling into his seat and giving the room the once over for well-known faces.

'Two kir royales,' he said to the waiter, without consulting Jack. 'God, that was a tedious meeting with Underworth. I can't believe Stuart thought we would go anywhere near that price.'

'I suppose they thought it was worth a try. They clearly don't fancy singing the Stars and Stripes every morning,' Jack said.

'Anyway, we should have our new offer out by seven-thirty tomorrow and then we can wade into the market and buy as much as we can. I'm sure Charlie will get hold of some of institutions at home tonight.'

'I still think we should have made it final. No bloody idiot is going to accept if they think we can go higher – Mr Big in particular.'

'Well, you're right up to a point. But as I hope I've explained, it's too early to box ourselves into a corner. Renasco's bid could run to the fourteenth of October.'

'Excuse me, Mr Armstrong,' said the waiter, serving the drinks, 'but you're wanted on the phone.'

Jack groaned and took a large gulp before going to answer it. It was Jane. 'How did you know I was here?'

She laughed. 'Haven't you guessed that I'm really a detective? The headhunter bit is just a front.'

'Look, things have been incredibly busy,' said Jack. 'But if you wanted to come here in an hour, we could go dancing at Annabel's later.'

Sarah acted as though everything was normal. She appeared not to react as Stern slowly and deliberately put his arm around her shoulders as they walked along the street to Frederick's in Camden Passage. And she managed to keep still when he laid his hand on her arm to make a point. But each time it set off electric shock waves throughout her whole body. They talked business throughout, and she tried to keep her expression equally business-like.

But he made her laugh. He had a wicked way of describing his fellow businessmen, demolishing them with viciously funny one liners, or telling hilarious anecdotes about drawn out negotiations, from which he inevitably emerged victorious.

She liked the airy atmosphere of Frederick's and the friendly service. Stern noticed her begin to relax, helped by the bottle of Château Latour he'd ordered. Her eyes shone, her skin glowed and her mouth looked warm and inviting.

They walked slowly back to his Bentley from the restaurant, enjoying the warm summer night around them. When he did not touch her, the disappointment was almost unbearable.

In the car, the conversation suddenly seemed stilted.

He stopped outside her flat and turned off the engine.

Sarah had decided not to invite him in. It seemed presumptuous. How could she Sarah Meyer, invite Sir Leo Stern into her flat for coffee? Yet somehow it seemed churlish just to jump out of the car and leave him there.

'Well, thank you for a very pleasant evening,' she said into the silence.

Slowly, calmly, as though it was the most natural thing in the world, he leant over and kissed her softly on the mouth. She felt her lips give way against the gentle pressure, and as his tongue tentatively explored the inside of her lips, every nerve ending in her body ignited. His hand moved to her breast and some distant voice, far away in the back of her brain, urged her to protest; but she knew it would be a pretence, a mockery – because her body was telling her she was utterly and irretrievably lost.

He pulled away for a moment, his eyes black. 'Let's go inside.' She led him straight to the bedroom then stood uncertain by the bed, waiting for him to make the first move. He pushed her down gently, his lips glued to hers, his fingers probing between her legs. When he entered her she felt she need never ask for anything again. For a moment, she caught sight of his face. It was contorted with lust, eyes blazing, lips furled in a grimace as he thrust inside her.

It was a face she would die for. She cried out his name, her body shaking and juddering, willing him never to stop.

Afterwards Stern held her hard against him as she shook with sobs. Only twice before in his long marriage had he been unfaithful, and both times he had sworn never again. He had found it impossible to remain emotionally detached. He envied friends of his who took mistresses the way they acquired new cars.

But once again his subconscious mind had sprung a trap and he had walked right into it. He told himself he would stop now. It wasn't sensible; it wasn't practical; he would end up hurting Sarah. He could never leave Paulette.

As she gradually became inert in his arms, her curls dark against his chest, he made a resolution not to see her again. And as he made it, he knew it was a resolution he would break.

Annabel's was pleasantly crowded with the usual assortment of pre-midnight faces, but Jack managed to get a table reasonably near the dance floor.

He waved to a couple of people as he and Jane came through the bar. He wasn't worried about being seen with her. Few men took their wives to Annabel's and no one would ring up Rosemary and tell her. It was an unspoken convention. In any case, Peter was coming down later with the completed announcement of the new offer. It could easily be a business meeting.

He ordered a bottle of Dom Perignon and settled back in his chair. 'It's hard work, all this high finance,' he said, flashing her his most heart-melting smile. He was delighted to see her.

'What's been happening?'

'Well, we've decided to up our share offer to 435p, which is 35p higher than Renasco at tonight's closing prices. We've also put in a cash alternative of 10p lower.'

'So will you win?' asked Jane, as the champagne arrived.

'Who bloody well knows? Their offer is cash, of course, but up to now the institutions have preferred paper. Anyway, we've left our options open. The problem is that now another bidder has come in, the sixty-day timetable starts from scratch.'

'And can they go higher again too?'

217

'Oh, sure,' said Jack.

'It's quite complicated, isn't it?' said Jane, frowning.

'Frankly, it's bloody terrifying. You really have to trust your advisers.' He picked up his glass and raised it to her. 'It's great to see you.'

'Should you be telling me all this?' She asked sipping at her champagne.

'Oh, there's no problem. The market's closed and we're announcing it first thing.'

'I could tip people off overseas.'

'New York's closed and they don't make a market in Tokyo in either Butlers or Empire.' He laughed at her. 'I think I'm safe.'

Jane looked as glamorous as ever, but her face had a strained look under her make-up.

'So am I forgiven for not returning your calls?' he asked.

'Of course.' Her voice was brittle. 'I should have realised how busy you were.'

Jack drained his glass and Frank Sinatra's voice suddenly enveloped them singing 'New York, New York'.

'Come and dance,' he said, feeling a wave of energy sweep over him.

'If I can make it there, I'll make it anywhere', sang Sinatra. They whirled round easily with everyone else, smiling and gazing into each other's eyes.

Their bodies came together as the music slowed down. 'I've missed you,' Jack said softly.

Jane pulled away from him, eyes flashing. 'Rubbish, Jack! What you mean is, now I'm here, you can't wait to get me into bed.'

Peter's arrival with a bespectacled member of his team and a female lawyer let Jack off the hook. He read the press release on his lap and OK'd it. Peter despatched his young man back to the bank.

'What does one have to do to get a drink around here?' he demanded. Glasses were fetched and suddenly the table became a stopping post. The extent of Peter's range of contacts never failed to amaze Jack.

'Good God,' exclaimed Peter with evident satisfaction, during a lull, 'at least half my clients are here.'

218

Jack decided Peter could buy his own champagne from now on.

'I'm going to get some sleep,' he said. 'You don't need me first thing, do you?'

Peter twinkled. 'Seven-thirty, you mean! No – Charlie and I can manage without you.' He glanced languidly at his watch. 'It hardly seems worth going to bed.'

The moment Jane and Jack got inside the flat, he pinned her against the wall, kissing her long and hard.

'You know what I was thinking while we were dancing?' he said.

'No.' Her eyes were half closed, her hand brushing against the hard bulge in his trousers.

'That we could very easily do it standing up.'

She started to stroke him, feeling her power.

'What a coincidence,' she whispered.

Sarah spent the weekend in a state of intense, unsatisfied longing. The image of Stern and their lovemaking floated before her like an endlessly playing movie in her head. She craved him like a drug. She wanted to touch him, smell him, talk to him.

She hardly knew the man. He hardly knew her. Yet she could think of nothing but him. She wanted to cook dinner for him, hear about his childhood, his marriage, his hopes, his fears. She wondered if a man like Stern had any fears.

She remembered how she had first loathed him, then liked him when Denis had been ill, then hated him again. But looking back, she saw that her feelings had been steeped in intensity from the moment they met. She could recall every word of their simplest telephone conversations.

She pottered around her flat, supposedly tidying up, putting things down and instantly forgetting where they were. On the Saturday, she lost her keys three times. She spent all afternoon trying to pinpoint exactly when she had fallen in love with him. The scene in the mountains haunted her. It must have been the skiing incident.

On Saturday night she took herself off to the cinema with a girlfriend in an attempt to stop the obsession.

Sunday morning brought with it a feeling of exultation. The

world shone in the sunshine, demanding she clean the windows – clean the entire flat. As she moved from room to room she danced to the raw thump of Bruce Springsteen, laughing at how demented she must seem to anyone walking past her neat bay window. But she felt truly alive for the first time in months.

Occasionally a thought like a dark shadow would darken her face. He was married. He was happily married, in fact. The whole world knew he was devoted to Paulette. But the force of her emotion swept the shadow away. Loving someone the way she loved him was worth some pain.

By lunchtime the world had turned bleak. The sky had clouded over and her flat felt grey and terribly quiet. She rang a couple of girlfriends but heard only breezy messages on answering machines. She almost rang her mother but recoiled at the thought of her probing, concerned questions. Nothing on the television appealed as she sat, flicking channels. A hot wave of longing for him swept over her and she pressed a hand between her legs to ease the ache. She could not even fall back on Simon. He had finally given up and started taking out one of the secretaries.

Chapter 15

The City of London sleeps in August. The big players vanish to the South of France or Marbella; their stockbrokers and merchant bankers retreat to farms in Gloucestershire or sailing boats in Cowes. Dealing desks are manned by juniors. Merchant banks drift on directorless.

In newspaper offices, deputy editors struggle to fill acres of white space and, in the absence of hard news, bully skeleton staffs into producing worthy articles on long-term trends or quoted soccer clubs.

Launching a bid or trying to raise money in August is the preserve of the eccentric. Stockmarket volume tumbles while the traffic in the tangle of narrow roads which make up the Square Mile flows strangely freely. The Savoy Hotel alternately shuts the River Restaurant and the Grill for two weeks each for a thorough facelift, and there is no need to book a table for lunch at Corney & Barrow in Moorgate.

The only social events of the British season take place around the Isle of Wight or in Scotland. Boredom spreads like a miasma, followed by desperate invention. If there is no news, business must still go on; therefore news must be made up.

Hence, August is a time of crazy rumours and occasional wild volatility in the market as inexperienced dealers over-react. Existing takeover battles such as Butlers/Empire/Renasco are gnawed at from every angle, buried and dug up. Gossip spreads like couch grass in an English garden.

'Shearman Drussel flew forty-five people over from New

York to defend Empire, and apparently they haven't come up with one original idea,' said Sarah to Simon over a drink in the Pavillion one muggy evening.

'I know,' he replied. 'All it's done is allow Marlow to treble its fee in line with Shearman.'

From their table by the window Sarah looked out over the bowling green to the bandstand in the centre of Finsbury Circus, and sighed. 'God, I'll be glad when September comes and things get back to normal.'

In the third week of August, Jack joined Rosemary and Mark on the Island of Elba off the Mediterranean coast of Italy. It was not Jack's first choice – he would have preferred either walking in Yorkshire or touring America. But Rosemary, who had done two years of Italian at evening classes, had rented an apartment just above Marciana Marina on the north side of the island and presented it to him as a fait accompli.

The second evening they had dinner at a small restaurant just off the main square of Marciana Marina, a small orange-roofed village. Afterwards they walked, arms linked, along the sea, glancing idly in the crammed shops selling clothes and souvenirs.

'I haven't seen you this relaxed for ages,' Rosemary said as they sat at a table outside a bar for some coffee.

He heard the reproach in her voice and smiled ruefully. 'I only do it for you, you know,' he said, his voice suddenly husky.

Rosemary shook her head. 'Don't kid yourself, Jack.' But she smiled too.

'Dad, Dad, phonecall.' Mark's voice penetrated a thick black sleep. Jack took the receiver, glancing at his watch. It was seven-thirty.

'Sorry to wake you this early, but I wanted to get you before you go off to the beach.' It was Charlie.

Jack resisted pointing out that no one sane goes to the beach before ten. 'Any news on the Monopolies Commission?'

'Yup. They've cleared us. It will be on the screen first thing.'

'Well, that's fantastic. Just shows what having an MP on the board can do.' Jack laughed. 'You can call me this time tomorrow if you like.'

'There is something else though,' said Charlie. 'We thought you ought to know that something strange has been happening to the Butlers share price.'

Jack's brain snapped into focus.

'How do you mean?'

'Well, the last two afternoons there's been a wave of selling – we think it's probably from the States because of the timing. The first day it happened we were taken by surprise and the price closed 20p down. Yesterday, we were ready and went in with some hefty buying – so we closed unchanged.'

Rosemary flung herself out of bed and stalked out of the room.

'But who would be selling?'

'Someone who wanted the price down,' Charlie said patiently.

'You mean, to make our offer worth less.'

'You got it sir.'

'Well, can't we do something?'

'All we can do here is to complain strenuously to the Takeover Panel. Peter's doing that first thing. We wondered if your friend Jean-Pierre might put a few feelers out? Obviously we suspect Renasco. If he could pin point the broker doing the selling from the States, it might help.'

'Right, but I can't ring him before twelve your time.'

'Fantastic,' said Charlie, 'talk to you later.'

Half an hour later Peter rang, followed by Edward.

Rosemary sighed angrily as she walked down the hill to get some fresh rolls for breakfast. 'Just as he was beginning to unwind,' she muttered to the pine trees.

Stern's irregular phone calls became the focus of Sarah's life. She thanked God for work, but cursed the fact it was August and business was half its normal level. She tried to occupy herself by analysing the portfolios of her major clients and drawing up a list of suggestions for when they returned in September.

But the work lacked urgency. She could afford to

daydream, reliving the first night with Stern like a movie on a video.

She indulged in long conversations with him in her head – where she told him of her true feelings, her fantasies, her horrors. The internal dialogue continued whether she was walking down the street, in bed at night, when she awoke in the morning.

But when he finally made contact, their real conversations were completely different from those of her imagination. Instead of lasting hours, they were short, often focused on work, leaving her wondering if she had imagined the whole thing. Could this man rapping out orders to her really be the same one who buried his face in her breasts?

Towards the end of August, during a brief call on a Friday, he promised to phone over the weekend.

Inexplicably, every single one of her friends rang her to catch up with the news. And every single one she cut off short, anxious to keep the line free. Every time the phone rang, she let it ring three times so he would not feel she was waiting desperately for his call. On the Saturday night, she forced herself to go out with a girlfriend, leaving her answering machine on. I can't stay in all weekend just for him, she told herself firmly.

But there were no messages when she got back. Sunday dragged by. Finally, when she was pretending to watch the evening news on the television, he rang.

She was so pleased to hear from him she could think of nothing intelligent to say. He did all the talking. He would be back on 2 September and could he take her to dinner one evening that week? He missed her.

That night she slept soundly for the first time since he had gone away. The promise of his return filled her with energy. In the office she became a whirlwind of efficiency, completing all the projects she had started, chasing up clients and flirting with Simon.

When Denis returned from three weeks' holiday in Marbella he seemed almost downcast to see how smoothly everything was going. 'Well, girl, you got it so under control, you don't really need me,' he said, only half joking. But despite the break, Sarah thought he didn't look that well – and he was putting on weight again.

224

Peter and Angela spent five days as guests of one of Peter's American clients in the Hamptons in Long Island. Every day brought new diversions: a barbecue by the pool; a steel band; a trip in a speedboat. And each night a new selection of celebrities flew in. On the last night Jean-Pierre Kransdorf arrived.

'It's that poof friend of Armstrong's I've told you about,' hissed Peter over his whisky sour just after they were introduced.

Angela was intrigued. What irritated Peter so much? At dinner she found herself placed next to Jean-Pierre and was struck by his Caribbean blue eyes and the hint of a French accent underneath the cultivated New York pronunciation. 'What is that accent?' she asked.

'My mother was from Montreal,' he explained, flattered by her observation. Not many people noticed.

He was clever, witty and charming. No wonder Peter loathed him – they were too similar.

'What I really don't understand,' Jean-Pierre said across the dinner table, dipping his soft-shelled crab in some salt, 'is why you haven't put Kroll on to Renasco?'

'Because we don't believe in fighting takeover battles with muck,' retorted Peter.

'Who's Kroll?' asked Angela.

'An extremely unpleasant financial detective agency,' snapped Peter.

'But you won't enquire too closely how I found out that a Swiss group were partly behind the shorting of Butlers shares?' said Jean-Pierre.

For once Peter was lost for words.

'Well,' Jean-Pierre continued, 'I bet someone is giving all the Butlers board the once over.'

'Then I expect your friends at Kroll are already engaged.'

'No way.' Jean-Pierre sipped at his champagne. 'Renasco are too tight and too WASP. They'll employ someone with a softer image. A firm which calls itself "consultant" rather than "private eye".'

Angela was rivetted. 'Are you really suggesting Butlers employ private detectives to try and dig up something incriminating on Renasco's directors?'

225

Jean-Pierre grinned, showing a perfect pearly row of capped teeth. 'Sure!' The last hapless crab disappeared between them.

'Don't look so shocked, darling,' said Peter loudly, his eyes glittering. 'It's all part of the great American way.'

Back in London, Peter had his office swept for bugs and told Edward Williams to do the same at Butlers. Whatever he thought of such tactics, there was no doubt they existed and one couldn't be too careful.

He was becoming increasingly irritated with the Takeover Panel who seemed disinclined to take any action over the tactical selling of Butlers shares nearly every afternoon. To be fair the Panel investigated the matter but reported back to him that they had 'received assurances that neither Renasco nor its advisers were behind the selling'.

What infuriated Peter was that the Panel seemed more inclined to pay attention to Renasco's accusations that the Butlers share price was being supported illegally.

He outlined the problems one afternoon at Hogarth Stein's regular four o'clock work in progress meeting, where all the corporate finance teams met to go over their deals. Listening to him, John Young reflected that Peter was reaping the results of his previous arrogance with the Panel.

'I suppose, he said,' those young tigers round there want to show the Americans that there is no bias against them in the London market.'

Peter snorted. 'There seems to be a positive bias *towards* them. It's absolutely ridiculous. Just because Jack Armstrong has attracted the support of some of the bigger institutions does not mean we are operating a concert party.'

'I appreciate that, Peter,' John Young said evenly, 'but I wonder if it might be better to try and work *with* the Takeover Panel occasionally, rather than engaging in head on confrontation the whole time?'

'Oh, they're a bunch of moaning minnies,' said Peter dismissively.

'Well, let's get on with the next transaction on the list.' John Young knew it was pointless to argue. Peter was the largest fee earner in the bank. It was just a pity he was such a prima donna.

226

He turned and smiled fondly at a blond young man a couple of years younger than Peter who hated him because his family owned tracts of land in Wiltshire. 'James! Have you found a buyer for Portland's property arm or have you decided to float it?'

David Bang returned from two weeks in the Algarve on the morning of 2 September – and he counted himself lucky to have had that much time off in the middle of a bid. As the plane dipped beneath the cloud above Heathrow, his heart lifted as drizzle spattered the windows. Good old England, he thought. He was sick of cloudless blue skies.

When he arrived at his office just before nine he was appalled to find his secretary, Penelope, manning the switchboard. 'Why isn't there a girl?' he demanded.

'There was one booked for eight-thirty but she hasn't turned up yet.'

'Well, please get one of the other girls to do it and get me some coffee. I need to talk to you.'

'No one else is in yet,' said Penelope calmly. She flicked a switch. 'David Bang Associates – just one moment, please, I'll check.' She looked up at him. 'It's Peter Markus. Shall I put him through to your office?'

'Fine,' he said, struggling out of his rain coat as he disappeared from reception, inwardly cursing Peter. As he went out one way, a tousled blonde girl appeared from outside. 'I'm sorry I'm late, I had a terrible time finding it,' she said in pure Sloane.

'Everyone does,' said Penelope grimly. 'I hope you can work a switchboard.'

Peter pitched straight in. 'David, we've got to get this press trip round the Butlers divisions motoring. Our young hero is getting restless.'

'Yes, I've been thinking about that while I was away. I'll whizz the proposals round on a bike if you like.'

'A fax would be faster,'

'Ok, but I'll send a bike as well – I hate those flimsy bits of paper.'

'Did we find anywhere feasible abroad? I don't think we can justify Hong Kong.'

'Well, there is the Swiss choccy business – it's only got a distribution agreement with Butlers but I think it will do. A quick flight to Zurich, lunch by the lake – or we could make it dinner and fly them back in the morning?'

'Sounds good,' trilled Peter. 'Can you send a copy to Jack as well? I'll talk to him about it and get back to you this afternoon.'

'Will do.' David put the handpiece down just as Penelope arrived with the coffee.

'Great,' he exclaimed. 'Get me Jack Armstrong, will you?'

By mid-morning a draft itinerary of a trip for financial journalists was on the desks of both Peter and Jack. And after a long telephone chat, Jack was clear most of it was David's idea.

The visit started with an early shuttle to Edinburgh from where a helicopter would take them to the original biscuit factory in Yorkshire and the Huntingdon sweet plant near Chester (to flatter Jack); lunch would be at the showpiece new recipe dish operation in the Midlands and then off to Bonard in Zurich to see how the Swiss make chocolate.

By that time everyone would be shattered. They would be whisked to the hotel, given time to have a bath and file their stories, and then treated to the best dinner Zurich could provide.

It was vital the journalists were given a real story – even though it was bound to upset the Panel. The combination of a genuine scoop with living like kings for a day should win them over to the Butlers side for the duration of the bid.

Patrick Peabody was gloomily deliberating on whether to use the article on the Condratiev Wave Theory or a freelance contribution entitled 'The cycles in the pepper market: the link with volcanic activity', when David's call came through.

'David, how are you? Thank God you're back. It's been appallingly dull without you.' Patrick had only been in the office a week himself, but it had seemed like a month. The previous Sunday he had been reduced to leading the City section on a broker forecasting the end of the eight-year

Thatcher bull market. The story had looked sensational enough – but he knew very well it was a cop out.

Someone's opinion did not constitute a scoop in his book. It was a *Sunday Times*-type story he had thought gloomily as he took the front page up to the editor on the Saturday afternoon.

'I wondered if you were free for lunch tomorrow?' David said.

Harry's Bar was quieter than usual, but the air of exclusive intimacy remained intact.

As he arrived, Patrick saw Michael Caine move away from David's table. 'It's my girlfriend,' said David by way of explanation. 'She's a showbiz agent, you know'.

They drank Bellinis and ordered tagliatelle alle cozze and veal with lemon.

'The point is, you are the Sunday paper that has followed Butlers most closely.'

'And most positively,' pointed out Patrick with a half smile.

'Yes, so it makes sense for you to come on the trip. We're going to pack a lot in – honestly, it will be quite a laugh.'

'Will Jack Armstrong be there?'

David looked abashed. 'It hasn't been decided yet.'

Patrick tossed back his black forelock and looked up from his tagliatelle. 'I'd settle for no Armstrong on the trip and a cosy exclusive chat the day after.'

'It's a deal. But you will come on the trip?' David sensed a get out.

'I'll even be on time for the plane. Who's that pretty girl lunching with Lord King?'

'His daughter,' replied David without looking up, 'and she's married to one of your rivals.'

Less than half a mile away in the green and gilt formality of the Connaught Grill, Peter was building up to broaching a difficult subject.

That morning his least favourite official at the Takeover Panel had virtually accused Butlers of bribing Unicom, its largest cocoa supplier, to support the share price.

He sipped his Chablis. 'By the way, Jack,' he began

229

carefully, 'did you know that Unicom had got nearly 2 per cent of your shares?'

An expression of childlike pleasure crossed Jack's face. 'Oh, have they? I am glad – I told them we could do with a bit of help.'

'Mmm. You didn't offer them any kind of deal, I hope?'

Jack frowned. 'Only the sort of thing you boys do every day.'

An alarm bell began ringing in Peter's head. 'Like what?'

' I just said we'd make sure they didn't lose out.'

'Anything else?'

Jack changed position and folded his arms. 'Well, I did mention that I thought our margins on cocoa could probably come down a bit.'

'You mean you offered to raise the price you pay for their cocoa?' There was no disguising the shrill note in Peter's voice.

Jack tilted his head back. 'Look, as I said, it's the kind of thing you and Charlie do all the time. I was having dinner with old Cantelli the other night and told him about the problem with the American selling every afternoon. He seemed only too pleased. . .'

'He's an old Mafiosi rogue,' cut in Peter. 'Well, it seems he's been boasting to the world and his wife that he's done a deal with you. I had the most uncomfortable conversation with the Panel this morning. At the very least you could have told me.'

'But you and Charlie . . .'

Peter cut in, softly furious, 'Charlie and I know what we're doing, and who we're dealing with. We are City professionals. You are a principal.'

Jack's eyes glittered green. His mouth was a straight line. 'How serious is it?'

Peter rammed his palms into his eye sockets, suddenly weary.

When he looked up he noticed the elegant frame of Stuart Anderson draped on a chair at the opposite side of the room. Behind the hooded eyes he could swear he spotted a glint of amusement. He must have arrived while he and Jack were talking.

230

Peter attempted to look normal. 'I have a very unpleasant feeling this could go to a full Panel hearing.'

Jack had no idea what that meant, but it sounded nasty.

'Is there anything in writing on any of this?' Peter asked.

Jack shook his head.

'Well, that's a relief. Let's have some coffee and then go through it in detail in your office.'

At six o'clock that evening Sarah was frantically searching for the fruit salad dish. She was beginning to think she had lost it in the move when she suddenly noticed her favourite pot plant standing in it.

What would her colleagues say if they could see her now? She had developed the reputation of being a dragon since she began working for Denis. As far as she was concerned it stopped people wasting her time – she got results, that was the main thing.

Her confident business persona seemed a million miles away as she watched Stern devour the meal she had put together. It was the first time they had met since dinner at Frederick's three weeks before.

He did not embrace her when he arrived. But just as she was disappearing into the kitchen to put out the smoked salmon, he caught her hand and pulled her back. She found herself looking up into his eyes. I've missed you, he said, and lightly kissed her mouth.

Later he undressed her slowly and stroked her body for what seemed like hours before they made love. She wanted him never to stop.

Later still they drank coffee and ate amaretti. 'Who do you think will win at Empire?' she asked idly as he caressed her breasts with crumby fingers.

'Whichever one gives me the best deal.'

Fear licked at her intestines. 'I hope you're joking?' she said. 'They really have tightened up on the regulations, you know.'

'Yeah, I do know.' There was a moment's silence. 'But it will be fun seeing what they come up with.'

The next morning Bertie Underworth and the head of

Renasco, John S. Ward III, both received calls from Stern Corporation, requesting meetings on behalf of Sir Leo Stern. Eagerly they both cleared their diaries.

Mr Ward would be delighted to dine with Sir Leo at Claridge's where he was staying for a few days. Bertie, anxious not to seem too keen, proposed tea.

In David Bang's office the red telephone, of which only four people had the number, shrilled it's high-pitched tune.

'Hi.'

The voice at the other end muttered a few brief instructions.

'Fine.' David put the receiver down and carried on dictating a letter to Penelope.

At the end he dismissed her. 'That's all for now,' he said, glancing at his Rolex. They had only done three out of the mountain of letters but Penelope had learned long ago not to query his instructions. He could have a vile temper.

David thumbed through his contacts book. It was five past four – an ideal time to plant stories.

STERN AND RENASCO IN EMPIRE TALKS shrieked the headline in the *Daily Telegraph* the next morning.

For the first time since the bid had started, Jack felt real panic. He had been woken by David, informing him of the story. Peter and Charlie had come on soon after, and by nine o'clock the Empire share price was flying.

'Leo's a bugger,' said Peter, 'but I think this time you're going to have to pander to his ego and ask to see him.'

Two hours later, Peter and Jack were seated in Stern's office. He was at his most charming, talking of everything but the matter uppermost in their thoughts.

'Now,' he said firmly, after providing them with coffee and home baked biscuits, 'I thought you might like to see Stern Group's video.'

Jack half choked.

Mercifully, the Stern Group video crammed fifteen years of impressive growth into ten minutes, and Leo had very sensibly kept out of it. But to Jack it seemed like a lifetime.

When it was over Stern pulled back the curtains, letting bright sunlight stream in, so he was for a moment to their blinking eyes, a menacing bulky silhouette.

'You won't win, you know,' he said softly, 'not without my shares.'

Peter put a restraining hand on Jack's arm.

'It's impossible to say that at this stage, Leo, as you well know.'

'Renasco want me to sell them my shares now.'

'Just what is your holding at the moment?' Peter was curious to get the accurate figure.

'The von Gleichen stake took me up to 8.4 per cent.'

'And your friend Schlosstein still has his 3 per cent.'

'Yup,' said Stern. 'I hope you're not suggesting that we might act in concert?'

'Of course not, Leo,' Peter said evenly.

Stern sat down on the armchair opposite and leaned forward confidentially.

'I'm told you have a very interesting new chocolate product in the pipeline.'

Jack smiled grimly. So that was it. 'So?'

'It will be launched in the autumn, and you have an exclusive marketing agreement with a major retail competitor of mine for the first six months. Right?'

'Right.'

'Scrap it.'

Jack couldn't believe his ears. 'Don't be bloody ridiculous. What's it to you anyway? Sandpiper only has a hundred outlets.'

Stern's eyes had turned to onyx. He spoke very slowly.

'I would like you to scrap the exclusive marketing agreement with Wingways – that's who it is, isn't it?'

Jack nodded. How the hell had he found out?

'And then I might think about accepting the Butlers offer.'

Jack protested. 'But Jim Hogan's banking on this. Their shares had a terrible pasting since that outbreak of botulism in their own label yoghurt. They're only just beginning to recover.'

'Exactly.'

'But I couldn't possibly switch the exclusive agreement to you.' Jack could not believe the man's cheek.

'I'm not asking for that. It would be far too obvious. Just scrap it. Launch the product on the market as a whole.'

'Why should you want their shares down?' asked Peter, suspecting he had already guessed the reason.

Stern ignored him; he was still staring at Jack, as a snake stares at a rabbit.

Jack was rapidly calculating the cost of the agreement in his head. The main problem was the joint advertising campaign which would have to be ditched. But it was still only at the concept stage. It might be a hundred thousand, a couple at most. Much more important, it would antagonise an important client. But there was no alternative. It would have to be done.

He uncrossed his arms and took a deep breath.

'Not possible, I'm afraid,' cut in Peter. Jack looked at him, astonished.

Stern said: 'I would have thought this was your client's decision.'

'My client pays me to know more about the workings of the City than he does. And you and I both know that this would be a flagrant breach of the Takeover Code.'

'That hasn't bothered you very often in the past.' Stern was brimming with fury.

Peter stood up, icy cool. 'One has to move with the times, Leo,' he spoke quietly. 'Thank you for your hospitality. Obviously this conversation never took place.'

Stern's eyes took on a dead look. He shrugged. 'Have it your way.' He pressed a buzzer for his secretary to show them out.

He stayed standing staring at the closed door of his office for a long time. What the hell was Peter Markus up to?

In the car, Jack exploded. 'I'm with him,' he said furiously, 'the bloody Takeover Code has never stopped you before.'

Peter concentrated on the traffic while Jack ranted on. Finally he said, 'It's actually got nothing whatsoever to do with the Takeover Code.'

'Well, what the hell did you say it was for, then?' Jack was fraying at the edges.

'I don't trust Leo. That place is bristling with electronic gadgetry. For all we know he was taping us, even videoing us. We had to say no in that situation.'

Jack looked at him, incredulous. 'Are you serious?'

'Very. Look, why don't I just ring him on his private line at home – I happen to know that's not bugged – and tell him we agree? Then you can sort out Jim Hogan.'

Calls from the business slots on television began to come through asking for Jack to appear. To begin with they were met with adamant refusal. Television both fascinated and terrified him. Few businessmen come across well in the medium, and despite David's camera training he was loath to make a fool of himself in front of millions.

Besides, he was having a crisis over his hairstyle. He had begun brushing his fringe back on some days as David had suggested, but did not feel comfortable.

Yet the idea of his face being transported to living rooms throughout the country had a compelling appeal. He would practise expressions in the mirror while shaving and compose no end of pithy comments.

As the bid entered the final weeks, the media pressure intensified and David persuaded the programme editor that all questions would be cleared first. Jack could see the edited version before it went out. 'I'm sure you would be terrific, Jack,' he said in his most flattering tones. 'You're a natural and it could just make the difference between winning and losing.'

Two days later Jack reported at the Stock Exchange studio, pale and soggy-palmed, to discover a camera crew but no interviewer.

'Don't worry,' said the production assistant brightly, 'Michelle will ask you the questions down this earpiece.'

'But this isn't what was agreed at all,' protested Jack.

'I know,' she said soothingly. 'The editor has become obsessed with this silly Benlox bid for Storehouse, and Michelle just can't be in two places at once.'

Jack looked accusingly at David. 'I knew I should never have agreed to this. If this goes wrong, I hold you responsible.'

David tried to look encouraging, willing him not to storm out. His faith paid off. On camera Jack's angular face looked the part while his fury with the editor came over as aggression and determination.

Poor Bertie Underworth on the other hand, who had also been seduced by the lure of fame, looked like a stuck rabbit.

The following Friday night, Jack sat semi-comatose in the back of the BMW, crawling through the six o'clock Chelsea traffic, his brief case unopened beside him. On top of everything else, he had lost his temper with Jane the night before. She had accused him of being a self-centred bastard, just because he had wanted to stay in. The trouble with intelligent women was they were too demanding.

Rosemary had a lot going for her, he thought, longing unexpectedly for her presence. He had barely seen her for more than a couple of hours since the holiday in Elba.

He would make an effort this weekend, he resolved. He and Rosemary would spend time by themselves. It would be inviolate.

He had been extraordinary lucky. Rosemary had great strength and very little guile. And – his eyes were pulled to a particularly shapely pair of calves in the Kings Road – it was just as well she hadn't been the jealous type.

Everyone he dealt with had some kind of an angle, be it for their careers, their next fee, a sale, a good word in the right place . . . but invariably an angle.

His diary was choked with appointments to see these people; they sat next to him at dinners, at lunches, on aeroplanes, the Opera, shooting parties – you name it.

Two days before he had taken Amanda to task: 'I don't believe half these meetings are necessary. You must learn to protect me.'

Not only were there lunches, dinners and breakfasts, there were meetings in between, and meetings in-between meetings. He hardly had time to have a pee some days.

Calmly she took him through the diary. Shamefaced he managed to cancel a couple of lunches, but for one reason or another the others all seemed perfectly valid. He had dates pencilled in six months ahead and all with people who had an angle.

But Rosemary had no angle. She just loved him. He

hugged the thought to him like a warm cushion. They would spend the weekend quietly. He would take her out to dinner. He could dig up all the summer's bedding plants and try to persuade Mark to have a game of tennis – although his son had officially given up tennis and taken up Tai Chi instead.

Jack had not even congratulated him on his A-level results, he thought with a stab of guilt. If only Mark could be a little more communicative. He wondered how his own flesh and blood could be so inscrutable.

His driver put his foot down, having made it to the relative freedom of the A3. God, he felt tired. He wondered which of Rosemary's delicious concoctions she would produce for supper?

He turned the key in the door and walked slap into his father-in-law. 'Nice house, Jack,' he said pleasantly. 'Not as big as Chester though.'

As he stood dumbfounded in the hallway it came rushing back to him; Rosemary's parents had come to stay for the weekend, the first visit since they had moved into the Esher house.

He found Rosemary in their bedroom putting on her make-up. She glanced at him coldly. 'You'd forgotten, hadn't you? I did ring and ask Amanda to remind you on Wednesday.'

'Why didn't you speak to me?'

'Have you tried getting through to you recently?' she asked acidly.

He stood behind her, disappointment flooding him. 'Come here, I want a cuddle,' he said in a little boy voice.

'What about all those times when *I* want a cuddle and you're not here?' she asked, painting on her lipstick with a brush the way Angela had shown her.

Jack could see it was going to be one of those evenings. 'Anyway,' she said, 'you'd better get ready. I've put a clean shirt out for you.'

'Ready for what?'

She swung round to face him, her lips taut. 'We're taking Mum and Dad out to dinner to celebrate Dad's birthday,' she said slowly, as if talking to a child.

'You can remember your lunches and dinners with the likes of Leo Stern and Peter Markus. You can remember your shooting engagements, your racing and your football. It's a great pity you can't remember your family occasionally.' Rosemary's eyes were blazing so he took the line of least resistance, disappearing downstairs to pour himself a very large Scotch.

'What about one for me, then?' his father-in-law's voice broke in. He had been the headmaster of a village school in Lancashire while his wife had brought up five children, of whom Rosemary was the eldest. Both had been actively involved in the local Labour Party all their lives. Jack marvelled that he had once felt respect for this man.

They dined at an overpriced local restaurant with snail-like service. 'I expect bill for this 'ud feed family for a week where we come from.' Rosemary shot a look at Jack, warning him not to rise to the bait. But he had drunk too much red wine to care.

'You're all right though, aren't you?' he challenged. 'With your inflation adjusted pension. You'll never go short.'

'I worked long and 'ard for that, lad, and lucky to do so. There's still 20 per cent of folk unemployed round our way, isn't there, love?' he appealed to his wife.

'Is there really?' said Jack. 'Well, if people like me didn't bust a gut every day, it would be a good deal higher.'

His father-in-law snorted and they all concentrated on eating. Why did they always have to go over this old ground? Rosemary looked wonderful tonight – although there was something different about her. Only over coffee did he realise what it was.

When they got home, after what had seemed like an endless meal, he caught up with her in the bathroom.

'You've gone blonde,' he said. 'It really suits you.'

'Well, fancy you noticing,' she said acidly. She had put on a thick shapeless nightshirt to discourage him. 'I've been blonde for three months.'

In bed she turned her back on him. 'Darling,' he wheedled, running a finger down her spine.

She sat up suddenly. 'Jack!' she exclaimed. 'You have been out every night for weeks on end – supposedly because of this wretched takeover which apparently involves breakfast, lunch and dinner at the Savoy, not to mention dancing until all hours in nightclubs where I am never taken.

'I have always been a tolerant wife because I deluded myself that at heart you cared about me. But you cannot come home, behave like a pig to my father on his birthday, and then expect to make love to me. It's not, not – ' she was groping for words ' – it's not logical,' she said finally, and burst into tears.

'We can't, not here.' Sarah pulled away from Stern who was insistently kissing her neck.

'Why not?' he said softly. 'It's my office.'

'Exactly!' she exclaimed. He slid his hands inside her jumper and undid her bra.

'Your secretary . . .' she protested.

'Is out, like everyone else.' His hand slid up between her legs and she felt her resistance ebbing away.

'Leo,' she pleaded, 'at least lock the door and take the phones of the hook.' Brusquely he did as she said and went back to where she was leaning against the sofa, her eyes languorous with desire, her skirt at her ankles.

As she wrapped her legs around him moments later, they heard the fax machine whir into action.

Afterwards she gazed at him in disbelief. She found her underwear and put it on. 'This is ridiculous,' she said.

'Fun, though.' He unlocked the door and put the phones back on the hook. One rang instantly.

'Oh, hi, Peter, Yes, we've been having trouble with the phones.' He winked at Sarah who had poured herself a glass of mineral water and was sitting demurely on the sofa.

'Venice! Sure. Let me check.' She watched him flick through the fat diary on his desk, his shirt still undone, showing the thick black hair on his chest. How could he be so in control?

'Yep. That looks fine.'

He put the phone down and walked across to her, planting a large kiss on her forehead.

'An invitation to spend the weekend in the Danieli with Jack Armstrong,' he said smiling down at her. 'They're beginning to get desperate.'

So am I, thought Sarah. So am I.

Stuart Anderson leafed through the press coverage of the bid for Empire so far. The *Herald* was the one paper that had swung wholeheartedly on to Butlers side and stayed there.

At the Empire morning meeting the next day he took Bertie Underworth aside afterwards. 'How well do you know this Patrick Peabody on the *Herald*?'

Bertie looked surprised. 'I've never met the chap. Our PR people said he had been bought by the other camp, so we'd be wasting our time bothering.'

'Mmm,' Stuart mused. 'Would you mind awfully if I took him out to lunch?'

Bertie's face lit up. 'Of course not, old chap. Splendid idea.'

Chapter 16

The thirty-ninth day after Renasco had put its counter-bid in writing was Empires last chance to defend itself with any new information.

True to form, Stuart Anderson, who was fond of comparing a bid defence to a striptease, was keeping the best until last.

He was well aware the company was indefensible, but it was his duty to ensure he got the best price. He had made it clear to his counterparts at Shearman Drussel, whose forty-five-man team had flown back to New York with only two minor suggestions taken up by Bertie, that underplaying the company's value was not what won brownie points in British takeover battles.

Stuart's team of young tigers (as he liked to call them) spent nights sitting up with the lawyers and company executives in a huge smoke-filled room known as 'the bunker', thrashing out the final salvo in the defence, line by line.

He wound them up to produce the most optimistic profit forecasts they could. 'Kitchen sink it,' he would say – meaning throw everything in but the kitchen sink. Some deft work on the property front had magically produced some cash which would be included as trading profits.

When they had done their best, he took it apart and put it together again, to make sure it stood up. Then he let the lawyers loose on it.

Bertie, who had become quite wily, waited until the last day before reading the final draft and grumbled that the figures were not high enough. Stuart patiently explained once

241

again that the art was to come up with a figure that was good enough to impress the market, but one which was also credible.

'If it looks remotely over the top, the press will crucify you,' he said, with emphasis firmly on the 'you'.

Until that weekend, Stuart had stuck to the letter of the Takeover Code, abiding by every wish and whim of the Panel. He believed in generating as much goodwill as possible, for you never knew when times might become difficult. To date, all Empires announcements had been made first through the Stock Exchange, and there had never been a suggestion of a leak.

But Stuart's adherence to the City rules stemmed from pragmatism rather than any innate belief in their justice. Keeping in with the authorities, flattering them into thinking he valued their judgement, gave him the edge in tricky situations. He liked to win every bit as much as the next man, but he had found it paid not to show it.

It was something young Peter Markus had yet to learn, he mused, as he alighted from the pearl grey Jaguar outside Mark's Club that Friday lunch-time.

If he was ever to cool Patrick Peabody's ardour for the merits of the Butlers bid, this was his chance.

The next day, David ordered one of his juniors to pick up the first editions of the Sunday papers and bring them to The Poppinjay, a few doors down from the *Herald*'s offices in Fleet Street.

Patrick generally came in for a couple of pints after the first edition on a Saturday evening. David had noted the unusual silence from him that week, but there was a great deal going on elsewhere and he had been so busy he forgot to ring him. He had totted up the figures in the *FT*'s bid table that morning. Apart from Butlers and Empire, there were £3.7 billion worth of takeover bids underway in thirty-eight separate transactions.

The pub welcomed him with its dark woody smell. A couple of Patrick's reporters sat at a corner table. They offered David a first edition of the *Herald* and in return he bought them both a pint and sat down with them. 'Cheers,' he said, raising the glass to his lips. Then he opened the paper.

EMPIRE STRIKES BACK screamed the headline with a strapline reading: 'Profits to rise by 35%'. There followed a fullsome account of the details of the Empire final defence document, which David knew was not due out until the following Monday.

Even more worrying, Patrick had written a large slug of his comment column on how the Empire management was getting its act together. He still commended the Butlers strategy, but his tone was noticeably cooler than in previous weeks.

'What do you think of my story, old son?' Patrick stood before him, rumpled from the day's work, his face half wary, half amused.

'I think it shows Empire is getting desperate,' David said. 'First they've started leaking, and second they'll never make that forecast.' He smiled affably to show there were no hard feelings. 'What would you like – pint of Guinness?'

Standing at the bar he ran through the possible sources for the story in his mind. It had to be Stuart Anderson. The PR company advising them just didn't have the balls.

On Sunday afternoon the head of the Takeover Panel played his regular weekend game of tennis with Stuart; the two men lived a couple of miles from each other in Gloucestershire. To his delight, he beat Stuart – a rare event.

He had decided to wait until they went inside for tea after the game, to bring the matter up. He settled in his armchair and took a breath.

'That piece in the *Sunday Herald* this morning looks like a blatant leak you know, Stuart – it simply will not do. Your people are usually so sensible,' he said, sipping the Earl Grey.

Stuart looked desolate as he offered him a home baked biscuit. 'I know. I really am most embarrassed about it. I really can't believe it was one of my team.' He sighed. 'I don't want to point fingers, but I just have a feeling it could have been the PR company on a frolic of its own.'

'Well, technically we should launch an official investigation . . .'

'Of course, I'm aware of that. Look, I'll have a crackdown tomorrow and let you know if I find anything.'

'Splendid,' said the head of the Takeover Panel, biting into a biscuit. 'Seen much of old Hugo recently?'

Jack kept the Topic page displaying the Butlers and Empire share prices permanently in his office so he could check them as he came and went. For days now, the Butlers share price had dropped after the American markets opened at two in the afternoon and he began to dread returning from lunch.

It took the combined skills of Peter, Charlie and Jean-Pierre's contacts in New York to keep the price above the lower Renasco cash offer. True, Butlers second offer had included a cash alternative higher than Renasco's – but they all knew Penasco was likely to raise its cash offer. Everything hung on keeping the Butlers share price as high as possible.

Yet some of those idiot institutions had chosen this moment to turn nervous of equities and start reducing their holdings. Jack was convinced it was a vendetta. But even Charlie privately believed the stockmarket was showing the classic signs of being at the top of a bull market. 'When Joe Public thinks the stockmarket is an easy way to make money, it's time to bail out,' he told his favourite clients. He dared not say the same to Jack.

Renasco had until the forty-sixth day of the bid to increase its cash offer from 400p and to top Butlers share offer, currently worth 420p – or nearly £3 billion for the whole company.

Jack knew he had convinced many in the City that he was the man who could weld Butlers and Empire into the biggest food group in Britain next to Unilever – which was, after all, half Dutch.

But he had been unnerved by the *Sunday Herald*'s change of heart.

At first he hoped it was just Patrick's Irish whimsy. But he had stopped ringing for his weekly chat. On the one occasion Jack had telephoned him, Patrick had been distinctly cool. He mentally wrote off journalists. They were two-faced, untrustworthy vermin.

His other problem was the handful of key institutions who

remained openly sceptical about his ability to turn his vision into reality. And with the sudden market nervousness, they made it clear they would have to consider taking Renasco's cash if they went higher.

Jack, Charlie and Edward returned to the treadmill of six presentations a day, concentrating on the institutions who were sitting on the fence.

Each day began with the 8 a.m. 'war cabinet' meeting and continued restlessly with presentations, drinks and dinner with someone who might influence events in the evening.

Jack's brain lost all ability to retain anything outside the bid. He ceased to care about his wife's coldness, the state of the house, his golf game, Jane Brompton, the two-year-old race-horse he had in training, his football club's problems. They all bounced off his consciousness like squash balls off a squash court. He even stopped going to the gym.

His portable phone went with him everywhere. Stranded on Northampton station after a day of presentations, Jack was in the loo when suddenly it rang.

Carefully, he fished it out of his briefcase. 'Oh, hello, Mr Armstrong, I hope I haven't caught you at an inconvenient moment. It's David Smith of Lex here.' It was a good job video phones were still at the development stage, Jack thought, zipping up his trousers.

In sleep, of which he never got enough, he dreamed of talking to rows of dozing fund managers who could not be wakened. Another night he found himself hemmed in by giant piles of documents whose vital pages had disappeared.

Peter told him it was normal.

He veered between an adrenalin high and total exhaustion. When he was not putting forward, yet again, the case for Butlers he attempted to keep up with the growing moutain of more routine work.

One evening, as Edward Williams worked late in his office, the kahki handset on his desk buzzed insistently. He shuddered. He hated the sound. It meant only one thing – Jack was on the other end demanding something impossible.

'Have you seen this proposal from Sean Macready for a management buy out of Pommodoro Rosso?'

'Yes, Jack, he sent me a copy,' said Edward quietly.

'One moment a bloody trade union militant, the next Italy's answer to James Hanson, eh?'

Edward kept quiet. 'Well, you can just tell him to forget it.' Jack said, slamming down the phone. He reached for one of the array of rubber stamps lined up on his desk like toy soldiers, smacked it on to the ink pad and then on to the letter. NOT APPROVED, it read in half inch capitals.

At the centre of Jack's grand obsession, like the flash of fire in the heart of a diamond, was the desire to win Sir Leo Stern over to his side. He became a suitor pursuing his bride. Stern's dark satanic head with its hawk's nose floated before him in meetings, his gravelly voice spoke to him in dreams. The closer the deadline of 14 October grew, the more intense became his desire and the greater the dread that Stern would find a last-minute escape clause.

Everything depended on how high Renasco was prepared to go with its cash offer. Butlers had bought just over 15 per cent of Empire shares in the stockmarket, leaving only about 15 per cent in the hands of the small shareholders.

The main block of the balancing shares rested with the institutions who had a habit of sitting on the fence until the last possible moment. Therefore Stern's 8.4 per cent and Schlosstein's 3 per cent had become crucial – just as Stern had always intended.

Then on day forty-five, Renasco increased its cash bid to 420p, 25p higher than Butlers cash alternative but still below the share offer which was hovering around 440p. As Lex concluded the following morning: 'Shareholders have a clear choice between cash that will see its value eroded by inflation and the management skills of an impressive, but nevertheless inexperienced new chief executive.'

Venice had emptied after the September film festival, but there were still tourists about. Rosemary and Jack stood on the Academia bridge looking back at the Grand Canal as it swept round towards the lagoon. 'I've wanted to come here all my life,' she said.

She glanced up at Jack and saw he was miles away. Over the past month he must have lost more than a stone and his cheek and jaw bones looked sharp under his skin. But for once she could not muster any sympathy. He chose this life of over-work, drinking sessions and other women. It was as if the well of patience and understanding inside her had finally run dry. She was sick to death of playing corporate wife.

They made their way to the Vaporetta. The metal gate of the landing stage clanged behind them and they swung into the centre of the canal, the engine whining, moving slowly past fading grand palazzos which were hung with wide red bands advertising current exhibitions.

Back in St Mark's Square they found Peter and Angela eating ice cream in Florian's. 'Anyone know where Leo and Max are?' asked Jack as the Palm Court orchestra played the Blue Danube.

'Don't worry, Jack,' said Peter, 'neither of them would miss taking dinner at Harry's Bar off you for the world.'

He was right. After eluding Jack all day, Stern got straight to the point over the Bellinis. 'How's this bid of yours going these days?' He sounded as if he were a casual bystander. Sensing Jack's anger simmering across the table, Peter cut in.

'It's going extremely well, Leo,' he said crisply. 'Several key institutions have given us private assurances that they will accept our offer in preference to the Renasco cash.'

'That's correct,' said Jack, struggling to keep a cordial tone. 'Our presentations over the past few days have gone very well.

'I was told the Guardian Royal fund managers all fell asleep,' said Stern, tucking a napkin into his collar as bowls of fettucine arrived.

'Oh, we all know the odd fund manager nods off in the afternoon, that's hardly a reflection on us,' said Peter. 'A good many of them rate the Butlers management style and will back the bid.'

'I'd say it was about fifty-fifty now the higher cash offer is on the table,' said Stern, shovelling pasta. 'You'll be in trouble if that Butlers price falls much further. It was looking pretty sick yesterday.'

'Oh, come on, Leo, you know the other side are shorting our stock like crazy.'

247

'So what's the Panel doing about it?' Stern demolished the last mouthful and wiped the sauce from his chin.

There was silence. Rosemary looked at Jack, who looked at Peter, who stared intently back at him as if to say: 'Now.'

'You're right as ever, Leo,' said Jack. His tone was almost humble. 'The fact is, we need your help.'

Stern's eyes glowed. He took a long slow drink of wine and put the glass down carefully as if afraid his big hands might crush it. The corners of his mouth turned up just a fraction. Those were the words he had been longing to hear.

'Why won't you at least give Jack irrevocable undertakings – there's only just over a week to go?'

Stern and Peter were walking through pale mist along the Zattare early the following morning.

'I'm teaching him a lesson. When he grows up, he'll be grateful.'

'But you're prepared to support the Butlers share price?'

Stern grinned. 'I might be going deaf but last night I thought I heard Jack Armstrong tell me I wouldn't lose money on my Butlers shares, whatever happens.'

Peter was silent. He had warned Jack not to indemnify Stern against loss. Apart from the potential cost to Butlers, it was blatantly illegal. But Jack was behaving like a man possessed. After dinner the three of them had gone to Stern's room for a *digestivo*, and two large *grappas* later Jack had seemed prepared to sign his life away to win the bid. At least, thought Peter, there were no outside witnesses.

'Anyway I want him to win – I think he'll do a good job,' Stern said, his eyes turning flat.

Peter felt he would explode with wrath. But they walked on as the sun began to penetrate the mist, a vision of serenity, bringing the island of Jeudecca into view on the opposite side of the water. Suddenly a hulk of a man, wide shoulders swathed in a purple cloak, emerged from an alley. He wore a broad-brimmed black hat and carried a large bunch of pink roses; a white poodle trotted at his heels.

He beamed at them and swept on.

'That's what I love about Venice,' said Stern. 'It's a city of surprises.'

Emerging from the scented darkness of the little church, Rosemary saw them walking slowly, unnecessarily close together. Next to Stern, Peter looked quite fragile, his shoulders half as broad. She was too far away from them to hear the conversation, but she could sense conspiracy.

But she had only a passing interest in them. She had woken at six overwhelmed by a heavy misery which she knew would not shift unless she got up. Finally she stole out of bed, dressing quietly in the bathroom.

In the church she had placed a candle to the Virgin Mary in the blazing circle and sat, head bowed. A vision of meeting Jack at the LSE freshers' dance filled her mind. Tall and skinny as a beanpole, he had drawn her to him like a magnet. She had loved his self-assurance and vigour. He had always been cocky, but for a long time his sense of humour had made it bearable. Every now and then a little boy would peep through the posturing, wanting only her. When she became pregnant she had felt the only thing worth doing in her life was to bring up Jack Armstrong's child.

They had been riotously happy for the first two years of marriage. Then the foreign travel started – and with it the infidelity. She had sensed it a long time before she had proof. Then one day there it was, the florist's bill in the inside pocket of his Hong Kong suit. She had stood looking at it while Susan, sixteen months old, staggered around her playpen, whooping with pleasure. It was funny how a flimsy piece of paper could change your life. In that moment, Rosemary heard the prison gates slam shut.

She did not confront him. Just once, she had taken her revenge with another man. But it was not her way. She folded her rage to her, buried it deep under layers of everyday.

She would stick to the contract. She had a lovely house, two healthy children, and a husband who turned the heads of other men's wives. When he became chief executive of Butlers she had enjoyed the razzmatazz, the attention, the reflected glory – although she told herself she knew it for what it was.

Inwardly she still balked at a system which said Jack was worth £300,000 a year when most of his employees earned less than a tenth of that. At Butlers they had entered the exclusive private world of the rich. She began to understand how the cocoon of money screens out the rest of the world.

Julian had brought a new dimension into her existence. You go through life for years, nodding, smiling, talking, never truly connecting. Then one day you walk into a gym, thighs a bit wobbly although not bad for your age, and there he is – ten years your junior with a body like marble, but fitting your soul like the missing piece of a jigsaw.

As she turned to stroll back to the Danieli the purple-cloaked man with the poodle hurried towards her, proffering a perfect pink rose. 'To the most beautiful woman I've seen today,' he said in a West Coast accent, and was gone. The smile lingered on her face all the way back to the hotel.

Max Schlosstein's tan looked yellow in the morning light and the rings on his podgy fingers glittered as he tore his brioche apart. He and Jack were breakfasting on the terrace, the early morning noises below drifting up to them – the Gondolieres making ready for another day, the omnipresent whine of the Vapporetti.

'Ya know me, Jack,' said Schlosstein, 'I'm only interested in one thing – and that's money.'

I'd never have guessed, thought Jack. 'Well, you've done pretty well on the Empire stake. I don't know what your average buying price was but . . .'

'Yeah, I've made nearly eight million bucks so far.' Jack tried to conceal his surprise. Who could have tipped him off that early on?

'Yep – and I've been loyally buying Butlers shares out of gratitude,' Max chuckled.

Jack's brioche sat untouched on his plate as he played with a toothpick. He desperately needed Schlosstein's 3 per cent.

'You know what I'd like?' Schlosstein gazed out dreamily across the Lido. 'I'd like to double that eight million.'

'Just how do you propose to do that?' Jack could hear his heart thumping. 'All shareholders have to be treated equally.'

'Oh, I understand the rules. But I'm not asking for a kickback. I'm not just an arb, you know.' Max sounded hurt.

'I'm a consultant. A fee for my services at a time when the boys on Wall Street were giving you trouble – paid into my bank account in Zurich. No different from your friend Krandsdorf.' Max chuckled. 'No sweat.'

But Jean-Pierre did not own any shares – that was the difference and Schlosstein knew it. Jack's stomach churned with dislike. If Schlosstein accepted the bid it would weaken Stern's hand, but was it enough? It would be good publicity and it might encourage some of the fence sitters. The bid closed on Wednesday week.

You two look as if you're plotting World War Three.' Peter's voice made Jack jump visibly.

Schlosstein rose to go, his annoyance plain. 'I'm going to take a walk around town. Catch you guys later.'

Peter and Angela sat down. 'Seemed very cosy?' Peter was oozing curiosity.

'You know what these Americans are like,' Jack said, trying to look relaxed. 'They meet you once and behave as if you're lifelong friends.'

Back in his hotel room he rang Jean-Pierre at home, where it was three in the morning. 'Don't worry, old buddy, I've been out partying.' He admired the lightly muscled buttocks of the Chinese youth mixing tequila sunrises on the other side of the room.

'I can't talk about this on the phone but I need to see you urgently.'

'Sure, I'll get on the nine-thirty Concorde.' He put the phone down and looked regretfully at his guest who was now moving gracefully towards the bed, glasses in hand.

'This will have to be a quickie, I'm afraid,' he said, taking a glass. 'I'm really going to have to get some sleep.'

'What's your friend Schlosstein up to?' Peter asked Stern. He had taken him aside over pre-lunch drinks.

Stern's lips twitched. 'He's usually up to no good. Why do you ask?'

Peter looked troubled. 'It's just that I saw him and Jack deep in conversation over breakfast. Jack nearly jumped out of his skin when I turned up.'

'Probably trying to do a deal.' Stern shrugged. 'Like the

251

rest of us. Only Max is perhaps a little less subtle, even than me,' he chuckled.

Peter ran out of patience.

'You had your way over Wingways. Why are you holding out on us?'

'Trust me I've said I'll go with you,' said Stern.

'Listen, Leo, we scrapped thousands of pounds of advertising and antagonised a major customer for you. It would really help us if you came over sooner rather than later.'

Stern put a fatherly arm around Peter's shoulder. 'Calm down. There's ten days to go yet. I just want to see if Renasco wants to play.'

Two days later, Jack, Charlie and Edward, or the terrific trio as David Bang had christened them, were sitting in London traffic with the rain beating on the car roof.

'How does it go again, Charlie?'

'We at Butlers are currently reviewing the management of our pension fund. Perhaps, once the bid is over, you would like to make a presentation to us.'

Jack repeated it word for word. Edward pursed his lips in disapproval. 'You're sure we're not breaking the rules?'

They were on their way to see one of the largest groups of pension fund managers for a last attempt to persuade them to accept the bid.

'It's perfectly above board,' declared Charlie. 'Just don't make any promises, that's all.'

By the last weekend before the deadline, every discretionary fund of Greenbag's and Hogarth Stein was bulging with Butlers shares. Hogarth Stein held over £250 million worth, Greenbag's around £200 million. Butlers price was holding steady 10p above Renasco's cash offer and as long as it continued that way, they should be home and dry.

Finally, the institutions were making supportive noises. Charlie's last ring-round indicated over 70 per cent of them would accept. But so far the level of formal acceptances was still less then 5 per cent. David, Peter and Jack focused on just one thing – press comment on the forthcoming weekend was crucial.

On the Friday morning Patrick opened his notebook at a fresh page, selected a biro from his drawer, and dialled David's number.

'Did you know that Jack was involved in a bribery scandal when he was at Renasco?' he said pleasantly.

There was a long, satisfying silence at the other end. Then: 'I don't believe it. where did you get this story?' For once David was unable to conceal the alarm in his voice.

'David,' said Patrick gently, 'I don't like this any more than you do. I've been a great supporter of Jack Armstrong, but I have to check out what I've been told and my source has been spot on in the past. I've checked and it is fact that his immediate boss in the Far East at the time was fired. Jack himself nearly got the chop.'

David was torn between throwing himself on Patrick's mercy and begging him not to run it, or being ruthlessly professional. He opted for the latter.

'Well, obviously we'd better talk to Jack about it,' he said, his voice sounding almost its usual honey-coated self. 'When was it?'

'As I understand it,' Patrick said, 'it was in 1976 in Hong Kong for bribing a major supplier of palm oil not to sell to a competitor.'

'But that's over ten years ago!' David grasped at the weakness. There was something odd about this story.

'So?' said Patrick.' Any man who was party to a bribe, however long ago, has a fundamental flaw in his character and should not be running a major public company.'

The 'something' clicked. 'Patrick, I don't know who your source is, but it sounds awfully like the dirty tricks brigade. If Jack had really been guilty, he'd have been fired.'

The story that had sounded so convincing to Patrick began to lose credence. Surely an eminent merchant banker such as Stuart Anderson wouldn't actually lie about such a thing?

'Well, I do need to talk to Jack,' he said. 'I tried him before I rang you but his secretary said he was out for most of the day. His mobile's not answering either.'

David thanked God. 'I'll get hold of him, don't you worry, although it may not be before this afternoon.'

Jack's face went white when David outlined Patrick's story.

'But it was normal practice,' he protested. 'That's the way everybody does business in the Far East. It was pretty small stuff – routine.'

'So why was your boss fired?'

'He was having an affair with that particular customer's wife. He threatened to withdraw all his business. The bribery business was a cover up for the affair.'

David believed him. 'That doesn't alter the fact that if the merest whiff of this story appears in print, it could wreck the bid,' he said. 'Could Patrick have any documentation?'

Jack thought and then shook his head. There was nothing in writing as far as I know that mentioned bribery outright. It was just put around that it was the official reason. Any Renasco director who was there at the time would know.'

'That's obviously where it has come from,' said David.

Jack regained a trace of poise. 'Patrick knows if he's wrong we can sue him and his paper for thousands.'

'Yup,' said David, lighting a Sullivan Powell. 'For once I think we're just going to have to stall.'

By four-thirty Patrick became concerned. At five he rang David who was at his most apologetic. Jack had been in non-stop presentations all day but was on his way back to London now and would probably ring from the car.

Around seven, Patrick tried Jack's mobile – nothing. At his home, Rosemary was charming but said she had no idea when he would be home. David, too, seemed to have gone missing.

He rang Peter at about nine and put the story to him. Peter sounded absolutely outraged at the very suggestion of bribery in Jack's past. He knew absolutely nothing about it, and no, he had no idea where Jack was.

Still, Patrick consoled himself, he could always catch Jack at home on a Saturday morning. But for the first time ever, the Esher number was permanently engaged until noon, when it rang with no reply.

Eventually he got hold of David. 'Hasn't he got back to you?' He sounded genuinely amazed. 'He was certainly intending to ring you last night.'

Patrick lost his temper.

254

'Look, don't go mad. I'll have another go,' said David sounding hurt.

By the time his four o'clock deadline came up, Patrick knew he'd been duped. Fury gripped him. Nothing was worse than having a story just outside his grasp. Instinct told him if Jack were too worried to speak to him he must be on the right track, but he dare not write anything without talking to him.

That evening, he was just sinking into an armchair around 9.30 when his phone rang.

'I know this is a bit late,' said Jack, all casual innocence, 'but David tells me you've been trying to get hold of me?'

'Well, as you know, my deadline passed some time ago.' Patrick could barely believe the man's gall.

You may as well tell me the problem anyway.'

Patrick did.

Jack laughed. 'It's complete rubbish. Those guys at Renasco have been trying to set you up.'

'It would have saved me having a nervous breakdown if you'd told me that earlier.'

'Come on, Patrick. You know how hectic things are. I've been out all day. Anyway, I thought you'd changed sides.'

Patrick sensed Jack was laughing at him. I have now, he thought. Condescending bastard!

Chapter 17

STERN TO SELL STAKE IN EMPIRE shrieked the headline in the *Daily Post* on the Monday morning. Under orders from Stern, Denis Jones had tipped off the *Post* he was poised to sell his stake in the open market. Stern also told Denis to offer a parcel of Empire shares to one of the larger market makers, to give the story credence.

The first edition of the *Standard* splashed a follow up version across its front City page, with a huge picture of Stern looking imposingly handsome. Next to it, a tiny grim-faced Jack looked young and gauche.

Peter felt his nerves stretch thin. He knew Stern enjoyed torturing Jack – the old stag teaching the young one a lesson – but until that morning he had believed he would stick to the deal. He had reassured Jack to that effect. Now, for the first time, he was not so sure.

Jack had been on the phone three times, each call increasingly abusive.

'Just get hold of that flash bastard you call a friend and find out what the fuck is going on!' he demanded the last time.

Stern had chosen this very day to go to Switzerland on 'urgent business'. His normal mobile phone number was switched off while his usually helpful secretary swore he could not be contacted despite Peter's pleas of urgency. He knew it was rubbish. Stern was never out of contact.

In Jack's office Jean-Pierre demolished the Danish pastry Amanda had bought specially for him.

'If you get Max to sell to you now, that would help, wouldn't it? I'll ring him.'

'But it's the middle of the night.'

'For eight million bucks he won't mind.'

'Try and beat him down,' asked Jack.

'Yup. He might settle for six.' Jean-Pierre licked sticky fingers.

'Right,' said Jack. 'Tell him there's a cheque on its way and we await his invoice by fax. But he has to sell his stock to us as soon as possible. Get his broker to call Charlie Briggs-Smith at Greenbag's.'

Jack's mind whirled on as he spoke. He needed a co-signatory – another director to sign the cheque. While he was thinking, he rang Charlie on another line to tell him to stand by for the call from New York.

'Let me know the instant it's done – we need to get this announcement out to the market,' Jack ordered. David Bang and Peter were summoned.

He had a choice between persuading either Sir Richard or Edward into signing the cheque. He plumped for Sir Richard.

'He's up in Yorkshire today, shooting,' said his secretary. 'But he will be ringing in. Can I give him a message?'

'No, don't worry about it,' said Jack. For a moment panic overwhelmed him. He could not face ten minutes of questions from Edward. Then it came to him. Of course! Sir Richard always left a few blank cheques already countersigned in case of emergencies.

He sauntered casually down the corridor into the board room and opened the safe concealed in the fake bookcase. His heart stopped for a second and then he saw the neat little envelope, marked 'cheques'. He took two just to be on the safe side. Thank God he had written the safe combination in his diary.

When he got back to his office Jean-Pierre was smiling. 'He's settled for six and a half, old buddy. I've got the details of his bank account in Zurich here. I'll leave you to it, I've got people to see.'

'Take my driver,' said Jack, grinning. He made out the cheque and told Amanda to send it off by courier.

Two minutes later, David came on expecting a stream of

abuse. Instead Jack sounded icily self-possessed. 'Get that story out of the *Standard*,' he commanded, 'and tell them Schlosstein has sold us his shares. Peter should get the announcement to the Stock Exchange before lunch. If they want to talk to me, I'm here. You can also tell them we have no knowledge of Sir Leo selling his stake to anyone at the moment. They can quote me on that if they want to.'

Jack put the phone down without waiting for David's reply, pushed himself back from his desk and walked to the window, smoothing back his hair. The panic of the morning had been replaced by glacial control. Every fibre in his body from the tips of his fingers all the way to his toes told him he was going to win. It had become a certainty; he was invincible.

The leaves on the trees in St James's Square were burnished with the colours of autumn. As he watched, the October sun came out from behind a cloud like a floodlamp bathing the square in light. A surge of jubilation welled in his heart.

Amanda popped her head round the door to tell him the letter had gone and the moment passed. His next problem was how to get hold of Stern.

Sarah! Why hadn't he thought of it before. He could barely remember the name of the broker – something beginning with T. Ah, Tulley, that was it.

Sarah sat alone at her desk, an uneaten tuna sandwich in front of her. She looked idly at the screen. The Butlers price was off the bottom and had actually put on 5p from its low point, but it was still down 25p on the day. Everyone else had gone out to lunch.

She hated what Stern and Denis were doing. It was so childish, not to mention reckless. If the story in the *Standard* was traced back to Denis he would be accused of creating a false market in Butlers shares. The authorities could then suspend him – it could even become a criminal matter.

A lone light on the key and lamp system began flashing. It was Jack at his most charming. 'Look, Sarah, you know the situation. I've got to talk to Leo and get this thing sorted out. He can't just let a rumour like this go unchecked.'

Sarah felt a wave of sympathy for him, and after all her

258

clients had done very well out of Butlers shares. Nothing would induce her to be disloyal to Stern but she said she would try and contact him. One call from her to his secretary would provide a number – she always knew where he was almost to the minute.

Half an hour later, Stern rang Jack. 'I'll be in my office at five this evening if you want to talk to me,' he snapped, and put the phone down.

At four, Peter arrived at St James's Square to talk strategy with Jack. He had grim news. Just before he left, the company registrars had told him that two of the institutions had withdrawn their acceptances. If Stern did not support Butlers, more would inevitably follow despite Schlosstein's sale.

Inside Jack's briefcase was a list of product lines that Butlers supplied to Stern; also a list of Empire products which he might be interested in buying. Peter and Jack went through them.

'You do realise we're sailing very close to the wind here? It's a clear breach of the Takeover Code to treat one shareholder differently from the rest.'

Jack looked at him stone-faced. 'What's the alternative?'

'We can call his bluff. He said he would accept our offer; he hasn't sold his shares yet. He could be just jerking the hook to see what comes up.'

'I can't afford to risk it – and he knows it. I need to offer him something else.'

Peter knew he was right.

'You've told me this kind of thing goes on all the time,' said Jack. 'It would be bloody difficult to prove.'

Peter was silent. Hogarth Stein's reputation was riding high on this bid and he had made sure his bank's fees were going to be the biggest ever paid to a British bank in a takeover – higher even than Guinness. He did not want to think about Guinness. His own reputation, too, was on the line.

But Jack and Stern were the principals after all. He could only advise. when push came to shove, they would do what they wanted.

They arrived on the dot of five, picking up a copy of the late

Standard from the news-stand near Stern House. David had done well.

The earlier story had been replaced by the Schlosstein share sale. Jack breathed a sigh of relief. There was even a picture of Schlosstein, looking every inch his unpleasant self. But they still needed Stern.

It seemed to Jack that Stern had taken on a demonic quality. In the fading light from the window his dark eyes seemed fathomless and his hair rose from his broad brow in a dark, lustrous mane. Jack remembered how he had briefly thought of him as a father figure and shuddered inwardly. He could think of no more malevolent, unforgiving father than Stern.

When they entered his office he did not invite them to sit on the easy chairs where he usually talked with visitors. Instead he motioned them to two chairs in front of the huge desk, behind which he lounged in blue shirtsleeves.

They sat down in silence. It was very quiet. Hard to believe that Oxford Street teemed less than one hundred yards away.

Stern made an expansive gesture.

'What can I do for you, gentlemen?'

The icy calm which had descended on Jack earlier had melted. They all knew it was a question of what they could do for him. Without mentioning his stake or the chaos of the morning, Jack opened his briefcase and got out a file.

'We've brought you a list of the main product lines that Butlers and Empire supply you with. We are open to reviewing the terms.'

'On all of them?'

Peter was studying Stern intently. He knew it was just a game. But Jack fell into the trap.

'Don't be ridiculous!' he snapped. 'You don't expect me to jeopardise my entire business.'

Silently, Stern leaned forward and took the file.

They stayed locked in his office for more than three hours. Stern examined every possibility and combination of possibilities. As the sun set, he had turned on the angle-poise lamp, throwing strange shadows on the desk while Jack and

Peter sat in semi-darkness. Finally he closed the file and re-lit his half-smoked cigar.

'I know you both think I've been a hard bastard.' He looked at Jack. 'But I put a deal to you two years ago. It was a deal that at the very least deserved consideration. With your talent and my experience we could have done great things.' He paused to draw on his cigar. 'And you didn't even bother to talk to me.' He blew out. 'Nobody does that to me.'

Peter and Jack sat looking at him through the furls of smoke. It seemed pointless to say anything.

'Now – ' his tone became brusque, businesslike ' – I agreed to sell you my shares in Empire in return for scrapping the deal with Wingways. I'm prepared to stick to that.'

Wait for it, thought Peter.

'If, however, as a token of your goodwill – and I do want us to be friends after this,' he said, 'if you care to give me a discount of 20 per cent below what any other customer gets on the basic Oaties biscuits, I would be delighted to accept.'

Jack could hardly believe his ears. So many days of torture and long wakeful nights and all Stern wanted was a gesture, a token of their esteem. He felt numb with relief.

'I can't see any problem there,' he said, finally finding his voice. 'Can you Peter?'

Peter simply shook his head.

Stern got up, snapped on the wall lights and opened a concealed fridge in the panelling behind him. It was crammed from top to bottom with bottles of Roederer Cristal.

He motioned towards the easy chairs and table. 'I think this calls for a little drink.'

As they moved across Peter noticed three elegant fluted champagne glasses already on the table. Stern poured the champagne and handed them both a glass. His face, so menacing a few minutes before, was transformed by a benign smile. 'Gentlemen, the toast must be "Butlers".'

The next morning, the reporter on the *Daily Post* arrived at the office at 8.30 to catch up on his expenses. He was in a good mood, whistling as he made himself a cup of coffee. The 'Stern to sell' story had been one of his best. He flicked on the Topic Screen, hoping to see the share sale confirmed.

Instead there was the statement that Stern had irrevocably accepted the Butlers offer. He stopped whistling, staring at the screen. 'I'll kill the bastard,' he muttered, and started punching out Denis's number.

'I know, I know, old son. I'm sorry. We've been used,' pleaded Denis. 'Yesterday, I swear he was going to sell to Renasco. Something must have changed.'

'Well, you can tell your major client from me that I'll have him in print.'

Denis put the phone down with a sense of unease. He could feel a faint but familiar pain in his upper chest. He breathed deeply and tried to relax. Gradually it ebbed away.

Within minutes the Butlers price had soared past the Renasco cash offer. By lunchtime, Butlers had 44 per cent of Empire shares. But they still needed another 6 per cent to win – and every time an institution accepted, Renasco's advisers got straight on the phone to persuade them to withdraw.

'They've got till one o'clock tomorrow,' said Charlie as if it were all the time in the world. 'I've told you they always wait until the last minute to decide.'

Peter pleaded an urgent appointment and drove round to talk to Stern about his bid for Wingways. Charlie and Jack sat up in the office until one, drinking whisky and sorting out the world. Nobody slept very well.

Jack woke at 5 a.m. his body rigid, his intestines knotted. He knew fear would trip the light fantastic through his low blood sugar level if he continued to lie there. As a food manufacturer he knew it better than anyone. But invisible steel straps bound him to the bed.

What if they lost?

He stared into a yawning chasm of blackness. Common sense told him he would just carry on running his business. It had happened to others. But the thought seemed unbearable. He knew it was not the truth. The truth was he would cease to exist.

The 8 a.m. war cabinet meetings had dwindled in number as the need for the lawyers, for advertising men, for Peter's juniors, disappeared. On that last morning a quintet of Jack,

Edward, Peter, David and Charlie sat around the table.

They went through the list of institutions they hoped would accept. If they did, they were easily through 50 per cent.

At half-past eight they listened to the news. 'As long as there are no scare stories in the market, or Mrs Thatcher doesn't get shot, we should be all right,' said Charlie.

The stockmarket opened steady.

Jack decided to go off to the gym. He could not concentrate on anything. Win or lose, he would need to be fit. But no matter how hard he pushed himself, he could think of nothing but the bid. Back in the office he took out the Scotch bottle. Then he put it back in the cupboard. He would wait until he knew the result.

At one minute past one Charlie rang. 'We're there', he said. 'You can open the fizz.'

Within seconds the dreaded buzzers were whining in every executive office in St James's Square, and for once the voice at the other end was cheerful.

Charlie's next call was to his brother-in-law at the stockbrokers advising Renasco. He sounded mildly surprised but was gracious in defeat. 'Well done old boy. Let's have lunch soon,' he said.

Peter rang Stuart.

'Yes, I've just heard,' he said, his voice warm. 'Well played. Between you and me, I always thought it was the best thing for the shareholders. We'll all have to get round the table and talk soon.'

Jack's office was becoming a little crammed. The central focus was the Topic screen. Suddenly there was an uncharacteristic whoop from Edward as the news flashed up.

'Butlers Group announces it owns, or has acceptances, covering 51.04 per cent of Empire Foods and declares the offer unconditional.'

Jack could hear everyone cheering as if the sound was coming from a long way away. He wanted to ring Rosemary. Suddenly the little crowd in front of his desk parted and Sir Richard plonked a Nebuchadnezzar of Krug on his desk. He reached out and shook him warmly by the hand for a long time. 'Well done, Jack,' he said, over and over again.

'Listen!' Jack held up a hand. Every single phone extension

in the place was ringing. Everyone laughed. Amanda appeared in the doorway with a huge bunch of pink and white balloons in one hand, a handkerchief pressed to her face with the other. 'Oh, Mr Armstrong, I'm so ha-happy,' she managed in between sobs.

Jack was near to tears himself. He stood up and flung his arms wide. 'Will someone go and get me some glasses so that we can drink this stuff?'

Flowers, telemessages, faxes and telephone calls of congratulation poured into the office throughout the afternoon. When he finally got through to Rosemary, he thought she sounded oddly detached. But then, she had never really been involved.

All the advisers were invited round for champagne. John Young showed up with Peter and the team, Charlie and his senior partner appeared, bottles in hand, trailing lawyers. 'I never thought I'd see these guys smiling,' joked Jack, filling up their glasses.

He was quite drunk by the time he and David Bang decided to go to dinner. 'I want to get laid tonight,' instructed Jack.

David smiled knowingly. He put an arm round Jack's shoulder. 'And so you shall. I know just the place.'

Amanda and Penny spent the next two days glued to the phone inviting people to the celebration party at the Savoy.

The room was already packed by the time Stern arrived, raven hair immaculate. He moved through the room, his magnificent shoulders cutting a swathe through the crowd, to shake Jack's hand and kiss Rosemary. 'You'll do a great job, my boy,' he said, putting an avuncular arm round Jack's shoulders. 'I wish you well. If you ever need any advice, you know where I am.'

'Thanks, Leo,' Jack found himself saying. 'I might just take you up on that.'

Peter pulled Stern gently away. 'Can we have a word about Wingways?'

Charlie arrived, charming as ever, slouching around chatting up the fund managers. David appeared in his baggy Prince of Wales check suit with a pink handkerchief in the pocket, wearing the tie with the Butlers logo he had had specially designed during the bid.

He gave Jack a bear hug. 'I always knew we'd do it,' he said affectionately. He turned to Rosemary. 'I hope you're giving him a quiet weekend? He's done a great job.'

'It will be nice to see him in the house for a change,' she said.

Max Schlosstein and Jean-Pierre shared a cab from Claridge's. 'I guess you'll be doing a little unbundling now,' said Schlosstein as they arrived. Jack looked mystified.

'It's the American term for breaking up the company and selling off the parts,' explained Jean-Pierre. Jack already knew exactly what he wanted to keep and what to sell, but he just smiled.

'If you need any help our side of the pond, let me know,' said Schlosstein, giving Jack's arm a harder than necessary squeeze.

The waiters kept everyone's glasses full of pink champagne and passed around plates of glazed smoked salmon canapés. Rosemary noticed Stern talking to a small dapper man, with a mane of glossy black hair and realised it was the same man she had seen him with at Ascot.

Sarah locked eyes with Stern across the room and they began making their way towards each other. There was a loud banging sound as David called for attention, standing on a makeshift dais to raise him above the crowd. 'Ladies and gentlemen,' he began, 'I'd like to hand you over to Sir Richard Butler, chairman of the group and great-grandson of the founder.'

There was a ripple of applause. 'I'm not going to make a long speech,' said Sir Richard, puffing on a Monte Cristo. 'When we took over Huntingdon Confectionery two years ago, Jack Armstrong was part of the package.' There were a few chuckles.

'I thought he was a punchy chap, if a bit young. But none of us realised how he would totally transform the company for the better. Butlers is now the largest food group in the UK next to Unilever.' There were mild cheers.

'The last four months have been tough at times, but last week I slept like a baby – every two hours I woke up and cried!' Everyone laughed obligingly.

265

'But it has all been indisputably worthwhile.'

There were cries of 'Hear hear'.

'So let us raise our glasses to Jack Armstrong.'

Over a hundred glasses were held in the air. 'To Jack Armstrong,' echoed the crowd, followed by cries of 'Speech, speech'.

Jack stood up on the dais, swaying slightly. A sea of drunken faces alight with goodwill beamed up at him. He had never been happier. Now he would be able to persuade the board he deserved that Bentley Turbo.

At Annabel's they were given the table favoured by Mark Birley himself from where Jack held court. A steady stream of people came by to congratulate them. Even Jacob Rothschild and Jimmy Goldsmith, in London on one of his flying visits, came over.

Jack was swirling Amanda round to Frank Sinatra when he saw Patrick Peabody watching him from the side of the floor. For a second, fear stabbed at him, but it was quickly replaced by anger.

'Journalists,' he told Amanda, ignoring Patrick, 'are nothing but scum.'

At a quarter to three Jack and Rosemary finally headed for the door. 'Be careful sir,' warned the doorman, 'there's a terrible storm out there.'

A fierce gust of wind ripped at their clothes as they emerged into Berkeley Square and, for a moment, stood transfixed by the noise and the sight of the trees swaying wildly. They climbed thankfully into the waiting taxis.

The next morning Jack awoke in the St James's Square flat with a head which felt two sizes too small. Then he remembered he had won the bid for Butlers and a wave of contentment passed over him. Rosemary slept soundly at his side.

He turned on the bedside lamp. Nothing happened. Wearily he got out of bed to look for a lightbulb. He shivered. It seemed colder than usual. He took one out of a lamp in the lounge. Still nothing happened. He tried the main light and realised there was no electricity. Damn it! He couldn't even make a cup of tea.

266

He went into the sitting room and turned on the portable radio. 'The storm has left many roads blocked by trees and large areas without electricity. The police are advising people not to go out unless they have to.'

Racing to the window he saw a tree lying across the road which was eerily free of traffic. The only people in the square were a few policemen standing in twos and threes. 'It looks like World War III's broken out,' he muttered.

He tried the telephone and sighed with relief as he heard the dialling tone.

Barely a mile away, Sir Leo Stern was losing his temper. 'What the fucking hell do you mean, I can't sell any shares? What does the London Stock Exchange think it's playing at?'

'I'm sorry, Leo, the whole system's down,' said Denis. 'They've stopped all trading. Maybe I can do something through New York once it opens.' Denis had stayed at the Tower Hotel the previous night and had not had too much trouble getting in.

It had taken Stern nearly an hour to get to his office from St John's Wood. He had intended to carry on liquidating his portfolio to realise some cash for the Wingways bid. He had already been quietly selling for a couple of months, but wanted to get rid of most of it by the end of October.

'Nah, don't worry,' said Stern, his temper ebbing. 'I don't suppose waiting till Monday will hurt that much.'

For once in his brilliant, hardworking career, Sir Leo Stern was completely wrong.

That afternoon Wall Street crashed more than 100 points. On the Monday the London stockmarket plunged as never before. On the Topic screens, the trigger page which showed the minute by minute movements was an unbroken sea of red.

By noon the market was 200 points down. When Wall Street opened it reacted by diving into free fall. At the end of the day it had registered the largest one day fall ever – tumbling faster and further even than in the crash of 1929. By the end of the week the London market was 21 per cent lower than at the start. And while the pace slowed a little, it kept on falling for the next few days. It was several weeks or so before the markets steadied – and by then many faced financial ruin.

267

Men like Sir Leo stern and Rupert Murdoch, who owned large stakes in their businesses, saw the values of their companies and thus their personal fortunes halved. Monday 19 October became known as 'Black Monday' and the events of the weeks following it as 'the crash of 1987'.

Every financial deal planned for that week in London and New York was put on hold. Many were never resurrected.

The crash dealt a mortal blow to Mrs Thatcher's dream of turning Britain into a nation of share owners – destroying in a day the confidence her government had spent seven years building up.

The beefy ageing WASP directors of Renasco congratulated themselves on their good fortune. If they had won Butlers, they would have been looking at an investment worth just half of what they had paid for it in hard earned cash. They were lucky enough to still have their money on deposit – and suddenly the world was full of bargains.

Those who had accepted the Butlers share offer pondered their recent past lives to discover what misdemeanour could have caused the fates to bring such misfortune on their heads.

But far unhappier, even than these, were the men who, out of respect for Jack Armstrong and his team, had supported the Butlers share price when mysterious forces were shorting the shares from the United States. They had believed; they had wanted to help out; to show their faith in his ability.

Surely this was no just repayment for their faith, their solidarity? Most of them conveniently forgot their true motives – a repayment for past favours or a hint of favours to come – and more than anything, the expectation of making a profit.

After four years of share prices moving relentlessly upwards, of new issues automatically being oversubscribed, rights issues fully taken up, underwriting fees regarded as nothing more than a gravy train for lazy fund managers, the true meaning of the word 'risk' once more became glaringly – obscenely – apparent.

Back in that gilded age of the bull market, in the comfort of the American Bar just two Christmasses before, Charlie had instructed Jack on the importance of 'fear and greed'. By 1987 greed had dominated for so long, only the old and wise still remembered its counterpart. Fear's comeback was no less spectacular for that.

People being what they are (and speculators are still people) looked around for someone to blame. Who had promised Paradise and failed to deliver?

Why Jack Armstrong and his advisers, of course.

They must be made to pay.

Chapter 18

'Just tell me why Butlers' share price is half what it was on the sixteenth?' Jack demanded of anyone who would listen. 'It's exactly the same company, it's going to make exactly the same profits, the debt ratio hasn't changed and business is good. These guys in the City don't know what day it is.'

To Jack, the world had gone completely mad. His recollection of the 1974 crash was hazy as he had been working for Renasco in the Far East then and the traumas of the British market had largely washed over him. So Black Monday had been a new and bewildering experience.

In the weeks that followed, the pundits shifted into overdrive, burning through tonnes of newsprint to describe and explain the phenomenon. Jack could understand that there had been a crisis of confidence, a financial melt-down; he realised markets had risen too high; that they needed a 'technical readjustment'.

But he could not grasp why Butlers' share price should halve along with the market. Could investors not see that Butlers with its quality of earnings, its superb brand names and outstanding management, was a special case? Sales were rising, and after all – people have to eat. He propounded this point of view to almost everyone he met. Every time he entered a room, tall and elegant as ever, his hair now swept smoothly back from his brow, he looked for someone to tell it to. It became his hobby-horse.

It also became the hobby-horse of every head of a major, decently run company and of some not so decently run. His fellow industrialists, men like Sir Richard, Sir Hector Laing,

Denys Henderson, the chairman of the mighty ICI, all joined in one long game of 'ain't it awful'.

The City, they collectively agreed, – was a crazy place. It lacked logic, reason and justice. It was full of greedy gutless people who refused to pay attention to the facts. Denys Henderson wrote an article in the *Sunday Times* condemning the City money men. Jack wrote one for the *Daily Post*.

The share prices stayed put.

Jack's City friends listened to him patiently. They did not argue. They looked wistful sometimes – because they knew the party was over and they had lost a lot of money (although the wise had salted away more than they had lost). They looked philosophical – because they believed that sooner or later the good times would return. Until then survival was the name of the new game in town.

'You know it's a bit like musical chairs,' Charlie explained to Jack. 'The main thing is, when the music stops, you have a chair.'

Meanwhile, they tended their gardens, improved their golf games and reacquainted themselves with their families.

They knew they could not provide an answer to satisfy Jack and the self-appointed posse of industrialists who were after the City's blood.

In their hearts they had contempt for these men who demanded logic, reason and justice. These so-called captains of industry had not complained on the way up. To berate the stockmarket for irrational swings was like complaining when the incoming tide swept away the morning's sandcastle.

One captain of industry who had no truck with the whingers was Sir Leo Stern. He remembered the crash of 1974 with nightmare clarity. His debt had been high and as interest rates had soared in a matter of weeks, his bankers had threatened to foreclose on him. But the episode had confirmed his faith in the retail business which gave him strong cash flow, while those whose money was tied up in assets such as property, which became unsaleable overnight, went under. He had always found enough money to pay most of the interest, even though, for a while, he had to stop paying off the principal.

He had also been lucky. He had persuaded the clearing banks to fund his expanding business in the good times and

271

they proved to be less jumpy than the secondary banks, which collapsed like a set of dominoes.

Young though he had been at the time, he went and talked to the bank's top managers. Despite his East End accent, he impressed them with his enthusiasm, drive and grasp of finance. He showed them his cash flow forecasts and pointed out that if they foreclosed, they would never get paid. But if they settled for a lower payment in the short term, their investment would remain intact. They had not foreclosed.

In 1987 Stern had again been cleverer than most. His experience in 1974 combined with instinct had told him the bull market fever could not last for ever. When his driver started asking Stern's advice about which shares to buy, he knew the top had to be near. The public always gets sucked in at the peak. He foresaw a time when cash would be king and nearly two-thirds of his portfolio had been sold before the crash. Most of the remainder was in Butlers shares.

But while others kept the Butlers telephone lines burning, Stern bided his time. Had he not had assurances from Jack in Venice that he would not lose any money through his supportive action? He stood back and watched while the financial world ran around like headless chickens. He took the opportunity to cut a few costs in his business, spent more time with Paulette, and went to synagogue each week to pray and catch up on who were the real losers this time round. He waited to see if those who ran a large respectable company such as Butlers, and the senior directors of one London's top merchant banks, would behave like gentlemen. He suspected not. On paper, he was more than £20 million down on his Butlers shares. It annoyed him. But he looked forward with a warm glow of anticipation to turning the screw in due course.

Klaus von Gleichen studied the screen in front of him. Every now and then his pale eyes flicked to the view from his office window. Lake Zurich sparkled in the autumn sunshine. The sky was blue. All seemed well with the world.

His computer screen told a different story. Klaus was the director in charge of investments for BANTA, the octopine Swiss group whose interests included chunks of real estate in Manhattan, Hong Kong and London, an Italian food combine, a French publishing house and a minority stake in a commercial bank. The investment portfolio which Klaus handled had, before Black Monday, accounted for just over a third of the group's assets. The crash had taken it to less than a quarter. Not only did that displease BANTA's major share-holders, a list of which read like a Who's Who of international finance, but of more importance to Klaus, in the past two weeks his own power within the group had accordingly been devalued. The directors who headed the property and food arms were, purely through the vagaries of the Wall Street and London stock markets, now more respected and powerful than him.

To his surprise he found Sir Leo Stern unmoved. They had worked together on and off for five years, swapping informa-tion, helping each other out from time to time. Stern had suggested the investment in Empire and had also helped coerce him into supporting the Butlers' share price.

On Empire, he had done well selling out to Stern, although not as well as if he had waited for Renasco to come in. But he was down nearly £2 million on his investment in Butlers and neither Jack Armstrong nor his finance director would return his calls. The clear implication had been if the worst hap-pened he would not lose money. Always in these support operations it had been the case. It was understood.

Stern had actually laughed when he brought up the subject and suggested that everybody was in the same boat. But Klaus von Gleichen had a strong suspicion that everybody was not in the same boat. He happened to know from a contact at a Zurich bank where Max Schlosstein had his account that two days before the end of bid for Empire he had received $6.5m from a British bank. And he felt Stern's manner was too self-satisfied not to have done some kind of deal. Klaus wanted some answers.

Peter could not remember a more depressing time. Simply everything had gone wrong. Two huge rights issues had been pulled and he had felt compelled to advise three sizeable companies not to float their shares on the stockmarket after all. The chances were they would lose their nerve and stay private now, even if conditions improved.

273

One company was insisting on going to the market anyway and he was offering it at half the original valuation – which meant half the fee for him. Flotations were supposed to be about cultivating long-term business, Peter reflected, but it still irked him.

As for takeover bids – they were out of the question unless they were for cash, and cash was a commodity in short supply.

One thing Peter liked about Leo was he understood the City and never banged on about the unfairness of it all. Jack had become obsessed with the low level of his share price. The fact that everyone else's shares had plummeted seemed to go over his head.

'You'd think it was their cocks that had halved in size,' Peter said to John Young. 'If I hear one more company chief executive claim his company is a special case, I'm off to Hong Kong.'

'I don't think I've had one cheerful phone call in a fortnight,' he complained to Angela on the last weekend in October. 'It will take more than a few prayers to help some people out, I can tell you.'

They were drinking coffee in the sitting room after a quiet dinner. Angela was embroidering a cushion cover. The crash had put something of a damper on Peter's hospitable impulses and the house was empty of guests.

'How much have we lost on the stockmarket?' Angela knew that most of Peter's salary went into the house, in pictures and antiques, but she was curious.

'We don't have to worry, I've got lots of boodle coming in from the huge fees of this year.'

'Yes, but . . .' Angela's needle moved smoothly. She refused to be deflected by his defensive tone.

'Oh, I suppose about fifty grand,' he said as casually as possible.

Angela looked horrified.

'I suppose that puts the kybosh on our Christmas in Gstaad.'

'Oh God,' said Peter, 'never make a promise to a woman.' He sighed. 'Things may well have picked up again by then. In any case, we can still go. We just won't drink so much champagne, that's all.'

Somehow, thought Angela, his voice lacked conviction.

'How do you get a stockbroker out of a tree?' Patrick Peabody asked. He was sharing a bottle of Mumm Cordon Rouge with David Bang and a couple of girls from his agency in Balls Brothers wine bar near St Paul's. They all looked mystified. 'Cut the rope,' Patrick said softly.

Max Schlosstein took Jean-Pierre to lunch at Le Cirque. Show biz personalities far outweighed the financiers, Jean-Pierre noticed, and he was sure the normally minuscule gaps between the tables had widened. Nevertheless it was still full, if subdued in atmosphere.

Schlosstein ordered with the abandon of a man who has decided to stay fat. 'I just wanted to thank you for your help with Jack Armstrong,' he said, tucking into his pasta primavera.

'Think nothing of it,' replied Jean-Pierre.

'Yeah, I'd have felt pretty uptight now if I hadn't done that deal with them.'

Jean-Pierre's turquoise eyes fixed him in an innocent gaze. 'How has that investment fund of yours performed since the crash?' he asked pleasantly.

At Schlosstein's behest, Jean-Pierre had put some of his bigger clients' money into it. And Jack had directed some of Butlers pension fund managers that way.

Schlosstein shifted in his seat. 'We-ell, pretty much like everything else, I guess. But you know,' he leaned forward confidentially, 'I have the feeling this is temporary. I mean, the world is the same place it was three weeks ago. There's been a crisis of confidence, but like the President says, the economy is as solid as a rock.'

'So the money Butlers' pension fund put in is safe, is it, in your view?'

'Oh, sure. Sure!' Schlosstein's voice rose to an unnaturally high pitch. 'Listen, my kids have got money in that fund and I'm totally relaxed about it.'

Sometimes, Jean-Pierre thought, crunching a piece of radiccio, Americans made him want to throw up.

One minute before the whistle blew the striker scored the

winning goal, his long blond hair flying as he gave the ball a massive kick. A surge of happiness swept over Jack. The home crowd went mad, cheering and clapping and waving banners as the theme song of the team rose above the general uproar. Even the police looked happy. Up in the directors' box the enthusiasm was more restrained. But there were plenty of smiling faces as they gathered for drinks afterwards.

'I hope Butlers will be able to carry on with its sponsorship of the club, Jack,' said the chairman over a gin and tonic.

'Of course,' said Jack. He still felt high from the winning goal. 'We can't let a few idiots in the City affect the future of the team.'

The chairman looked relieved. 'Mind, this isn't the time to go on a spending spree. Need to let it blow over,' added Jack.

Inwardly he knew there was little chance of extracting much money for the club at the next board meeting. Sponsoring the club had been a far from unanimous decision – in fact he had steamrollered it through.

Edward had oozed disapproval like a maiden aunt sanctioning a visit to a strip club. 'It's good for our image, it's good for their image,' Jack had insisted. Ever since he had captained the school soccer team he had longed to be a director of a football club. He had come to understand exactly why Stern kept a controlling shareholding in his company. Edward could go to hell.

Since the crash nothing had turned out the way he anticipated. He had expected the few weeks after the bid to be hard work, sorting out the Empire directors and sending in the 'hit squads', as he called them, to the various subsidiaries.

In fact, the Empire directors had all gone quite meekly, content with fat compensation cheques. Men without ambition, Jack thought with contempt. No wonder the company was such a mess. Only Bertie Underworth had held out for a seat on the board, arguing that he knew the company better than anyone and could be of considerable assistance. As Bertie's service contract was more lucrative than anyone's, he had risen in Jack's estimation. And he would be useful – just so long as he didn't have any power.

But the real problem had been the shareholders. He was amazed to find leading fund managers of unit trust groups and insurance companies demanding compensation for their losses, claiming they had been given indemnities. On top of that he had more than a dozen calls from fund managers asking when they could make their presentation to take over the management of the Butlers pension fund.

Charlie and Peter were behaving most strangely about the whole thing; they rarely returned his calls and suffered from extraordinary lapses of memory. No gratitude, he thought, absolutely none.

Two days later he received a call from Klaus von Gleichen, demanding a meeting.

'I can fly to London any time you want. In any case I have to talk to Sir Leo about certain things.' His clipped tones were quietly menacing. Jack felt trapped. Gleichen was well aware of what had gone on during the bid and by mentioning Stern was making sure Jack realised the extent of his knowledge.

But he did not want von Gleichen seen in the office. Edward would immediately jump to the right conclusion. So would Bertie who had taken to drifting around the corridors, popping into people's offices – far too much for Jack's liking. If he arranged to meet von Gleichen for lunch or dinner somewhere, he felt certain he would be seen. If one of those bloodsucking fund managers got the idea deals were being done, he would have to pay every single one of them off. There was nothing else for it.

'Well, actually, Peter Markus and I have some business in Zurich. Why don't we come and see you?'

'An excellent idea,' said von Gleichen, understanding immediately, 'and so much more discreet.'

'It would help if you could be more specific about what you wanted to discuss?'

'Regretfully, that must wait.' Von Gleichen's voice was soft but firm.

Jack arranged for his secretary to do the necessary liaison work.

Then there was the matter of Hogarth Stein's fees. The bill had been for more than £19 million and when Jack had complained it was more than three times what Stuart Anderson had charged Empire – a tab Butlers was also having to pick up – Peter merely said: 'Empire lost.'

Shearman Drussel had also charged a fee for its advice to Empire, although fortunately it had been even more geared to success than Hogarth Stein.

Jack felt drained. The previous day, he had gone through the figures with Edward. After the merchant bank fees, which admittedly included all the sub-underwriting, came the PR and advertising, which was up to nearly £3 million. The security bill was nearly £1 million. But what had really hit Jack like a slap in the face was the bill from Krandsdorf Consultancy for £2 million. Edward had been outraged and Jack had a feeling that Sir Richard's attitude would be much the same.

Somehow, Jack knew, it had to be paid. Worse, was Edward's discovery of the $6.5 million consultancy fee to Schlosstein. Jack had never quite got round to broaching the subject. Edward had become pale and tight-lipped. 'I do hope we're going to be able to explain all these bills satisfactorily to our auditors,' he said.

And then there was the matter of Stern. It was as though someone filled his stomach with ice cubes every time he thought about it. He had delayed asking Peter whether he thought what had been said in Venice held good now. After all, the circumstances were extraordinary. But he knew the answer. There had not been a peep out of Stern, not a call, not a mention of him by Peter; not so much as the snapping of a twig. It was like waiting for a great bear to wake from sleep and emerge, hungry, from its lair.

It was pouring with rain when he and Peter landed at Zurich airport two days later. The flight had been so bumpy they had slopped orange juice down their suits and Jack had nearly gouged his eye out with a forkful of sausage when the plane had taken a particularly violent dive. As they walked across the wet tarmac to the airport bus, Peter shivered under his Burberry. He loathed deals that dragged on like this with tedious loose ends to be tied up. He loathed Klaus von Gleichen and he loathed Zurich. Still, he thought miserably, it was not as if he had a full diary to keep him busy.

278

The small anonymous offices of BANTA were warm, quiet and thickly carpeted. Jack and Peter were relieved of their coats and shown into Klaus von Gleichen's office where they drank some excellent coffee and listened to him explain once more that he was £1.8 million down on his investment.

Jack had decided to play tough guy. 'I am not responsible for the vagaries of the stockmarket,' he said tersely. 'We can't go around doling out cash to everyone who lost money on Butlers during the stockmarket crash. We'd break the company.'

'Mr Armstrong,' said von Gleichen, who believed in formality, 'for a start I am not "everyone", and secondly I have no intention of demanding anything as crude as a cash payment.' He opened a slim manila folder in front of him.

'You have a canning subsidiary called Pomodoro Rosso with its main operations in Italy, I believe. It doesn't really fit in with the rest of your company. I gather the management wanted to do a buy-out earlier this year but you could not agree on a price.'

Jack and Peter exchanged glances. On several occasions since the crash Jack wished he had accepted Sean Mac-Cready's proposal. It would have got his potentially dangerous presence out of Butlers forever and the price of just over £3 million he had offered now looked generous.

'I am prepared to buy it for a price of £1 million.'

'Out of the question,' Peter rapped out before Jack could stop him. 'That's barely a third of what the management were offering six months ago.'

'£1.2 million is my final offer,' said von Gleichen impassively.

'It's outrageous,' protested Peter.

Von Gleichen ignored him. He had been staring at Jack intently.

'Six months ago is a long time. The world has changed. Even a well-known supermarket chain like Wingways has halved in value.'

Peter stared at the floor. There were a hundred better examples than Wingways and the three of them knew that. He hated to give in to a hoodlum like von Gleichen, but he was clearly a psychopath. It was better he was off their backs.

'Perhaps my client and I could have a few moments alone to discuss the matter?'

'Of course.' They were shown into a small prettily furnished waiting room.

They emerged twenty minutes later.

Jack said: 'The managing director is a man called Sean MacCready. I want written assurance that he will be kept on.'

Von Gleichen nodded. 'Yes, that should be possible. In fact I understand he's quite good – speaks Italian too, something quite rare with you British.'

'£1.3 million and it's yours,' said Peter.

A glimmer of a smile passed across von Gleichen's bloodless features.

'Dealt.'

They all shook hands.

It did not take Sean MacCready long to work it out. A formal letter from Jack had arrived saying BANTA was in the process of buying the company in order to merge it with its own canning interests in Italy. The BANTA food group had been trying to bribe his suppliers away from him for some months. How much simpler just to buy his company – he considered it his – and close it down. Cold fury overwhelmed him. This was what he got for betraying his class, for selling out to the capitalist pigs.

He noted there was no mention of price. He would not have minded betting it was less than what he and his management had offered.

He flew to London and asked for an appointment with Jack. It was refused. The next morning he was waiting when Jack arrived at the office at eight o'clock.

Jack's face turned to stone when he saw him. Unwillingly, he invited him in.

'I think you owe me an explanation,' said MacCready, his blue eyes glittering with controlled rage.

'It was a simple business proposition,' said Jack curtly. 'The timing of their offer was better than the timing of yours.' His fingers played with a biro. 'I am looking after your interests, you know. They're giving written assurances they'll keep you on.'

'As what?' Sean spat out the words. 'Don't you realise they want to close us down? They've been trying to break us for over a year, so that they can screw the growers around Puglia into the ground.'

Jack wished he would get out.

'The deal is virtually signed,' he said, his tone icy. For a moment he thought Sean was going to hit him. Then suddenly he slumped in his chair.

'Please, please, reconsider,' he begged. 'This job has meant everything to me. My wife and I have been happy for the first time in ten years.'

With a jolt Jack realised he was close to tears.

'I'm sorry. The deal will go ahead. It's for the good of the rest of the group.'

Sean stood up slowly, regaining his dignity as he did so.

'And how much did they pay you to wreck one of your own subsidiaries?' he asked in his desolate scouse twang.

Jack found he could not meet the man's eyes. 'We are receiving a fair commercial price. There has been a stock-market crash.' He felt impotent guilt at the anguish before him. 'Now, please, I have work to do.'

Sean stood in front of him, a tall, gangling figure who had betrayed his ideals and his fellow union members on the say-so of the man before him. Hatred filled his soul.

But there was something else bothering him.

There was no logic to this deal. He could not see a motive for suddenly selling out to the Italians, or the Swiss, or whoever they were, for less than he and his team had offered.

'I'm going to get to the bottom of this,' he said, suddenly calm. He turned on his heel and was gone, leaving Jack's office door wide open.

Sean had already planted two spies and quite soon they found the right people to bribe. It took him three weeks – a little longer than he expected – to discover the price BANTA had paid.

By then, he had remembered BANTA was a significant shareholder at the time of the bid – and that there had been a big story when it sold its stake to Sir Leo Stern.

He went to the registrars of both Empire and Butlers and

found that diligent company secretaries had uncovered other shareholdings, through using the powers of section 212 of the Companies Act. At the end of the bid these records, which were by law available to the public, showed that BANTA still held 2 per cent of Butlers.

He calculated the loss on the holding from the Thursday before the crash – it was £1.7 million, exactly the difference between the price he had offered Jack for Pommodoro Rosso and the price von Gleichen had paid.

As the days passed Sean's worst fears were realised. BANTA offered him the choice between a lowly factory manager's job in one of their olive oil plants – 400 kilometres from where he had bought his dream Italian farmhouse six months before – or one year's salary. He took the money, left Lucia and his two children in the farmhouse, and went to stay with an old trade union friend in London.

By mid-November, Denis found his clients' potential bad debts amounted to £877,000 and that was money Denis was bound to pay to the firm. The sum fell just short of the cash he had amassed over the previous three years.

To Irene, it was an action replay of what had happened in 1974 and to a lesser extent 1980. Only this time, she feared it could kill her husband.

Denis never complained to anyone about what had happened. It was the market, it was his life. Inwardly he cursed himself that with all his experience he always ended up giving his profits back. It was not as if this bull run hadn't been long enough. And he had been careful. He had stashed away just over £1 million in various offshore hidey holes so that the Inland Revenue didn't get their hands on it. At the time of the crash he had only a small amount of his own money invested. It was just that he chose to deal for unreliable people who left him with a mountain of bad debts.

Sarah watched him going through his books and sighing. They were the only ones left in the office. Someone had turned the Topic screen off and the lights of other offices glowed through the dark outside even though it was only 5.30. Christmas was coming.

'Why don't you have a thorough clean up of your clients

and next time refuse to deal for the suspect ones?' she suggested.

'That wouldn't be very interesting, would it?' he muttered without looking up. 'Anyway, who says there'll be a next time?'

Sarah realised with a shock that the lovable, irrepressible and forever optimistic Denis Jones was seriously depressed.

She got up from her desk and stood by him, putting a comforting arm around his shoulders.

'Nah,' he said, 'don't give me sympathy. You'll find it in the dictionary between shit and syphilis.' He sat up straight. 'I need a good blow job, not bloody sympathy.'

Instinctively she withdrew her hand.

'Nah, not from you, don't worry. Save all that for Leo.'

Sarah's heart began pounding in her throat. Unconsciously she backed away from him as though he were on fire, her face white.

'Sorry, sorry, shouldn't have mentioned it,' he said. 'You could try not hanging on his every word, though.' Denis closed his book and started putting things in his briefcase. It was a warning.

Sarah felt as if she were choking. 'Denis, I . . . you wouldn't . . .'

He gave her a long hard look. 'Mention it to anybody else? Never. Not even him.'

She realised she was shaking with fright.

'Listen, you've turned quite pale. Come on, girl. Put your coat on. Uncle Denis will buy you a sherbert and make you feel better.'

It was only lying in bed that night, reliving those moments that she understood the fear. It was not being found out – she could live with that. But if they were found out, she would have to stop seeing him. That was what terrified her.

Chapter 19

Jack snoozed fitfully in front of the television, his long body sprawled indolently in the armchair. He had spent the morning playing golf and inevitably drunk too much in the clubhouse at lunchtime. Rosemary had gone for a long weekend to Leningrad with a girlfriend. He wished she would come home.

The world had turned suddenly precarious, with enemies at every turn, and he felt the need of her commonsense approach. He hated the house without her in it. He glanced at his watch. Another hour before she was due. He drifted off again.

'Jack, Jack, wake up!' Rosemary's voice came to him through a dark fog. Relief that she was back flooded through him and his green eyes were already smiling when he opened them.

But Rosemary was not smiling. Beside her stood a tall bronzed man in his mid-thirties with long, casually cut blond hair. Jack had never seen him before.

Before he could ask, Rosemary spoke. 'Jack, this is Julian. I don't know how to tell you this gently but we're in love and want to spend some time together. I'd like – I want a trial separation.'

'What, now?' asked Jack, incredulous. This must be a dream! Rosemary had always been the model of fidelity. He would have bet anyone she had never been with another man.

'You wouldn't want me to stay now I've told you, would you?' Rosemary's voice was gentle, almost as if she was talking to a child.

Jack stood up, feeling foolish in his stockinged feet in front of the stranger. He was a good ten years younger than Rosemary – healthy and strong. Jack's brain refused to take it in.

He slipped on his shoes. 'I don't know what to think. Can't we talk about it on our own?' He motioned to Julian.

'I'm sorry.' She looked at him, her cheeks flushed from the cold outside. 'But it's what I've got to do. I'll ring you tomorrow and we'll talk it over.'

Jack noticed Julian dispassionately summing up the decor. Even as he wondered if he should hit him, Rosemary took his hand and moved towards the door.

Jack took a step forward. 'But I need you.' His voice was a bewildered whisper. 'You are my wife.'

She turned on him, guilt firing her anger. 'I needed you. But you always preferred your career.'

He stood in the dimly lit, rumpled sitting room with the curtains still open, listening to the sounds of departure. He heard the slam of the front door, the footsteps on the path, the sound of a car engine starting and the tyres squelching on a wet road.

She would be back. Julian was no more than a toy-boy after all. It was the mid-life crisis. She'd become obsessed with looking younger. She would be back, he told himself again. The bitch! And until she saw sense, he could see more of Jane. His cock stiffened but his spirits failed to lift.

Anyway, he had more important things to worry about. He walked to the window, drew the curtains and poured himself half a tumbler of whisky.

During his late twenties, Sean MacCready's politics had swung so far to the left he had regarded most members of the Labour Party as capitalist tools. His contacts were built up with extreme left-wing back-benchers, representing constituencies in deprived areas of Scotland and the North.

In the new look Labour Party, none of his friends had much power or influence. For his message to have an impact in high places, he knew it must not come from the 'loony left'. He needed somebody with credibility, who would be listened to at shadow ministerial level.

His first step was his old friend, Len Weaver. Like Sean, Len had started out on the far left but had become a moderate, a high up in the electricians' union which had sold out to Rupert Murdoch during the Wapping dispute, sacrificing the hard line printers as a result.

At the time, what Sean had seen as collusion with the capitalist 'enemy' had almost broken their friendship. But Sean's recent experience in management had changed his attitude. He had come to know the difficulties of operating if the workforce has you by the balls – something newspaper owners had experienced for more than twenty years.

During his time as managing director of Pomodoro Rosso, he had renewed his friendship with Len and now felt he was the right man to give advice – although he was careful not to tell him the story in detail. He did not want his grand plan going off at half-cock.

Len suggested the obvious. Sean's local MP from the North-West just happened to be the ideal carrier. Donald Reece was one of the new breed of Labour MPs. The second son of a Ford junior manager, he had grown up in the wasteland of Tottenham in North London, attended the local grammar school and gone on to Warwick University where he obtained a degree in economics.

His father's career had been held back because of his unstinting trade union activity, something Donald did not recognise until his mid-twenties.

Always active in political societies, his career developed naturally. As a Labour councillor he attracted the attention of Ken Livingstone and became involved with the GLC. Livingstone had started out as his hero, but Donald soon detected the self-destructive flaw – and became a pragmatist.

He saw no point in fighting for something you couldn't hope to win. He entered the House of Commons at twenty-nine after a swing to Labour in a by-election. In debate, he was clear thinking, articulate, persuasive and unemotional. He had stamina and a good memory and his hard work had been rewarded by nomination to various committees and quangos. But at thirty-four he was ready, in his own opinion, for a shadow junior ministerial post.

Most important, he knew Len well and could be persuaded

to hear Sean's story. Sean arrived at the Houses of Parliament early and had to wait in the Central Lobby for fifteen minutes before Donald emerged. He led Sean down seemingly endless low-ceilinged corridors and finally into a small scrappy half-timbered office, cluttered with desks and filing cabinets.

For the first few minutes Donald wondered why on earth Len had been so keen for him to see this man. He could sense an irrational, burning hatred. People with grudges rarely had accurate or helpful tales to tell. But he had pledged his time.

'Right, how can I help.'

'That's it,' said Sean after twenty minutes of solid talking.

By then Donald had changed his mind. The story made sense, and while Sean's anger still worried him, it sounded interesting on its own merits. He was impressed, but he knew it was pointless pressing for action unless they were sure of their ground.

'They are big contributors to the Tory Party, you say?' he was mulling it over.

'Yes, £50,000 for the last two years. And the chairman, Sir Richard Butler, is always round at Number 10.'

Donald was still uncertain. 'It's extremely interesting, but it's largely circumstantial. We don't have massive research facilities in the House, you know. You *are* sure about the share stakes and the purchase price?'

'The share stakes are a matter of public record. And I have a copy of the letter of agreement for the purchase for my company where the price is mentioned. In any case, it will have to appear in the Butlers' accounts.'

Donald smiled inwardly at this former communist's possessiveness about a company.

'There has been a stockmarket crash. Could it just be that the lower price reflects that?'

Sean shook his tousled black curls. 'Listen, they paid less than a third of what an independent firm of consultants valued it at seven months before on the basis of historic profits. Armstrong has given it away.'

Donald picked up the emotion in the other man's voice.

'Forgive me,' said Donald, 'but I'm always suspicious of cases where there's personal malice involved. What do you personally hope to gain by exposing this?'

To his surprise, Sean laughed. But it was a laugh without mirth. 'Oh, you have every reason to be suspicious. There *is* malice involved – I'd like to see Jack Armstrong in jail.' He fixed Donald with a chilling stare. 'But I'm right, too.'

'OK,' said Donald. 'Bring me the documentary evidence, chapter and verse. I'll see what I can do.'

Jack studied the now familiar menu at Mark's Club but it did nothing to stimulate his appetite. Peter, sitting at Stern's side, felt much the same. Jack and Peter ordered lobster salad to start, followed by plain Dover sole. Stern ordered caviar and grouse.

By his side Peter had a revised copy of the dossier of any Butlers subsidiaries which might appeal to Stern. Peter could not think he wanted another supplier's deal. His shops did not buy enough of any one product to make up for anything like the £25 million he calculated Stern was out of pocket on his Butlers shares.

Jack and Peter had been summoned that morning to dinner. Both had prior engagements but had recognised a command when they heard one.

Stern had already arrived at the table, rising as they joined him, all towering benevolence. 'Let's have a bottle of Krug. We mustn't let the market get on top of us,' he had said, shaking hands warmly with them.

'Cheers,' he continued, playing up the simple East End lad bit. 'Happy days.' They all drank. Stern drained his glass, placed it thoughtfully on the table and began to speak.

'Now Peter here is a clever City chap, and Jack, you've learned a lot in the last couple of years. Tell me, just exactly how would you define an indemnity?'

Nothing like getting straight to the point, thought Peter.

At that moment the waitress brought the lobster salads.

'Mayonnaise?' Her voice Was high-pitched, Italian-accented.

Peter was irritated. 'You know perfectly well, Leo. An indemnity is a guarantee against a loss.'

'And remind me – because I am only a simple retailer – when is it legal and when is it not?'

Peter sighed. Jack could feel his heart thudding. 'It is quite

288

legal to indemnify someone against loss if they buy shares in a bid target, for example. But it is not legal,' he coughed despite himself, 'to indemnify someone against loss if they buy shares in your company, or the company which you are advising.'

'I see,' said Stern. 'So effectively those assurances that you gave to me in Venice were illegal?'

Jack and Peter munched their lettuce. As if he hadn't known so at the time, thought Peter.

'So I suppose that is why you haven't offered to honour them?'

'Actually, Leo,' Jack began, but Stern held up his hand. His caviar still lay, dark and glistening on his plate.

'I'm surprised at you, Peter,' he said softly. He mixed some egg white and chopped onion into the caviar, pressed it on to a piece of toast and pointed it in Jack's direction. 'This Johnny come lately here, I can understand getting in a muddle.' His tone became aggrieved. 'But you, Peter, you should have known better. I might almost think you took advantage of my lack of knowledge of City matters.'

Jack tried again. 'We have got some suggestions for you, Leo. We've been thinking hard about what to do.' He mustered some of his old confident charm. 'Of course we appreciated your help during the bid and we wouldn't want to see you lose out. But it has been a difficult time, as I'm sure you realise.'

'I do, Jack, I do.'

Peter cut in. 'So perhaps when we've finished dinner you could look through my file? I'm sure we can find something that keeps us technically within the law, but which makes you feel better.'

Stern's voice was icy. 'Nah, forget it.'

Peter and Jack exchanged glances. Surely he wasn't letting them off the hook?

Stern finished his caviar, wiped his mouth, leaned back on the banquette and smiled. 'I'd like to sell Butlers something for once. I don't want any of your rubbish.'

So that was it, thought Peter.

'I've got a couple of warehouses on the outskirts of New-castle on Tyne, superfluous to my uses. As you know, I don't like hanging on to property and since my latest reorganisation I don't need 'em. As a food manufacturer I'm sure you have unlimited use for warehouse space. But my property friends tell me it could be a very valuable piece of land. You could make a lot of money out of it sometime.' He smiled again, this time with real pleasure. 'I'll sell it to you for £30 million.'

They both gaped at him. Finally Peter drew breath.

'But Leo,' he pleaded, 'that's a price beyond reason.'

Stern's black eyes glittered. 'Call it what you like,' he smiled. 'It's my price.'

Two weeks later, the shadow secretary of state for trade and industry sat in his less than spacious office and tenderly fingered the typed pages on his desk. It was a briefing note left by Donald Reece and he loved it.

A true blue Tory board of directors: The chairman, a leading light in the CBI with the ear of the Prime Minister; the chief executive one of the rising stars of British industry and tipped for a knighthood; one Tory MP on the board and £50,000 a year to the Party.

'And,' he said gleefully, 'all breaking the rules like they were playing Monopoly on a wet Sunday afternoon.'

With him sat his Parliamentary Secretary and a junior.

'Now what do you chaps think we should do about this interesting document, for maximum damage?' he asked them.

'You could bring it up at Question Time,' said the younger one.

'No, no,' said the other. 'If we try that, it will be so far down the list it will never get asked. Everyone is obsessed with tabling questions about the Health Service at the moment.' He reached for his cigarettes.

'What about a simple letter to your counterpart in the government simply stating the facts?' He lit up and took a long draw. 'You understand that Butlers Group, Britain's second largest food company after its opportunistic takeover of Empire Foods, is in breach of the Companies Act, section whatever. You therefore call upon him to institute an enquiry into the matter.'

'That seems pretty low key,' said the shadow secretary of

290

state. 'Can't we make something of the fact that they are huge contributors to the Tory Party and that their chairman spends half his life whispering sweet nothings to the Prime Minister?'

The other man grinned. 'Well, it's a gamble. The idea is if we play it low key to begin with, they might fall into the trap of thinking we will forget about it and therefore won't take action.' He paused for effect.

'That's when we can bring it up at Question Time and publicly imply the reason there is no inquiry is because the company is such a huge Conservative supporter.'

The shadow secretary of state leaned back in his chair and grinned. 'Excellent,' he exclaimed. 'Truly excellent'.

Two evenings later, his counterpart in the government sat gloomily at supper with his mistress – a thin, nervous-looking brunette. He had received the letter that lunchtime but had not been fooled by the tone.

Something would have to be done, he knew, much though it irked him. He had become genuinely fond of Sir Richard and valued him as an adviser. It seemed likely that if an investigation led to anything he would lose him.

Jack Armstrong was a bit cocksure and aggressive for one so young. But youth and vigour were what was needed these days. And then there was the problem of charles Fookes-Wilson, the MP on the Butlers board. His career had been looking quite promising.

He had the world baying at his heels about corruption in the City. This was all he needed. God knew what the Prime Minister would make of it all – probably reshuffle him. He decided to talk it through with his colleagues in the morning, and wondered how long it would be before the letter hit the press.

If the newspapers were to be believed at all, it had been the government's intention to make the Guinness scandal the scapegoat for the wrongs of the City. 'Let's get the handcuffs on,' one Cabinet minister was reputed to have said.

The government image had become too entangled with that of big business and high finance – something on which the opposition traded. If the result of a criminal trial could throw a few high-profile City figures into prison, and some who had been entertained at Downing Street, it should prove the government's impartiality once and for all. It could not be seen to condone commercial and financial crime while continuing to fill the prisons with petty criminals.

But the case was proving incredibly difficult to bring to trial and it seemed unlikely a jury would ever understand it when it did.

Senior civil servants had come to think that if there was a case that was less complicated and messy, something more cut and dried that the public could understand, it would be much better to get on with that. It would at least go some way towards satisfying the critics of the City, who since the crash had been baying for blood.

So the Prime Minister and her public relations advisors pounced on the Butlers case as a way out of the quagmire to possible glory. His fears of reshuffle were replaced by hopes of greater things.

The government were not going to fall into the trap of dragging their heels and have it all leak out as if there was some kind of cover up. Those days were over. It was a pity about Sir Richard, he was awfully nice and very supportive. But at the end of the day, if thine eye offend thee . . .

The opposition gave the government just twenty-four hours before leaking the letter to all the lobby correspondents. The story exploded across the front pages and television news. Sean was euphoric. But because there was no detail as to just how the Companies Act might have been breached, no paper followed it up and the story died. Sean's pleasure gave way to disappointment. It was a long way from the campaign of public persecution he had envisaged – and he was not to know the government's plans.

If he could only tell the full facts of the BANTA purchase of his beloved Pomodoro Rosso to one newspaper. But his own contacts with the national press were non-existent. Then he remembered a man on the *Herald* with whom Jack had been very pally. They seemed to have fallen out just at the end of the bid. He would compose a dossier.

On Friday morning, Patrick Peabody read Sean's letter with extreme interest. His attempts to follow up the initial story had got nowhere and now here was someone offering to tell him the full details behind the opposition's demand for a DTI enquiry. He reached for the telephone.

Two hours later Sean sat in his office. Patrick's first reaction to his story was much the same as Donald's. He had listened to too many people motivated by spite, people who felt they had a good tale to tell. But when Sean produced photocopies of the evidence he had given the opposition, Patrick's attitude changed.

Sean promised him total exclusivity and for once Patrick judged he could keep the story to himself. This time he had more than enough information to run it without talking to Jack, but it would be tremendous to get a quote. Jack had not forgiven him for siding with Renasco in the last instance, but victory had soothed his pride. Anyway it was his own fault Patrick thought, flicking open his loose-leaf telephone book. There were five numbers: Butlers' main number, Jack's private line, his car telephone, the flat and the Esher house. If he could get to him without the switchboard alerting him, so much the better.

'The vodaphone subscriber you have called is not available,' said a clipped female voice.

He tried Jack's private line – it was engaged. He really wanted to see him face to face. There was so much you could not tell over the telephone. It was already twelve-thirty and he was due at the Howard Hotel at one o'clock for lunch with someone you could not lightly stand up. He tried the private line again. Still engaged.

He would take the risk and leave it till the afternoon. Jack was either going to talk to him or not. He rang the main switchboard and left a message with his secretary.

Jack stared at the cuttings. The letter simply referred to breaches of the Company's Act – and Jack was at a loss to know which particular breaches might be referred to. The ever present knot of fear in his stomach pulled tighter.

The letter had been published on Wednesday and since then, absolutely nothing had happened. Sir Richard had been on to him; Peter had been on to him; Jack had been on to the company lawyers and to David Bang, but they all seemed as much in the dark as each other. But the fact that the letter came from the Labour Party gave him a clue. Somehow, the whole thing had Sean MacCready stamped all over it. Amanda popped through with a note.

'Patrick Peabody wants you to call him.'

'Bloody journalists!' said Jack. 'Can't trust them further than you can throw Sir Leo Stern.' He smiled grimly at his own joke.

Amanda hovered in front of his desk. He had refused all press calls so far, but something about Patrick's tone made her push his case. 'He said he was running an important story and would prefer to talk to you about it if at all possible.'

He looked out of the window at the already darkening sky. Perhaps Patrick knew something he did not. 'OK, put him through.'

It was already dark when Patrick went to see Jack at St James's Square later that afternoon. Little appeared to have changed.

'Come and have a drink, Patrick. I'm sorry we fell out at the end of the bid, but there's no reason why we can't be friends. I won after all.'

He was laying on the North country accent a bit, thought Patrick, but as they sat in the office like old times he felt himself relaxing. He told him the stockbroker joke, sipped his glass of wine and remembered why he had been fond of Jack who poured himself a huge Scotch.

But when Patrick finally broached the subject of the sale of an Italian tomato plant to a mysterious Swiss company which had owned shares in Butlers – and saw the blood drain from Jack's face – he knew there could never be a reconciliation between them.

The *Sunday Herald* led its City pages on the story with the headline BUTLER'S ITALIAN CONNECTION. To Patrick's fury he had been unable to persuade the editor to run it on the front page as well. The numbers involved were too small. But he had written a pithy tailpiece in his column, demanding a DTI investigation.

Patrick's instinct told him he was pulling the thread of a

294

skein of intrigue which would make it the best story of his career.

After Patrick left his office on the Friday night, Jack had weighed up the options. He felt no desire to call in David Bang who had been vague and unhelpful when the letter had been published. Jack had ceased to trust him.

He had a sudden childhood memory of sitting on a rough mat at the top of a helter skelter at the local fair. Only one thing could postpone the moment when he pushed himself away, down the swirling path. He had to stop Patrick.

He poured himself another drink. He was the silver-tongued Jack Armstrong, after all. He had met the managing director of the company that owned the *Herald* at a party some weeks before.

They had exchanged cards.

His heart thudded as he dialled the number. Charmingly, he reintroduced himself and explained the situation. Just as charmingly he threatened to withdraw Butlers advertising forever, if the coverage was 'negative'.

The managing director sounded genuinely sympathetic but regretted he had no direct power over the editorial decisions, however valuable the advertising.

It was raining the following Sunday morning in Esher and the house was quiet and grey. There was a vacuum where Rosemary should´ have been. He missed the sound of her voice, the smell of her in the bathroom, her warm, reassuring body at night.

He re-read the *Sunday Herald* articles over and over again and then the follow ups in the other Sundays. He had been so anxious about the story, he had driven up to Kings Cross the night before to pick up the first edition. He had thought it would help him to sleep to know the worst. Instead it made him anguished and he had tossed and turned all night, waking at six as if it were a weekday.

He considered going to church, but he found the thought facing the Vicar too daunting, although he didn't suppose the Vicar read the business pages. He had never realised Rosemary read so much. The place was full of new novels and self-improvement books such as *Pulling Your Own Strings* and *The Road Less Travelled*, which began 'Life is difficult'. But whatever he picked up, his mind would not focus. It kept flicking over the mental Rotaflex of what they could get him on.

If they started with BANTA, why should they leave it there? Patrick's article had touched on Schlosstein, although it was clear he didn't have much detail. But what about those discontented fund managers, so many of whom had been pacified in one way or another? And who exactly were 'they'?

All the secretary of state had said was that the matter was being 'looked into', and clearly neither Patrick nor his rivals had been able to get any further. Was he to expect DTI officers on his doorstep when he arrived at St James's Square, or even the police? He had a vision of being handcuffed and led through the office like the American insider dealers.

He thought of phoning the company lawyer. Was it appropriate? Fear smothered his brain in fog. Had he actually done anything illegal? He knew he had been sailing near the wind, bending – well, perhaps breaking – the rules of the Takeover Code. But there had been no crime exactly. 'At least, he did not think there had been a crime – not a real crime.

In any case he had been advised by the best merchant banker in town. Peter did not know about the Schlosstein fee, of course. But Jean-Pierre had been pretty relaxed about it.

What an idiot he had been to buy those warehouses from Stern – the local estate agents had estimated they were worth £5 million at the most. He felt his confidence drain away like bathwater.

The house closed in around him, forcing him out into the park to walk in the rain. He pulled his jacket collar up around him, feeling miserably furtive. Jane was in Hong Kong again on business. Until Rosemary left he had not realised how busy Jane was. She was fine for occasional sex, but he needed more than that.

On his way back he passed the local pub; caught sight of a darts match underway through the doorway as a group of laughing young people entered. The Christmas lights were already twinkling inside and the fat double-sized bottles of spirits gleamed on the optics.

It might as well have been a mirage, he thought with a great tug of longing for that woody, male atmosphere of a British pub on a Sunday morning.

At the house there was a brief message from Peter on the ex-directory answering machine asking him to ring back. He rang back.

Peter said: 'I thought you might need cheering up. Did you know about this article?'

Jack felt a wave of affection for him. 'Well, Patrick came to see me on Friday.' He laughed wryly. 'Said he wanted to get a balanced view.'

'What on earth possessed you to see him?'

It was a question that Jack had asked himself several times.

'I hoped to make him see our point of view.'

There was a long silence. 'Did he mention me or Hogarth at all?'

The wave hit the sand. So that was it. A call to find out if his own position was endangered.

'No, he didn't, strangely enough.'

'Well, I do hope you remember, Jack, that I never wanted to do that deal. When Klaus first mentioned the price, I said it was out of the question.' Peter's voice had lost its initial cheeriness. He sounded eerily calm.

'You came round quite quickly, I seem to remember,' Jack replied, an edge of anger in his voice. How interesting that Peter called him Klaus.

'Only because you were so hellbent on doing it.'

Jack realised Peter was trying to push him into a clear statement that he was not party to what happened. And over the phone.

'I don't think it's sensible to talk about this on the telephone,' he said. 'From what I hear they bug you at the drop of a hat these days. Come round on Monday morning and see me at the office.

'I can't, I've got three meetings one after the other. Listen, I must dash, we've got guests arriving for lunch.' Peter put the phone down, turned off the tape recorder and felt ashamed. Then he felt scared.

Jack's listed number started ringing around lunchtime as the keen reporters for the Monday papers began their follow-up calls. After three conversations Jack's resolution to sound calm and confident began to falter.

'But my editor will kill me if you don't give me a quote,' pleaded a whining girl from *The Times*.

'I'm sorry, but I have no comment to make,' he said for the fourth time, putting down the phone and taking it off the hook. 'I hope he does,' he muttered to himself.

He arrived at the office the next morning expecting a milling throng of reporters and DTI inspectors. Everything was exactly as normal. As he sat down at his desk absorbing the comfortable familiarity it flashed through his mind that it had just been a bad dream. Then Sir Richard appeared, knocking briefly on the door but not waiting for a reply.

'I just wanted a few words before the others arrived – I know you get in early,' he said. His face wore a sheepish 'sorry to do this to you, old boy' look. In his hand was a copy of the *Herald*.

'I do wish you'd told me about this,' he said, sitting down heavily opposite Jack.

'I didn't know.' Jack saw the look of incredulity. 'I mean, I didn't know for certain he would run the story, or how large.' Sir Richard's large flabby features had settled into concern. He said nothing.

'In any case, I know it seems like a big story, but it's just an embittered old union man stirring up trouble. Everyone will forget it in a week.' Jack had decided on the stance he would take on the drive in.

Relief flitted across Sir Richard's features for an instant, then doubt took hold again. He cleared his throat.

'I don't recall this sale ever coming up at a board meeting.'

Jack managed an ingenuous smile. 'It didn't seem worth bothering the board about, a deal this size.'

'No, I suppose not.' Sir Richard cleared his throat again. 'What concerns me is the allegation that the sale of this subsidiary was in some way linked to the buying of shares in Butlers.'

Jack breathed in. 'Me too, Richard, and I shall talk to the lawyers first thing.' He reached for his cigar box and continued: 'It's absolute rubbish, of course – it was purely circum-stantial. And there was a stockmarket crash between Mac-Cready offering to buy the company and the sale to BANTA.'

The look of relief lingered longer on Sir Richard's face this time. 'Yes, of course. Would you mind awfully if I sat in on the meeting with the lawyer? It's just – what with us being blue-eyed boys round at Downing Street . . .'

Jack had already mentally kissed his knighthood goodbye, but did not think it was a good idea to tell Richard he would now never sit in the House of Lords.

The next two weeks passed in a strange kind of limbo. There was no sign of the DTI and after the first couple of days the press seemed to lose interest too, more fascinated by the predictions of massive job losses in the City.

He stayed up in London the whole of the first week, but ironically, now he knew Rosemary was not at home in Esher, the flat seemed lonely.

He took Jane out when she came back from Hong Kong on the Wednesday, longing to talk things over. They dined in Mark's as usual, but she seemed too distracted about her failing business to be interested in his problems. Still, at least there was sex. When they got home she took him straight into the bedroom and began taking her clothes off. He looked at her pert breasts, the curved stomach and russet triangle. For a moment he knew this was not what he wanted.

But lust stirred in him and he began making silent, desper-ate love to her. Then, for no reason, he could not go on.

'What's the matter, Jack?' Jane's green eyes were half puzzled, half annoyed.

'I'm sorry.' He rolled off her, his penis limp and soft. 'I must have drunk too much.'

'Mmm. I think it's simply that you don't fancy me any more.'

'God, Jane.' He glared at her. 'My entire life is falling apart and all you can do is talk about your potty little busi-ness, and screw. Just for once I need some understanding, someone to listen. Life isn't just about sex. I thought we were friends too.'

She got up and began to dress. 'Well, maybe we were. But

you and I are bull market animals. We need the adrenalin of winning.'

He stared up at her. She seemed utterly in control. 'But in case you'd failed to notice, I have to tell you I'm not the motherly type. I can't cope with men wallowing in self-pity and wondering why their long suffering wives have finally left them.' Her tone had turned venomous.

'That's not fair. Rosemary had a good life with me.' Jack rose and put on a robe.

'Really?' Jane ran a comb through her hair. 'Well, my view is she had a dog's life. And I have absolutely no inclination to take her place.'

'Nobody's asking you,' he snarled, his temper rising.

'That's just as well,' Jane said, dropping her voice. 'I'll let myself out.' She walked to the door and turned. 'And by the way, it may be a potty little business to you, but it's more important to me than any man could ever be. Goodbye, Jack.'

The house in Esher began to deteriorate. Washing up mounted in the sink, cups ran short, newspapers lay strewn everywhere, and Jack's supply of clean shirts and underwear dwindled. He knew vaguely that there was a cleaning woman, but what day she might come was a mystery.

Rosemary rang midweek saying she wanted to talk things through calmly. Jack told her to go to hell. He wished he'd remembered to ask about the cleaning lady before he'd done so. And to ask how to use the dishwasher and the washing machine.

The approach of Christmas depressed him. His red *Economist* diary bulged with stiff white invitation cards to this grand dinner or that smart cocktail party. Despite the crash, and the smallness of company p/e ratios, low interest rates meant business was holding up well. The Captains of Industry were determined to celebrate Yuletide 1987 with as much gusto as ever. Jack accepted most of the invitations in a spirit of bravado. But when the time came for him to turn up at Claridge's Ballroom, one of the Savoy's private rooms or an austere City Livery Hall, he found his relish for business gossip had dulled.

300

He had the additional problem of being without a partner which ruled out the invitations to the opera and to dinners with other chief executives and their wives.

Stern dragooned everyone he knew into attending at least one performance by the London and City Ballet. A succession of 'intimate dinners' for twenty-five couples each time were preceded by Swan Lake, the Sleeping Beauty or Giselle. Stern also threw his regular party at Claridges, before Christmas this year, sprinkling it with celebrities from the arts and the media as well as every City luminary he could find. Jack stuck it for twenty minutes. The dinners and the ballet he turned down. Although he thought ballet idiotic, he hated feeling left out.

Hoping Rosemary would return he told no one about her departure. In her absence she suffered three attacks of food poisoning, a throat infection, and the first of that year's 'flu bug, which had a nasty tendency to recur.

'How is poor Rosemary?' asked Charlie on the phone one morning.

'Much better,' replied Jack. 'Still a bit weak after the 'flu, but coming along nicely.'

Charlie said: 'Gosh, has she had 'flu as well as food poisoning? Poor thing. She's always looked so healthy.' Jack was sure he picked up a mocking note.

Then Edward's wife went into hospital with what he described as 'something gynaecological' and Jack noticed that no one ever asked a follow up question about it.

Shortly afterwards, Rosemary too, developed 'something gynaecological'. He had found the magic cure for people's well-meaning curiosity.

Sir Richard remained gloomy Although Jack's prophecy that the BANTA story would soon be forgotten appeared to have come true in the short term, he knew better. He had received a polite but definite snub from his old friend the secretary of state, saying he regretted that after all he would not be able to attend the 21st birthday party of Sir Richard's daughter as he had hoped. And as Christmas approached he received not one single invitation to the regular soirées at Downing Street.

A number of his CBI colleagues also failed to invite him to

their annual dinners and cocktail parties, and it had become abundantly clear he would not be asked to the Boxing Day lunch at Chequers. He had been dropped.

And as far as he could see, it was all Jack's fault.

The business itself remained Jack's only pleasure. The rationalisation had gone more smoothly than anyone dared hope and sales were powering ahead in every division. All over the globe, managers of surprising ability had emerged from beneath the bureaucratic layers at Empire, while those who had been quietly devouring the company's overheads in idleness were mostly delighted to take the money and go.

Even Edward began to display signs of genuine enthusiasm.

He bounced into Jack's office two days before Christmas, alight with excitement.

Jack was delighted to see him. He'd kept him away from the BANTA problem as much as possible, leaving him to mastermind the merging of the two companies.

Edward had a sheaf of photographs in his hand. 'Do you know what this is?' He handed them to Jack. They were of a tall tower block near the waterfront in Hong Kong.

Jack frowned. 'Isn't it where Empire's Hong Kong office is?'

'Right,' said Edward. 'And we own it!'

Jack stared at the picture again. 'How much of it?'

'The whole thing,' said Edward. 'Those idiots didn't even know they owned it, or they had forgotten. It's in their books at less than £5 million – they picked it up in the Hong Kong property crash. It's worth nearer £50 million today.'

Jack wanted to cheer. He leapt up from his desk and grasped Edward by the shoulders. 'Well done well done! That's wonderful.'

Edward looked slightly alarmed. Jack was almost in tears. 'I must ring Richard and Peter,' he said, and started pacing around.' It means we've knocked £50 million off the purchase price. It's a real Christmas present. Well done.' Edward carried on smiling, but warily.

'Amanda.' Jack buzzed through. 'Find some cold champagne and bring it in, and ask Sir Richard to join us.'

Peter was out but Jack found Charlie. 'Listen, my brilliant finance director has just found a £50 million pound building buried away in Empire's accounts.' Edward began to feel faintly embarrassed. It wasn't that fantastic considering the size of the bid.

Jack put the phone down, chuckling. 'That should get the share price moving,' he said as Sir Richard entered, looking irritated.

'Edward has just given me a terrific Christmas present,' Jack explained while Amanda poured the champagne. 'You have some too,' said Jack, patting her shoulder. She flushed with emotion. He had been a real pig to work for recently.

'Happy Christmas, everyone.' They all raised their glasses. 'Happy Christmas,' they echoed. Even Sir Richard cheered up. Jack insisted on a second bottle but Sir Richard and Edward pleaded early lunch appointments and disappeared. Amanda went off to do the washing up and Jack settled down to drink the rest on his own, spreading out the photographs of the building before him.

He answered the phone automatically. 'Armstrong.'

A man's voice, faintly tinged with South London said: 'My name is Arthur Robinson. I'm an official with the investigations division of the Department of Trade and Industry. We'd very much like to talk to you.'

Chapter 20

On the morning of 23 December 1987 Jack sat in the reception area of Pike Marston & Co, one of the big City firms of accountants, two cups of tepid tea on the low table before him. With him was the company lawyer, a thin grey-haired man wearing rimless glasses. Jack stared sightlessly at the front page of the *Financial Times*.

His telephone caller had explained he was speaking on behalf of two inspectors appointed by the Department of Trade and Industry. Would Jack be prepared to visit them the following day?

'But it's two days before Christmas,' he had protested.

He understood that, the man persisted, and apologised for the inconvenience. But under the Financial services Act 1986, the inspectors had the power to require that he attend. And they would be most grateful if that was as soon as possible. He could, of course, bring a lawyer.

Eventually Jack agreed. 'But what exactly is it concerning?' he asked for the third time.

'I can only say we are investigating affairs which happened during or after the Butlers bid for Empire,' said the toneless voice at the end of the telephone.

'And I would ask you, sir, to keep the matter confidential. Currently this investigation is under section 432 of the Companies Act, which means it is a private investigation. The DTI will not be commenting to the press and we would ask you to do the same.'

'But if a journalist asks me a direct question and I say 'no comment', they will assume it's true.'

The man appeared not to understand.

'I can only ask you not to comment,' he had repeated like a machine.

A freckled secretary asked them to come in. Jack checked his watch. They had been waiting exactly eight minutes.

They were shown into a featureless room with a large square table in the centre. Behind it stood two men, one dark, short and stocky, the other pencil slim with steely grey hair and eyes to match. To the right sat a young woman, a notebook and tape recorder in front of her. To the left, an older woman guarded a pile of files.

The two men moved around the table to greet Jack. The short one got there first. He smiled and shook Jack's hand warmly. 'Glad you could make it at such an inconvenient time. We do appreciate it. I am Thomas Butcher – I am a chartered accountant – and this is Nicholas Courtney, QC.'

Expressionless, the lawyer proffered a slender, limp hand.

The accountant said: 'It is our duty to inform you that you are required to answer any questions we may put to you. You do not have the right of silence as in a court of law.'

The nerves in Jack's stomach contracted. He looked enquiringly at his lawyer who nodded. 'They've had these powers since 1986. There was a bit of a fuss at the time.'

No wonder, thought Jack. The accountant produced a Bible. 'I have to ask you to swear an oath.'

The questioning began. 'We want to ask you about the sale of a company called Pomodoro Rosso to BANTA, a few weeks ago.' Just as he had thought. Three hours later they were still at it. The inspectors would have doubled for Mutt & Jeff, thought Jack. If he had been less angry and scared it would have been funny.

'So, Mr Armstrong, can we just go back over your state of mind when you agreed to sell Pomodoro Rosso for £1.3 million? Mr MacCready had offered you £3 million just six months before, which you turned down.' The QC had taken off his jacket, but still exuded a dry elegance.

'My state of mind,' said Jack, 'was as I've stated before. Following the stockmarket crash it became imperative to raise cash. And after the bid for Empire, the Italian canning company did not exactly fit in anywhere.'

The accountant had got up and was pacing around in a manner designed to intimidate. 'Yes, yes, I see all that. But why didn't you go back to Mr MacCready?'

'Well the BANTA deal promised to be quick and tidy. I was unsure Mr MacCready could still raise the money.'

'Really?' said the QC. 'And you were not inclined to give him the chance against someone who had supported the Butlers share price so helpfully during your bid for Empire?'

Jack's lawyer began to mutter in his ear about entrapment. Jack was silent.

'Well?'

'Was that a question?' His tone held a dangerous hint of mischief. These guys were beginning to get on his nerves.

'Mr Armstrong! Were you aware that BANTA was buying shares in Butlers during the bid?' The QC raised his voice.

'Yes, of course,' said Jack, feeling confidence flow through him, 'we noticed their name come up on the share register.'

'No, no, Mr Armstrong. I mean through talking to BANTA executives directly or through a third party. You have already told us they were associates of Sir Leo Stern.'

Yes, he had, hadn't he? His stomach muscles contracted again. Things were beginning to tangle in his brain. He was hungry. Since they had entered the room they had not been offered so much as a cup of coffee, let alone a biscuit.

'Well, we hoped, after the meeting in the South of France I mentioned earlier, that they would, naturally.'

'Why naturally?'

Jack's fuse blew. 'Because we needed all the help we could get. I would have thought that was obvious.'

He heard the sharp intake of breath from his lawyer and the sound of the tape recorder clicking in the silence as it came to the end of that side. The stenographer turned it over.

'Well, perhaps we should call it a day,' said the accountant, looking smug. 'We will, of course, want to see you again after Christmas.'

Jack nodded. He needed a drink.

Sarah lifted the handset quickly to check the dialling tone and replaced it. Of course it was working. It had been working all day. It was working when her mother rang to check what time she would be over on Christmas morning and to ask her for the thousandth time if she was sure she didn't want to stay overnight in her old bedroom on Christmas Eve.

It was working when her best friend rang from New York to say she had just got engaged. And it was working half an hour before when she had snatched it up, sure that this time it must be Leo because he often rang between six and seven. Instead she had got a very small child in search of his grandmother.

'No, sweetie, I think you must have the wrong number,' she said gently, marvelling at her own patience.

Leo had promised he would ring before leaving for Gstaad. She didn't know what time he was flying. That was the problem with multi-millionaires, she thought ruefully, they did not fly on scheduled airplanes like ordinary mortals; they travelled in their own jets at their own whim. So she could not know when finally to douse the fragile spark of hope – all that was left of the previous night's glowing certainty that he loved her.

It was two days before Christmas, and she should have been out there trawling the shops. Her mother's present still eluded her, and she needed some smaller gifts for visiting children.

But she had stayed in nearly all day, desperate not to miss his call. When she popped out at lunchtime to pick up a few provisions, she had left the phone off the hook. If he got the answering machine, he might assume she was out for the day and not ring back.

She had busied herself cleaning, using the hoover in short bursts in case its sound muffled the ring of the phone. She washed her hair and twice ran naked and dripping from the bathroom into the hall, imagining she had heard it through the noise of the shower.

The evening stretched before her, terrifying in its emptiness. Her shoulders were rigid with tension; every now and then she felt a strangling sensation around her neck.

She told herself it was not his fault; he was incredibly busy; he had a wife and teenage children and they were all going off together; he had probably tried anyway when she had been talking to her mother. She must get another telephone line at home, she decided. She knew she was over-reacting. Any sensible woman would just go out shopping anyway and leave him to talk to the machine.

She must not shout or cry when he did phone – if he ever did phone again, she thought, panic gripping her. No, it had happened before. Sometimes it was inevitable. She must simply be grown up. He just had not had the opportunity and he thought she would understand.

Part of her understood. The other part prayed he was OK and that God hadn't struck him down with a heart attack or a stray drunken Christmas driver. And a last part raged against him. How dare he jet off to Gstaad for a whole ten days without ringing to say goodbye? It was Christmas!

He could have found a way to reach her if he wanted. He'd have found a telephone if he thought she had a business deal for him. He couldn't love her, it was obvious. Nobody who loved someone would leave them wondering and waiting two days before Christmas. She sat on her sofa and sobbed. She wouldn't do it to him, whatever the circumstances. She wouldn't do it to a dog.

Angela looked with dismay at the huge pile of luggage on the bed. All morning she had stuffed anoraks, salopettes, heavy jumpers and boots into cases. To make matters worse Peter insisted on having his own skis. Not that there was any snow. The reports said the mountains around Gstaad were as green as springtime.

She wondered what an earth Paulette Stern and her friends would wear in the evenings. Angela was used to casual chalet skiing holidays where she never got out of trousers. She had packed one smart blue wool shirtwaister, a silk Ralph Lauren blouse, a couple of calf-length skirts and two elegant jumpers from Brown's. She had not liked to lash out. Peter kept saying they were all right for money, but he grumbled loudly at every bill that came in. She hoped they weren't expected to dress up every single night. At least there had been no mention of a dinner jacket for Peter.

But The Palace was the smartest hotel in Gstaad. 'Ready, darling?' Peter appeared in the doorway. 'We should have left half an hour ago. Have you turned everything off.'

'Well, I've been here for some time,' she said pointedly. 'Yes, I have.'

They heaved and humped everything down the oak staircase, through the hall and into the Range Rover as there was not room in the Aston Martin. Leaving the house in the care of Mrs Warren, they drove off to Field Aviation at Heathrow to meet up with Leo and some of the other guests for the flight.

Jean-Pierre Krandsdorf checked in at Kennedy Airport for the early morning Eastern Airlines flight to Fort Lauderdale looking like an advertisement for Louis Vuitton luggage. He wore a dark green Loden coat, a paler green check cashmere scarf and Gucci loafers. His tan, as ever, was immaculate but in need of a top up, his auburn curls newly cut. He settled into his seat in the plane with a sigh of excited anticipation. He was off to pick up a college boy for Christmas.

When he had found one he liked – and there was a considerable selection in Fort Lauderdale's many gay bars – his plan was to spirit him off to a Christmas house party being given by one of his oldest friends in Eleuthera, one of the Bahamian out islands. He was looking for a boy with powerful shoulders and a tight ass. He'd gone off Orientals for the moment.

He sighed and wondered if the DTI would find out about Schlosstein. Something deep in his gut told him they would. Just as well he never bought shares in client companies. He wondered uneasily just how much he might be implicated in advising Schlosstein and resolved to stay out of England for a while.

'I'll do that if you like,' said Rosemary taking control of the gravy.

'Thanks, Mum, but you're supposed to be a guest.' Somehow, Mark had managed to get both his parents to come together for Christmas Day.

They sat down to eat in the dining room which had hardly ever been used except to entertain Jack's business contacts. Mark tried hard to keep the conversation going but it was impossible to ignore the haunted way his father kept looking at his mother, and how she kept looking away. He wished he had not forced the issue.

309

They managed to eat only half the normal quantities of Christmas pudding and mince pies. The moment they were finished Mark leapt to his feet, anxious to escape the charged atmosphere.

'I'll bring you in some coffee,' he said. Perhaps they needed to be alone.

The unspoken question hung between them. Rosemary looked at Jack, her eyes calm. 'I can't come back.' She saw his dark hair, swept back City-style, the green triangular eyes and sharp cheekbones, and wondered why they seemed the features of a stranger.

'I don't understand,' he said. He reached out, touching the back of her hand. 'You know I've always loved you.'

There was silence. They could hear the clatter of washing up in the kitchen.

'No, Jack. You may have thought you loved me, I didn't know. You married me because I was pregnant, remember?'

'But I wanted to be with you. I knew we would be a good team, and we have been.'

Rosemary stared at him, unconvinced. 'In any case, I've been the last thing on your list for the past two years.'

'But that was work, my career,' he protested. 'That was for both of us' – he gestured hopelessly – 'for all of us. Not just me.'

She sighed. 'Well, maybe, but it never felt like that. It's just so wonderful to be with someone who actually notices my existence.'

'And what about our children?' he asked, going on the attack.

'Oh, come on, Jack. Susan left home three years ago because you refused to see her point of view on anything. Mark is practically grown up. And did you ever spend time with either of them?'

'I care about them both. I still love Susan, even if she has decided to live elsewhere. I've spent a lot of time with Mark trying to teach him tennis and golf. It's not my fault if he isn't the sporty type. I just don't seem able to talk to him.'

'He's not your son, that's why,' she said quietly.

Jack first thought she was making it up to hurt him. But the pity in her eyes told him it was true.

Then everything made sense. Mark did not have one tell-tale likeness to him. It had disappointed him that the boy had looked so like Rosemary. Temperamentally, though, Mark was quiet and moody, unlike either of them. Jack had always put that down to having such a bouncy elder sister.

He put his head in his hands and gave a short, mocking laugh. 'I've never doubted you,' he said, incredulous. 'Never.'

'It was when we were in America and you were always travelling around. I was lonely and exhausted – Susan was tiny. You remember how difficult she was? The neighbours were OK but I had nothing in common with them.'

'But who was it?' Jack burned with curiosity.

'One weekend you invited one of your directors to stay with us – a man called Jerome and his wife Sally.' Jack remembered a tall weedy man with glasses and a slightly sour woman.

'You didn't notice, of course, but he was terribly sweet to me that weekend. He was wonderful with Susan, read her stories, and he helped with the drying up. We talked a lot. His wife couldn't have children and . . .'

Jack exploded: 'But surely you didn't do it with everyone in the house?' He would have staked money on Rosemary.

She shook her head. 'No, of course not. He rang me on the Tuesday and said he was passing through. Could he come by for coffee?' Rosemary spoke as if in a trance. 'It just happened that Susan was out with the lady next-door and her little girl. When he arrived, we both knew. It was as if we were powerless.' She looked at him questioningly as if to say 'Surely it has happened to you too?'

'It was only the once,' she finished. She could still remember the lemony smell of his aftershave as he had pushed her down on the bed.

'I always trusted you,' Jack said accusingly.

Rosemary ignored him. 'Mark doesn't know,' she said. 'It would be pointless to tell him.'

'That bastard got fired,' Jack said suddenly. 'You lousy, lying bitch! You betrayed me in our own house. On our own bed.' He was incredulous. 'And you never told me.'

'How could I have told you?' asked Rosemary, her heart thudding. 'It would have ruined our marriage.'

311

Jack drew a deep shaky breath and stood up. 'I think I'd like you to go.'

Jean-Pierre ran his middle two fingers lightly down the young man's spine as he lay sleeping. He stayed sleeping and Jean-Pierre, marvelling at youth, slipped out of bed and walked on to the balcony. The turquoise of the sea was brilliant against the pale sand. Two snorkellers were already hard at it, their fins plopping about as they marvelled at the teeming multi-coloured world below them. It was a world away from New York which he had left cloaked in snow.

He thought about Jack and felt his cock stir. All these years and he'd never managed to stop wanting him. It was the long legs and green eyes that did it – and that whole insolent air. He remembered a holiday they had spent together in Cape Cod when Jack and Rosemary had been living in America. Jack had been so elegant, so amusing, and somehow so very physical. For a while Jean-Pierre had wondered – had hoped all the overt womanising might be a cover.

Then one evening he had been on the verge of bringing up the subject when two tall beautiful boys had walked by hand in hand, their shadows long on the sand.

'Bloody pooters,' Jack had laughed. Then, realising his gaffe, had coughed and quickly changed the subject. They had never mentioned the subject again but there were times when he felt Jack was teasing him, flirting quite overtly. And there had been the time with the blackgirl. Jean-Pierre smiled ruefully now as one of the snorkellers came up for air.

As he walked back into the bedroom the young man turned on to his back and opened his eyes. Jean-Pierre smiled at him. 'Merry Christmas,' he said.

The youth held out lightly muscled arms. 'Merry Christmas to you.'

The noise of the propeller was almost deafening at the helicopter lifted off the snow. As it moved over the mountain edge it plummeted into an air pocket and everyone shrieked with fear and pleasure. They were being taken to the top of an unpisted mountain to ski in virgin powder snow. Leo looked round from his seat next to the pilot and grinned.

312

'Everyone OK there?' His glance fell on Angela, the least chic but the most cool of the three women aboard. On the runs the day before she was easily the best skier. She and Peter were well matched, he decided. His ego and temperament needed somebody with a stable head.

The chopper bounced around in the thermals and by the time they landed twenty minutes later, they all felt slightly sick. Somebody produced coffee and brioches. It was as if they were the last people on earth, this strange band of skiers in their vivid suits. Looking down on the sparkling mountain tops beneath them, Stern had a fleeting vision of finding Sarah up to her neck in snow nearly two years before.

Then the guide was motioning them to follow, and one by one they slid down into the silky smooth whiteness. The lightly frozen surface gave under the pressure of the skis with the merest scrunch, and they flew down the mountain, the snow sighing against their ski tips. Behind them they left curved trails for lesser mortals to wonder at as they stared down from the chair lifts later.

They returned from the mountain for lunch still high on the experience and instantly drank more *vin chaud* than was good for them. Their skin shone, their eyes were alight, they felt alive in a new way. They could take on the world and win now. Leo kept everyone in fits of laughter over the meal, taking off people in the City. The atmosphere became raucous with everyone wearing funny hats, blowing whistles and laughing. Peter felt the tensions of the City slip off him and found himself giggling helplessly at everything. Only Paulette was quiet.

She watched Leo hold the table in his thrall with an uneasy heart. He had been strangely distant for several months now. She knew it was partly her own fault – if only she felt like sex more often; she should have made more effort. But she felt sure there was someone else. Looking at him now, he was just a touch too animated, too amusing to be true.

At around four they suddenly flopped like rag dolls and retired to bed. In their room, Leo took Paulette in his arms. 'Why so sad, my darling?' The mere fact that he had noticed sent the tears coursing down Paulette's face and she clung to him, sobbing. He stroked her head gently, wondering if somehow she had found out about Sarah.

She was his wife of twenty-two years, mother of his sons; she rarely complained about his neglect, his overriding passion for the business. And she was still beautiful.

When he picked her up, she was like a piece of thistledown in his arms. He placed her on the bed and lay down beside her.

'I do love you,' he said truthfully.

'I know.' Her voice was still choked with sobs. 'I love you too – I know I'm cold – I don't know why – but it does not affect my feelings.'

He kissed her and they made love slowly and deliciously with the wonder of old lovers coming together anew.

Then afterwards as he lay still, stroking her softly, he found a small lump the size of a pea just under her left breast.

His fingers stopped moving and when he looked at her he saw from the fear in her eyes that she had already discovered it. 'What have you done about this?'

'I have to see the specialist when we get back,' she said. 'The doctor said it could easily be nothing bad.'

He held her very close.

Chapter 21

As the days of the New Year went by with no call, Jack's moods swung from acute anxiety to desperate hope that the DTI inspectors had given up. Then at the end of the first week they summoned him again.

Jean-Pierre rang in good spirits.

'Happy New Year, old buddy, how ya doin.'

For the first time in their long relationship, Jack found the American bonhomie a bit much to take.

'How do you think I'm doing? There's a DTI investigation going on here,' he snapped.

'Shit, I ain't read nothing about it. You mean like Guinness?'

Jack shuddered. 'Not quite like Guinness. The investigation's private,' he hesitated, 'so far.'

'Anything particular?' Jean-Pierre tried not to sound too interested.

'Well, I'm told this phone is almost certainly bugged, but as it's been all over the papers I might as well tell you. It was that deal with BANTA to sell the Italian tomato canning business.'

'That's all?'

'So far,' said Jack grimly.

Jean-Pierre sounded very chirpy. 'So nothing this side of the pond?' he was being deliberately vague in case of a tape.

'No,' said Jack. 'When are you coming over?'

'Well, I've got a hell of a lot on just at the present. Every corporation in town wants advice on how to buy back its own stock. It's all the rage here.'

'Mmm, it's being talked about here, but companies need to

315

change their articles of association. Can't your people manage without you for a few days?' Despite his irritation Jack longed to see an old friend.

'I can't, old buddy.' The insincerity was becoming blatant. 'A couple of my key guys smashed themselves up skiing in Colorado over Christmas. I'll see you later in the year. Keep me posted. Love to Rosemary.'

No way was he leaving the good old USA, he thought as he put down the phone.

Jean-Pierre's secretary brought in his mid-morning coffee and his favourite apricot Danish, shiny with sugar glaze. He swivelled round on his leather-padded chair, swung his hand crafted shoes on to his desk and flicked the television screen onto the CNN financial news channel – and nearly choked.

A shot of Max Schlosstein's head surrounded by police filled the screen. As the camera panned away, he could see that Schlosstein's fat little wrist was handcuffed to one of the policemen who was leading him, none too gently, down Wall Street.

It was Peter's turn to be interviewed by the inspectors. He tried to conceal his irritation.

'Just remind us of your frame of mind when you arrived in Zurich.'

Peter said: 'I was extremely annoyed to be out of London. I was feeling very impatient and slightly sick. We'd had the most awful flight.'

'And you say you opposed the sale of the company?'

'Inititially, yes.'

'On what grounds?'

'That it wasn't enough money.'

'So why did you change your mind?'

Peter hesitated. He didn't want to be a total shit. But it was the truth.

'My client insisted – and von Gleichen increased the price slightly.'

'And why do you suppose Mr Armstrong insisted?'

Peter's fuse began to fizz. 'How should I know? He seemed to want to get shot of this company.'

'What did he say?'

'I don't remember.'

'Well, what was the tenor of what he said.'

'I think it was that the business didn't fit in any more.'

'Was there any suggestion that he wanted to repay von Gleichen for any past favours? For instance, supporting Butlers share price during the bid.'

Peter was on very dangerous ground and he knew it. If only he knew what Jack had told them. He presumed they hadn't been able to tempt von Gleichen out of Switzerland.

Sensing his inward struggle the accountant said: 'You are on oath, Mr Markus.'

The room seemed to get hotter. 'Well, von Gleichen had certainly made it clear he was unhappy about the loss,' he paused, floundering. 'But nothing was actually said as far as I remember, about making it up to him.' He could feel his heart thumping at the half truth.

'But why, as a merchant banker, did you agree to a price that was less than half the management buy out offer, seven months before?' persisted the accountant.

'Well, there had been a stockmarket crash.'

The QC glanced meaningfully at the accountant. 'Mr Markus, we have asked a leading management consultant's for their view and they say that the value of an Italian tomato canning company would hardly be influenced by crashing share prices in London; certainly not by the amount in question.'

Peter stared straight ahead. He had wondered how long it would take them to realise that.

Sir Leo Stern played the videotape of Max Schlosstein being arrested several times trying to gauge the expression on the man's face. He did not like it. Max had been charged with insider dealing, but the details were unknown. The trouble was, in the US these guys had a nasty knack of spilling the beans on all their associates in return for a lighter sentence.

Max knew nothing of Stern's direct dealings with Jack and Peter, but he knew all about the stake-building exercise in Empire. Stern froze the frame on Max's face. It didn't give him confidence. Still, the worst that could come out was allegations of a concert party. Perhaps he shouldn't have used the same broker. A picture of Sarah standing in the witness box, her pale face distraught, flashed into his mind. He closed his eyes, willing the vision to go away.

He glanced at the carriage clock on the mantelpiece. Paulette was due back from the hospital any moment. Even as the thought entered his mind he heard the soft scrunch of the Bentley's wheels on the gravel drive and the muted thud of the door as the driver closed it behind her.

He jumped up and went into the entrance hall to greet her, trying not to look anxious.

One glance at her face told him everything. He put his arm round her shoulders and guided her into the sitting room. They both sank on to the couch. He gripped her firmly by each shoulder.

'When's the operation? I want to know when to put in my order with the flower shop.'

As he had intended, she smiled despite herself.

'They can take me in on Monday,' she said. 'Oh Leo, I'm so frightened.'

'Rubbish!' He stood up suddenly and paced to the fireplace. 'You're frightened because that's what people expect you to be. Plenty of people have this operation and make a full recovery.' He pointed a big finger at her. 'You are going to be just fine, do you hear? Just fine. And that's an order.'

The next day, he took Sarah to lunch in the Raffles restaurant in the Portman Hotel. It was not the kind of place where they were likely to be seen by anyone in the City. For although he had a perfectly legitimate reason for having lunch with his stockbroker, his instinct advised discretion.

The large airy room with its sumptuous central buffet was only half full that rainy January day. They sat by the window.

Sarah knew something was wrong. He was solemn and serious, his dark eyes hard. She wondered if it was Max. His arrest in his office had been all over the financial pages. She kept telling herself she would be all right; that she had just been acting as an agent. But it made her jittery all the same.

Stern snapped a grissini stick in two and handed her a piece.

'Did you know that Jack and Peter have been interviewed by DTI inspectors?'

So that as it. She wasn't that surprised.

'No, I didn't. In connection with what?'

'Well, the bid, of course. But mainly some deal they did with von Gleichen. They sold BANTA some factory in Italy for a silly price, to get him off their back.'

'Oh, yes, the *Herald* ran the story,' she said, nodding.

'But you realise they've arrested Max Schlosstein in New York too?'

She nodded.

'Have they been in touch with you?'

'No, but Denis and I have talked it through. We're just agents. We buy shares for clients. There shouldn't be a problem.'

'How are you going to explain buying shares in Empire for Schlosstein while you were also buying them for me?' He started on the second packet of grissini.

'I'll just say you recommended him as a client.'

Stern nodded approvingly. 'Your firm doesn't use tapes, does it?'

'No, thank God.'

'So just say that when you came to see me that day, I recommended an American client to you in passing.'

'Fine,' said Sarah as her melon arrived.

They both relaxed slightly.

'So how was your Christmas?' she asked, wanting to take the conversation away from business.

His eyes slid away from hers. 'Paulette's got cancer.'

An armoury of emotions assailed Sarah. There was a wild flash of hope that Paulette might die, instantly doused by guilt at such an unworthy thought; then a wave of panic at what might happen if she did.

She reached out her hand and touched his arm. 'How awful. I'm sorry.' She paused until curiosity won out. 'Where is it?'

'In her left breast.'

'Well, she'll probably be all right then,' she said soothingly.

Stern looked out of the window. 'I hope so,' he said fervently.

319

'Leo Stern! Always with a pretty girl. How are *you*?' The greeting was delivered from about three feet away. They had both been so involved in their conversation they had not noticed the approach. The speaker was a slim dapper man, immaculately dressed in a dark double-breasted suit, with the faintest of chalk stripes. From his breast pocket tumbled a maroon silk handkerchief. His hair was as black and glossy as the shine on his handmade shoes. Dark eyes twinkled mischievously in a tanned face.

'I'm surprised you could tear yourself away from the Suvretta House, Baron,' said Stern, rising to his feet to greet him. Sarah instantly recognised the name of the hotel.

'Sarah, do you know Baron Marks? He's one of my oldest friends. Baron, this is Sarah Meyer, the best little stakebuilder in town.'

He winked at Baron who said: 'Delighted to meet you.' He held out a small, perfectly manicured hand. 'Trust Leo to find the only attractive stockbroker in the City.'

'I'm also quite good,' Sarah snapped defensively, irritated by the sexist tone.

'No one's suggesting you're not,' said Baron. 'It doesn't hurt to be pretty as well.' He dropped his voice. 'What about Max then?'

Stern nodded and their eyes locked knowingly.

'Let's have dinner soon,' said Stern.

'Fine. I must fly, I'm forty minutes late for lunch as it is.' They shook hands again. 'Don't let him lead you astray,' Baron teased as he took Sarah's hand.

She resisted the temptation to say she was already about as far astray as she could go.

She looked at Stern questioningly.

He said: 'That is one of the cleverest property dealers in the country. What and who he doesn't know, isn't worth knowing.'

'Is he public?'

Stern grinned. 'Like I'm public. He owns 54 per cent of a quoted company called Yorkbridge Holdings.'

Sarah's eyes lit up in recognition. 'Oh, yes. The stock was doing very well before the crash. But you never read anything about them.'

'That's right. He never talks to the City, or gives interviews. He's hardly known outside the property sector. He's an expert at keeping his head below the parapet.'

'Why so paranoid?'

'He had a bad time in the 1974 crash. That's when we met.' Stern smiled fondly. 'I helped save him from going bust.' He stroked the back of Sarah's hand. 'Now, young lady, let's just go over what you are going to say to those nice DTI inspectors. I have a feeling they could be in touch very soon.'

Stern's instinct was unerring as usual. The next day, Sarah and Denis both received phone calls. Charlie Briggs-Smith at Greenbag's was also asked to attend the offices of Pike Marston. A few days later Stern himself was summoned. Jack had been called back three times, Peter twice.

Miraculously, the news that a formal DTI enquiry was underway had still not found its way into the press which remained obsessed with the aftermath of the stockmarket crash and the waves of sackings swathing through the City. The fall from grace of young men and women who months before had commanded annual salaries of between £100,000 and £200,000 after two or three years' experience excited feverish *schadenfreude*.

Financial journalists, where the pinnacle of success after years of hard slog brought in £50,000, could barely contain their glee.

Patrick Peabody was amazed and annoyed at how quickly interest in the story had died. Slowly and quietly he beavered away, rekindling his old contacts in the DTI and the Fraud Squad, sometimes drinking into the early hours with them. It was the kind of story it didn't pay to get wrong. Finally he was there. He went to the editor. He had a particular idea for the way it should be handled.

Towards the end of January, Jack felt life veer towards normal. It was a cold sunny Saturday and he played a round of golf in the morning and joined some fellow members for lunch at the club. In the afternoon he got down to some forward planning for the company.

Now the basic rationalisation was done he needed to think

strategically about where the group was actually heading. He got the Scotch bottle out. He found it helped him to think – up to a certain point.

He felt his life had no underpinning. He still hoped Rosemary would come back. He could not believe she would stay with Julian. Maybe his first instinct had been right and he just needed to stick it out. He was certain she still loved him. Everyone knew women went peculiar in the run up to forty.

At just past midnight he rolled into bed and fell asleep with a forgotten feeling of contentment. He knew there couldn't be anything about him in any of the Sunday papers, as the others would have been on to him by now, wanting confirmation.

Patrick had become increasingly irked at seeing his scoops followed up in second editions of rival Sunday newspapers and passed off as if they were their own. He persuaded the editor to hold it back for the second edition, which did not hit the streets until after ten, long after rival City staffs would have gone home.

So when Jack picked his *Sunday Herald* off the mat along with the cartload of other papers, he felt as if someone had kicked him. DTI PROBE BUTLERS read the headline on the front page.

The Department of Trade and Industry is conducting an investigation into Butler Group's bid for Empire Foods last summer. The investigation is being conducted under section 432 of the Companies Act and is believed to focus on the sale of the Italian subsidiary Pomodoro Rosso to the mysterious Swiss holding company BANTA, revealed exclusively by the *Sunday Herald* in November. At the time of the revelation, The *Sunday Herald* called for a DTI enquiry into the matter. However, it is also thought the investigation nay shortly be widened to include a share support operation during the bid, involving the American arbitrageur, Max Schlosstein, who was recently arrested in New York.

Jack's heart started thumping at the last paragraph: 'The DTI is understood to have passed an interim report to the Serious Fraud Office.'

The phone rang. It was a journalist on the *Daily Post* whom Jack knew slightly.

'Sorry to ring you on a Sunday morning,' he said pleasantly. 'It's just that I'll be on duty later and I thought I'd catch you now, before everyone else gets on to you.'

'That's all right. How can I help you?' Jack's tone was equally pleasant.

The reporter was slightly thrown. 'Er, well, I wondered if you could comment on the story in the *Herald*?'

Jack sighed. 'I am as much in the dark as you are, I'm afraid.'

'You mean it's not true!' said the journalist incredulously.

'I mean, that I don't know what the article is about. I'll be talking to the other directors tomorrow. I really have no comment to make.'

Eventually the journalist got bored and said goodbye. Jack put the phone down and immediately turned on the answering machine. There was only one thing to do. Brazen it out as long as he could, and hope for a miracle.

He decided to call a board meeting for that afternoon. That should make them all realise how concerned he was, he thought as he rang Amanda. He marvelled at how calmly he was behaving, compared to the turmoil in his head.

David had rung, sounding hurt Jack had not contacted him before Patrick's original story. 'There are several damage limitation tactics we can employ,' he had said. Jack agreed to see him the next day although something told him damage limitation tactics would be about as effective as a band aid on a haemorrhage.

A lifetime later he got back home. He poured half a glass of Scotch and drank it while he played the answering machine. Journalists from every single newspaper had left messages. Their tones varied from brisk and cheerful to pleading. Radio and TV were also doing their bit.

The phone rang. Wearily he picked it up.

'I just wondered how you were,' Rosemary said. 'I've seen the *Herald*.'

323

'The board have asked me to resign.' She was the first Person he had told.

That night, he drank the best part of the bottle of whisky but it seemed to have no effect on him. In bed he lay awake, his head full of vivid images and loud voices. He kept seeing his father, standing over him as he had the day he had come home from school with a terrible report. 'I'm not angry, lad, just disappointed,' he had said. In sleep his father became Sir Richard. It seemed he had only just drifted off when three thunderclaps on the front door woke him. He lay, ramrod-still in bed, half wondering if they had been in the dream when they came again. BANG BANG BANG.

Mark? Surely not Rosemary? He swung out of bed and grabbed his dressing gown, full of dread.

Two men stood on the doorstep. Tall and broad-shouldered, they stood with their legs apart as if planted in the pathway. Jack needed no identification. They might as well have had a police siren on their heads.

His memory of that moment was for ever afterwards like a snapshot – the rosebushes crystallised in white frost standing out eerily in the blue light from the street lamp. It was a freezing January morning. Somewhere up the road in the darkness someone was having trouble starting a car.

Tikatikatikkatikkateee.

Jack absorbed all this as he stood shivering – or was he shaking? – in his dressing gown. The idea that one of the children had been hurt vanished. This was no sympathy visit.

The detective spoke: 'Are you Jack Albert Armstrong?' Jack flinched at the sound of his hated middle name.

'Yes, I am.'

'I am Detective Inspector Harrison from the City Fraud Squad. I am arresting you for conspiracy to defraud in rela- tion to the takeover bid by Butlers for Empire, and offering indemnities to Sir Leo Stern, which is a contravention of section 151 of the Companies Act.'

Jack's brain refused to take in the message.

'What! There has to be some mistake.' He now knew for certain he was shaking. For a millisecond he contemplated running for it – dashing past the plainclothes man – into the arms of the constable at the end of the drive. He wondered if they were armed.

'No, sir.' The policeman shifted his weight slightly. I can assure you there is no mistake. I must ask you to come with me to Bishopsgate police station. You are not obliged to say anything, but I must warn you that anything you do say will be taken down in evidence and may be used against you. We would also like to search the house.'

'I'd rather you didn't, officer,' he said, a shadow of his normal confidence returning. 'Do you know who I am?' Even as he spoke he remembered he was no longer chief executive of the second largest food company in the country. He noticed his head was pounding.

The policeman looked at him patiently. 'You are within your rights to refuse, sir, but we will only go back and get a warrant. It's much simpler if you agree now.'

Why were they treating him like this? This was what happened to burglars! Jack's brain finally ground into action. 'I need to phone my lawyer.'

'By all means, although arrangements to contact him can be made at the station.'

Jack finally stood aside. 'I assume I can put on some clothes?'

'Of course, sir.' The officer's tone mellowed a fraction. 'One of my officers will accompany you upstairs.' A third detective emerged from the back of the house.

What did they think he was going to do – leap out the bedroom window? He dressed as if he was going to the office out of habit, holding in his stomach as he took off his pyjamas and clambered into his underwear. The young constable silently watched his every move.

He took three aspirin and found his pocket diary with the home and office numbers of Martin Jennings, his lawyer, in it.

'Is it OK to ring my lawyer now?' he found himself asking the detective.

'Of course, sir.'

His wife answered. Martin Jennings had already left home for an early appointment, she said. He would be in the office later.

When they came downstairs Jack was handcuffed to one of

325

the policemen and marched to an unmarked black Rover saloon which had appeared just outside the gate. As he walked to the car he looked up for an instant and saw the net curtains move in the upstairs window of the house opposite.

Sitting in the back of the Rover, his mind, now on full alert whirled back over the entire bid. The South of France, Stern, von Gleichen, Max, Venice, Mark's Club . . . What did these charges actually mean?

Peter had said these kind of deals went on all the time in takeover bids. Why was he being singled out? Did they know about the warehouses in Newcastle? What had possessed him to hand over £30 million to Stern?

Peter had said: 'You can't let a man like Stern down. He is too powerful to have as an enemy – these are exceptional circumstances.'

Why hadn't anybody stopped him? A head of fury welled up in him. Edward should have threatened to resign. He conveniently forgot the force with which he had railroaded the land sale through – and after it had been signed. He had then presented the deal as a fait accompli to the board for ratification. Edward had been tight-lipped, disapproving. But there had been nothing he could do. He had, in fact, considered resigning, but he believed in loyalty.

Jack had waited until Richard had been away shooting, and backed up the logic for the sale by producing an obscure local land agent's report about prospects for the area. After reading it, his co-directors had rubber stamped the deal. Jack knew the report had been commissioned by Stern.

The facts were that Lincolnshire had escaped the property boom.

He had asked someone independent to nose around the property agents in the area and concluded that the warehouses and adjoining land were not worth a penny more than £5 million. It made the payments to Max and the BANTA deal look like peanuts.

Max was obviously blabbing about everything he had ever done in an effort to get clemency. And what about the £2 million to Krandsdorf Associates? Surely that must be OK? Jean-Pierre, at least, had not bought any shares in Butler.

He wanted to ask if they had arrested anyone else that

morning. A vision of Stern being dragged from his Bentley flashed through his mind.

His immediate problems reasserted themselves. How would he let anyone know where he was? How would he stop the world finding out?

Let it be some terrible mistake.

The tornado of anger in his head turned towards Stern. None of this would have happened without him. You would have lost the bid though, whispered a voice.

At that moment, driving through the early rush hour, with the feel of hard steel on his wrist, he felt it would have been a small price to pay.

The car pulled up with a squeal of tyres and he was ushered out none too gently and taken quickly into the police station, through a door and down some stairs.

'I want to phone my lawyer.'

'Hold on a minute, sir.'

He was taken to the charge desk. Detective Inspector Harrison said: 'This is Jack Albert Armstrong. I've just arrested him. If you could do the necessary, Sergeant.'

The desk sergeant took down Jack's details. 'Right, I'd like your money, any valuables you have, your shoelaces, belt and tie.'

Jack looked at him dumbfounded.

'It's normal procedure, sir.'

The charge sergeant gave him a form which stated that he had the right to ask for a solicitor. He gave them Martin Jennings's number and was taken to a cell. There was a bed along one wall and a lavatory without a seat in an alcove. About a foot above his head was a small window with bars. Aeons later the sergeant reappeared.

'Mr Jennings is neither at home nor in the office yet, but they are expecting him.'

Around mid-morning, Jack was taken out of the cell and photographed. He had no idea how he looked, but tilted his chin at the camera. Then they took his fingerprints, leaving his fingers covered in black ink. They gave him some white spirit to clean off the ink, but most of it stayed on. It made him feel unclean.

Martin Jennings did not arrive until lunchtime.

Finally Jack was shown into an interview room. It was one of those cheaply furnished rooms found in institutions such as schools and hospitals. But there was a starkness about this room and an indefinable feeling in the air that spoke of custody. It could have been nowhere else but in a police station.

Martin Jennings prepared him. 'They are going to ask you question after question and tape the whole thing. They may well have evidence. They will have been preparing this case for weeks. Simply say 'no comment' to every question, no matter how tempted you are to answer.'

Jack was not going to argue.

Afterward they took him back to the jailer. Detective Inspector Harrison then read out details of the charges against him and cautioned him again. He found himself staring at the floor.

'You will be held here overnight until tomorrow morning when you will appear before a magistrate,' said Harrison.

He turned, leaving Jack alone with the jailer who showed him back to the cell. He had no option. He walked in. The door slammed behind him and he heard the scraping of keys.

Peter narrowly missed a motorcyclist who shouted abuse and thumped his car three times before roaring off. 'Cretin,' he muttered. He was crawling along Brook Street, wildly late for his meeting at Claridge's with the head of a large American oil company looking to buy chunks of the North Sea.

He flicked the radio on to hear the pre-news jingle on LBC. 'And this is the news at twelve. The head of Butlers Foods, Britain's second largest food group, was arrested early this morning at his home in Esher. Jack Armstrong, the chief executive, was taken to Bishopsgate police station in the City. No charges have yet been made but the arrest is thought to be in connection with Butlers bid for Empire Foods last autumn, just before the stockmarket crash. Mr Armstrong . . .' There was a jolt as the Aston glided into the taxi in front.

'God!'

Peter leapt out of the car, extracting his card from his wallet. 'Where are you, Guv, on another planet this morning?' said the taxi driver pleasantly.

'Sorry. Look, I'm in a terrible rush. Here's my card.' He scribbled his registration number on it.

'Hold off, I just want to see what damage you've done.'

Peter sighed. The man, who had no passenger and was clearly feeling in need of a chat, got out of his cab as if he had all the time in the world and ambled round the back of his vehicle.

'Mmm, haah, well.' He lovingly caressed the back bumper, then examined the front of Peter's car.

'Well, I'll send you an estimate. Mind how you go, Guv.'

Two minutes later Peter leapt out of his car, thrust a ten-pound note into the hand of the doorman and dashed into Claridge's.

'Can you tell Mr Bromberg that I'm on my way up? I've got to make a phone call,' he said to one of the men on reception.

He popped into one of the booths and rang Stern's private line.

It was engaged.

He rang the main number and asked for his secretary.

'Can you tell Leo it's Peter Markus on the phone and it's mega-urgent.'

Leo came on. 'Yup, I've heard, Peter. It's been on the news.'

'What's the best thing to do, do you think?' asked Peter. How could Leo be so calm? Peter noticed his hand was slippery on the handset.

'I know what I'm gonna do,' said Stern. 'I'm gonna talk to my lawyer pronto and make sure if they want to arrest me, they do it by appointment. I suggest you do the same.'

Peter put the phone down and rang the lawyer he had approached after the DTI enquiry had begun. Hogarth Stein's lawyers would face an uncomfortable conflict of interest, but the lawyer was out and Peter was already unacceptably late.

In the lift he found he was shaking so much he had to stop his teeth chattering. He willed himself calm.

Minutes later, as he greeted Art Bromberg in his suite, the only expression in his azure eyes was a look of intelligent interest.

The days which followed were the longest in Peter's life.

Every phone call or knock on the door sent his nerve ends into spasm.

His lawyer promised him he would not be the victim of a dawn arrest like Jack. But he wasn't convinced.

Jack had been released on bail and had asked for a meeting. Peter had invited him to the flat, praying that no one would see him come in. It had not been a pleasant couple of hours.

Nervousness rippled across the entire City. Anyone who had been connected with the bid was overnight regarded with suspicion – fund managers who had helped out, analysts close to the company, the company accountants, lawyers, not to mention the brokers. Lunch invitations plummeted.

The scandal monopolised conversation in bars and restaurants. The lack of business meant everyone had more time to discuss it and, worse, brood on it. The City became a profoundly jumpy place.

At Greenbag's, Charlie suffered from a feeling of impending doom. He had splashed out on a £1 million house in the Boltons in the summer before the crash, and his monthly mortgage repayments were the equivalent of many people's annual salaries. Charlie also had a number of transactions on his conscience which kept him awake at night.

The next arrest was not of Stern or Peter but of an unknown Newcastle land agent. Stern had once bailed him out of trouble and had finally called in the favour. Against his better judgement, he had written a wildly optimistic report and valuation on the Newcastle properties on the strict understanding the report was only for private consumption and would never see the public eye.

Luckily for him, he had been paid merely handsomely. Enough maybe to raise an eyebrow, but not enough to constitute a bribe. He was not a brave man and he did what seemed the sensible thing at the time. He turned Queen's evidence.

A week later Stern received a call from his lawyer, Sir Matthew Makin. 'I'm afraid the police want you to go in,' he said. 'Bring your passport.'

It might be the civilised way of doing it, but it was an experience he would rather not go through again, thought

330

Stern five hours later. The police had been well prepared, with the evidence piled up on a table.

The officer had explained that, like Jack, he would be interviewed in the presence of his lawyer and the entire interview would be taped.

'I don't want to appear disrespectful,' Stern said, 'but couldn't that tape be edited?'

'No need to worry, 'said the officer cheerily. 'All these new machines have a device which records the time the tape has been running. If we started mucking about with it, there would be gaps. It would be instantly noticeable.'

Stern nodded. After two three-hour sessions of detailed questioning he had passed through anger to a state of numbness. Like Jack, on the advice of his lawyer he had replied 'no comment' to everything.

The police then formally charged him with six offences. There was a general charge of conspiracy to defraud covering his activities throughout the bid; obtaining money through deception relating to the warehouse sale; two charges of 'conspiracy to act in breach of Section 205 of the Companies Act', accusing him of acting in concert with Max and von Gleichen. He was also charged with conspiracy to manipulate the market – a breach of section 47 of the Financial Services Act, and contravening section 151 of the Companies Act.

The most serious charge was 'obtaining money by deception' which related to the sale of the Newcastle warehouses which he had so enjoyed negotiating in Mark's Club.

Three days later Peter went through the same procedure.

He was charged with conspiracy to defraud Butlers; conspiracy to manipulate the market; conspiracy to dishonestly conceal material facts from the market, and contravening Section 151 of the Companies Act.

331

Chapter 22

Peter rocked the screaming child in his arms, full of wonder that such a tiny scrap of humanity could make such a huge noise. His daughter's face was puckered and red, her head like a coconut covered in spiky black hair.

'Here, let me take her.' Angela appeared at his side in the garden. 'Darling, it's far too cold out here. Are you trying to give her pneumonia?'

'Nonsense, it's a wonderful early spring day. She likes the fresh air.'

'It's February,' declared Angela firmly, and disappeared back into the house through the French windows with the noisy bundle.

Peter stayed outside in the winter sunshine, admiring the view, made all the more precious by the fear he might lose it. For one brief moment he felt utter contentment. How strange that he should feel happier now, after a year out of work, than when he had been at the peak of his career at Hogarth Stein.

After the waiting, his arrest had come almost as a welcome relief. Two of his favourite clients had put up the £400,000 bail between them. The worst thing was having his passport taken away. But after a certain amount of haggling, the Serious Fraud Office had agreed to let him have it whenever he wanted to travel, provided he told them where he was going and why.

Hogarth Stein had fired him almost exactly a year ago. They had no choice, they said. John Young and the bank's chairman had summoned him to the boardroom where he found them looking acutely uncomfortable. John Young had spoken. 'We feel that for the overall good of the bank and all its employees, we must ask for your resignation.'

'But I was acting in the best interests of my client,' Peter protested. 'It was that same client who brought this bank nearly twenty million pounds worth of fees. You must remember that after the crash we were dealing with very exceptional circumstances.'

John Young was gentle but firm. 'The circumstances were exceptional, I agree. But frankly, Peter, I don't feel it is in the client's interest to encourage him to neglect his fiduciary duties.'

Peter had refrained from saying that his client needed no encouragement. His dismissal took six minutes.

He had burned with injustice. 'Strange how the law says you are innocent until proven guilty, but your employer, for whom you have earned millions of pounds, does not,' he had said to Jack when they met again for a discreet and modest lunch a few weeks later. He had felt less sensitive about being seen with him now they were both in the same boat.

Jack had every reason to agree. He, too, had been released on bail, put up by one of his big customers. Peter had heard that Sir Richard had been deeply saddened, some said almost heartbroken by what had happened.

'If he was so upset, how come he couldn't bring himself to tell me in person?' Jack had said scathingly. Sir Richard had left it to Edward and the rest of the board. Edward had almost broken down in tears.

Peter had not seen Jack since then. His lawyers had advised against it. But in just a few weeks, he had seen the change in Jack His hair had grown, his face looked gaunt and his shirt had a grubby look – so unlike the elegant, vain man he was used to. He demolished two large gin and tonics before the meal and insisted on a second bottle of red wine over lunch. Most of it he drank himself.

Then a couple of weeks after that, the tabloid press, who had been hounding them all, finally discovered that Rosemary had left him. Angela had pointed out an article in Mr Warren's newspaper which had devoted a whole page to the subject.

WIFE LEAVES DISGRACED BOSS read the headline. The story was written in the usual sensationalist idiom, but worse were the pictures of Jack – unkempt and drawn – standing in the garden of the Esher house. The photographers had clearly caught him by surprise, but he had made a vain attempt to look dignified. The result was pure pathos.

Peter had realised that Jack would have been too proud to tell him about Rosemary, but he was irritated that Angela had kept it a secret.

'Rosemary knew if I told you it would be round the City in two ticks. She didn't want to damage Jack any more,' she had said. It explained the catalogue of illnesses Rosemary had suffered from that winter.

Peter had felt a wave of sympathy as he looked at the picture, but at the wire he blamed Jack for the whole mess. If he hadn't been so prepared to deal so generously with his supporters, they would still be dining twice a week at Mark's Club.

Deep in his heart, he blamed himself too. He should have known better – but it had seemed a way out of the mess created by the market crash. John Young had not enquired too closely what was going on at the time, he thought bitterly.

After his arrest, the tabloids gave him the same treatment. But when news of his firing hit the press he barely had time to feel despair before sympathetic and supportive letters started pouring through the door.

More than half his clients had written. He was also touched by the letters and phone calls that came from his rival merchant bankers.

Well, they could afford to be generous now, he thought, after reading one particularly fullsome note, finishing up with a quote from Kipling. They had never really liked him when he was around.

But after a couple of weeks, as if at a given signal, radio silence began. It was as if the City and those who used its services had pulled out the connecting wires. 'It's like watching your ship go steaming by while you sit becalmed on a raft in the middle of an empty sea,' he said to Angela one evening.

She squeezed his arm and smiled. 'We'll be all right.'

334

Their friends and acquaintances in the country remained cordial, but there was a definite fall off in the number of dinner invitations from those with connections in the City – as if his problems were somehow contagious.

He read the financial press as if from a great distance. It was like watching a movie in which he had once starred. He knew all the characters, but instead of being one of them, he was now part of the audience.

What irked him most was knowing he had done nothing particularly out of the way. Yes, he had stretched the rules – even broke them – or allowed Jack to break them. But any number of his peers would have done exactly the same in the circumstances.

He struggled to grasp that his life was in ruins through breaking a few irritating rules. It was not as if anyone had been hurt. The shareholders of Butlers had fared no worse than those in any other major company in the crash. And in the fullness of time he was convinced they would do better.

Peter's anger turned outward and he became obsessional about the wrongdoings of others in the City. The evils of insider trading became his hobby horse. He viewed the subject from a great moral height, proclaiming to anyone who would listen that he had never done anything for his own personal gain.

For decades, senior brokers, bankers and company chairman had lunched and dined together. It was a City habit. And for decades it had been thought perfectly normal practice to buy a few shares if the chairman had been cheerful and optimistic and perhaps even dropped a few hints that exciting times were on the way. In truth they quite often revealed hard facts, usually around the port stage.

When insider dealing became illegal in 1980, the lunches went on even though most company directors became more circumspect about what they said. You can't prosecute someone for buying shares because the chairman seemed in good spirits or selling them if he was subdued.

Peter would point out to anyone who would listen that all this went on quite blithely – people making money illegally, in spirit at least. Yet he, who had done nothing for his own financial gain was treated like a pariah simply for looking after his client. He preached the message to journalists, to visiting guests, to the local farmers, and most of all to his lawyers. They nodded in sympathy.

The world whirled on. The injustice was driven home as he watched his fellow practitioners at work. Most of them had at the very least bent the rules at various times, when the pressure was on. They knew it too, which was why there had been such a wave of sympathy after his sacking. 'There but for the Grace of God' had taken on a very personal meaning.

And, although Peter found it hard to believe, his fellow merchant bankers actually missed him. He had brought a lightness of touch and a unique style to their business. He had tinged it with glamour. They might outwardly have disapproved of the racy suits, flash car and the grandiose house in the country, but they had secretly enjoyed being outraged at his cold calling of their clients with daring deals to do – and his constant baiting of the authorities.

He had added colour to their lives. The City landscape seemed drear without him.

They did not thank him for the scandal, though, and the spotlight it put on all their doings. Eager young compliance officers clustered in corporate finance departments like metal filings on a magnet.

Merchant bankers stopped taking notes at confidential client meetings, fearing that, if there were an enquiry, they would be taken and used as evidence. There were dire warnings from merchant banking chairmen about sticking to the letter of the law and memos forbidding leaks to the press from the Takeover Panel.

Those who until the crash had liked to model themselves on Peter began shunning the press, preferring a low profile. It was a time for discretion, for keeping heads well below the parapet.

In those first couple of months of purdah, Peter's only regular contact with the outside world took place with his lawyers. He spent seemingly endless hours in their offices helping them piece the story together for their 'proofs of evidence' – the basis of the brief for the barrister. Finally, it had been done.

His other main preoccupation had been haggling with the

personnel department of Hogarth Stein who had turned maliciously stingy about his terms of severance. He had never felt more lonely in his whole life.

He understood why Jack was disintegrating on his own. Without Angela he knew he would have gone insane. Women were strange. She had seemed almost pleased.

'You're always complaining you don't have time to do the things you enjoy,' she said. 'You'll even be able to spend more time with me. You can come out riding.'

He had got to know Angela all over again. Beneath the cool no-nonsense manner which she affected to protect herself, he rediscovered a gentle, understanding woman.

Some inner key had been turned and in April their daughter, Charlotte Angela, had been conceived.

Peter had been horrified. 'Of all times, Angela, this was not the moment to choose. What kind of a future can I offer a child? I may never work again.'

She laughed. 'Children need love and order, not money,' she had said. 'Anyway, it's rubbish that you'll never work again. You may never work again in the City, but your brain will always be in demand.'

Peter had thought her a foolish optimist. Then one day in June when he was admiring the newly opening roses she had come running across the lawn, hair flying, her face alight with excitement.

'It's Jim Hogan of Wingways,' she gasped. 'He says he needs your help.'

He hugged her. 'Darling! Be careful. You are pregnant, you know.'

Hogan sounded almost apologetic to be bothering him: 'I hope you don't mind me ringing you at home,' he had said – as if there were anywhere else. 'We're trying to do this merger, and your old colleagues simply can't seem to find a way of doing it. I wondered if you could give us some ad hoc advice?' He hadn't even mentioned Butlers.

Peter had sorted out the problems in a few days; and once the news leaked out that he was prepared to advise unofficially, the telephone had started to ring.

His biggest surprise came when the chairman of one of the stuffier merchant banks had invited him to lunch and offered

337

him an informal consultancy. 'We have enormous respect for your intellect and expertise. All this business seems such a waste,' he had said. 'We can't officially employ you, but we'll put the fees on deposit until this whole thing is over.'

Peter stood in the garden, smiling at the memory of it. The truth was he was earning more now than he had ever made at Hogarth Stein. A cloud suddenly passed over the sun and an east wind bit into him. It was all very fine, he thought, turning to go inside, but he might well be facing a prison sentence, not to mention a legal suit from Hogarth Stein for negligence which could wipe him out financially.

It was the uncertainty which undermined him. The date for the trial had been postponed twice. Now it was set for June. It was one thing to use him now, while he was still technically innocent. But how would people feel about employing a convicted criminal?

Stern and Sarah stood silently together as the coffin slid out of sight, trembling as it went. The crematorium chapel was packed. Denis had been much loved, in and out of the City. Dickie made a moving address, bringing out all Denis's warmth and humour, looking the perfect City senior partner. For most of the service Sarah stayed dry-eyed, beautiful in black Valentino. Then, in piercing tones of innocence, the leading chorister sang Psalm 121:

> I will lift up mine eyes unto the hills, from whence cometh my help.
> My help cometh from the Lord, which made heaven and earth.
> He will not suffer thy foot to be moved: he that keepeth thee will not slumber.
> Behold, he that keepeth Israel shall neither slumber nor sleep.
> The Lord is thy keeper: the Lord is thy shade upon the right hand.
> The sun shall not smite thee by day, nor the moon by night.
> The Lord shall preserve thee from all evil; he shall preserve thy soul.

The Lord shall preserve thy going out and thy coming in from this time forth, and even for evermore.

By he end of it, the tears were coursing down Sarah's pale cheeks.

She cried for Denis, who in the end had died painlessly in his sleep, and for Irene and the children. But she also cried for herself. She loved Stern as she had never loved anyone. She knew she would never love with such passion again. She felt the power of his presence beside her and looked up at him, tall and magnificent, his thick black hair gleaming on his leonine head. He was the love of her life. But it had ceased to be enough to be his mistress.

She longed to wake up next to him, to scrub his back in the bath, to go for walks with him, to cook supper for him – to do the normal things of life together.

Since the scandal they had to be doubly careful about being seen together. After the arrests they did not meet for more than a month. She had felt as if part of her had died.

Then they began seeing each other again, but the routine of dinners and lovemaking had closed in on her. Not once did he ever stay the whole night with her. One morning she woke up, alone as usual, and in a moment of snapshot clarity realised that this was the sum total of their relationship. This was all it was ever going to be.

Paulette had recovered and Stern showed no sign of wanting to leave. He still made love to Sarah with genuine passion but for her there was a sterile quality about it. Whatever he and Paulette had together, it was stronger than her. Once she accepted that, she began slowly, almost imperceptibly, to detach.

As they fled out of the chapel into the garden of remembrance and stood awkwardly around, pretending to admire the huge displays of flowers, she made up her mind. Once the trial is over, I'll get out of England, she thought.

Stern squeezed her arm gently. She looked up into his black eyes and smiled. It was too soon to tell him.

Stern had not been fired. As chairman and major shareholder of Stern Group he was his own employer and not about to dismiss himself, however much the pundits might call for it.

The worst ordeal had been attending a glittering reception given by Integrated Leisure the evening after his arrest. Paulette had begged him not to go.

'You can say that I was ill,' she had pleaded.

'It's like having a car accident,' he had said. 'If you don't get behind the wheel and drive again straight away, you lose your nerve. Besides,' he added, 'I don't want all those toffee-nosed pricks thinking I'm chicken.'

It had felt like taking a dive from the high board as they stood just outside the entrance to the ballroom at Claridge's, waiting to be presented. Stern looked as imposing as ever, Paulette as elegant. But that night their faces had been taut, their eyes a little brighter than usual. Stern whispered into the flunkey's ear and as they moved forward his voice rang out: 'Sir Leo and Lady Stern.' For a moment no longer than a heartbeat the silence rippled before them like a wave lapping against the shoes of the assembled guests. Then out of the abyss had come a familiar voice.

'Nice to see you, Leo, Paulette.' It was their host, Bob Benson. He shook Stern's hand and kissed Paulette with unprecedented warmth. Stern had guided Paulette towards a group of their old friends willing them not to turn away. They hadn't.

But Stern had remained grim-faced throughout the evening. He was not going to pretend that everything was just as usual. He was not going to smile with relief that everyone was still talking to him. But he was not going to stay at home either.

Paulette had been wonderful, he thought afterwards. His greatest worry had been that the stress of the scandal might have accelerated her cancer. But the operation had been a total success and the best cosmetic surgeon in the land had ensured that her left breast was hardly less perfect than the right.

Stern had called a board meeting of Stern Group the day after his arrest. It was a small board, with only four executives, all devoted to Stern. In each case, he had plucked them from mundane jobs, motivated them and made them rich men.

340

But the same kind of folie de grandeur which had allowed Paulette to bully him into taking on the chairmanship of the London and City Ballet had also persuaded him to appoint two non-executive directors, both from outside the retailing sector.

One was the former chairman of a large industrial group, the other a director of one of the big four clearing banks. The former chairman had spoken at the meeting. He was an affable clever man, steeped in industry.

'We all value your leadership tremendously Leo, and it is obvious that Stern Group would not be the success it is without you,' he had said in genuinely sincere tones. 'But do you not feel at for the good of the outside shareholders, you should perhaps stand aside from the role of chairman?'

Stern looked at him coldly. 'You think it will make the share price go up again if I stop being chairman?'

'You would still run things, Leo,' the banker had said soothingly, 'but you would have made some concession to the outside world. You only have 47 per cent, you know. A shareholders' meeting could vote you out.'

It was highly unlikely, but Stern took the point. After the meeting he ordered Charlie and Denis to start buying Stern Group shares. 'Stop when you get to 51 per cent,' he told them.

That had solved that little problem.

The clearing banker resigned from the board a week later. The industrialist stayed on. He liked and admired Leo – and besides, the £20,000 a year came in handy.

Apart from spending hours closetted with his lawyers, Stern carried on much as before – if anything with a little more flamboyance. Any sign of weakness he believed would be interpreted as guilt.

The DTI had been thorough and clumsy. Once the enquiry became public, they had taken every file, every diary, every fax stub they could find, first from Butlers offices, from Hogarth Stein, and finally from Stern Group.

They had gone through the bank accounts, the suppliers' contracts, the customer contracts, the computer systems and all the invoices. They uncovered his special agreement on the price of Oaties. For a while he thought he would be safe as far

341

as Wingways went. Why, after all, should they connect him with Butlers dropping an agreement for the exclusive distribution rights of a chocolate bar?

But Jim Hogan, Wingways chief executive, had done his own detective work and was only too happy to make his findings available to the inspectors. At the time he had suspected it was a ruse to make him vulnerable, and had noted the huge selling orders in the days afterwards.

But in Switzerland the police came to a dead end. Klaus refused to co-operate, pleading the Swiss confidentiality laws. But they had seized all Denis and Sarah's records (in fact the records of the entire firm) which had infuriated Dickie. Those showed the sales under a nominee name, which after a search under section 212 of the Companies Act eventually revealed BANTA. Even so there was no proof that Klaus and Stern were acting in concert.

Klaus had, fortunately, placed the selling order with Sarah direct, which was all she had to say. It was unlikely the case would even come to court, his lawyers told him.

The DTI's insider dealing branch had interviewed Stern unsuccessfully from their point of view. He had appeared nerveless.

But the charges of market manipulation and breaking section 151 of the Companies Act worried him. And then there was the warehouse deal . . .

Sometimes when he went home in the evening and sat in his pretty sitting room, with its gilded French furniture and Impressionist paintings on the wall, he could hardly believe it was happening to him. Outwardly he gave little sign that he was under pressure. But he had taken to waking at four in the morning, feeling a cold, empty space between his ribs. And he would go over it – and over it – and over it.

Sometmes he argued the case so powerfully in his head, he emerged pristine – innocent on all counts. Other times, he heard the prison gates clang shut.

He had been totally honest with his lawyers and had employed a leading silk to represent him in court at a cost of £5,000 a day. If money could buy his acquittal, no expense would be spared.

He redoubled his efforts at work but his moods swung

unpredictably. One day he would feel secure that an eloquent barrister must be able to persuade the jury of his innocence – that he had no intention to break the law.

The next, someone would make a remark which would destroy his confidence. One friend, who was also a barrister, declared that it all boiled down to whether the jury liked the look of you or not.

How would he look to a jury of council house dwellers? Any jury at a long trial consisted of housewives and the unemployed. Anyone else could plead that they were needed at work. He doubted that the sympathy of the jury would be with a man still worth £500 million on paper and living in a £2 million house in St John's Wood.

He knew, too, that he was up against anti-Semitism. As the year had worn on the whispers had grown louder. Somehow the City had invented a Jewish conspiracy. Stern, Schlosstein and Sarah were all Jewish – it was a good enough peg for the establishment to hang their prejudice on.

Of course, no one said anything to his face. But he had friends who reported back. The most telling occasion had been at a drinks party at Hogarth Stein. 'They do all seem to have been Jewish, don't they?' one director had said smugly to the head of one of Stern's big suppliers.

'Do they?' he had replied. 'Armstrong's not Jewish, Peter Markus isn't Jewish, those Swiss aren't Jewish.'

'Oh, come on,' said the director scornfully, 'Peter's father was Jewish – he was supposed to be distantly related to the Rothschilds. It's in the blood, you know.'

Stern tried not to waste his energy thinking about it. It made him too angry.

A whole year had gone by while the police struggled unsuccessfully to extradite Max Schlosstein from New York and Klaus von Gleichen from Zurich.

They were wasting their time with Schlosstein. The US authorities were much too keen to hang on to him for themselves. Von Gleichen they might get – but first they had to find him. Stern occasionally smiled at the thought. BANTA protected its own.

The death of Denis Jones had eliminated the last possible witness who could have convicted Stern of insider dealing.

Something had always stopped him using Sarah on those occasions.

So he was not that surprised when the DTI decided to drop the insider dealing charges. They had the solace that the newly created Serious Fraud Office would almost certainly nail all three defendants on other offences.

The latest news was of a June trial. Now, a year after the arrests, Stern congratulated himself that he hadn't done too badly in the circumstances. It had been business as usual. He hadn't gone under. As far as he was concerned, the trial couldn't happen too soon.

As for Sarah – apart from when they met, he tried not to think about her.

Jack sat bolt upright in bed. He had thought for a terrifying moment that his heart had stopped. He sank gingerly back down again on the grimy pillows. Little men with hammers were trying to get into his skull. Or were they inside, trying to get out? Pain reached at him from various parts of his body. His stomach felt like a wet sponge. A wave of nausea swept over him and he lurched, grey and sweating, out of the bed along the small hallway to the bathroom. His knees buckled as he clutched the lavatory bowl. Five minutes of retching produced nothing.

He staggered to his feet and reached for a toothbrush with a shaking hand. In the shaving mirror, with the north light shining in his face, Jack saw bloodshot, watery eyes barely visible under the puffiness of his eyelids in an ashen face. But tiny red veins were beginning to form a tracery on his cheeks.

What was happening? He stared at his reflection in terror, as if the man in the glass might somehow speak and give him the answer. 'What's going to become of me?' He heard himself speak the words out loud and knew he had no idea of the answer. The future gaped before him like a yawning, featureless chasm. He squeezed the toothpaste onto the brush watching his hand shake; then as the paste stung his mouth he felt a faint surge of hope.

Today, he wouldn't drink! That was the only way. In fact he wouldn't drink for a whole week. He would get fit. Just because he couldn't pay the gym membership any more didn't mean he had to let himself go. He did not have to be a victim. He could go to the local swimming pool, go for a jog on the common. In fact he would go now. Well, perhaps a walk rather than a jog.

Feeling better already, he had a bath and made himself a pot of tea in the flat's cluttered kitchen. He had put the Esher house on the market three months after Butlers had fired him. For the first month he had been under siege anyway. Then the press seemed to forget about him. There was the odd phone call from Patrick and one or two others to see if he had any plans for the future, but gradually even they died away.

The world of public companies had turned out to be much less forgiving than the City. He had been quite optimistic at first. He hoped that one of the big food companies would have employed him on a consultancy basis. When they didn't ring him, he rang them – but it had been embarrassing and humiliating.

Men who had dined at his table and played golf with him, months before, vanished into endless meetings. Their secretaries said they would ring back. They did not. Jack rang back. They were still in a meeting, they would ring back. They didn't. He tried writing letters. That at least felt more productive.

Back came polite little notes expressing sympathy, wishing him well, but regretting they couldn't offer him anything at the moment. Some were more honest than others. 'We cannot risk besmirching the reputation of our company,' said one.

Pompous southern oaf, thought Jack.

One day, about a month after Butlers had fired him, he got a letter from his football team. He looked at the envelope and turned it over several times, fearing to open it.

He read: 'Dear Jack, as you may know, Sir Richard Butler has seen fit to withdraw Butlers sponsorship of the club, following the stockmarket crash and your departure. However, we would very much like you to stay on as a director and wish you well in your current difficult time.' He had almost cried.

His visits to the matches had been like points of light in the bleakest of winters. And when the team made it from the third division into the second division he forgot his troubles for nearly an hour.

He had been hopeful, even confident, that Rosemary would come back. His male ego had refused to believe she could really prefer someone else. He had seen her several times, but although she showed concern, gradually, she extracted her belongings from the house. On one occasion, a weekday evening when he had been feeling particularly low, she had tried to talk. She had said how difficult it must all be for him, how she was sorry it had all happened at the same time.

He had screamed at her, called her a disloyal bitch.

A few weeks later, he had rung Angela.

'I wondered if you had seen Rosemary?' he said, coming straight to the point.

'Yes, I have Jack,' said Angela quietly.

'And was she happy?'

'I'm afraid so, Jack. I got the impression she was very happy.'

He decided to sell the house. He cleared a profit of nearly £200,000 on it after he had paid off the mortgage. Meanwhile he rented a three-bedroom flat in Clapham, near where Mark was living with some friends.

There were some very good pubs in Clapham, he discovered. He soon got to know the locals. After a few weeks he settled into one, treating it like a second home. He liked the landlord. A small group of them used to stay on and drink, all through the afternoons sometimes.

He'd somehow lost interest in women; they had mysteriously become the enemy. A conciliatory note from Jane had arrived two days after his arrest, but she had not rung him. Secretly he was relieved.

A few of the wives in his newfound drinking school eyed him hungrily – but for the first time in his life, he couldn't be bothered even to flirt with them.

To begin with it was just a couple of hours that went missing, then it became whole days. At Christmas he'd picked a fight with someone. At New Year he picked another and actually landed up in hospital with a black eye and two broken ribs.

The pain had been excruciating. It had become an effort to go out, to move, especially to sit in a bar and laugh. He found a local off-licence that would deliver and took to solitary drinking.

Mark pleaded with him.

'You're drinking too much, Dad. You'll kill yourself.'

'Rubbish,' Jack had said, still able to muster bravado. 'It dulls the loneliness a bit, that's all.'

Mark knew his father's temper too well to argue. Once he had come round for Sunday lunch. Afterwards when he was clearing up he found the dustbin full to the brim with empty whisky bottles and beer cans.

He saw his father less and less.

Jack walked round Clapham Common for about half an hour. Some boys were kicking a ball about in the late-February sunshine. He wished he were one of them. They looked so healthy and carefree. He stood watching them for a moment, listening to their shouts of glee, and his eye wandered to the road.

That was interesting. He had never noticed that pub before. How extraordinary, he thought he'd been in them all. The church bell began chiming noon.

He thought about popping in, just to see what it was like.

But you're not drinking today, you're getting fit, said a voice in his head.

Well, that was first thing, he argued back. I feel fine now. It could have been that Indian takeaway upset me. I'll only have a half of bitter.

One drink leads to another, said the voice.

No, really, I'll just have half a pint. Then I'll go straight back home.

He marched through the door and up to the gleaming bar. The woody pub smell made him feel instantly warm and relaxed. The barman beamed at him.

'Yes sir, what would you like.'

He flashed the man a friendly smile. 'I think I'll have a pint of your best bitter.'

347

Chapter 23

Sarah leaned back in her chair in post-lunch weariness. She had never felt as tired in her life as during the past few months. Once it had come out that she had been Stern's and Schlosstein's broker, many of her clients had simply melted away. But the lack of work was more than compensated for by the stress. The publicity in the weeks after the news broke had been relentless.

Somehow, one of the tabloids had got hold of a picture of her in a bikini. 'Beautiful broker at heart of Butlers scandal' the caption had read. A group of depressed-looking men and women burdened with cameras and tape recorders had laid seige to her flat. She had even got on to speaking terms with some of them. Despite her parents' pleas to move in with them, she had stayed put. She knew these people would somehow track her down wherever she went. Then, after about a week, they mysteriously vanished like morning mist – it was hard to believe they had ever been there.

But if the journalists were a pest, they were nothing compared to the DTI inspectors and the Serious Fraud Officers, alternately matey and threatening.

The Serious Fraud Office had spent more than twenty hours with her on the Butlers case. Now Denis was dead, she was a crucial witness. She had stuck broadly to what Stern and she had agreed over lunch, but they had extracted the exact timing and details of every bargain she had done in connection with the bid and her recollection of every telephone call. She had thanked God several times there were no tapes at Tulley.

She had astounded everyone at work by her resilience. If they had only known! She had astounded herself by her ability to cry herself to sleep, wake at five and lie in bed rigid with tension for two hours before getting up and appearing in the office as though everything was perfectly normal.

It was not only that she was a crucial witness. She was a crucial witness for the prosecution.

Stern's image had been catapulted from the cosy world of the City press on to the front pages of the tabloids. It had not travelled well. Everything he owned – his house in London, the villa on the Cote d'Azur, his car – was photographed and plastered across double-page spreads. Such wealth, they seemed to be saying, could not have been accumulated honestly.

Then there were the stories about Sarah – all innuendo and no facts, but clearly hinting that if she was his broker she must also have been something else. Fully recovered from her operation, Paulette was outraged.

'There's a law against sexual discrimination in this country, but they allow this kind of sexist rubbish. It's a disgrace,' she declared one Sunday morning at the peak of the publicity. For once she found Stern totally in agreement on the subject.

Peter fared little better – Charlton House, his pride and joy, became a positive disadvantage. His lawyer suggested he move out and had almost begged him to sell the Aston Martin.

'And get a Mini, I suppose?' Peter had said scornfully. 'No way.'

Angela agreed with him. After all, where would she keep the horses? 'In any case, I fail to see why the fact that we've got a big house and a fast car should make a jury think you are guilty. Grandiosity isn't a crime, you know.' The lawyer wasn't totally sure if she was joking or not.

'Yes, and we need the space for our daughter,' said Peter. He and Angela both burst out laughing. The strain was getting to them, the lawyer thought.

The contrast between them and Jack could not have been

more stark. At the time of the arrests, the press had taken shots of the Esher house, but someone tipped them off about Rosemary leaving and Jack moving into the flat.

So far there had been three court hearings, where they all turned up, gave their pleas and the prosecution said it needed more time to prepare its case. At the last hearing the press had caught Jack leaving his flat, looking terrible. They flogged the human wreckage angle just as hard as they could and tracked down Mark.

'Life has been incredibly difficult with my parents splitting up, and now this. Why don't you leave us alone?' he told one Sunday tabloid. There was a picture of him looking waif-like in his jeans.

To Jack's embarrassment the only person the press had found to stand up for him – and they had collectively decided that he was the victim – was the publican of his nearest local. 'Jack Armstrong is being driven to drink by worrying about his trial,' he told the same Sunday newspaper. In a half-page lurid colour photograph, he appeared standing behind the bar, beaming, with a picture of Jack inset, unshaven and haggard. It was all good for trade.

But if the public saw Stern and Peter as rich City fat cats whose come-uppance was long overdue, and Jack as an innocent, beguiled victim, the view from inside the extended Square Mile was just the opposite.

At first the reaction had been to pluck out the eye that offended. But Stern and Peter were two of the most talented men in their respected fields. Calibre like that did not grow on trees and there was no doubt both had shown a lot of pluck in adversity. More than a year had gone by and they had both kept their dignity. In the spring of 1989 their names were bandied around the lunch tables in merchant banks, the Savoy Grill and the Connaught as much as ever – and with a new affection.

They were seen in these places less frequently, but as time went on they made occasional appearances and were initially surprised and then delighted at the welcome they received. They had achieved celebrity status.

Under the surface, Peter found it the most difficult. He steeled himself against the same question whenever he showed his face.

'What are you doing now?'

The problem was that most of his 'consultancies' were for people who did not want it shouted from the hilltops that he was working for them.

'Oh, scraping a living,' he would say with a grin. It generally sufficed.

But the City had turned its back on Jack Armstrong.

'Let's face it, Charlie, he got carried away,' said one of the fund managers who had not been involved in the bid. They were having lunch at Café Pelican in a draughty converted wharf called Hays Galleria at London Bridge. Greenbag's new owners had moved them into London Bridge City – a gleaming complex of glass and steel next door.

Charlie thought gloomily about his mortgage. 'Well, they were very heady times, if you remember. I rated him. He'd done a good job. It's a miracle that we didn't get our fingers burned, looking back.'

The fund manager sipped his wine.

'Maybe. Or maybe you just have better instincts. You've seen it all before. He came from nowhere, suddenly found himself the centre of attention. It went to his head.'

'Do you think they'll get off?'

'Hard to say. How are you going to explain all this to a jury? The warehouse sale is about the only straightforward thing. Persuading someone who owes you a large favour to buy property from you for five times the market price looks pretty cut and dried to me.'

Charlie moved the grey pâté on his plate around. 'Yes. And the jury may just look at Leo and Peter and think, rich fat cats, they deserve to go down.'

'Don't underestimate the British public. I don't think they are as against success as everyone seems to think. They are a lot more anti the police.'

Charlie flicked back a lock of blond hair and idly watched a smart redhead in a sage green outfit walk towards them. He was just thinking what wonderful legs she had when she waved.

'Hello, Charlie. Still practising the art of the long lunch. How are you?' It was Jane Brompton and she looked gratifyingly pleased to see him.

351

'Splendid. Why don't you join us for a drink?' He introduced her to the fund manager.

'We were just talking about poor old Jack.'

Jane's eyes clouded. 'Yes, it seems very fashionable to think of him as a victim, a pawn in the hands of the wicked City.' There was a sharpness in her voice.

'Well, Peter was supposed to know the rules. Jack wasn't,' said Charlie.

'Yes, but from what I gather, most of those rules got broken all the time. And I remember Jack being fanatical about winning. He could talk of nothing else sometimes. It was just that extraordinary property sale that seems so stupid now. One can't think what possessed them.'

Charlie sighed.

'They were under a lot of pressure. Nearly every major shareholder was screaming at them after the market crashed – certainly everyone who had helped out during the bid.'

'Mmm. And Sir Leo is not exactly a man you want against you.' Jane's drink arrived and her face lit up in a smile. 'Well, here's to you anyway.' She had always liked Charlie – he was good fun and uncomplicated. 'Has the trial been definitely fixed yet? I suppose you will be a witness?'

'They think it will be June,' said Charlie uncomfortably. 'They seem to be giving up the idea of ever getting the American or the Swiss over here to testify. How about you? Have you seen Jack?'

'Not for over a year – and he looked awful then.'

'Yes, eighteen months is a long time to wait to be brought to justice.'

The fund manager broke into their dialogue. 'Well, I really must be going, Charlie. Thanks for lunch. I'll be in touch. Nice to have met you.' He shook hands with Jane.

Left alone they started to giggle. 'He was a bit of a boring old fart,' said Jane.

'He's a very senior fund manager. Got to be nice to these people,' grinned Charlie. 'Shall we have another drink?'

She smiled back and crossed her stunning legs. 'Yes, please.'

Patrick was resolutely not feeling sorry for Jack. He had

vowed to get even with him for trying to get the managing director to kill his story.

David Bang, who on some whim was buying him lunch in the cosy jade opulence of the Connaught Grill, was doing nothing to disillusion him.

'Quite honestly, all this poor Jack stuff makes me sick,' David said. He was wearing a new double-breasted dogtooth suit. 'The man is an egomaniac. I mean, there was no doubt who was in control at those morning meetings.' They both looked up at the arrival of a silver trolley bearing a magnificent whole roast rib of beef. Three waiters hovered anxiously.

'Ow wood you like ze beef?' asked the most senior.

Patrick ruminated pleasurably. 'Quite rare, I think.'

David nodded. 'Same for me.'

Perfect pink slices of beef, served with featherlight puffs of Yorkshire pudding and sizzling roast potatoes, were placed before them.

'You know,' said David oozing satisfaction, 'I'd forgotten how nice this place is.'

'And what do you think of Stern? Is he the real evil genius?'

David sipped contemplatively at his claret. 'Isn't that that wild property dealer, Paul Bloomfield, over there?'

'Yes,' answered Patrick. 'But what about Stern?'

'Well, I have done a bit of work for him from time to time, actually.'

Patrick raised an eyebrow.

'I've always found him pretty straightforward. He just hated to lose. And after all, Jack had promised him the world in Venice.'

'Oh, did he? I hadn't realised that.' Patrick's journalistic instinct snapped to attention.

'Oh, sure, that's the whole problem. Jack offered him a verbal indemnity against loss as long as he continued to support the Butlers price. It's a flagrant breach of Section 151 of the Companies Act – but on the other hand it has happened to a greater or lesser extent in practically every major bid this decade.'

'But it only came to light in Butlers because the indemnities were actually called after the market crashed, of course,' said

Patrick. 'You are well informed,' David said with a hint of a question mark.

'God, this beef's good.'

'And presumably the discount on Oaties was an inducement to get him to accept the bid on behalf of his eight or so percent?'

'Yes, I guess so,' Patrick sensed that David had gone deliberately vague.

He changed the subject. 'What I don't understand is why they are all pleading 'not guilty' to everything. I mean, all these things will have gone through the company accounts. The warehouse sale is utterly flagrant and the land agent has turned Queen's evidence.

'Schlosstein has apparently confessed he demanded $8 million from Jack as a consultancy fee in lieu of supporting the share price. There's this union bloke blowing the whistle on the Italian deal. I don't see why they are bothering. I think they should go for the sympathy vote and plead guilty.'

David gave a low, cynical laugh. 'Sweetheart, sometimes you journalists can be touchingly naive. The evidence suggests that practically everyone in financial fraud cases get acquitted because firstly, the jury doesn't understand what the case is about, and secondly they see all these nice-looking, smart people and don't want to convict them.'

'But Peter seems to think just the opposite,' said Patrick. 'That they will take one look at him and say he deserves to go down, even if he's innocent, because he's rich.'

David put his knife and fork together and leaned back with a sigh of contentment.

'I'm not so sure. These is going to be a long trial. The jurors will be mainly housewives and the unemployed. A friend of mine did jury service recently and said he was the only man out of the twelve.'

'And you really think women won't want to send smart businessmen down?' It was Patrick's turn to think David naive.

'You wait and see,' said David as another trolley, piled up with puddings, arrived.

'We also 'ave some fresh berrees such as raspberrees, blueberrees and fraises du bois,' said the waiter.

'I'll have the crème brulée and some fruit salad,' said David. 'My money's on Stern,' he continued. 'He's a winner, you wait and see.'

The following morning Sarah surveyed the row of designer suits hanging in her wardrobe. There was Valentino, Chanel, Max Mara – and all paid for out of her own salary. It had been a surprisingly mild winter and she hadn't needed to wear an overcoat once. This particular March morning she stared at them with sudden dislike.

She had gone back to helping out her old boss on researching the food companies, as her own 'sharp end' business had grown so sparse. She was supposed to be visiting a company that morning, but for some reason the idea seemed overwhelming.

She tried on the least unpleasant-looking of the suits but could not find a blouse to go with it. She threw it on the floor angrily. One after another she tried them all on. One had a stain down the front, one was too loose – she had lost nearly a stone in the past few months. The colour of the next one made her look yellow. After twenty minutes she was still standing in her dressing room in her underwear. She could not wear any of them. Her feet seemed glued to the floor as she stared at the five suits lying in a jumble on the floor. Take charge, take charge, a voice whispered. She put a hand to her face and found her cheeks were wet.

Leo would know what to do! She would phone Leo. But she could not reach the telephone. Panic bubbled up in her like a spring and she started to shake. She made for the only safe place in the flat.

'Dickie, you don't know where Sarah is, do you?' The head or research sounded anxious.

Dickie paused in his study of the Topic screen. He could not understand why every single share in the oil sector seemed to be going up apart from the one he had bought for his own account the week before.

'No, why should I know?'

'Well, she was supposed to be visiting a company this morning, and the chairman's secretary has just rung in and said she hasn't turned up.'

'And she's not here?'

'No, of course not,' the head of research snapped. 'I'd hardly be bothering you if she was.'

'Have you tried her at home?'

'I've only got her old number where she used to live with her parents.'

Dickie gave him the new number. 'It's most unlike her. Maybe her car broke down.'

The head of research rang the number. There was no reply.

Well, he'd just have to wait for her to contact him.

Later that morning Stern rang for Sarah at Tulley. Nobody seemed to know where she was. He got put through to Dickie.

'Where's my favourite stockbroker?' he said, trying to sound unconcerned.

'Well – we're a bit worried actually,' Dickie said. Stern tried Sarah's number. It was engaged. He looked at his watch. The head of a major Italian design house was meeting him for lunch to discuss designing an exclusive range of knitwear for his stores.

He'd try again after lunch.

Sarah turned the heating up. She was feeling very shivery for some reason. She decided to have a bath. She turned on the taps and opened the bathroom cabinet to get out the bubble bath. God, her head hurt. Her eye fell on the aspirin bottle.

Her grandmother had killed herself with aspirin. She had always wondered how many it took. She'd have her bath first, see if that shifted her headache.

She turned the taps off, still in the full-length petticoat she had been wearing when trying on the suits.

The bathwater beckoned, calm and blue. Drown in me, it whispered. I'm not getting in that, she thought, backing away. I'll never get out. She shut the bathroom door, returned to the bedroom and got back into bed. She started to shake again.

Stern stood on the pavement outside Cecconi's and shook hands warmly with the head of the Italian design house. '*Ciao! Cevidiamo ancora*,' he said.

She smiled at him through huge glasses as she pulled up the

collar of her sable coat. 'I hope so. It has been an enjoyable meeting.' She turned to where her driver was holding open the door of a long two-door Mercedes, the calf-length sable swinging as she moved. A final wave and she was gone.

She was probably the most sophisticated woman he had ever met, thought Stern. It was good to know there were still some nice surprises left in life. As he was just round the corner from Savile Row he decided to pop into his tailor, Kilgour French & Stanbury, and look at the new season's fabric. They were delighted to see him. He loved the feel of the shop, the smell of fine wool, the dark surroundings and huge bolts of cloth piled up apparently at random.

He wanted something lightweight for the summer. Sarah always said she liked him in paler colours. Sarah! How could he have forgotten?

'I'm sorry, I've just remembered I should be somewhere else,' he said.

He walked briskly back to the car and called Sarah's number again. It was still engaged. He handed his driver ten pounds. 'Get a taxi back to the office, will you, Louis? I'll take the car.'

As he drove, he checked Tulley to make sure she hadn't turned up.

'No, her phone is permanently engaged,' said Dickie. 'We were thinking of calling the police.'

'No, don't do that for a bit. I've got an idea,' said Stern. 'I'll get back to you.'

The light was beginning to fade when he arrived. It was a ground-floor flat in a terrace so he could not get round the back. The curtains of the front room were drawn. He rang and knocked. Then he got out his key.

Thank God she hadn't put on the Chubb. 'Sarah!' he shouted as the door opened. 'Sarah, it's me.' The flat was absolutely silent. He walked straight into the bedroom.

She was huddled against the pillows, the billowy cream duvet drawn up round her neck, her face almost the same colour and running with sweat. From the door he could see that her whole body was shaking. Her dark curls were plastered almost flat on her head. Her eyes shone with fever, huge and black.

As Stern moved towards her, she started to scream.

Chapter 24

Sir Matthew Makin was sunk deep in a brocade armchair, admiring the Magritte above the fireplace when Stern arrived. He had been invited for a quiet dinner with his client to discuss the latest developments in the case. As ever, Sir Matthew reflected, he was the one who was waiting.

He struggled from the low cocoon-like comfort to shake hands and was startled by the manic expression in Stern's eyes. It was the first time since the arrest, or indeed ever, he had seen Leo look anything other than fully in control.

'Is something amiss?' he asked as Stern strode to the Louis XV cabinet used for drinks and poured himself a large Armagnac. Hardly a pre-dinner drink, thought Sir Matthew. He was used to humouring Stern in all kinds of ways. Considering the legal fees this case would bring in, he didn't mind at all.

'I want to change my plea to guilty at the next hearing,' announced Stern.

'Good heavens, whatever for?' Sir Matthew's feeling of benign tolerance gave way to alarm. 'We have one of the best young QCs in the land to defend you and you stand a rattling good chance of acquittal. The latest news from the prosecution is excellent. They have refined the charges. If they stick to what they say, you are facing only ten charges under an umbrella of four main counts.'

The news froze Stern, glass in hand. Then his whole body seemed to sag. He shook his head.

'But at what cost to everyone involved?' he asked slowly. 'Some of the witnesses are showing signs of strain. I don't want a suicide on my hands.'

358

Sir Matthew coughed, trying to conceal his irritation. His instincts told him which witness Stern had in mind.

'I haven't told you the best piece of news.'

Stern looked up.

'The prosecution has been persuaded that there is no case to answer on the distribution agreement with Wingways, or the 20 per cent discount on Oaties. Frankly, because you, Peter Markus and Armstrong were the only ones present when those decisions were taken, there is no evidence that any reciprocity was involved. They are just slightly sharp commercial deals – some would even say skilfully negotiated deals that are advantageous to Stern Group. The charges will be dropped at the next hearing.'

For the first time that evening Stern smiled.

'You're not such a bad lawyer, are you?' he said drily.

Sir Matthew smiled too.

'What about the rest?'

'As we've discussed, Leo, I believe we have a good chance. The majority of the charges – those regarding the conspiracy to manipulate the market, and the charge of acting in concert – are all notably light on evidence. Even if the evidence stands up, and I'm afraid a lot of it does rest on Miss Meyer, the jury may well be persuaded that there was no 'mens rea' – no intent on your part to break the law. Such evidence as there is, is circumstantial. Without Schlosstein or von Gleichen they will have extreme difficulty persuading the jury that you are guilty beyond reasonable doubt. You are primarily a businessman after all. You cannot be expected to know every nuance of the Companies and Financial Services Acts, particularly when there have been so many changes. We have ample evidence that this kind of behaviour went on in other bids.'

Stern had sunk into a deep armchair opposite Sir Matthew, his face impassive.

'The final point is that the shares were purchased on behalf of Stern Group, so there was no personal gain – although the prosecution will doubtless point out that you own half the company.'

Stern drummed his fingers on the brocade arm of the chair.

'What about the big one?'

Sir Matthew coughed. 'Yes. The sale of the warehouses for five times their market value just a month after the stockmarket crashed.'

Stern looked straight at him.

'It is a pity the amount of profit you made out of that so precisely relates to the loss on your Butlers shares,' said Sir Matthew.

Stern ignored him, tossing back the second half of his Armagnac.

'So if I stick with the plea of 'not guilty' you're saying I could get acquitted of nearly all the charges, except that one, which is what? Conspiracy to defraud?'

Sir Matthew nodded.

'If I pleaded guilty to everything but that, what kind of sentence might I get?' Stern had risen and was pacing up and down the room as he spoke.

Sir Matthew became irritated. The idea of Stern changing his plea to save the nerves of one witness he found distastefully melodramatic. He decided to put things clearly.

'Well, pleas of guilty always get a sympathy vote of course. The rule of thumb is that you get a third off 'the tariff' – that is, the average sentence for that crime.'

'Good God, I hadn't realised there was anything as crude as a tariff,' exclaimed Stern, continuing to pace.

Sir Matthew continued, 'So on those Companies Act charges I reckon you might get away with two years imprisonment and a hefty fine, bearing in mind who you are.'

'Two years!'

Stern sank into a seat on the far side of the room.

There was a long pause. His expression changed. 'Why the discount?'

'Oh, a reward for contrition and remorse; encouragement for others to do the same. And also,' Sir Matthew smiled wryly, 'it is a tremendous saving of the Court's time and therefore the State's money. The barristers don't like it much, mind you, does them out of a job, but that's their problem.' He sipped his sherry.

Stern looked stricken

'You're right. I shall plead "not guilty" to everything.'

'Very sensible.' Sir Matthew refrained from mentioning

360

that if Stern were convicted on the warehouse deal, the prison sentence could be considerably longer than two years. 'I have some ideas on the warehouse problem,' Stern said.

'Really?'

'Let's talk about it over some food.' Stern rose from his seat and motioned to the doorway. 'Paulette has gone to a concert with some friends. Shall we have dinner?'

Sir Matthew struggled out of his chair. Again he was struck by the look in Stern's eyes.

'Are you sure you're feeling well, Leo?'

Stern paused in the doorway, his eyes intense. 'Never better,' he said quietly.

Someone was sucking Jack's cock. The room was dark and he wondered if he was dreaming, but his head was pounding in the normal way it did in the mornings. Suddenly a strident woman's voice with a strong North country accent said: 'Ooh, you can still get it up then? Amazing after what you shipped last night. You managed all right then too.' There was a disembodied giggle from around his groin. Then he felt the soft warm wetness envelope him once again.

The woman moved up the bed to lie next to him. 'Was that nice, love?' she asked and he felt large rolls of flesh nestle up to him.

He got out of bed, found his dressing gown and turned on the light. In his bed was an overweight woman in her fifties with jet black hair and a kindly expression.

'Who are you?' he asked.

She looked hurt. 'Don't you remember, love. The old Anchor? We had a game of darts and a few bevvies. Then we came back here for a bit of nookie.' She giggled again.

Jack shuddered. His mind was blank, then it came back to him. The day before had been his forty-second birthday. 'I'll call you a minicab.' he said.

When she had finally gone, reasonably mollified by the fifty pounds he had given her for the fare, he went into the kitchen to see if there was any Scotch left. He did not want to think about the night before. He did not want to think about anything.

All he could find was a quarter of a bottle of rum left by

some of Mark's friends. He hated rum but he drank it just the same. He drank it fast, straight from the neck so he hardly tasted it.

Stern went to see Dickie and told him Sarah must have a couple of months off. He also went to her parents saying he felt responsible for her collapse. The least he could do was to send her to one of the best recuperative clinics in Switzerland.

That meeting had been difficult. Sarah's mother had emanated hostility at the beginning of his visit, but he gradually convinced them of his genuine regret and his wish to make amends.

That summer, the high streets of Britain had their worst trading in years. Although Stern's middle of the road, quality merchandise stood up relatively well, compared with some of his more gimmicky competitors, life was still tough. The food business also held up, with sales of Oaties maintaining their reliable pattern.

Jane Brompton's head hunting firm felt the squeeze tighten as the huge investment and recruitment made during Big Bang began to unwind. In the City, salaries drifted downwards and jobs grew scarce. Despite the rise in share prices, the level of turnover – the number of shares traded each day – stayed well below that of the summer of 1987 when Butlers had made its overwheening bid.

Huge takeovers came briefly back into vogue again, but unlike the mid 1980s they were mainly financed by debt instead of shares. The term 'leverage' became the City's favourite buzzword.

June blazed, the water authorities warned of drought and got ready to be sold to the public.

And as Sir Matthew had predicted, the charges relating to the Wingways deal and the Oaties discount were both thrown out at the final hearing before the case came to court. Peter, Jack and Sir Leo Stern prepared themselves as best they could for trial.

And what of those supposedly on the side of justice? Despite the collapse of some of their charges, the Serious Fraud Office

362

senior personnel were not too unhappy. The evidence from Douglas Coles, the Newcastle land agent who was to be the chief prosecution witness, they viewed as definitive. He had sung like the proverbial canary. Barring anything happening to him – and they had lengthy tape recorded interviews with him to be safe – they were confident their case was as watertight as it could be.

The big debate at the Serious Fraud Office had been whether to go for theft or conspiracy to defraud. They had opted for the latter on the advice of counsel who said jurors were traditionally reluctant to find people guilty of theft where there has been no obvious, personal financial gain.

Even so, on the charge of conspiracy to defraud, they felt quietly confident that all three defendants could go down for more than five years each. It would more than justify the case.

These middle-aged detectives whose reputations were riding on the case were well aware that they were on less firm ground regarding the breaches of the Companies Act and the Financial Services Act. In essence, they had to prove the defendants deliberately broke the law.

In the case of Peter Markus this was clear cut as he was paid to know the law – it was his field of expertise. But both Stern and Jack could plead they had no idea what they had done was wrong, let alone criminal.

Only on the charge of theft against Jack on the payment to Schlosstein did they have a straightforward case. The US authorities were hanging on to Schlosstein. But the British police, still had their hopes.

The trial was due to take place in Court 16 – the end court on the first floor at the Old Bailey and one of the larger courts, traditionally used for financial cases because of the mountains of documentary evidence the prosecution accumulated. And in this case it would need to accommodate large numbers of public and press. It was the last trial of its nature to be held at the Old Bailey; from then on, all trials of a complex financial nature would take place at Southwark Crown Court.

At 10.30 a.m. on Monday 5 June the clerk of the court called their three names and Jack Armstrong, Peter Markus and Sir Leo Stern filed into the dock at the back of the court facing the judge. Leading the way was a young shirtsleeved police officer.

On the first day, the public gallery was jammed full, mainly with journalists. Angela, Paulette and Mark had all been told to arrive early. They trudged up the dingy staircase round the side of the building, and took their seats in the front row.

They gazed forth over apparent confusion. Situated in the modern part of the building, Court 16 was uninspiring in terms of atmosphere. Half-panelled walls in blond wood contrasted pleasantly enough with the deep green of the carpet and leather bucket chairs, but here was no sense of history.

The courtroom was cluttered with files, paper and people. Every available surface was covered with piles of ring binder files bursting with evidence. The long desks facing the judge and clerk of the court groaned under their weight and room had been made for a free-standing circular file holder at one end of the court. Even the judicial bench was laden.

Eight barristers were due to sit at the first long desk facing the bench and the clerk of the court. It was already scattered with papers and files. Peter, Jack and Stern each had a QC and his junior to represent them. The desk in front of the clerk of the court was also piled with files and had a sophisticated, multi-function telephone sitting or it. Several microphones were strategically placed throughout the courtroom.

'This isn't at all how I imagined it,' Angela whispered to Paulette. She hardly heard. Her body was rigid with tension, her eyes anxiously roaming the courtroom.

What was going on below seemed irreverently casual. The stenographer, a blousy blonde wearing bright lipstick, leafed through a copy of the *Sun* while the bewigged barristers chatted amiably to the solicitors and each other, their black robes casually slung over Savile Row suits.

The only sign of tradition in the room itself was the coat of arms of the City of London hanging behind the judge's high-backed leather chair – a splendid red, gilt and white shield bearing the motto 'Honour is as honour does' in Latin.

The trial had been due to begin at 10.30. By 10.45 nothing had happened. The three defendants sat solemn-faced, their feelings concealed. They were spaced well apart, giving no hint of friendship or association.

Peter was the first to look up, his blue eyes searching the public gallery until he found Angela's face. They grinned spontaneously at each other, fleetingly comforted.

Then Stern turned his head to look straight at Paulette as if he knew instinctively exactly where she would be sitting. His face softened slightly, and sitting next to her Angela felt the intensity coming from Paulette. There was a depth of passion there she realised she could only partly comprehend.

A loud knock heralded the entrance of a court user from a door behind the judicial bench. She was a pleasant-looking woman of about thirty-five who would have looked more at home in a suburban supermarket than Britain's central criminal court – if she had not been wearing a short black robe.

'May the court rise!'

The judge entered, resplendent in purple, black and red, moving quickly to the bench, and Angela and Paulette glanced at each other in surprise. The judge was a woman.

The clerk of the court turned to the defendants and confirmed each man's identity. Then, one by one, he read out the charges asking them after each one, 'Are you guilty or not guilty?' It took over an hour.

Four times Sir Leo Stern responded: 'Not guilty'

Three times Peter Markus responded: 'Not guilty.'

Twice Jack Armstrong responded: 'Not guilty.'

Once he responded: 'Guilty.'

Peter and Stern both strove to look unmoved. A murmur of surprise ran round the court and the judge adjusted her tinted Dior spectacles. The prosecution barristers' white curled heads bent together, startled, concerned.

'Er, excuse me, Your Honour, I would like to confer with the defence counsel.'

The judge nodded. She scribbled some notes with a gold plated pen.

The barristers huddled.

'When was the plea changed?'

'Oh, I see.'

'Fine, fine.'

'Would have been nice to know.'

Angela leaned across to Paulette, keen to impart her

365

superior knowledge. 'Apparently, Jack has decided to plead guilty to the theft charge regarding his payment to Max Schlosstein on the hopes of a light sentence.' Paulette nodded. Whether or not she understood, Angela had no idea.

The jury filed in – nine women of varied ages, two of them black, two white men of middle age and an Asian man in his thirties. Between them they had less style than a crimplene two-piece. None of them looked as if they would earn in a lifetime what Stern made in a week.

Angela was struck by the casualness of it all, the mundanity. Trials went on every day here. Elsewhere people spent their days pounding typewriters, teaching children, conducting board meetings, selling stocks and shares, running shops.

Here in this Crown Court individual lives hung daily in the balance, often after years of waiting. They were here for murder, robbery, drug dealing and fraud. Mostly there were wives, children, parents and sweethearts looking on – suffering, loathing, loving. Above all wishing that it had never happened; all subject to the same off-hand workmanlike ritual, day in, day out.

Finally the jury were all sworn in and the indictments and pleas read out again. The jurors were not told of Jack's plea of guilty to paying off Schlosstein for fear it would prejudice their view of him.

The leading barrister for the prosecution rose to his feet to begin his opening speech. The courtroom quietened in expectation.

For two and a half days the audience in the public gallery ebbed and flowed while the opening speech continued. Jonathan Dangerfield, QC, tall, grey and lanky, started by describing the background to the bid, the takeover itself. He warned the jury of the complexity of the issues involved. How they would have to grapple with areas unfamiliar to most of them. But in the final analysis, what they had to decide was the same as in a simple robbery.

'In all these charges, complicated though they seem, we are talking about dishonesty. You the jury, ladies and gentlemen, have to decide whether the defendants were dishonest. Firstly, did they, beyond all reasonable doubt, break the law?

366

Secondly, at the time they broke it, did they intend to break it?

'To those of you familiar with criminal cases this may sound strange. After all, surely somebody knows if he broke the law or not? But the laws governing conduct in the financial world have been subject to great change in the last few years. The amendments to the Companies Act in 1985 and the new Financial Services Act in 1986 have tightened up the workings of the City. That was their intention – to protect ordinary shareholders, customers and employees of big public companies.

'The three gentlemen you see before you are sophisticated businessmen capable of buying or giving the best advice. Nevertheless they have pleaded not guilty to wilfully breaking the law on nine counts.'

On the afternoon of the third day he began to call witnesses. In the majority of criminal trials, one of the chief witnesses is the victim of the crime. But in this instance the 'victims' were the shareholders of Butlers whose money had theoretically been squandered on paying off those who had supported their share price during the bid.

The witnesses came in four groups. Firstly, there were the Butlers directors, Edward Williams and Sir Richard Butler. Next came the stockbrokers who had bought shares for Stern, Sarah and Charlie, and thirdly the other directors of Hogarth Stein. Finally there were the star witnesses, Sean McCready and Douglas Coles, the land agent from Newcastle who had produced the inflated valuation on the warehouses.

Day by day, week by week, the prosecution plodded its way through. Once the barristers had asked all the questions they wanted – their job was to help the witnesses paint a picture for the jury, not to lead them in any way – it was the turn of the defence barristers to cross-examine those witnesses.

Sir Richard and Sarah were the best value for the press. Sir Richard sat in the witness box, look of bemused grief on his face. His voice was heavy with sadness, particularly when he was questioned as to how the payment to Max Schlosstein came about. At times his voice sank almost to inaudibility. Towards the end of the prosecution's questioning he suddenly exploded.

'I trusted Jack Armstrong like a son! Of course I left a few signed cheques in the safe. It was necessary for the smooth running of business. He abused that trust.' It made front-page headlines of every national paper the next morning.

Sarah had been told that the evidence she could give would be circumstantial. She had co-operated politely with the prosecution counsel all through.

She was questioned by the younger barrister, good-looking and confident, who subtly tried to flirt with her across the courtroom. She looked pale, almost ethereal, having lost so much weight. But she was composed.

The questioning seemed interminable, going over the share purchases for Stern and Max. She could tell her interrogator was becoming frustrated. The facts were she had bought shares for both of them. Stern had indeed introduced her to Max Schlosstein, but he had never spelt out his reasons. Wearily he tried again.

'So Sir Leo never told you why he wanted you to act for Schlosstein?'

'Only that he was a friend and business associate.'

'Did that not imply to you there could be a possible concert party?'

Stern's counsel was on his feet. 'Your honour! That is a leading question and my learned friend is going over old ground.'

'I agree,' said the judge. 'Get on with it.'

She breathed again. She never knew why, but they never found the right question to elicit the information they needed. Nobody had ever told her directly it was a concert party – she had simply overheard it.

The trial moved on to the allegedly fraudulent sale of Pomodoro Rosso to BANTA. Jack had hoped that Sean MacCready would be over-emotional as a witness, but Sean had vowed not to fall into that trap and in parts his evidence even sounded apologetic.

'I was convinced that there had to be a reason why Jack Armstrong was prepared to sell the company so cheap,' he said when asked why he had decided to investigate the matter.

Even without von Gleichen's presence, the evidence

against Jack and Peter in the BANTA charge seemed damning. The share buying, the loss on the shares, and evidence of the meeting in Zurich. Large chunks of the DTI interviews with Peter and Jack were played in court. But the most critical evidence was in writing.

Uncharacteristically, von Gleichen had dropped Jack a letter of thanks for agreeing to do the deal. Distracted by a phone call summoning him to an urgent meeting, Jack had allowed Amanda to file it, instead of putting it in the shredder.

Even more damning was the evidence against them in the Newcastle warehouse deal.

Douglas Coles took the stand after lunch one day, resplendent in a loud check suit with a scarlet lining. He was a big bluff man with a hearty manner of talking that disguised a faint heart. Sir Leo Stern had frightened him. The police had frightened him. Then the prosecution solicitors had frightened him. He had agreed to confess everything.

'Mr Coles,' began the prosecuting lawyer,' please tell us your profession.'

'I am a land and property agent in and around Newcastle.' His voice held a genteel Geordie twang.

'How long have you been a land agent in Newcastle?'

'Thirteen years.'

'And would you say you are successful at what you do?'

Coles smirked. 'Reasonably so.'

'Your reputation is good in the area?'

'I believe so.'

'How long have you known Sir Leo Stern?'

'I first met him in 1974.'

'And what is the nature of your relationship with him?'

Coles looked confused.

'Is it business or personally based, would you say?'

'Oh, business, mostly.'

'Have these business ventures with him been profitable?'

'Your honour.' The defence was on its feet. 'The question is leading. The past relationship is irrelevant and aimed at creating bias.'

'I will endeavour to prove that it is relevant.'

'You may go on for the moment,' said the judge.

369

'What was your most important business venture with him, would you say?'

Coles hesitated. The barrister gave him an encouraging smile. He knew what to say.

'He introduced me to a buyer for an office block in Holborn.'

'And how much was the sale worth?'

'Twenty million, which at the time was quite a big deal.'

'Quite so. And when was this?'

'February 1974.'

'And could you tell the court the state of the London property market at the time?'

Coles actually laughed. 'It was hopeless. You couldn't sell anything.'

The courtroom had gone quiet.

'Now let us move on to your valuation. When did Sir Leo Stern approach you?'

They continued through the details of where and when. The jurors were instructed where to find copies of the valuation in the evidence.

'Your Honour, we also have valuations of the same warehouses and surrounding land made by two other local firms of commercial estate agents.' These were distributed to the jury by the ushers.

'As you will see, one valuation puts it at £4.5 million, the next at £5 million against Mr Coles's valuation of £30 million.'

Everyone nodded, although the jury was totally bemused by the lengthy description of the property and land and the various assumptions used to come up with one simple figure.

The barrister drew a deep and solemn breath. It was the moment he had been waiting for.

'Mr Coles, will you tell the court how you account for the differences between your valuations and the others?'

Douglas Coles glanced fleetingly at Stern before he said in a low voice: 'Sir Leo Stern made it clear that nothing less than £30 million would be acceptable.'

Up in the public gallery, Angela felt Paulette tremble. She reached out her hand and put a comforting hand on the other

370

woman's arm. She looked down on the dock and to her astonishment, for one fleeting instant, saw unmistakably the glimmer of a smile pass across Stern's face.

It was what lawyers call half time. When the prosecution finally rested its case the trial had been running for six weeks and three days. Then it was the turn of the defence.

Outside the Old Bailey the summer blazed on. At lunch-time barristers, defendants and jury would come blinking out of the air-conditioned artificial light of the court into the brilliant heat of the street.

Peter and Angela took to eating lunch in Le Gamin brasserie opposite the court or sometimes at the Chinese restaurant next-door where they occasionally put tables outside. Stern generally had his chauffeur take him and Paulette and sometimes his counsel along the road to Le Poulbot in Cheapside. Jack would disappear, heading for one of the Fleet Street pubs, usually with his solicitor.

Attendance at the public gallery grew sparse. Angela retreated back to the country for three days a week. Mark found watching his father in the dock too painful to bear and sensed Jack would rather he were not there. His appearances became less frequent.

Only two journalists from the news agencies stayed day in, day out, noting the proceedings in perfect shorthand.

Paulette Stern came each day, although she would leave after an hour or so if the questioning was not directly concerning Stern.

To her, much of the trial was as arcane as it was to the jury. She had never really understood the stockmarket and had always regarded it simply as one of Leo's hobbies, like the Casino in Monte Carlo.

The witnesses for the defence were on the whole colleagues and workmates who would vouch for the good character of the accused. They had been hard to find.

In the case of Stern it was impossible to bring directors of Stern Group as witnesses, as he quite clearly held the power of their livelihood over them. The defence solicitors had however found a senior banker and the head of one of Stern's big customers who were prepared to go on the record and declare how impressed they had always been with Stern's business methods.

Jack's solicitors had found life more difficult as his former board had all testified against him. However Greenbag's senior partner, Anthony Fulbright, who had not been called as a prosecution witness, was prepared to go into the stand on his behalf.

The defence's problem with Peter was deciding who would be the most relevant witnesses. A large number of former clients and colleagues wanted to defend him.

Peter was touched. But he noted wrily that none of his rivals, who had privately told him they would have done the same under similar circumstances were prepared to stand up and say so in court.

Right from the beginning of the defence, it seemed that the barristers were determined to bore the jury into a 'not guilty' verdict.

The judge began to show signs of impatience as each witness underwent the most tedious list of questions. Jack, who managed to keep his drinking down to half a bottle of Scotch a night for most of the trial, went on a bender and appeared in court shaking and shiny with a sweat that had nothing to do with the heat outside.

During September the temperature began to fall, but the sunshine continued to pour down. Then, one Tuesday at the beginning of October, a chill north-east wind began to blow.

Peter sensed there was something different about the court that morning. Maybe he had picked it up from Stern. Maybe it was just the weather, but the jury looked less asleep, the public more expectant.

As the morning session began, Stern's junior barrister rose to his feet and requested permission to call a new witness. Jonathan Dangerfield raised an eyebrow at his junior.

'I swear by Almighty God that the evidence I shall give, shall be the truth, the whole truth, and nothing but the truth.'

Baron Marks stood in the witness box, gleaming like a new pin. His cuffs dazzled, his dark blue double-breasted pin stripe bore not a speck of dust and his glossy black lair shone like a shampoo commercial.

In the public gallery Angela's mind raced back to Ascot two years before. He was the man talking to Stern on the racecourse!

Lawrence Balentine QC was a good fifteen years younger than the two eminent barristers representing Jack and Peter. Stern had chosen him for his youth and ambition. He had taken silk only a year before. He had a lot to prove, in every sense of the word.

'Mr Marks, can you tell the court what you do for a living?'

'I am a property developer,' said Baron pleasantly.

'Could you explain a little more what that means?'

'I buy buildings, or land, or both and redevelop them. I turn them into something else such as a new office building or a shopping centre. Then I usually sell it again – for a profit, naturally.'

'You are, I believe, familiar with the piece of land sold by Sir Leo Stern to Butlers?'

'Indeed I am.'

Something in his tone made Peter's heart start beating faster. He looked at Stern. Under the mane of raven hair his face was closed – but his body lounged. Jack was staring at Baron Marks as if he expected him to vanish in a puff of smoke.

'How much would you say it was worth?' Lawrence Balentine's voice was deliberately casual.

'At least £35 million.'

There was a rustle of astonishment. Jonathan Dangerfield leapt to his feet.

'Your honour, the witness is not a qualified chartered surveyor to my knowledge.'

'Your honour. I think you will see the validity of this witness's views if we proceed,' retorted Lawrence Balentine. The judge nodded and Jonathan Dangerfield started scribbling a note, his brows knotted.

Lawrence Balentine addressed his witness again. The casual tone had been replaced by one of great portent.

'And how would you account for the huge difference between that valuation and that given by local agents in 1987?'

Baron glanced round the courtroom, relishing the moment. There was total silence.

'My company exchanged contracts with the directors of Butlers to buy it from them at that price last night.'

There were gasps of surprise from the public gallery and the jury looked totally confused.

Lawrence Balentine, smiling slightly, pressed on in tones of considerable reverence: 'And can you tell the court why you feel this land is now of such value?'

'Well, I think it has had that potential for some while. It has excellent access to the motorway system and is ideal for development. Any valuer who did not take that into account needs his head examined – chartered surveyor or not,' he added with the touch of a sneer.

The advocate interrupted.

'Are you telling the court that it could have been worth that two years ago?'

Baron Marks looked straight at the jury. 'Look,' he said patiently, 'all valuation is subjective. The fact is this particular piece of land has the potential to be turned into something much more valuable than £5 million – and to anyone who bothered to do some homework, it had that potential two years ago.'

'And can you tell the court what your company is planning to do with the land?'

'Indeed. We have lodged a Master Plan for a £90 million scheme to build a business park and a housing project. We have every confidence we will obtain the necessary detailed planning consent for the scheme.'

Peter's face was aching from trying not to laugh out loud. He saw tears of relief streaming down Jack's face. Stern's expression had barely altered. Only the corners of his lips twitched.

Chapter 25

Jean-Pierre switched on CNN's financial station as he did every morning when he awoke, to see Stern beaming and waving to the camera as he disappeared into his black Bentley.

'Meanwhile Sir Leo Stern was acquitted on all counts after the appearance of a surprise witness who effectively validated the price he had charged Butlers Group for a property purchase,' said the news reader.

'What about Jack?' Jean-Pierre asked out loud, instantly wide awake. The news reader ignored him. 'Peter Markus was found guilty on one count, relating to the sale of a Butlers subsidiary to a Swiss company, but acquitted on another three charges. He was given a suspended sentence.' The picture on Jean-Pierre's television showed a weary-looking Peter leaving the court with Angela on his arm. Jean-Pierre sat up in bed and tutted impatiently.

Then came a shot of a man – a jumble of angular bones with a bewildered, desperate expression on his face – being helped into a police van. It took Jean-Pierre a few seconds to realise who it was.

'Jack Armstrong, the former chief executive of Butlers Group was found guilty of unlawfully selling a Butlers subsidiary to a Swiss company and of paying illegal fees to the American arbitrageur, Max Schlosstein, during the bid for Empire Foods,' said the news reader. 'He was sentenced to three years imprisonment.'

Jean-Pierre watched the rest of the bulletin without seeing it and when he reached out his hand for the remote control pad he noticed it was shaking – 'Three years! Poor old buddy,' he murmured.

Thank God he had stayed out of London.

'The question is,' said Patrick Peabody, as his smoked salmon was Placed before him, 'did Stern know the value of the land would shoot up all the time – or did he just get lucky?'

David Bang glanced round the room, making sure he knew just who was eating with whom at the pink-clothed tables, and stubbed out his Sullivan Powell.

'Difficult to say really, isn't it? I think it was just a question of instinct. Gambler's luck. The fact is, the man is a winner.'

'Or a crook?'

'If he's a crook, he's a very clever one.'

Patrick puzzled over David's defensive tone.

'Peter was lucky to get off with a suspended sentence, don't you reckon.'

David glanced at him, incredulous. 'If you think it's lucky never to be able to operate in London again,' he said quietly. 'Still, it could have been worse. I suppose they took pity on him because he didn't make any money p.a.,' he conceded. 'And although in law there's not supposed to be any difference between a principal and his advisor, his role in the sale of Pomodoro Rosso was very much advisory. Jack admitted as much in court.'

'Yes, he's the one I feel really sorry for.' Patrick speared his langoustine with his fork, swirling it round in the coral sauce.

David lifted his hand to wave at a boyish-looking man with a mop of blond hair who was being escorted to a window table by the head waiter.

'I just can't imagine what possessed him to pay Schlosstein that money,' he said. 'I think it must have been that American poofter friend of his, put him up to it. People just get carried away by their own success.' He smiled wickedly at Patrick and sipped his champagne. 'They believe everything we tell them.'

Patrick frowned. 'How much time do you think Jack will actually serve of that three years?'

'No more than one and a half. He'll go to Ford Open. They say it's like a holiday camp in there.'

'Really? I wonder if they let journalists in for interviews.'

Around them, the clink of knives and forks on china and the murmur of contented lunchers made a soothing atmosphere. Glasses, polished to within an inch of their lives, sparkled in the sunlight.

'Who is that chap you were waving at?' asked Patrick changing the subject.

David's rumpled face lit up. 'He's my newest client. He's in property but building up a leisure side. He floated his company about two years ago although he's kept low profile up to now. He's going to be one to watch. I'll arrange for you to meet him if you like. There'll be lots of good stories.'

'Mm, love to.' Patrick sipped his wine and gazed out over the bare branches of the trees to the river.

A silver trolley bearing a saddle of lamb appeared before them.

'Ah, that looks splendid,' said David, beaming at the carver.

'One yellow metal watch.' The prison officer took the Rolex and handed it to another man who was putting all Jack's clothing and valuables in a cardboard box noting down the contents as he went.

'Twenty-two pounds, eighty-seven pee,' he continued 'One jacket.'

Finally he came to the end. 'This will be kept under your surname and prison number.'

They had given Jack a prison number almost the moment he walked through the gates.

He was then escorted to have a bath. Afterwards he was given a towel to put round him and taken for a medical check up.

The doctor was a surprisingly cheery man in the circumstances. But then, thought Jack, he wasn't a prisoner.

He asked about Jack's blood pressure, tapped his chest, looked down his throat and tested his reflexes.

'Sit down.' He had a large check sheet in front of him. 'Now, I'm going to ask you a lot of questions.' And off he went.

'Date of birth?'

'Marital status?'

'Current health?'

'Any regular prescription drugs?'

'Any serious illnesses?'

'Do you smoke?

'How much do you drink?'

And so on.

A warder took him back to what could only be described as a holding area. Another man appeared, this time a prison red band who started cross examining him about his measurements.

'Neck size?'

'Waist size?'

'Inside trouser measurement?'

'Shoe size?'

He was left alone again, sitting on a bench of wooden slats. The entire decor had a sludge-like quality.

There were plenty of people around, but he had never felt more isolated. The other admissions seemed quite cheerful. In fact the atmosphere had something of a reunion about it. Men were standing about in little groups chatting to each other and every now and then there was a subdued burst of laughter. He longed to go up to one of the groups and see a familiar face. He found himself searching for someone he knew – anyone to give him some sense of identity. But he was a stranger here, a new boy.

After a while – it could have been ten minutes or an hour – his surname and the last three digits of his identity number were called out. He went up to the desk.

'Shirts, two,' said the warder to his colleague.

Two blue and white striped shirts were placed in front of him.

'Vests, two.'

'Y fronts, two.'

'Dungarees, one.'

'Socks, three pairs.'

'Shoes, one pair.'

'Greys, one.'

'Two sheets and one pillowcase.'

The pile mounted before him. He was led away to get dressed. Slowly he put on the shirt. It was quite old and had the prison code stamped in black on the back. He put on the rest. Finally he put on the shoes.

378

Once dressed, he was marched off to another holding area and after more waiting around, his name was called. They gave him another number – 3/21 – representing the landing and cell number.

He stood for a moment looking down at the black plastic shoes. They were so unlike the pair of Lobb's hand-made loafers which he had handed in, that he blinked his eyes in disbelief. A sudden wild flash of hope that he might wake up, swept over him. It vanished as quickly as it had come.

Gone was Jack Armstrong, free to walk and sleep where he willed; free to pick up the telephone to his children; to eat what took his fancy; to drive a car; write a letter; choose a brown jumper rather than a grey one; pick up a woman. A few simple, painless procedures had changed him from a citizen to prisoner 3/21.

Stern pulled Sarah's pink skirt up around her hips and began stroking her inner thigh. She half giggled, half moaned as he pushed her towards the wall. 'Check-in's in half an hour,' she pleaded. He knelt, pulled down her panties and started licking her softly, his tongue moving insistently, round and round. Then he stood and unzipped the skirt, lifting her so that it slipped to the floor. He pinned her against the wall and she gasped as he thrust inside her, moving gently at first, lips glued to hers as she shuddered and moaned.

He uncoupled from her and wordlessly Sarah lay on the floor her eyes begging him to come inside her again. He moved on top of her, driving into her like a piston. Somewhere, above the ecstasy, she could hear her voice sobbing and calling his name. When she came, she dug her fingernails into his back.

After a few minutes, he drew away from her and smiled.

'I don't want you to forget me in New York.'

He took her cases and put them in the Bentley. 'This is terribly risky, Leo. What if we're seen?'

'I was taking my loyal stockbroker and friend to the airport,' he said. 'Paulette knows I was very concerned when you became ill before the trial – and that I blamed myself. She thinks I look on you as a kind of daughter.'

'Well, don't you?'

His eyes were tender. 'In some ways, maybe. It was strange how Paulette took your side when you were getting all that flak from the press.'

Sarah smiled. She was fond of Paulette. 'Anyway, I suppose it's unlikely we'll be seen. The main problem,' she said a touch crossly, 'is getting there in time. If the traffic is bad. I've had it.'

But Sir Leo Stern was the kind of man for whom the traffic is rarely bad and they were soon speeding along the flyover past all the familiar landmarks – the Wang building, the Mowlem headquarters. She felt a wave of gratitude that he was free, and a pang of sadness for Jack Armstrong because he wasn't. The difference was that Leo was a creature of the jungle. He had been born into it and he understood it. Jack had been an innocent who had blundered into a pleasant glade and believed the whole jungle was like that.

She looked up at him, the smile still playing at the corner of his mouth, his shoulders hugging the black leather of the seats, the broad brow, the mane of black hair, the beak of a nose, the molten black eyes. Her heart lurched in the same way as the time she had seen his car in the hospital grounds.

'I do love you, Leo.' Her voice was wavering with emotion. He caught her hand and kissed her fingers.

'You can always change your mind.' To their left an aircraft hurled itself into the sky.

She said quietly, 'We both know I've got to go.' She glanced at him once more and saw that the smile on his lips had died.

Minutes later, Sarah strode purposefully into the Concorde lounge. The flight was Stern's parting present to her, with a return ticket to use whenever she wanted. They were already boarding and she walked straight through, a vibrant figure in a fuchsia suit. She sank into her window seat with a feeling of relief and accepted a glass of orange juice. She gazed out on to the tarmac, idly watching the plane in the next space back out.

She was due to start work at Shearman Drussel the very next day. And for once this had been a job she had found all on her own, winning it against fifty-two other applicants.

380

They had wanted someone with sound experience of the London market and plenty of push to sell British equities to the American institutions. When Sarah had told her mother she had got it, she had cried and laughed alternately.

She was pleased to have made her parents happy for once. They had never actually talked to her about Stern, but it was obvious they had guessed – particularly when he had gone to see them after her breakdown. She could sense that they liked him. But then, she defied anyone to dislike him when he was at his best.

The captain rattled through the PR pitch and the plane began its long trip down the runway, gathering speed until it shot into the air like a well-made paper dart.

She turned as the steward offered her a glass of champagne. The man who had taken the seat next to her smiled. He was tanned and lean with aquiline features and steel grey hair. Something about her made him raise his glass. 'Here's to good trip.' They drank. 'My name is Bud Hershfield.'

'Sarah Meyer.'

They shook hands.

'And what do you do, Sarah?'

'I'm an investment banker,' she said with an inner glow of happiness.

She looked out of the window. The plane edged through the grey fog of cloud and then they were through into the wide blue arc of the sky, gliding above a carpet of billowy white cumulus. Wall Street beckoned.

Peter sat in the wood-panelled, velvet-curtained luncheon room overlooking the trading floor of one of the big American investment banks in London.

One of the Vice Presidents sat opposite him.

'The fact is, Peter, we would love to offer you a full-time job, but the regulatory authorities just won't wear it,' he said. 'You and I know that what you did may not amount to a row of beans, but the fact is it has resulted in a criminal conviction.'

He clasped his hands in front of him on the table. 'I'm sorry. Every single director wants you on board, but it just ain't possible.'

For once, Peter made no attempt to put on a brave face. It was the fourth such conversation in a fortnight and it was beginning to get him down.

'What about ad hoc consultancy work?'

The American nodded. 'Sure, we can use you. But we can't put your name on documents. You'll get paid but you won't get any glory.'

The Financial Services Act 1986 makes it clear that anyone giving financial advice must be licensed by one of the regulatory authorities. Anyone with a recent criminal record was automatically deemed to be unfit, and therefore no authorised merchant bank could employ him.

'So, effectively the whole of the City of London is barred to me,' he said gloomily to Charlie and his wife who were standing him and Angel dinner that evening.

They nodded sympathetically. 'Yes, we checked it out with our people,' said Charlie. 'We'd have liked you to come on the corporate broking team. But it's absolutely out of the question, although there is nothing to stop one of your former public company clients taking you on as an employee.'

'But not as a director,' said Peter drily. 'Yes, I've thought of that and one or two of them have been kind enough to offer. But you know I'd get bored stiff acting for just one company.'

Charlie said brightly: 'You could always go to Hong Kong. They don't have any of these damn fool regulations there.'

'Please don't even think about it,' said Angela sharply.

Peter grinned. 'It's too far away. And as you can tell, Angela would hate it – not to mention my daughter.'

Charlie looked despondent. 'Well, what are you going to do?'

Peter stared moodily at the pot of flowers on the table. Suddenly he looked up and smiled. 'Leo owes me a favour or two. I think its time to give him a call.'

Jack began to fall in to the routine of prison life. In fact there were days when he almost liked it. He was feeling a lot healthier. He began to wonder what all that heavy drinking was about. After the first few days, which had been torture, the lack of alcohol had ceased to bother him. One of his cell mates was a drugs dealer, the other a used car dealer. Dealers of one kind or another dominated the prison.

Once he learned how to work the system he discovered there was quite a lot of freedom. The second morning he had decided he wanted to write a letter to Rosemary. He had asked one of the warders.

'All letters have to be requested before 9 a.m. You will have to wait till tomorrow.'

'Well, why didn't somebody tell me?' he asked, furious at his own lack of control over such a simple matter.

'You didn't ask,' said the warder.

He turned to find his cell mates with silly grins on their faces.

'Yeah, you'll find it's the case with most things. Know what I mean,' said the car dealer. 'Gotta whack in the request before nine. We all get caught at the beginning.'

It took him until lunchtime to cool down.

The first week there was an induction course which told new prisoners of the facilities and activities. Someone had given a talk on alcoholism.

'We have Alcoholics Anonymous meetings each week on a Wednesday for anyone who thinks they might have a problem.'

Jack shuddered at the idea. He was fine now. It had just been all the pressure.

After the talk was over the man had appeared at his side. 'Think you might give the AA meetings a whirl?' Jack looked at him, startled. How had he been singled out?

'I understand you had a bit of a problem before coming in here,' said the man quietly.

'Well, yes, I did a bit,' Jack said defensively. 'But I'm fine now thanks.' He turned away.

'Of course you're fine!' said the man, grinning. There's no booze in here. We go to the meetings so we don't go back to square one when we get out. The first few days out there can be pretty lonely. The pub seems the natural place to go.'

His tone was friendly, slightly teasing.

'Look, it's something different to do for an hour and a half on a Wednesday evening. You don't have to say anything.

There are no musts in AA. You won't have to come back if you don't like it.'

It was as if a burden that had been weighing Jack down shifted slightly and lightened.

He sighed. 'OK, I'll come along – just to see.'

'Fine.' The other man's tone was matter-of-act. Then he smiled. 'See you then.'

Jack had gone to the meeting.

A few weeks later Stern's sleek motor boat edged its way out of the marina at Beaulieu-sur-Mer. Stern lounged darkly against the white leather banquette, next to Angela and Peter. Baron Marks sat opposite.

'How is your apartment?' he asked Peter.

'Very much like all Monte Carlo apartments, I imagine,' answered Peter. 'What did Somerset Maugham say about Monte Carlo? 'A sunny place for shady people.'

'But there are compensations,' cut in Angela, picking up the melancholy tone in Peter's voice. Stern had fixed everything.

'And what will you do now?' she asked Stern.

'Business as usual, of course.' He glanced knowingly at Baron and then back at her and Peter.

Baron smiled, white teeth brilliant against his tanned skin. 'We're going to do a few deals, make a bit of money, have some fun.'

Stern chuckled in agreement, his mouth twisting into its sarcastic smile.

'You're very clever,' Angela said, only half admiringly.

'You've got to be lucky to be clever, never forget it,' Stern said.

She stared coolly back at him, feeling the goose pimples rise on her arms.

The engine growled as the boat picked up speed, bouncing over the astonishingly blue waves. The spray hit her in the face and she felt a shudder of excitement. Or was it revulsion?

Movers and shakers – did they really serve any purpose? They made life more interesting certainly; they made those around them feel more alive. It was as though some of their adrenalin spilled over into the ether.

Angela liked Stern. He made her laugh, made her forget her mundane problems. He transported her into a fantastical world. But would she trust him? Did he care about anything or anyone outside the dark tunnel of his own ambition?

Suddenly the young driver lifted his arm.

'Look! Dolphins!'

As their eyes followed his pointing hand, they saw the smooth rounded shapes effortlessly arching in between the waves. There was a shoal of about six, leaping and plunging, seemingly for the sheer joy of being alive.

Angela forgot her deliberations. 'Where are we going now?' she yelled into Stern's ear as they zipped along the coast.

'We're going to eat the best lunch in the whole of the South of France.'

He lay back and turned his face to the sun, a small, contented smile on his lips.

The dolphins played.

When the heart attack struck, he barely felt a thing.

You have been reading a novel published by
Piatkus Books. We hope you have enjoyed it and
that you would like to read more of our titles.
Please ask for them in your local library or
bookshop.

If you would like to be put on our mailing list to
receive details of new publications, please send a
large stamped addressed envelope (UK only) to:
Piatkus Books: 5 Windmill Street
London W1P 1HF

PIATKUS

THE SIGN OF A GOOD BOOK